The Light We Left Behind

Adelaide Vaughn

Published by Adelaide Vaughn, 2024.

This is a work of fiction. Similarities to real people, places, or events are entirely coincidental.

THE LIGHT WE LEFT BEHIND

First edition. October 7, 2024.

Copyright © 2024 Adelaide Vaughn.

ISBN: 979-8227224590

Written by Adelaide Vaughn.

Chapter 1: Beneath the Willow Tree

I settled deeper into the embrace of the willow's cascading branches, the tendrils of green curling around me like an old friend. Each rustle of the leaves was a whisper, carrying the scent of damp earth and memories I thought I had tucked away neatly in my mind. The sun flickered through the canopy, casting playful shadows that danced on my arms. I could almost hear the echoes of laughter from my childhood, the shrill calls of friends who had faded into the backdrop of my hurried life in the city. Here, everything felt suspended in time, a soft lullaby urging me to stay a little longer, to breathe in the past.

I shifted on the mossy ground, a patch of comfort amidst the discomfort of my return. The nearby creek gurgled softly, its water a crystal-clear ribbon winding through the trees, a sight I had once taken for granted. As a child, I would spend hours skimming stones and daring myself to jump into its chilly embrace. Now, I felt the coldness creeping in—not from the water, but from the memories of sunlit days where I felt invincible. I squeezed my eyes shut, imagining I could freeze time again, wishing to capture the joy of summer afternoons and the sweet taste of homemade lemonade poured from my mother's cherished glass pitcher.

But reality beckoned, and I opened my eyes to the present, the sun now fully drenching me in its warm embrace. The neighborhood hadn't changed much; the familiar creaking of Mrs. Granger's porch swing still echoed across the street, and the old dogwood tree stood proudly at the corner, its blossoms bursting with color. Yet, the absence of my mother's hand on my shoulder, guiding me through the maze of our town's history, felt like a void that swallowed the vibrancy whole. Each step toward our house was an act of defiance against the memories that clamored for my attention, a stubborn refusal to let the past dominate my future.

As I pushed open the weathered door, the hinges protested, a sound that resonated deeply within me. Dust motes swirled in the sunlight filtering through the windows, illuminating the long-forgotten corners of our living room. The faded floral wallpaper, once a vibrant pink, now hung in tatters, peeling away like the layers of my heart. I inhaled sharply, my breath hitching as the scent of lavender and freshly baked cookies wafted through the air, evoking memories of my mother baking on lazy Sunday afternoons. I could almost hear her humming softly, a tune that seemed to float in the air even now, wrapping around me like a cherished blanket.

I wandered through the house, each room a snapshot of time, a collage of moments that I had either clung to or tried to forget. The kitchen was a particular sanctuary, where the sunlight spilled over the worn countertops, revealing the scratches and scars of countless meals prepared with love. I traced my fingers over the smooth surface of the table, memories flooding back of family dinners, the laughter that filled the space, the way my mother's eyes sparkled when she spoke of her childhood adventures. I had often watched her from the other side of the counter, trying to absorb every detail as she whisked batter, her laughter bubbling over like the pots on the stove.

But the heartache came rushing back, uninvited and relentless. My mother had been my anchor, a guiding star in my tumultuous sea of childhood emotions. And now, with her gone, I felt adrift, left to navigate the stormy waters of grief alone. It wasn't just her absence that stung; it was the echoes of my father's abandonment, a shadow that had always loomed large. I could almost hear his distant voice, a fading whisper in the back of my mind, urging me to be strong, to forget the pain, to focus on the future. But the future felt daunting, a vast expanse filled with uncertainty and longing.

I stepped outside again, the air thickening with the promise of rain, each droplet a reminder of the tears I had yet to shed. I wandered toward the garden, where my mother had nurtured her flowers with unwavering dedication. The once-lush beds had become wild, a tangled mess of overgrown weeds and sporadic blooms fighting for sunlight. My fingers brushed against the petals of a daisy, bright and defiant against the encroaching chaos. I felt a flicker of hope, a tiny spark in the darkness, reminding me that even amid decay, beauty could flourish.

As I knelt down, my hands sinking into the cool earth, a sense of purpose ignited within me. This garden had been her sanctuary, a place of healing and creativity, and perhaps it could be mine as well. The weeds were a tangible representation of the chaos in my life, but pulling them out one by one felt symbolic, a way to reclaim what had been lost. Each tug at the roots was cathartic, a gentle release of the grief that threatened to consume me.

The sky above began to darken, ominous clouds gathering as the wind picked up, whispering secrets among the trees. I looked up, feeling the first drops of rain kiss my skin, mingling with the sweat from my labor. There was something exhilarating about the storm, an electric energy that coursed through me. It felt like a reset, a cleansing of sorts, washing away the remnants of sorrow that clung too closely.

I rose, brushing the dirt from my knees, and surveyed the garden. It wasn't perfect, but it was a start. I could almost hear my mother's voice encouraging me, reminding me that growth was a process, not a destination. Perhaps, if I tended to this place, it could become a sanctuary for me too, a reminder that life, with all its unpredictability, still held moments of beauty worth cherishing.

As the rain began to fall in earnest, I felt the weight of the world slowly lifting. I turned back toward the house, a new resolve bubbling within me. I was not just a visitor in this home; I was its guardian now, a keeper of my mother's legacy. The journey ahead would be fraught with challenges, but beneath the willow tree, I felt a sense of belonging that I had not realized I had been missing. Willow

Creek was not just where I had come from; it was where I would find my way back to myself.

With the rain falling softly, a rhythmic patter that felt like a soothing balm on my restless heart, I returned to the shelter of the porch. The old swing creaked in familiar protest as I settled into its embrace, letting the cool air wash over me like a gentle reminder of life beyond my grief. The droplets danced around me, glistening in the fading light, and I closed my eyes, allowing the sound of the rain to fill the empty spaces of my mind. Each drop seemed to carry with it a piece of the past, transforming sorrow into something more manageable, as if the earth itself was reminding me that healing was a journey, not a destination.

The memories were still raw, of course, but something about this place felt alive, breathing alongside me. I opened my eyes to see the garden glistening, the flowers swaying as if they were rejoicing in the rain's arrival. The colors seemed more vivid, more alive, each petal shimmering like a precious gem. It was a beautiful contradiction—chaos mingling with grace, just like life itself. I noticed how the daisies, their heads drooping under the weight of the water, mirrored my own heaviness, while the resilient marigolds stood proudly, defiantly, as if they had taken on the world and said, "Bring it on."

In the distance, a rumble of thunder echoed, deep and reassuring, as though it were nature's way of offering solidarity. I felt a smile creep onto my lips, a small victory against the gloom that threatened to engulf me. The world kept moving, the storm didn't ask for permission to come, and somehow, in that chaotic dance of nature, I found a flicker of strength. It was the perfect metaphor for my life—dark clouds looming, yet beneath them, a garden waiting to bloom.

As the rain softened to a mist, I made my way inside, the air now rich with the earthy scent of rain-soaked soil. I couldn't ignore the boxes that awaited me, their flaps slightly ajar, eager to divulge their contents. Each box represented fragments of my mother's life, snapshots of who she had been and who I had become in her absence. I pulled one closer, dust motes swirling in the air like whispers of stories yet to be uncovered.

With trembling hands, I opened the lid, revealing a jumble of old photographs, brittle with age yet vibrant with memory. The first image that caught my eye was of my mother, her smile wide and her hair a wild halo of curls, dancing barefoot in a field of sunflowers. I could almost hear her laughter, feel her joy as she twirled beneath the sun. The photograph radiated warmth, a stark contrast to the emptiness that had settled around me since her passing. I traced her face with my finger, a silent promise that I would remember her this way—full of life, a beacon of love.

As I sifted through the collection, each photograph opened a door to the past, revealing fragments of family gatherings, summer barbecues, and lazy afternoons spent on the porch, sipping iced tea while the world drifted by. There was my father, awkwardly holding a fishing pole, his smile strained, and my mother standing proudly beside him, as if to say, "This is my family, flaws and all." The tension between them was palpable, an invisible thread woven through the fabric of our lives, and I felt a knot tighten in my chest.

I could feel the familiar ache of abandonment, but it was softer now, muted by the love that surrounded me in those photos. I forced myself to focus on the joy—the silly poses, the spontaneous moments of laughter. A part of me wanted to lock away the memories of pain and heartache, yet I knew that to heal, I needed to embrace the whole of it, the laughter and the tears, intertwined like the roots of the willow that stood guard outside.

I tucked the photographs back into their box and pulled out a small, worn diary, its leather cover cracked and faded. It felt heavy in my hands, as if it held within it the weight of unspoken thoughts and dreams left behind. I hesitated, my heart racing with anticipation and fear. Would I find my mother's dreams laid bare? Would I uncover the words she had never shared aloud?

With a deep breath, I opened the diary, the scent of aged paper filling the air, a nostalgic aroma that spoke of long-lost secrets. The first pages were filled with her elegant cursive, swirling like the vines that climbed our porch. She wrote about her days, the mundane and the extraordinary, capturing the essence of life in Willow Creek. I couldn't help but smile as I read her musings about the changing seasons, the comfort of community, and the challenges of raising me, her only daughter.

As I turned the pages, her voice became clearer, weaving a tapestry of hope, love, and resilience. There were entries about her dreams of travel, her desire to explore the world beyond the confines of our small town. She had written about my childhood—my first steps, my first day of school, and all the milestones in between. Her words shimmered with love, and I could almost hear her voice echoing through the hallways of my memory, urging me to chase my own dreams, no matter how far they seemed.

Tears filled my eyes, a bittersweet mixture of love and loss. I felt her presence so strongly in those pages, as if she were sitting right beside me, urging me to embrace life fully. I could see her, hair blowing in the breeze, eyes sparkling with the light of a thousand stars. She had always believed in me, had always pushed me to soar, even when I felt tethered to the ground by grief.

And there, tucked between the pages, was a small photograph of us—a candid moment captured at my high school graduation. I was beaming, wearing the cap and gown that seemed to shimmer in the sunlight, and she stood proudly beside me, a glimmer of tears in her eyes, reflecting joy and hope. That day had been a celebration of everything we had overcome together, a testament to our unbreakable bond.

As the rain continued to tap against the windows, I closed the diary, clutching it to my chest as if holding onto my mother herself. The warmth of her spirit wrapped around me like a comforting embrace, and for the first time since my return, I felt a flicker of clarity. The pain of loss would always be a part of me, but so would the love she had poured into every moment, every word, and every memory.

In that moment of quiet reflection, the shadows that had loomed over me began to dissipate. I understood that it was okay to grieve, to miss her, but it was equally important to celebrate the legacy she had left behind. Willow Creek wasn't just a town of my past; it was a canvas for my future, a place where I could cultivate my own dreams while honoring her memory.

The storm outside began to wane, the clouds slowly parting to reveal patches of blue sky. I felt a sense of renewal coursing through me, a commitment to breathe life into my mother's dreams and my own. The journey ahead would be uncertain, but as I stood in the heart of the home she had created, I felt ready to embrace whatever came next.

The next few days blurred into a whirlwind of memories and responsibilities as I navigated the bittersweet task of sorting through my mother's belongings. The air remained thick with the scent of rain-soaked earth, and each time I breathed it in, I felt as if the town itself was welcoming me back, urging me to reclaim my place within its embrace. The golden afternoons melted into one another, and I lost myself in the rhythm of unpacking and rediscovery. Each box I opened felt like unearthing a part of her, pieces of the woman who had shaped my world with her laughter and unwavering love.

In the living room, I found a box of her journals tucked behind a collection of faded cookbooks, their pages stained with the remnants of flour and sugar. The moment I lifted the lid, I felt an electric current of familiarity and nostalgia. Her handwriting was as fluid as her thoughts, swirling with the ebb and flow of her emotions. I sank onto the worn couch, its cushions bearing the imprint of countless family conversations and late-night heart-to-hearts, and began to read.

The entries reflected not only her thoughts but also the heart of Willow Creek. She wrote about the annual fall festival, where pumpkins adorned every doorstep and children raced through the streets with sticky candy fingers. I could almost hear the music, the laughter blending with the crisp air, as the town came alive in a vibrant tapestry of colors. She spoke of the friendship she forged with Mrs. Granger, a bond formed over shared recipes and whispered secrets. It was as if each line she penned wove a connection between her past and my present, a bridge that I could walk upon if only I could summon the courage.

One passage struck me particularly hard: she had documented her struggle with the absence of my father, painting it with a palette of heartbreak and resilience. She wrote of the nights she lay awake, staring at the ceiling, wondering what could have been, yet still managing to find light in the small joys around her. "Life has a funny way of giving you what you need when you least expect it," she had written, and I felt the warmth of her optimism wrap around me like a favorite sweater. It was a stark reminder that, even in her darkest moments, she had chosen to embrace hope.

Inspired, I decided to take a walk through town, craving the familiarity of its winding streets and friendly faces. The air was still tinged with the remnants of rain, but the sun peeked through the clouds, casting a golden hue over everything. I passed the local bakery, its windows fogged up with warmth, the smell of freshly baked bread mingling with the floral notes of blooming gardenias. I paused for a moment, nostalgia washing over me, and stepped inside, greeted by the familiar chime of the bell above the door.

The baker, a stout man with flour dusting his apron, looked up and broke into a broad smile. "If it isn't the prodigal daughter," he boomed, his jovial tone pulling me into the warmth of his presence. "We missed you around here."

"Thanks, Mr. Thompson," I replied, my cheeks warming at the attention. "It's good to be back, though I wish it were under better circumstances."

He nodded, his expression turning momentarily somber. "Your mother was a fixture here. We all miss her. The way she used to bring in those chocolate chip cookies—made the best batch in town, if you ask me."

A lump formed in my throat, but I managed a smile as I remembered those afternoons spent helping her in the kitchen, the sweet scent enveloping us like a hug. "I'll have to try and fill her shoes. I think I owe it to her."

"Take your time, dear. Willow Creek will always be waiting for you," he said, handing me a warm croissant that crumbled slightly at the touch, its buttery scent wrapping around me like a comforting blanket. I thanked him and stepped back outside, holding the pastry close, a little piece of home nestled in my palm.

As I wandered through the town, I felt the weight of eyes upon me, familiar faces peering out from behind hedges and front doors. I waved at Mrs. Granger, who was pruning her roses, and she offered a small, knowing smile that ignited a warmth in my chest. Willow Creek, with its small-town charm and interconnected lives, was a living tapestry of shared experiences and unspoken bonds.

I continued my stroll, my feet guiding me to the park where I had spent countless afternoons, lost in the wonder of childhood. The playground stood as a nostalgic monument to simpler times, the swings swaying in the gentle breeze as if beckoning me to take a seat once more. I approached, the echoes of laughter whispering in my ears. I couldn't help but imagine the little girl I had been, her laughter ringing out with unrestrained joy, the world her playground.

Sitting on the swing, I let my legs dangle, feeling the cool metal beneath me, and with each gentle push, I was transported back in time. I could almost hear my mother's voice calling to me, urging me to be brave, to find joy even in the smallest moments.

A sudden burst of laughter pulled me back to the present. Two children raced past, their faces alight with delight as they chased each other around the playground, their energy infectious. In their laughter, I found a piece of myself I thought I had lost—a reminder that life, even amid heartache, could still be filled with moments of pure joy.

As the sun dipped lower in the sky, painting everything in hues of amber and gold, I felt the weight of my mother's love wrap around me like a gentle embrace. I returned home with a new resolve, clutching my croissant and the fragments of her life, both fragile and beautiful.

That evening, as I sat on the porch with the diary on my lap, I found myself dreaming of ways to honor my mother's legacy. The garden, once wild and tangled, now felt like a canvas waiting for my touch. I envisioned a space bursting with colors, fragrant blooms, and laughter—an homage to the woman who had cultivated beauty in all things.

The stars began to twinkle overhead, their light sparkling against the deepening dusk. I closed my eyes, feeling the warm breeze on my face, and in that moment, I understood that I was not just a visitor in Willow Creek; I was a part of its story, intertwined with my mother's in ways I was only beginning to comprehend. I would plant her dreams alongside my own, allowing them to take root in this fertile ground, nurturing them until they blossomed into something magnificent.

As I closed the diary, my heart swelled with a renewed sense of purpose. I was ready to face whatever came next, equipped with the love of my mother and the strength of this town. Tomorrow would bring its own challenges, but for now, I was content, my heart whispering softly that life, with all its unpredictability, could be a beautiful journey—if only I dared to embrace it.

Chapter 2: The Stranger at the Café

The sun hung low over Willow Creek, casting a warm, golden glow that painted the streets in rich amber hues. As I pushed through the weathered door of Maple Café, the scent of roasted beans enveloped me like a cherished embrace. The chatter of regulars mingled with the clinking of ceramic mugs, a familiar symphony that filled my heart with comfort. It was a small-town haven where dreams were shared and laughter echoed off the exposed brick walls, each person a character in this cozy, unchanging play.

I settled into my usual spot by the window, the one with the perfect view of Main Street, where life unfolded in a slow dance of familiarity. The barista, a cheerful woman with a shock of purple hair, recognized my order before I even had to speak. "Medium roast, two sugars, right?" she chirped, her voice bright like the morning sun. I smiled, nodding as she prepared my drink with practiced ease.

That's when I first saw him—Luke. He stood tall at the counter, his presence commanding yet effortless, like he had strolled in from a different realm altogether. Dark hair tousled casually, he pushed it back with a single, languid motion, revealing sharp cheekbones and a jawline that seemed sculpted by an artist's hand. My breath caught for just a moment as I watched him interact with the barista, an easy banter exchanged that made the air crackle with an unexpected energy. He was not like the others who frequented this café, all too accustomed to the rhythm of Willow Creek. There was an undercurrent of mischief in his smile that suggested he had stories to tell—stories that might disrupt the predictability of our quaint town.

As I sipped my coffee, the warmth spreading through my fingers, I found myself caught in a silent battle between curiosity and caution. My heart raced as I stole glances, hoping to decipher the mystery that surrounded him. Most of the people in Willow Creek were lifers, entrenched in their predictable routines, their lives seemingly scripted. But Luke was different; he exuded an air of possibility, as if he were a rare comet passing through our starlit skies, illuminating everything in its wake.

Finally, our eyes met—a fleeting moment that ignited something deep within me. He held my gaze with a calm intensity, the world around us fading into a muted backdrop. It was an unspoken connection that lingered in the air, thick with anticipation. I had to resist the urge to turn away, to break the spell, but instead, I felt a smile tug at my lips, a playful invitation dancing between us.

"Coffee in hand, I see," he said, his voice smooth like aged whiskey, drawing closer as if our conversation were a well-kept secret. "I hope you're not a connoisseur who judges the brew here too harshly."

"Not unless it's absolutely terrible," I replied, trying to sound nonchalant. "But fortunately, Maple's is pretty solid. It's the only place in town that gets it right."

He chuckled, a rich, warm sound that made the corners of my heart flutter. "Then I'm glad to be here, in that case. I wouldn't want to offend a local."

There was a playful glint in his eyes, and I was struck by how comfortable he seemed, how effortlessly he navigated the café's familiar chaos. It wasn't just his looks; it was the way he engaged with those around him, as though he belonged to a world that thrived on spontaneity. I could sense my pulse quicken, excitement brewing at the thought of someone shaking up our staid little bubble.

We drifted into a conversation that felt both exhilarating and natural, punctuated by laughter and shared observations about the town. I learned that Luke had just arrived from a bustling city where dreams and disappointments raced past one another on crowded streets. He described his move with a mixture of nostalgia and hope, the way a painter speaks of their canvas—every stroke imbued with intention. I found myself leaning in, hanging onto his every word as if they were droplets of rain on parched earth, soaking in the possibility of a life less ordinary.

As the minutes turned into an hour, the café began to quiet down, the regulars filtering out into the evening. The sun dipped lower, casting elongated shadows that danced across the wooden floor. I stole glances at the clock, each tick a reminder that reality awaited beyond the sanctuary of our conversation. Yet here I was, entranced by a stranger whose very presence threatened to unravel the predictable tapestry of my life.

"Are you planning to stick around Willow Creek?" I asked, my voice laced with an eagerness I couldn't quite hide.

He paused, his smile fading for just a fraction of a second, as if weighing the significance of my question. "That depends," he said, a teasing glimmer in his eyes. "What's it like living in a town where everyone knows your business?"

I laughed, unable to resist the magnetic pull of his charm. "You'd find it both comforting and suffocating. It's all about balance—knowing when to join the chorus and when to step back."

"Maybe I'll stay long enough to learn the rhythm," he replied, his voice imbued with a playfulness that felt like a dare. The way he leaned closer suggested he wanted to know more, to dive deeper into this new connection we were forging.

But beneath the surface, I felt a tremor of apprehension. A stranger could easily become a catalyst for change, and change was a double-edged sword. My heart raced, eager for the adventure he represented while simultaneously questioning the safety of my well-worn path. In this small café, with coffee swirling in the air like dreams waiting to be realized, I stood on the precipice of something new, and I couldn't help but wonder how far I was willing to leap.

The atmosphere buzzed with potential, and in that moment, the future stretched out before us like an uncharted map, daring us to explore its every crevice and hidden treasure.

The conversation flowed with a rhythm that felt both foreign and exhilarating, like the gentle swell of waves teasing the shoreline. I could hardly believe how easily our words intertwined, each shared laugh peeling back layers of hesitation. Luke's eyes sparkled with mischief as he recounted tales from the city—a place that pulsed with life, the air thick with opportunity. The way he described crowded sidewalks, street vendors peddling wares that reflected a kaleidoscope of cultures, made Willow Creek feel like a quaint, albeit charming, museum piece.

"I'll admit," he said, leaning closer as though sharing a tantalizing secret, "there are days I miss the chaos. The thrill of bumping into strangers who become instant friends, if only for a moment." His voice dipped, gaining a conspiratorial tone. "But then, I imagine a life of quiet mornings in a café where the coffee is good and the people, well, a bit predictable."

A smile tugged at my lips, and for a fleeting moment, I entertained the thought that perhaps predictability had its merits. But there was something liberating about Luke, a magnetic pull that beckoned me to step outside my own carefully curated boundaries. The sun slipped behind the horizon, painting the windows with golden hues, casting soft shadows that danced across the café.

"You could always stir things up around here," I challenged playfully, feeling the warmth of camaraderie seep into my bones. "People might need a bit of disruption."

"Oh, I plan to," he replied, his eyes glinting with a blend of mischief and determination. "Every place has its pulse, and I'm here to find out what makes Willow Creek tick." His confidence was contagious, and I could almost hear the faint echo of my own heartbeat quickening in response.

I pondered the implications of his words, the audacity of someone willing to unravel the threads of our well-ordered lives. A tingle of excitement coursed through me, and as I looked into his eyes, I felt a flicker of something I had long thought buried—an insatiable desire for adventure, for stories yet untold.

The café's door swung open with a jingle, interrupting our moment. A group of familiar faces shuffled in, their laughter a soothing reminder of the community I was a part of. They settled into their usual corners, their easy chatter a stark contrast to the electric undercurrent I felt with Luke. I couldn't help but wonder what they would think if they knew I was sharing this space with a stranger—an enigma that could unravel my carefully structured life.

"Mind if I join you?" Luke's voice drew me back, his curiosity evident. He motioned toward the empty chair across from me, his invitation both thrilling and terrifying.

"Go right ahead," I replied, surprising myself with how welcoming I sounded. I was not typically one to embrace the unknown, preferring the safe familiarity of my circle. Yet, here I was, welcoming this new chapter, eager to discover what lay beyond the borders of my comfort zone.

As he settled in, our conversation transformed, drifting between light-hearted banter and deeper revelations. Luke shared his love for the outdoors, recounting hikes that had taken him through breathtaking landscapes, where the mountains kissed the sky and rivers whispered secrets to the wind. His passion was infectious, igniting a spark within me that I hadn't realized had dulled over the years.

"Have you ever climbed to the top of Willow Peak?" he asked, his tone casual yet probing, as if testing the waters of my adventurous spirit.

I shook my head, a hint of regret surfacing. "No, it's always seemed too daunting. I'm more of a stroll-through-the-park kind of girl."

"Then it's settled," he declared, his excitement palpable. "We'll go together. You'll see that the view from the top is worth every step." His eyes held a challenge, a dare to break free from the mundane, and I felt an undeniable thrill at the prospect of exploring something new with him.

The evening wore on, the soft glow of the café's lights creating a cocoon that felt both intimate and inviting. I glanced at the clock again, time slipping through my fingers like grains of sand. Each moment spent with Luke felt significant, filled with a warmth that contrasted sharply with the cool autumn air outside. The familiar sounds of the café faded into a soft hum as I lost myself in our exchange, a dance of words that felt choreographed by fate itself.

But amid the laughter, I felt a stirring of apprehension, an internal voice reminding me of the risks that came with opening up to someone new. Was it wise to welcome this stranger into my life? And yet, as I looked across the table at him, I saw not a threat but a promise—a glimpse of what could be if I allowed myself to embrace the unknown.

"I should probably get going soon," I said reluctantly, not wanting the evening to end.

Luke raised an eyebrow, his playful smile unfaltering. "And miss our chance to plot world domination over coffee? I wouldn't dream of it."

The lightheartedness of his comment drew a genuine laugh from me, dispelling the remnants of doubt that clung to my thoughts. "Okay, fine. One more cup," I relented, signaling to the barista for a refill.

As I settled back into our conversation, I couldn't shake the feeling that this was more than just an ordinary meeting of two strangers. There was an energy between us, an unspoken bond that hinted at shared adventures and secrets waiting to be discovered. With every word, Luke seemed to peel back the layers of my carefully constructed façade, revealing parts of myself that had long been tucked away, gathering dust.

I found myself sharing stories I hadn't told anyone in years—my childhood dreams of traveling the world, my hidden passion for painting, the way I had always felt more alive when lost in nature. He listened intently, his gaze unwavering, as though I were the most fascinating story he had ever encountered. It felt refreshing to be seen, to share my hopes and fears with someone who seemed to genuinely care.

And just like that, as the stars began to twinkle in the indigo sky outside, I realized that I was no longer merely a spectator in my own life. I was a participant, eager to embrace the journey that lay ahead. Luke was not just a stranger; he was a doorway to something more—an unexpected twist in the narrative of my life, daring me to leap and discover where this new path might lead.

As the café clock ticked softly, a rhythmic reminder of time's passage, I felt the world outside gradually slipping into the hush of evening. Maple Café, with its warm lights and rustic wooden tables, created a cocoon that seemed to insulate us from the encroaching darkness. The golden glow from the overhead lamps glinted off Luke's features, emphasizing the shadows that danced across his face, making him look almost ethereal. With each laugh we shared, it felt as if we were drawing a fine line around our little universe, one that excluded the routine of Willow Creek and the familiar faces that would soon filter out into the night.

"You mentioned you're here to discover what makes Willow Creek tick," I said, taking a sip of my coffee and savoring the rich, nutty flavor. "What exactly are you hoping to find?" I was intrigued, perhaps a bit possessive of my hometown, protective of its quirks and charms.

Luke leaned back, fingers lacing behind his head, the gesture exuding a casual confidence that made me both curious and envious. "I'm looking for stories," he replied, his eyes narrowing as if he were evaluating the landscape of the town, not just the café. "Every place has its hidden narratives—people who've experienced love, loss, joy, and despair. I want to know what drives them, what shapes their lives."

I couldn't help but admire his ambition. The way he spoke ignited something deep within me, a flicker of the writer I had buried beneath years of predictability. I had always found solace in crafting stories, yet somehow, I had allowed my own narrative to stagnate. Listening to Luke, I realized that my life was more than the routine I had come to accept. It was rich with moments that had shaped me, and perhaps, they were stories worth telling.

"I've lived here my whole life," I confessed, a hint of vulnerability creeping into my tone. "But I feel like I've barely scratched the surface of what this town has to offer. I know the obvious things—the best fishing spots, the hidden trails behind the old schoolhouse—but I think there's more."

"Then why not explore it together?" he proposed, his tone light, yet laced with an earnestness that sent my heart racing. "We could unearth those stories, peel back the layers of this town and see what it really holds." His proposal was a spark of inspiration, igniting a longing in me that I hadn't felt in years.

A part of me hesitated; the echo of my cautious nature whispered warnings. What would it mean to embark on this adventure with a stranger? Yet another voice, quieter but insistent, reminded me that sometimes the most rewarding journeys began with a single leap of faith. The thought of sharing this exploration with Luke thrilled me, the idea blooming like a wildflower in the cracks of my predictable life.

"Okay," I said, barely able to contain my excitement. "Let's do it. Let's find those stories."

His grin widened, lighting up his features and making my heart flutter in response. "Excellent! We'll start with the locals. I bet they have tales that would make even the most seasoned traveler envious."

As we brainstormed our plan, the café filled with the comforting scent of freshly baked pastries and the soothing hum of conversations. We talked late into the evening, crafting an informal itinerary filled with visits to the farmers' market, local artisans, and even the annual town fair that was just around the corner. Each idea felt like a step away from the ordinary, and I reveled in the thought of what lay ahead.

The atmosphere shifted as the last of the customers departed, leaving only the two of us surrounded by remnants of laughter and clinking dishes. Outside, the sky had darkened into a deep navy, the stars flickering like tiny beacons, winking in on our little secret. The moon hung low, casting a soft light that spilled through the windows, illuminating Luke's face, his expression a mix of enthusiasm and focus as he sketched out plans on a napkin.

"What's your story?" I asked, genuinely curious, wanting to peel back the layers of this man who had already begun to feel like more than just a stranger.

He paused, his gaze flicking up to meet mine, a shadow of something deeper flickering behind those dark eyes. "It's not as exciting as yours," he replied, a hint of self-deprecation in his voice. "I grew up in the city, surrounded by ambition and noise. It was thrilling and exhausting. I've been searching for a place that feels... real, where I can reconnect with the quieter parts of myself. I thought maybe I'd find it here."

"Sounds like you're looking for solace," I said, understanding the undertone of his words, feeling the weight of his longing.

"Maybe," he admitted, his voice softening. "But more than that, I want to create something meaningful. My job used to consume me, and I lost sight of what mattered."

His vulnerability resonated with me, revealing that beneath his confident exterior lay a depth I found alluring. I wanted to know more—the reasons behind his desire to reconnect, the dreams that had led him to Willow Creek. But before I could press further, the moment was interrupted by the barista, who appeared, collecting empty mugs with a smile that suggested she had seen our budding connection.

"Closed for the night, folks," she chirped, glancing at the clock as if we needed the reminder. "But don't worry, we'll be here bright and early tomorrow!"

Luke glanced at me, a playful glint in his eye. "Tomorrow, then? We can kick off our adventure bright and early. I promise I'll bring the enthusiasm; you just bring your best stories."

I laughed, feeling an unexpected surge of excitement. "Deal. But you'll need to keep up with my caffeine consumption."

He chuckled, rising from the table with a grace that spoke to his ease in this unfamiliar setting. "I think I can handle that."

As we stepped outside, the cool air wrapped around us like a shroud, invigorating and charged with possibility. The stars twinkled above as if cheering us on, and I felt a surge of anticipation bubbling in my chest. This wasn't merely an encounter with a stranger; it was the beginning of a partnership, an uncharted adventure that promised to breathe life into the stories hidden in the crevices of Willow Creek.

With each step away from the café, I felt the weight of my past routines start to lift. The streets, lit by the soft glow of streetlamps, beckoned us like old friends eager to share their tales. I glanced at

Luke, his silhouette outlined against the backdrop of a small town filled with dreams waiting to be uncovered. For the first time in a long time, I felt alive, as if my life were a canvas once again, ready for vibrant strokes of color and experiences yet to come.

As we parted ways, a gentle breeze ruffled my hair, and I couldn't help but smile, knowing that tomorrow held a promise of exploration. With Luke by my side, Willow Creek transformed from a mere backdrop to an expansive landscape brimming with possibilities, each moment a chance to rewrite the narrative of my life. And as I drifted off to sleep that night, I couldn't shake the feeling that this was only the beginning—a first chapter in a much larger story waiting to unfold.

Chapter 3: A Past Unraveled

The attic was a realm of shadows and echoes, the air thick with the scent of musty paper and faded memories. I felt like an intruder in my own past, tiptoeing through the labyrinth of old trunks and peeling wallpaper that whispered tales of lives once lived. Each step sent a tiny cloud of dust spiraling into the dim light, dancing like lost souls trying to find their way home. Sunlight filtered through a small window, illuminating motes that glimmered like stars in this forgotten universe, and I couldn't help but wonder what stories lay hidden beneath the surface of this cluttered sanctuary.

As I rummaged through the decaying relics of my childhood, I was struck by the weight of nostalgia mixed with sorrow. The faded letters—yellowed and brittle—spoke of a time before my birth, when my mother was a woman with dreams and desires far removed from the shadowed figure I remembered. Her laughter, once vibrant and full of life, seemed muffled in the dusty corners of this attic. I clutched the edge of a weathered trunk, feeling the rough wood beneath my fingertips as if seeking solace in its solidity.

That's when I saw it, half-buried under a tattered quilt and a stack of outdated magazines—a locked box, its surface polished to a dull sheen, glimmering faintly like a beacon of secrets. My heart quickened, an involuntary reaction to the discovery. The engraving on the lid was unmistakable, a careful script that spelled out my mother's name. I felt a magnetic pull toward it, as if the box held not just her belongings but a part of her soul that had been hidden away. With trembling hands, I turned it over, searching for the keyhole that guarded whatever lay inside.

It didn't take long to pry the box open; the lock yielded easily to my persistence, releasing a soft click that echoed in the stillness around me. As the lid lifted, a rush of stale air escaped, carrying with it the scent of time and untold stories. I hesitated for a moment, my breath caught in my throat. What if the contents revealed a side of my mother I could never reconcile with the woman I knew? My heart raced with both excitement and dread.

Inside the box, neatly folded letters lay stacked like a collection of secrets begging to be unraveled. Each envelope was addressed not to my father, as I had always assumed, but to a name that was unfamiliar and oddly foreign. With each letter I read, the world I had known began to shift and twist, blurring the lines between love and loss, truth and deception. The ink was as vivid as the emotions that spilled forth from the pages—longing, regret, and a heartache that transcended time.

The letters chronicled a relationship I had never fathomed. My mother's words flowed with a poetic cadence, revealing a woman deeply in love yet tethered by obligations she could never fully escape. This other person, a mysterious figure tucked away in the folds of her past, was an enigma that pulled at my heartstrings, igniting a curiosity that burned bright. How could I have grown up believing I knew her entirely when I was now confronted with this unfamiliar piece of her?

As I continued to read, the warmth of the attic began to feel stifling, the weight of the letters heavy in my hands. My surroundings faded, and I was transported into the landscape of her memories. I could see her—young and radiant—laughing in sun-drenched fields, dancing barefoot on the cool grass beneath a sky painted with the hues of dusk. Her joy felt palpable, yet so distant, as if I were peering through a veil of time. She wrote of adventures that seemed larger than life, filled with secrets shared under the stars and whispers exchanged in the shadows of trees that stood witness to their love.

But as the letters continued, the tone shifted, revealing the tangled threads of her reality. Words like "sacrifice" and "duty" stood out starkly against the backdrop of affection, hinting at the choices that had led her to build a life that, to me, had always seemed singular and uncomplicated. The exhilaration I felt turned to a hollow ache as I recognized the price she had paid for the life she had chosen. I was left grappling with the knowledge that my mother had not only been a nurturing figure but also a woman of depth, grappling with the weight of her own heart's desires.

The realization settled over me like a heavy cloak. I wasn't merely here to pack away memories; I was embarking on a journey to understand a woman who had been both a mother and an individual long before I entered her world. My childhood was wrapped in the warmth of her love, but it was this newfound understanding of her complexity that ignited a yearning deep within me—a desire to uncover the truth about not only her life but my own.

In that moment, the dust of the attic transformed into a tapestry woven from threads of my mother's past and my present. Each item, each letter, held a piece of a puzzle I was determined to complete. I felt a surge of determination coursing through my veins, igniting a flame of curiosity that had long been dormant. If I could piece together the fragments of her life, perhaps I could discover more about myself in the process.

I inhaled deeply, allowing the air thick with nostalgia to fill my lungs, a reminder that the past was not something to be feared but embraced. I was no longer just the daughter of a woman who had crafted a life of hidden complexities; I was on the cusp of a journey that would unravel the truths that had been left unspoken. With each letter, each revelation, I would navigate the intricacies of love, loss, and identity, forging a connection to the woman who had shaped my existence in ways I had yet to comprehend.

The air in the attic felt electric, alive with unspoken stories swirling around me like a dance of ghosts. As I sat cross-legged on the wooden floor, surrounded by the remnants of a life once vibrant, I realized that this locked box was not merely an artifact of my mother's past; it was a portal. With every letter I unfolded, I could almost hear the echoes of her laughter and the gentle cadence of her voice, weaving a tapestry of emotions that intertwined with my own.

I surrendered to the words, each one unfurling secrets like petals of a flower blooming under the weight of sunlight. The letters spoke of a love that felt both foreign and familiar, a love that illuminated the shadows of my mother's existence while casting new ones over my own. This mysterious figure, whose name I'd yet to fully grasp, had clearly played a pivotal role in her life—a role that made me question the narratives I had clung to throughout my upbringing.

In one particularly poignant letter, my mother described an afternoon spent in a secluded park, the air heavy with the scent of blooming lilacs, a memory imbued with a bittersweet glow. Her words flowed like a river, rich with affection as she recounted stolen glances and laughter that rang like music against the backdrop of rustling leaves. The joy in her prose was palpable, yet beneath it lay an undercurrent of something more profound—an aching desire for freedom that was both liberating and suffocating. I could feel the weight of the choices she had faced, the crossroads where love and responsibility collided with consequences that rippled outward.

As the afternoon sun began to set, casting a golden hue through the attic window, I felt a newfound determination take root within me. With each letter, I unearthed fragments of her spirit that resonated deeply with my own long-buried hopes and dreams. I was not just the sum of her sacrifices; I was a continuation of her story, woven together with the fibers of her past. I longed to understand not just the woman who had raised me, but the girl she had once been, fearless and alive, filled with aspirations that seemed to have dimmed as the years wore on.

I shifted my weight, the floorboards creaking softly beneath me, as I reached for another letter, the familiar handwriting like a gentle caress against my fingertips. This one was different. The tone shifted dramatically, revealing a struggle cloaked in vulnerability. My mother's words expressed a heartache that felt both raw and intimate, detailing moments of doubt that hung like storm clouds over her choices. She wrote of sleepless nights filled with what-ifs, of the weight of unspoken words lodged in her throat, and the incessant nagging of dreams deferred.

I leaned back against the wall, the reality of my mother's complexity wrapping around me like a thick fog. How had I been so blind? The woman I had known was so tightly bound by her choices that I had forgotten she was once a dreamer, too, battling the quiet chaos of her desires against the harshness of reality. I could see now that my childhood memories had painted her in shades of perfection, a canvas unmarred by the struggles that had surely shaped her.

With the sun sinking lower, the attic became a sanctuary of revelations, a cocoon of discovery that enveloped me in its embrace. I reached for the final few letters, my heart racing with anticipation and trepidation. Each one felt like a key, unlocking another layer of understanding that would connect me more intimately to her essence. The last letter, the one that felt both heavy and light in my hands, was addressed simply to "My Dearest."

My breath caught as I unfolded the paper, feeling the fibers whisper against my skin. The words that flowed from her pen were a symphony of love and despair, a raw honesty that felt like an offering. She spoke of a decision she had made—a choice that had sealed her fate and mine in ways I had yet to comprehend. The name of the mysterious figure resonated throughout the letter like a haunting refrain, a name that now danced on the tip of my tongue, tantalizing and elusive.

Suddenly, the walls of the attic closed in around me, constricting with the gravity of my discovery. The shimmering reality that I was more than my mother's daughter, that I was an extension of her life, began to weave itself into the fabric of my being. My heart raced not just with revelation but with the weight of expectation. I realized I could no longer merely exist as a reflection of her choices; I had to explore the depths of my own desires and confront the shadows of my past.

With newfound resolve, I set the letters aside, the sunlight fading into dusk, casting an ethereal glow across the attic. The contours of the room became soft and inviting, transforming the once-stifling atmosphere into a sanctuary filled with possibility. I rose to my feet, brushing the dust from my knees as I began to gather the letters and tuck them carefully back into the box. Each one felt like a fragile treasure, a piece of my mother that I was determined to safeguard.

I cast a final glance around the attic, my heart swelling with gratitude for the time I had spent there. I had unearthed not just remnants of the past but an opportunity to redefine my future, to embrace the unknown and explore the depths of my own identity. The echoes of my mother's life would resonate within me, guiding me as I ventured into a world filled with uncharted territory.

As I descended the attic stairs, the weight of the box cradled in my arms, I felt a sense of liberation wash over me. I was no longer simply the daughter living in the shadow of her mother; I was becoming the woman my mother had always hoped I could be. With every step, I carried with me the knowledge that the journey ahead would be fraught with challenges, but it would also be rich with discovery—a chance to carve my own path while honoring the legacy of the remarkable woman who had come before me.

The weight of the box felt like a steady heartbeat in my arms as I navigated the stairs, each creak of the wood beneath me resonating like the ticking of a clock, counting down to something significant. My mind buzzed with the implications of what I had discovered. It wasn't just a collection of letters; it was a lifeline to my mother's soul, a map that hinted at the contours of her hidden life. As I reached the bottom of the stairs, a newfound urgency coursed through me. I needed to understand the depth of her choices, to delve into the narrative that had shaped her and, by extension, molded me.

Once in the cozy chaos of the living room, I placed the box on the coffee table, its dark wood gleaming ominously in the soft glow of the lamp. I took a deep breath, steadying myself as I prepared to explore the depths of my mother's past further. I had spent countless nights wondering who she had been before the family dinner tables, the PTA meetings, and the Sunday church services claimed her. Each letter had peeled back layers, revealing a woman whose heart pulsed with longing and dreams—a stark contrast to the quiet life I had always known.

I reached for the first letter again, eager to immerse myself in her words. The first few letters had spoken of clandestine meetings and stolen moments in hidden cafes, where whispered dreams were exchanged over steaming cups of coffee. I envisioned my mother, youthful and full of life, animatedly discussing her passions with someone whose laughter mingled with the aroma of fresh pastries, the world outside a blur of vibrant colors. There was poetry in those letters, an intoxicating energy that contrasted sharply with the pragmatic woman who had guided my life.

But as I progressed through the collection, the tone shifted once more, revealing the underbelly of her existence—the guilt that gnawed at her, the suffocating grip of responsibility that left little room for her desires. I found myself captivated by the duality of her world, the bright hues of love contrasted with the somber shades of duty. I could feel the weight of her struggles pressing against my chest, drawing tears from my eyes as I recognized the unfulfilled dreams that echoed in her words.

One particular letter stood out, marked by a fragile crease that suggested it had been opened and read many times. In it, my mother recounted a moment of heartbreak, detailing a confrontation with her love—a man whose name now danced tantalizingly in my mind but remained just out of reach. The intensity of her emotions spilled onto the page, the ink smudged as if her tears had mingled with the words. She described the finality of a choice made not out of desire but necessity, a choice that reverberated through time, shaping not only her life but mine.

Reading her confession, I felt as though I were peering into the very marrow of her being. The walls of my childhood home seemed to dissolve around me, revealing a new landscape filled with possibilities. What if I could step beyond the boundaries of my current life and embrace the complexity that lay within me? What if I could forge my own path, unshackled from the expectations that had always held me captive?

The box suddenly felt lighter in my hands, as if the very act of understanding my mother's past had liberated me from my own self-imposed limitations. I tucked the letters back into the box, a promise to myself that I would revisit them, savor their wisdom as I began to navigate the uncharted waters of my life.

The following days were filled with a fervor I hadn't felt in years. Each morning, I woke with the rising sun, eager to explore the city that had once felt like a maze of obligations and routines. With each step down the familiar streets, I began to see them through a new lens. The coffee shop around the corner, once merely a stop for caffeine, transformed into a haven of possibility where I could pen my own dreams. The park where I had jogged countless times became a canvas of inspiration, each rustling leaf whispering tales of my mother's unspoken desires.

I revisited the letters often, savoring the rhythm of her words as if they were a balm for my restless spirit. I found myself drifting into reveries of what might have been, weaving together her stories with my own hopes, sketching a future that embraced the vibrant chaos of life. It was exhilarating and terrifying, this newfound sense of freedom that came with understanding my mother's choices. I began to craft my own narrative, each decision becoming a brushstroke on the canvas of my existence.

One fateful afternoon, I decided to visit the quaint bookstore that had long been a refuge for my soul. Its creaky wooden floors and the scent of aged paper always invited me in. As I entered, the familiar jingle of the bell overhead felt like an old friend greeting me. I wandered through the aisles, my fingers grazing the spines of books that seemed to beckon me with their untold stories. It was here, amidst the towering shelves, that I first caught sight of him—an intriguing stranger who appeared lost in the pages of a novel.

He had dark hair tousled in a way that suggested he had just emerged from an adventure of his own, and his eyes, a striking shade of green, sparkled with an intensity that made my heart race. There was something effortlessly charming about him, a presence that felt electric. I couldn't help but wonder if he was carrying his own secrets, perhaps even a story of love and sacrifice that mirrored my mother's.

I found myself gravitating toward him, drawn in by an inexplicable urge to connect. "What are you reading?" I ventured, my voice barely more than a whisper, as if I were stepping onto sacred ground.

He looked up, surprise flickering across his features, quickly replaced by a warm smile that lit up the dim space around us. "It's a tale about second chances," he replied, his voice smooth and inviting. "The kind where the protagonist learns that it's never too late to chase what truly makes them happy."

As we fell into conversation, sharing snippets of our lives, I felt an exhilarating connection—one that pulsed with the promise of new beginnings. It was as if the universe conspired to lead me here, to him, at this very moment. I could feel my mother's spirit nudging me forward, urging me to embrace the unpredictable tapestry of life.

In that small bookstore, surrounded by stories both old and new, I began to envision a future that combined my dreams with my mother's. The man before me was not just a stranger; he was a part of a narrative that was unfolding, a testament to the idea that connections could spark from the ashes of the past. My heart swelled with the possibility of what lay ahead, the prospect of love, adventure, and self-discovery swirling around me like the dust motes that danced in the afternoon light.

And so, in the midst of unraveling my mother's past, I began to weave my own story—one that was vibrant, complex, and uniquely mine. Each moment became a thread, interlacing with the legacies of those who had come before me, forging a path that was as unpredictable as it was beautiful. I was no longer just the daughter of a woman shaped by her choices; I was becoming the author of my own life, ready to embrace the future with open arms.

Chapter 4: Luke's Secret

The summer sun cast a golden hue over Willow Creek, bathing the town in a warm, inviting glow that seemed to promise healing. The streets, lined with quaint Victorian houses adorned with blooming hydrangeas, sang a soft lullaby of nostalgia. Each home held stories whispered between neighbors and laughter echoing from backyards. Yet, beneath this picturesque facade lay the undercurrents of life that flowed with the speed and unpredictability of a river, occasionally swallowing those unprepared for its depths.

I often found myself drawn to the old oak tree in the park, its gnarled branches spreading wide like a protective embrace. It was here, beneath its leafy canopy, that I felt the presence of my mother most keenly. I could almost hear her laughter mingling with the rustling leaves, urging me to push through the pain. But it was also here that Luke first entered my life—a whirlwind of dark hair and earnest eyes that made my heart flutter with both hope and trepidation.

From our initial meeting, Luke seemed to slip into my life with the effortless grace of a dancer. His laughter was infectious, each chuckle spilling into the air like the gentle tinkling of wind chimes. When he was around, the world seemed to blur into a softer focus, the edges of my grief dulled by his steady presence. Yet, I couldn't shake the feeling that there was an unseen storm brewing beneath his calm exterior, one that threatened to pull him away just as quickly as he had come.

We often spent long afternoons strolling through the town, exploring the tiny antique shops and quaint cafes that lined Main Street. Each visit to the local bookstore felt like a treasure hunt, searching for lost words among the dusty shelves. Luke would find obscure novels and share passages that left me pondering long after we left, his enthusiasm igniting a spark within me. In those moments, I could almost forget the hollow ache of loss that nestled in my chest.

But as the days stretched into weeks, I began to notice the shadow that flickered in his gaze when he thought I wasn't looking. The way he would pull his sleeve down over the scar on his forearm like it was a secret too heavy to share. Each time I tried to dig deeper, he skillfully redirected our conversations, weaving laughter and charm into his responses, leaving me with more questions than answers.

One sultry evening, as the sun dipped below the horizon and painted the sky in hues of orange and pink, we sat on the porch of my favorite café, sipping iced tea that shimmered like amber in the fading light. The scent of blooming jasmine lingered in the air, mixing with the aroma of freshly baked pastries from inside. It was the perfect backdrop for confession, yet I hesitated, feeling the weight of my curiosity pressing against the delicate fabric of our budding connection.

"Luke," I began, my voice barely above a whisper, "what's your story?" The question hung between us like a fragile thread, ready to snap at the slightest tug.

He turned to me, his expression shifting from playful to serious, his eyes darkening like a storm cloud gathering on the horizon. "You know, sometimes the past is best left buried," he replied, his tone heavy with an unspoken burden.

I felt a pang of disappointment, the distance between us expanding like a chasm. "But it's a part of you. It shapes who you are." I tried to keep my voice steady, but the tremor revealed the truth of my own scars—those invisible marks left by grief.

He sighed, rubbing the back of his neck, a gesture that revealed his discomfort. "Some stories are harder to tell, especially when they don't have a happy ending." The flicker of vulnerability in his gaze ignited a flicker of empathy within me. I wanted to reach out, to bridge that widening gap, but the shadows lurking in his words held me back.

As twilight settled around us, I caught a glimpse of something in Luke's eyes—a mix of pain and longing that struck a chord deep within me. It was as if we were both wading through murky waters, trying to find solid ground while grappling with our own histories. "You can trust me," I urged, my voice barely louder than a breath, filled with the earnestness of someone desperate to connect.

He hesitated, and for a moment, I thought he might finally let me in. But just as quickly, that flicker of hope dimmed. He laughed, a hollow sound that echoed in the stillness. "Maybe one day, I'll share it with you. Just... not today."

And so, the night carried on, laden with unsaid words and unbroken silence. The stars began to twinkle overhead, tiny diamonds scattered across the velvet sky, but the warmth between us felt like a fragile candle flickering in the wind. As the café's lights dimmed and the patrons trickled out, I couldn't shake the feeling that beneath the layers of charm and laughter, Luke was caught in a storm of his own making, one that might sweep him away before I could understand the depths of his heart.

The next morning, the sun rose with an urgency that pierced the tranquility of Willow Creek. The air was thick with anticipation, a heavy stillness settling over the town like a shroud. I could feel it deep in my bones, the whisper of change brushing against my skin. As I stepped onto the porch, my coffee steaming in hand, I sensed that today would not be just another ordinary day.

The remnants of last night's conversation played in my mind like a haunting melody. I resolved to unravel the mystery of Luke, to draw him out of the shadows he so carefully curated. Little did I know, the answers I sought were tangled in the fabric of his past, woven with threads of pain and secrets waiting to unravel in the most unexpected ways.

The morning sun poured through the window, casting a warm glow over my small kitchen. I stood at the counter, coffee in hand, the rich aroma swirling around me like a comforting embrace. With each sip, I felt a flicker of determination light within me, fueled by the notion that today might finally unveil the secrets that clung to Luke like a second skin. I needed to find a way to breach the walls he had built, even if it meant risking the fragile connection we had formed.

After a quick breakfast, I slipped on my worn sneakers and headed out. The air was thick with the scent of blooming lilacs, intoxicating in its sweetness. The world felt alive, bustling with activity as the townsfolk went about their daily routines. I waved at Mrs. Hargrove, who was tending to her garden, her wide-brimmed hat shielding her from the sun. The smile she offered was filled with the warmth of community, a reminder of the love that surrounded me even in my darkest moments.

I decided to take the long way to the park, weaving through the winding streets and savoring the morning light. I thought of Luke and the walls he had erected around his past, impenetrable yet intriguing. What haunted him? What memories lay buried beneath the surface? I felt a mix of frustration and empathy churn inside me, pushing me to delve deeper into his story.

As I arrived at the park, the old oak tree stood proudly in the center, its branches swaying gently in the breeze, beckoning me closer. I spotted Luke sitting on a bench beneath its sprawling canopy, a book resting on his lap, his brow furrowed in concentration. The sunlight danced through the leaves, casting dappled shadows across his face, accentuating the strong angles of his jaw and the way his hair fell slightly over his forehead. He looked up as I approached, a smile breaking through the seriousness of his expression, and my heart did that familiar somersault.

"Good morning, stranger," he teased, closing his book and setting it aside as if it were a mere distraction from the world around him.

"Mind if I join you?" I asked, sinking onto the bench beside him, the wood cool against my skin.

"Not at all. I was just pondering the mysteries of life," he replied with a playful smirk.

His charm never failed to draw me in, and I couldn't help but laugh. "Or just pretending to read that book?" I nudged him lightly, feeling a familiar rush of warmth flow between us.

"Guilty as charged," he admitted, feigning a look of remorse before breaking into a grin. "But I was thinking about you."

"Me? What about me?" I asked, a teasing lilt in my voice, even as my heart raced at the thought.

He leaned in slightly, his expression shifting from playful to sincere, a shadow of seriousness passing over his features. "I was thinking about how much you've shared with me lately. Your dreams, your fears... but I feel like I haven't reciprocated."

I held my breath, the air around us thickening with anticipation. "I'm here to listen if you want to talk," I encouraged gently, my heart hammering in my chest.

Luke hesitated, glancing away as if searching for the right words in the leaves rustling above us. "It's not that simple," he said finally, his voice low. "I don't want to burden you with my past."

"Your past doesn't burden me. It makes you who you are," I insisted, feeling a pull of connection urging me to dig deeper. "We all have our stories, Luke. I promise I can handle it."

His gaze locked onto mine, and for a heartbeat, I thought he might finally let me in. "You really want to know?" he asked, the challenge hanging in the air.

"More than anything," I replied earnestly, willing the sincerity to shine through.

He took a deep breath, as if steeling himself against the tide of memories threatening to spill forth. "I grew up in a small town, not too different from this one," he began, his voice steady but laced with an undercurrent of tension. "Things were... complicated. My parents had their issues, and I often felt like I was caught in the middle."

I nodded, my heart aching for the boy he once was, trapped in a cycle of family strife. "That's tough," I said softly, feeling the weight of his words settle between us like a tangible thing.

"Yeah, well, it got worse," he continued, his gaze drifting back to the ground. "I made some choices that I'm not proud of—choices that hurt people. I thought I could escape it all by leaving."

The vulnerability in his voice struck a chord deep within me, resonating with my own struggles. "We all make mistakes," I offered, hoping to reassure him. "It's part of being human."

He chuckled, but it lacked humor. "Some mistakes have consequences that follow you, no matter how far you run." His eyes darkened, a storm brewing beneath the surface. "I've had to look over my shoulder ever since."

The gravity of his words weighed heavily, and I felt the air grow colder around us. "Are you... in danger?" I asked, my heart racing at the thought of something lurking just beyond the horizon.

"I've learned to navigate my life carefully," he said, a hint of defiance sparking in his eyes. "But it's hard not to feel like the past is always nipping at my heels."

A silence enveloped us, thick with unspoken fears and shared vulnerabilities. The vibrant colors of the park faded into the background, leaving only the two of us suspended in this fragile moment. I reached out, brushing my fingers against his forearm, tracing the faint scar that lay beneath the fabric of his shirt. "You don't have to face this alone," I whispered, willing him to understand.

Luke turned to me, surprise flickering in his gaze, and for a brief second, I could see the conflict warring within him. "You don't know what you're asking," he said, the gravity of his past pressing down on his words.

"Maybe not, but I'm willing to learn," I replied, my heart full of determination. "Whatever it is, we can figure it out together."

He searched my eyes, a moment stretching between us like an elastic band, ready to snap with the weight of our confessions. In that instant, I knew that the connection we shared was more than just a passing fling; it was a tether binding our fates together, challenging us to confront our truths.

As the sun dipped lower in the sky, casting long shadows that danced beneath the oak, I felt a sense of purpose swell within me. Luke's past might have been a tempest, but I was ready to weather the storm with him. In the heart of Willow Creek, amidst the memories and mysteries that lingered like ghosts, we would navigate the uncharted waters together—healing, discovering, and perhaps even learning to forgive ourselves along the way.

The air was electric as I sat beside Luke, the weight of his revelations hanging between us like the heavy humidity of a summer afternoon. As the sun sank lower in the sky, its rays filtered through the leaves, creating a mosaic of light and shadow that danced on our skin. The park had taken on a dreamy quality, the distant laughter of children mingling with the chirping of crickets preparing for twilight. It was a backdrop of serene normalcy, yet beneath it lay the tumult of unspoken fears and buried truths.

I felt a sense of urgency settle within me, a fire ignited by the flicker of vulnerability Luke had shown. The secrets he carried felt like a tapestry woven with threads of pain, and I longed to unravel it, to see the full picture. "You can tell me anything, Luke," I urged, my voice steady, even as my heart raced. "I promise I won't judge. Whatever it is, I can handle it."

His expression shifted, uncertainty mingling with a flicker of something else—hope, perhaps? He looked out at the park, his jaw tightening. "It's not that simple. Sometimes, it's easier to carry the burden alone. Trust me."

"I understand the desire to protect yourself," I said softly. "But I also know the weight of carrying secrets alone. It can be suffocating. Let me share that weight with you." I watched as his gaze flickered back to mine, the battle of resolve playing out behind his dark eyes.

He leaned back, exhaling a breath that felt like it had been trapped for far too long. "When I left my town, I thought I could escape everything—my family, my mistakes. I moved here to start fresh, but the past has a way of creeping in when you least expect it." His voice trembled slightly, the tension palpable.

"What happened?" I pressed, my heart aching for the burden he bore.

He hesitated, wrestling with the memories that danced in his mind. "There was an incident—a mistake I made that hurt someone. It was never my intention, but it had consequences. I didn't think it would follow me, but it did. And now..." His voice trailed off, frustration lining his features.

"Now what?" I urged gently, willing him to push through the hesitation.

"Now I'm stuck in this cycle of fear, always waiting for the past to catch up with me." He glanced down, the flicker of vulnerability replaced by an armor of defiance. "Sometimes I wonder if I'm just running in circles, trying to outrun my own shadow."

I reached for his hand, intertwining my fingers with his, feeling the warmth radiate between us. "You're not alone in this. Whatever it is, we can face it together. I'm here." My voice was steady, filled with sincerity, and I felt him relax slightly, the tension easing from his shoulders.

The park around us seemed to fade into the background, the world narrowing to just the two of us, bound by unspoken promises.

"You really want to know?" he asked again, his voice low and cautious, as if testing the waters of my resolve.

"Yes," I affirmed, holding his gaze with unwavering determination. "Please."

He took a deep breath, and I could see the internal struggle etched on his face, the battle between the urge to share and the instinct to protect. "A few years ago, I was involved in a car accident. I wasn't drunk or reckless, but I was distracted—thinking about everything I was trying to escape. I hit someone."

The words fell heavily between us, like stones sinking into still water. "They survived, but the aftermath was a storm I never saw coming. The guilt gnawed at me, and the whispers in town grew louder. I left to find peace, but the echoes of that night never faded."

My heart twisted as I absorbed his confession, the complexity of his pain washing over me like a tidal wave. "Do you know how they are now?" I asked softly, my mind racing with the implications of his revelation.

He shook his head, eyes dark with regret. "I've tried to stay away from that part of my life. It's easier to forget, to start anew without the constant reminders of my failures. But sometimes, I see faces in the crowd, and I wonder if they know...if they're waiting for me."

In that moment, I understood the depth of his fear, the suffocating grip of anxiety that had woven itself into his very being. "It's not your fault," I whispered, feeling the weight of his grief pressing against my chest. "We all make mistakes. It's what we do afterward that defines us."

Luke turned to me, his expression softening. "You're too kind, you know that? It's hard to accept kindness when you feel unworthy."

"Maybe it's time to start believing you are worthy of it," I replied, squeezing his hand tighter, grounding him in that moment. "You're not that person anymore. You've shown me a different side of you—one that cares, one that can heal."

As the evening deepened, the sky transformed into a canvas of indigo, speckled with stars that twinkled like distant dreams. A cool breeze swept through the park, rustling the leaves above us and wrapping around us like a comforting blanket. I sensed a shift in Luke, a cautious willingness to shed the armor he had worn for so long.

"What if I told you I wanted to make amends?" he asked, his voice barely above a whisper. "What if I went back, faced my past instead of running from it?"

A flicker of hope ignited in my chest. "Then I would support you, every step of the way. You don't have to go through it alone." I searched his eyes, desperate for him to see the sincerity in my words.

He nodded slowly, the weight of the moment settling on his shoulders. "I want to believe that's possible. But it terrifies me."

"Fear is just another part of the journey," I reassured him. "It's what makes us human. But think about it—facing the past could be the first step toward finding peace. Imagine how freeing it would feel."

The light of determination began to flicker in his gaze, and for the first time, I saw a glimmer of hope emerging from the shadows.

"I'll think about it," he promised, a tentative smile breaking through the lines of worry on his face. "With you by my side, maybe it's not as daunting as I thought."

In that moment, under the sprawling branches of the oak tree, I felt the fragile beginnings of something beautiful—a bond woven from trust and shared burdens, a connection that promised the possibility of healing. The night deepened around us, the stars shining brightly above, and I realized that perhaps the pull I felt toward Luke was more than mere attraction. It was a chance for both of us to confront our demons, to rise from the ashes of our pasts and forge a new path forward together.

As we sat in comfortable silence, the world around us faded into a gentle hum, the symphony of crickets serenading us into a future that seemed a little less uncertain, a little more filled with promise. It was the beginning of something extraordinary—two souls, united by their scars, ready to face the storms ahead.

Chapter 5: The Letters

The sun hung low in the sky, casting a warm, golden hue over the streets of Charleston, South Carolina, as I sat cross-legged on my childhood bedroom floor, surrounded by an assortment of letters that had somehow become both a lifeline and a burden. The letters were penned in my mother's delicate, looping script, each word a brushstroke painting a portrait of a woman I had never fully understood. My heart thudded with a mix of anticipation and trepidation as I unfolded another piece of her past, the musty scent of aged paper filling the air like a whisper from another time.

As I read, the world outside faded into a distant hum. The aroma of salt from the nearby ocean mingled with the earthy notes of blooming magnolia trees, but all I could focus on were her words, the rhythm of her emotions echoing in my mind. With each letter, I was transported into her secret life—a vivid world filled with unspoken desires and longings that had remained locked away for far too long. Her ink bled passion onto the pages, vibrant and alive, telling tales of stolen moments and whispered secrets beneath the swaying oaks draped in Spanish moss.

"Henry," she wrote, his name a recurring motif like a haunting refrain in a forgotten song. Who was he? The intensity with which she described him—his laughter like summer rain and eyes that held entire galaxies—made my heart ache for the mother who had always seemed so steadfast and grounded. In my memories, she was a beacon of strength, a woman who endured the storm of my father's departure with a quiet grace, yet here, in these letters, I saw glimpses of vulnerability, of a yearning that seemed almost insatiable.

I imagined her as a young woman, her hair dancing in the breeze as she laughed with Henry on a sun-drenched porch overlooking the river. The vivid imagery was intoxicating, pulling me deeper into her world, leaving me breathless with questions. Did she think of me when she was with him? Did she wonder about the future she had sacrificed for the safety of our little family? The dissonance between my perception and this new reality was jarring, like stepping from a sunlit day into the depths of a stormy sea.

"Henry makes me feel alive," she wrote in one letter, and my breath caught in my throat. What could possibly have kept her from him? The pain of it clawed at my insides as I reread the passage, desperate to uncover more of the mystery that enveloped her heart. I wanted to scream at her, to shake her gently and ask why she hadn't shared this part of her life with me. Why hadn't she sought comfort in the arms of a man who clearly adored her?

Luke, my younger brother, knocked gently at the door, breaking the spell. I glanced up to see him leaning against the doorframe, his brow furrowed with concern. He had always been my rock, the one who would jump in to lighten the mood with a well-timed joke or a cheeky grin. Today, however, he seemed weighed down, as if he had sensed the gravity of my discovery.

"Hey, what are you up to?" he asked, his voice casual but his eyes searching mine for a hint of what lay beneath. I folded the letter carefully, a silent promise to return to it later.

"Just... reading some letters," I replied, my voice faltering slightly. I wanted to tell him everything, to unburden myself of the turmoil brewing inside me, but fear gripped my throat. Would he understand? Would he share my fascination—or my dread—over our mother's past?

"Yeah? Anything interesting?" He stepped inside, his interest piqued.

I hesitated, my heart racing at the thought of revealing the name that had become a shadow in my mind. "Just some stuff about Mom," I said finally, keeping it vague. I didn't want to draw him into the emotional labyrinth I was navigating. The shadows of secrets were far too intricate, and I was afraid they would ensnare us both.

"Mom had a pretty intense life before us, huh?" Luke said, trying to keep it light, though I could see the worry etched on his face. "I mean, there's a lot we don't know."

His words hung in the air like an unanswered question. I wanted to explore the depth of that statement, to unravel what he meant, but the tension crackled between us, a barrier formed by years of unspoken truths.

"Yeah," I agreed, my voice barely above a whisper. "But why keep it all hidden?" The frustration boiled inside me, and I could feel the hot sting of tears pricking my eyes.

"Maybe some things are just too hard to share," he said, and I could see he was struggling to offer solace. I wished I could tell him about Henry, about how his very name seemed to peel back the layers of our mother's carefully constructed life, exposing the raw, tender parts that had been stitched up for so long.

"Do you think we'll ever know her whole story?" I asked, desperation creeping into my voice.

"I hope so," he replied, crossing his arms as if to shield himself from my anguish. "But you have to be careful. Some stories are better left untold."

His words hit me hard, echoing the unspoken fears that were clawing at my insides. I wanted to dive deeper, to confront whatever it was that had kept our mother's heart captive, but I couldn't shake the sense that the more I uncovered, the more I might lose the mother I had known. Would knowing Henry shatter my illusions? Would it tear apart the fabric of the life we had shared, the love that had nurtured me?

As Luke slipped out, I returned to the letters, feeling the weight of the world pressing down on my shoulders. Each sentence I read was a step into a different universe—one where my mother was not just a caretaker but a woman full of dreams, desires, and a love that had burned bright yet flickered in the shadows. I was caught in a web of her past, grappling with the threads that held our lives together, and I realized I had to find Henry. To understand him was to understand her, and maybe, just maybe, I could piece together the fragments of her soul that had been left behind.

The next few days felt like a disorienting dream, each moment tainted with a bittersweet blend of nostalgia and confusion. I found myself combing through the letters with an urgency that felt almost primal, a need to unveil the truths hidden within the parchment. It was as though each letter held a fragment of a life that had not been fully lived, and I was determined to piece it together, like a jigsaw puzzle scattered across the table of my mind.

The sun-dappled streets of Charleston became my backdrop as I scoured through the vibrant town, searching for hints of Henry. My footsteps echoed against the cobblestones, a rhythmic reminder of the weight I carried in my heart. The rich scent of low-country cuisine wafted through the air from nearby restaurants, mingling with the fragrance of blooming jasmine. Families laughed and strolled, unaware of the internal storm that raged within me. I was captivated by the notion that my mother's world, vibrant and colorful, had intertwined with the history of this very town, and that somewhere amidst the historic homes and bustling markets, the shadows of her past lingered.

I stopped by the local library, its weathered facade standing sentinel over countless stories—some read, some forgotten, and others like my mother's, yet to be unearthed. The musty aroma of old books enveloped me as I navigated through the aisles, the whispers of those who had come before me echoing softly in my ears. I felt the weight of generations pressing down as I searched for anything that might connect to Henry. I was looking for a photograph, a newspaper clipping—anything that would give me a glimpse into the life my mother had kept hidden.

As I rifled through the archives, I stumbled upon an old newspaper, its brittle pages crackling as I opened it. A headline caught my eye: "Local Woman Hosts Art Exhibit: A Night of Passion and Expression." There, nestled between articles about local events and the mundane chatter of community happenings, was a photograph of my mother standing beside a man whose features were shadowed by time but bore an unmistakable resemblance to the descriptions she had woven into her letters.

Henry.

The realization washed over me like a tide, pulling me deeper into the depths of my mother's past. There she was, radiant and alive, a kaleidoscope of emotions painted across her face. My heart raced as I traced my finger over the image, yearning to bridge the gap between the girl in the picture and the mother I knew. She wore a flowing sundress that danced around her knees, and her laughter seemed to leap off the page, a ghost of joy trapped in the sepia-toned confines of the newspaper. Beside her stood Henry, his expression one of adoration, his eyes sparkling with a warmth that seemed to reach out across the years.

The librarian approached me, her curiosity evident as she noticed the photograph in my hand. "Ah, that was quite a night," she mused, her voice tinged with nostalgia. "Your mother was the heart of the community back then. She had a light about her that drew people in."

I could hardly respond, my thoughts swirling like leaves caught in a tempest. "Did you know her well?" I managed to ask, desperate to draw more from this well of memories.

"Oh, we all did," she said, her smile softening. "She had a way of making everyone feel special, of finding beauty in the ordinary. But she had her own struggles, too. Everyone does. You know, Henry was quite a mystery. People talked, but it seemed your mother was always so... composed. Even when her heart was heavy."

Her words struck a chord deep within me, reverberating through the chambers of my heart. My mother had fought battles I had never seen, and Henry had been a part of those struggles, a bittersweet connection that still tethered her to a past I was only beginning to grasp.

"I'm trying to learn more about them," I said, gathering my thoughts. "Do you have any idea where I might find him?"

The librarian's brow furrowed slightly. "Henry? He moved away after the exhibit. Some said it was to follow a career in art, while others whispered of a broken heart. But there's an old gallery on King Street that sometimes features local artists. You might find something there."

I thanked her, feeling a spark of hope igniting within me. I left the library, clutching the photograph like a talisman, a key to unlocking the doors of my mother's hidden world. As I walked through the bustling streets, the vibrant colors and sounds of Charleston began to blur together into a symphony of life—a contrast to the solitude I felt within. The more I uncovered, the more I felt like I was tethered to a legacy of longing and love that had shaped my mother into the woman I had known.

The gallery was a cozy nook tucked between a bustling café and a vintage bookstore, the air thick with the scent of fresh paint and wood. I entered, heart racing, scanning the walls adorned with paintings that whispered stories of their own. Each canvas radiated emotion, but none drew me in like a piece hung at the back of the room—a striking portrait that seemed to capture the very essence of longing. The artist's name was scrawled at the bottom: Henry Blake.

I stepped closer, the world around me fading as I became immersed in the painting. It was my mother, her face illuminated by a soft light, her eyes reflecting the complexity of her soul. It was as if Henry had poured every unspoken word and unfulfilled dream into this work of art. A sense of familiarity washed over me, and I felt a connection to both my mother and this man whose existence had shaped so much of her heart.

"Beautiful, isn't it?" a voice broke through my reverie. I turned to find a middle-aged woman with an artist's apron tied around her waist, her eyes sparkling with admiration for the piece.

"Yes," I breathed, my heart thundering in my chest. "Do you know him? Henry?"

The woman nodded slowly, a knowing smile playing on her lips. "He was here not long ago. A quiet man with a profound understanding of emotions. He left behind more than just his art; he left behind a legacy of love and loss."

My heart raced with anticipation, and I leaned in closer, eager to hear more. "Do you know where I can find him?"

"Last I heard, he was upstate, near the mountains. He found solace in the landscapes there, but he would return from time to time. If you're looking for closure, I think you should go after it. Life's too short to let the past linger without resolution."

Her words ignited a spark within me, transforming my yearning into determination. The pieces were starting to align, and I felt an urge to chase the remnants of my mother's story, to grasp the threads of love and loss that had woven through her life.

As I left the gallery, the sun dipped below the horizon, painting the sky in hues of pink and orange. With each step, I felt a resolve solidifying within me, a promise to unravel the enigma of Henry and, in turn, the layers of my mother's heart. I was no longer just a daughter seeking answers; I was a seeker of truth, driven by the echoes of a past waiting to be uncovered.

The road wound through the lush South Carolina countryside, dotted with wildflowers swaying gently in the breeze, their colors vibrant against the backdrop of an endless blue sky. As I drove, I felt a mixture of excitement and trepidation, the weight of my mother's letters still fresh in my mind, guiding me toward the unknown. I was on my way to find Henry, a man who had become an almost mythical figure, an echo of a past that had yet to be fully revealed. Each mile seemed to blur the line between who I was and who I was becoming—a seeker of truth, a daughter trying to reclaim a fragmented history.

The mountains rose majestically in the distance, their silhouettes against the horizon inviting me into their embrace. I had never ventured this far beyond Charleston, and the change in landscape felt almost symbolic of my journey. The air grew cooler, crisp with the scent of pine and damp earth, a stark contrast to the warm, salt-kissed breezes of home. It was as if I were shedding layers of my previous self, peeling away the comfortable yet confining cocoon of my life to uncover the vibrant butterfly waiting to emerge.

When I finally reached the small town nestled at the base of the mountains, it felt like stepping into a storybook. Quaint cottages lined the streets, their wooden façades adorned with colorful flower boxes, while the sounds of laughter floated through the air like notes of an old melody. I parked the car in front of a charming café, its awning striped in cheerful yellows and whites, and stepped inside, the bell above the door chiming a soft welcome. The aroma of fresh coffee mingled with the sweet scent of baked goods, wrapping around me like a warm hug.

At a corner table, I spotted an older gentleman, his weathered face illuminated by the soft glow of the afternoon sun streaming through the window. He was sketching in a tattered notebook, the edges frayed and worn, a testament to the stories it held. Gathering my courage, I approached him, sensing that he might know something of the man whose name had become a lifeline to my mother's past.

"Excuse me," I said, my voice trembling slightly. "I'm looking for someone—Henry Blake. Do you know him?"

His eyes lifted from the page, and a slow smile spread across his face, as if he were welcoming an old friend. "Henry, you say? Quite the artist, that one. Lives up on the ridge, in a cabin surrounded by trees. You might even catch him at the gallery down the road; he has a few pieces displayed there."

My heart raced at the thought of finally reaching the man who had loomed so large in my mother's life. "Do you think he'd be willing to talk to me?"

"Henry is a solitary soul, but he has a good heart. If he feels your intentions are genuine, I reckon he'll welcome you." He paused, his gaze thoughtful. "He carries his own shadows, though. Approach with care."

I nodded, the gravity of his words settling in. The shadows of the past were not merely echoes; they were living things that breathed and pulsed with the memories of lives intertwined. After sharing a few more pleasantries, I thanked him and made my way to the gallery he had mentioned.

As I entered, the atmosphere shifted. It was hushed, reverent, as if the artwork itself demanded silence. Each piece told a story, vibrant colors leaping from the canvas, shadows dancing in the corners, evoking feelings that stirred deep within. And then, there he was—Henry.

He stood at the back, immersed in conversation with a young woman, her laughter light and effervescent. I couldn't help but notice how the lines on his face seemed to soften in her presence. He was older than I had imagined, perhaps in his sixties, with graying hair that curled just above his collar. There was a ruggedness to him, a sense of a life fully lived, yet something tender glimmered in his eyes—a warmth that hinted at stories untold.

Gathering my courage, I approached, my heart pounding like a distant drum. The young woman glanced my way, her expression curious yet kind. Henry turned, and in that moment, the world faded away, leaving just the two of us, two souls connected by a thread spun from the past.

"Can I help you?" he asked, his voice deep and resonant, tinged with an accent I couldn't quite place.

"I'm looking for you," I managed, my voice steadier than I felt. "I'm the daughter of Anna, your—" My breath hitched at the weight of the word, "your friend."

The flicker of recognition that crossed his face was swift, but it was quickly followed by an emotion I couldn't quite decipher—surprise, perhaps, tinged with something more profound. "Anna," he repeated softly, as if testing the name on his tongue. "It's been years."

There was a pause, a shared silence that spoke of memories and missed opportunities. "I found some of her letters," I continued, emboldened by the sincerity in his gaze. "They revealed a side of her I didn't know—a part of her life that you were so deeply woven into."

Henry's expression shifted, vulnerability creeping in. "She wrote letters?" His eyes held a depth of emotion, a mixture of joy and sorrow that seemed to mirror my own feelings.

"Yes," I replied, feeling the weight of those letters behind me like a quiet army. "She loved you, didn't she?"

He nodded slowly, the corners of his mouth turning up slightly. "She was the light in my life. We were young, caught up in the reckless abandon of our dreams. But sometimes, love isn't enough to conquer the world's expectations."

I felt the words resonate within me, an echo of my own life's struggles. "But she never told me," I whispered, my heart aching at the thought of the secrets she had carried. "Why didn't she come to you when Dad left?"

Henry's gaze turned distant, lost in the labyrinth of memory. "Life had a way of leading us down different paths. Your mother was a brave soul, and I admired her for that. She made her choices, but it didn't lessen what we had. We all have shadows that haunt us, choices we wish we could change."

A rush of empathy surged through me, realizing how intricately tied our stories had become. "She was so strong," I said, my voice barely a whisper. "But it feels like I've lost part of her by not knowing you."

"Perhaps," he mused, his eyes glistening with unspoken words. "But you're here now, and that counts for something. You have the chance to learn about her, to honor her truth."

The young woman who had been at his side cleared her throat, reminding me of the world outside this intimate moment. "I should go," I said reluctantly, feeling the weight of time pressing upon us. "Thank you for speaking with me. I—I hope to learn more about her, about you both."

Henry nodded, his gaze warm yet sad. "If you ever want to talk more, I'll be around. You're welcome to visit."

As I left the gallery, the cool mountain air greeted me like an old friend. My heart swelled with the knowledge that I was not alone in this quest for understanding. I had glimpsed a piece of my mother's soul, and now I held the key to unlock the door she had closed so tightly. The journey ahead would not be easy; it would require courage to face the shadows, but I was ready to embrace whatever truths lay ahead.

The mountains loomed majestically in the distance, steadfast guardians of the stories hidden within their depths. And with each step I took, I felt the bond between mother and daughter weaving stronger, the tapestry of our lives rich with colors of love, loss, and ultimately, the promise of discovery.

Chapter 6: The Night It All Changed

The night was a tapestry of vivid colors and sounds, weaving together the joyous laughter of children, the clinking of carnival games, and the intoxicating aroma of sweet cotton candy mingling with the savory scent of grilled corn. Willow Creek was a small town where everyone knew each other's names and secrets were traded like baseball cards. Under the glow of fairy lights strung between the trees, the fair thrummed with a pulse of life that seemed to resonate in my chest.

I moved through the crowd, feeling Luke's presence at my side like a storm cloud threatening rain. Despite the cheerful chaos surrounding us, a weight hung in the air, thick with unspoken words. Each step felt like an exercise in restraint, my heart racing against the quiet war brewing within. Luke's hand brushed against mine, but the connection felt fragile, like a thread ready to snap. He was supposed to be my anchor, yet instead, he felt like a riddle I couldn't solve.

As we wandered past the booths adorned with brightly colored banners, the thrill of the fair buzzed around us—laughter erupted from a nearby game where someone had just won a giant stuffed bear, the operator shouting in delight. I forced a smile, but my thoughts spiraled back to the letters hidden in my mother's attic, their words heavy with history and longing. What had she kept from me? Why did it all lead back to Luke?

It was at that moment, as the crowd cheered for a thrilling ride, that the first fireworks lit the night sky, illuminating faces with bursts of color. My breath caught in my throat, a kaleidoscope of bright greens and brilliant reds painting the dark canvas above us. I turned to share the moment with Luke, but my words froze when I noticed him stiffen, his eyes fixed on something—or someone—across the fairgrounds.

My gaze followed his, and my heart plunged into icy water. There he was: Henry. A figure from my mother's past, his face framed by the flickering lights, casting shadows that seemed to dance with the fireworks. He stood alone, his eyes locked onto mine, a mix of surprise and recognition flickering in the depths of his gaze. In that instant, everything within me ignited, a fire fueled by curiosity and dread.

Before I could take a step toward him, Luke's grip tightened around my arm, his fingers biting into my skin. "Not here. Not now," he hissed, urgency lacing his voice as he tugged me away from the crowd. I stumbled slightly, torn between the pull of my past and the concern etched on Luke's face. He was afraid—of what, I couldn't yet comprehend.

"Who is he?" I asked, trying to keep my voice steady despite the tremor of uncertainty lacing my words. The fair around us buzzed with life, but within the tight circle of Luke's grip, time seemed to slow, the laughter fading into a muffled echo.

Luke's expression darkened, shadows pooling in his eyes as if they carried secrets he was loath to share. "It's complicated, Willow," he said, his voice dropping to a near whisper as we stepped away from the dazzling lights and into a quieter corner of the fair.

"Complicated?" I echoed, feeling the sting of betrayal seep into my veins. "You've been hiding things from me, Luke. Why didn't you tell me about him? He's a part of my mother's life!" The intensity of my words surprised even me, but the depth of my confusion demanded an answer, the air heavy with questions.

His jaw clenched, and for a moment, I saw a flicker of the boy I once knew—bright and carefree—before the shadows enveloped him again. "Trust me, you don't want to get involved with him. Not tonight. Not ever." The fervor in his voice made my heart race, but the reasoning behind his fear eluded me, clouded by the kaleidoscope of emotions swirling around us.

"Why? Is he dangerous?" I pressed, desperate to untangle the web of fear and uncertainty that had woven itself into this night. The sky exploded with color again, but all I could focus on was the man who had slipped into my life, a specter of my mother's past whose significance loomed larger than the fair itself.

"Not in the way you think," he replied, his tone softening, but the shadows lingered in his eyes. "He's... complicated. You don't know the full story, and I don't want you to get hurt." His expression shifted, vulnerability breaking through the fortress he had built around himself. It was a glimpse of the boy who had always been my protector, yet now I felt trapped in a cage of secrets.

"What does he want?" I asked, my voice barely above a whisper, as if the very act of speaking his name could summon the past.

Luke hesitated, the weight of his silence stretching between us like a taut rope. "You'll have to ask him that," he finally murmured, glancing back toward the crowd, where Henry had started to blend into the shadows, a ghost slipping away.

Before I could respond, the fireworks erupted again, a symphony of light that dazzled the crowd. But my eyes were locked on Henry, his figure growing smaller, more distant, as if he were being swallowed by the very night that had brought him back into my life.

"Let's just enjoy the fair," Luke urged, his grip loosening, but the warmth that had once radiated between us was fraying, replaced by the chill of unspoken truths.

I nodded, though the taste of unshed tears clung to the back of my throat, and my heart beat a mournful rhythm. Each burst of color above us felt like a cruel reminder of the confusion wrapping around my thoughts. I wanted to lose myself in the laughter, the music, and the light, but all I could see was Henry's haunting gaze, the question lingering in the air like smoke from the fireworks.

What did he want, and why was I so drawn to the enigma of my mother's past?

The crowd swelled around us like a tide, pulling laughter and excitement in all directions, yet my mind anchored itself in that fleeting moment with Henry. The distant boom of fireworks vibrated in my chest, a heartbeat of chaos against the tumult of my thoughts. I felt as if I were caught in a dream, teetering between the shimmering allure of the fair and the murky depths of my past that Henry represented.

As we moved further away from the lights and sounds, the fairground faded into a soft hum behind us, a cocoon of warmth and familiarity that began to feel alien. Luke led me toward the edge of the festivities, where the trees stood sentinel, draped in strands of twinkling lights like stars captured in branches. Here, the laughter faded to whispers, the joyous chaos replaced by a tense silence that settled heavily between us.

"Why don't you want me to talk to him?" I demanded, my voice a mixture of confusion and determination. The scent of freshly popped corn lingered in the air, a reminder of the carefree fun we should be having, yet it only served to heighten the tension. I searched Luke's eyes for answers, hoping to unlock the secrets swirling around us.

"It's complicated," he replied, the edge of urgency sharpening his tone. "You don't understand the whole story. Trust me, Willow." His gaze shifted, scanning the darkened perimeter as if he expected Henry to materialize from the shadows, his presence looming larger than life, a specter just beyond reach.

Trust. The word danced tantalizingly close yet felt weighted with betrayal. The flickering lights in the trees reflected off Luke's face, casting a glow that illuminated the lines of worry etched around his mouth. This was the boy who had shared dreams and secrets with me, who had whispered promises beneath the stars, yet here we were, estranged by unspoken fears and hidden truths.

"I want to understand," I insisted, refusing to back down. "How can I trust you when you won't tell me the truth?" The sharpness of my words hung in the air, a challenge I didn't mean to throw but felt compelled to voice.

He ran a hand through his hair, the gesture so familiar, yet it felt as if it belonged to a different life. "It's not that simple," he said, his voice barely above a whisper, vulnerable and strained. "I just want to protect you."

The sincerity in his eyes softened my resolve, but the burning curiosity inside me refused to be doused. "Protect me from what? From him?" I felt the weight of my mother's secrets pressing against my chest, the desire to unravel them battling against the instinct to heed Luke's warning.

Luke took a deep breath, the tension in his shoulders easing slightly. "Henry has a complicated history with your family. I can't explain it all here. Just... promise me you won't seek him out. Not tonight." His voice was laced with a plea that tugged at my heart, making it difficult to disregard his concern.

I nodded slowly, though inside, a storm raged. The fireworks continued to burst in the sky above, casting a shimmering glow on our secluded space. Each explosion of light mirrored the chaos within me, a beautiful but tumultuous display that begged for release.

Before I could respond, a sudden shriek of laughter erupted from the fairground, shattering the stillness. I turned, catching a glimpse of a group of children racing toward a ride, their faces painted with joy. The contrast to my own turmoil felt sharp, a reminder of the innocence that wrapped around this town.

"I can't just ignore him," I said, feeling resolute despite the dissonance swirling within. "He's a part of my mother's past, and I need to know why he's here."

"Sometimes, the past is better left buried," Luke replied, his voice laced with an intensity that made me shiver. "Your mother—she had her reasons for keeping that part of her life a secret. You don't know what you're asking for."

The words struck me like a sudden downpour, drenching me in doubt. What if uncovering those secrets only brought heartache? Yet the thrill of discovery was intoxicating, igniting a fire in my soul. "But how can I move forward if I don't know where I come from?" I implored, desperation creeping into my tone.

His gaze softened, and for a moment, the storm in his eyes was replaced by something warmer—concern, perhaps, or affection. "You're strong, Willow. Stronger than you realize. But sometimes strength lies in knowing when to walk away."

The earnestness in his voice hung in the air, a fragile thread woven between us. As the last firework crackled in the sky, its fading light mirrored the waning warmth of our connection, each second that passed stretching the distance between us.

"I need time to think," I murmured, the weight of his words settling heavily on my heart. "Can you give me that?"

He nodded, though the look in his eyes spoke volumes—a mixture of relief and lingering worry. "I'll be here when you're ready." With that, he stepped back, giving me space, and I felt the cool night air wrap around me, as if the universe itself were urging me to confront my fate.

As I lingered on the outskirts of the fair, I watched the crowds—families huddled together, friends laughing over funnel cakes, lovers sharing cotton candy. Their joy felt like a distant echo, an idyllic scene playing out while my heart tugged me toward the shadows where Henry had vanished.

With each passing moment, the thrill of the night began to fade, and in its place rose a palpable sense of longing. The thrill of the fair couldn't chase away the questions gnawing at my insides. What lay behind the curtain of my mother's past? What stories lingered in the letters hidden away in that dusty attic?

Taking a deep breath, I turned toward the heart of the fair once more. The laughter and lights beckoned me back, but my gaze wandered to the edges, where shadows danced in the flickering light. Henry had looked at me as if he knew something profound, something that might change everything I thought I knew.

In that moment, I made a silent vow. I would uncover the truth, whatever it took. The fair, with its vibrant atmosphere and infectious energy, could not drown out the hunger for knowledge simmering within me. I would face whatever shadows awaited, even if it meant confronting the very heart of my mother's secrets.

The night stretched before me, an open canvas waiting to be painted with the colors of revelation. Each breath I took filled my lungs with resolve, fueling the flickering flame of determination. I was ready to dive deeper, to uncover the layers of my past, even if it meant braving the darkened corners where truth and fear entwined.

As the echoes of laughter danced around me, I felt the warmth of the fair fade, replaced by an unsettling chill that crept down my spine. Henry had vanished into the throng, yet his presence lingered, a whisper of intrigue that pulled at the edges of my consciousness. The colors of the fair, once vibrant and inviting, began to blur into shades of uncertainty, a surreal landscape filled with hidden meanings and unanswered questions.

Luke walked a step behind me, his eyes scanning the crowd as if he feared Henry might reappear at any moment. I could sense the tension radiating from him, like heat from a rising sun—visible but elusive. With every breath I took, the weight of his silence pressed down harder, and the exhilaration of the fair slipped through my fingers like grains of sand. The sounds of distant music swelled, a merry tune that felt increasingly out of place amid my swirling thoughts.

In my heart, I knew I had to find Henry. I needed to piece together the fragments of my mother's past, no matter how jagged or uncomfortable they might be. Each explosion of color from the fireworks above cast fleeting shadows on the ground, and I felt as though they mirrored the complexities of my own life—brilliant but fleeting moments overshadowed by the obscurity of what lay beneath.

"Willow!" Luke's voice broke through my reverie, snapping me back to the moment. "Where are you going?" His concern was palpable, a lifeline thrown into the tumult of my thoughts, but I couldn't allow myself to be pulled back into the comfort of ignorance. Not when I stood on the precipice of discovery.

"I'm going to find him," I declared, my voice steady despite the tumult within. The glow of the fair seemed to brighten in response, illuminating the path before me like a neon sign flashing "Go." I took a step forward, and the crowd parted around me, unaware of the storm brewing just beyond their cheerful façades.

"Willow, wait!" Luke's plea wrapped around me like a vine, attempting to reel me back, but I had already taken another step. Each footfall echoed the rhythm of my heart, a steady pulse pushing me forward into the unknown. "Please, just listen to me," he implored, desperation lacing his voice.

I paused, glancing over my shoulder to catch the flicker of emotion in his eyes—a tumult of worry and something deeper, perhaps fear for what I might uncover. "You need to trust me, Luke. I can't ignore this. He's part of my story."

The plea hung in the air, heavy with unspoken truths, but I turned away before he could respond, the thrill of purpose igniting a fire within me. I navigated through the crowd, weaving past families, friends, and couples, their faces illuminated by the fairy lights, each one a reminder of the connections that tethered them to one another.

As I made my way toward the edge of the fair, where the laughter and music faded into the distance, I spotted him—Henry stood by a forgotten booth, the bright colors dulled in the waning light. He looked older than I remembered, his hair flecked with silver, but the intensity of his gaze remained sharp. There was a gravity to him that drew me in, as if the very air around him hummed with secrets waiting to be unveiled.

"Henry!" I called out, my voice slicing through the night like the fireworks above. He turned slowly, his expression shifting from surprise to something softer, a flicker of recognition in his eyes. The distance between us felt vast, yet it diminished with each step I took toward him.

"Willow," he replied, his voice a mix of warmth and wariness. "I didn't expect to see you here."

"Neither did I." I paused, trying to gather my thoughts, the questions swirling like leaves caught in a storm. "I've been looking for you. I need to know about my mother."

His gaze darkened, shadows pooling in the corners of his eyes. "Your mother... she had her reasons for keeping the past buried."

"Reasons that don't matter anymore," I insisted, my resolve hardening. "I need to understand. I've found letters—things she wrote. They connect to you."

He hesitated, the weight of my words settling heavily between us. "Sometimes, the truth is more complicated than it appears, Willow. Your mother wanted to protect you from things you might not be ready to hear."

"Protect me or hide the truth?" I challenged, feeling the fire of determination burning brighter within me. "I can't move forward unless I know what happened back then."

With a sigh, Henry shifted slightly, the fairy lights casting a soft glow on his lined face, revealing a lifetime of stories etched into his features. "What do you want to know?"

"Everything," I replied, my heart racing. "Why did you and my mother stop talking? What happened?"

He took a deep breath, the sound filled with memories both bitter and sweet. "Your mother and I shared a bond that was forged in the fire of youthful dreams and secrets. We were close once—too close for the town's liking. And then, things changed. She chose a different path, and I... I let her go."

The weight of his words settled over me like a heavy blanket. "But why? Was it me? Did I change everything?"

"No, Willow." His voice softened, and a flicker of sadness crossed his features. "Your arrival changed nothing. It was life, choices, and the complicated mess of love and fear that pulled us apart."

The honesty in his tone cut through my confusion, and for a moment, I saw my mother reflected in his eyes—a woman caught between the world she wanted and the reality she lived. "What did she write in those letters?"

Henry paused, searching my face as if trying to gauge my strength. "She wrote about love, loss, and the secrets that haunted her. There were dreams she abandoned and fears she couldn't face. It all tied back to me, to us."

A wave of emotion surged through me, an echo of my mother's struggles resonating deep within my core. "I need to read them," I said, feeling the urgency of my request bubble to the surface. "I have to understand."

His gaze pierced through the night, revealing a vulnerability I hadn't expected. "You may not like what you find, Willow. Some truths are harder to bear than the lies we tell ourselves."

"Then I'll bear them," I replied, the fierceness in my voice surprising even me. "I owe it to her, to myself."

He nodded slowly, the acceptance in his expression like a fragile truce. "Alright. Meet me tomorrow at the old café on Maple Street. We can talk there—away from prying eyes."

"I will," I promised, a thrill of anticipation coursing through my veins. As I turned to leave, a surge of hope began to unfurl within me. The firework finale above erupted in a cascade of color, each burst of light reflecting the burgeoning sense of purpose I felt.

As I made my way back toward the heart of the fair, my thoughts spun like the carousel spinning in the distance, a whirl of possibilities and potential. With each step, I could feel the pulse of Willow Creek surrounding me, a vibrant reminder that life was not merely about the shadows of the past but also the promise of what lay ahead.

The laughter, the joy, the connection of this small town was alive and throbbing in my chest. I had taken a leap into the unknown, and while the shadows would always linger, so too would the light of discovery. The letters awaited, and with them, the pieces of my mother's story—and mine—were finally within reach. The truth beckoned like the bright lights of the fair, illuminating the path toward understanding and connection. And for the first time, I felt ready to embrace whatever lay ahead.

Chapter 7: Confrontation

I paced the dimly lit living room, the flickering shadows from the nearby streetlamp dancing across the walls, illuminating the remnants of a life I had thought I understood. The scent of freshly brewed coffee lingered in the air, mingling with the faint smell of the lavender air freshener my mother had loved. I could hear the echo of her laughter, a sweet sound that had filled these rooms, now replaced with a silence so oppressive it felt like a weight on my chest. Luke stood by the window, his silhouette outlined against the dull glow outside, his expression unreadable.

"Why didn't you tell me?" My voice cracked, each word laced with the disbelief and anger boiling within me. "You've known all along. You've been here, watching me, and you didn't say a word about who he is—or who you are."

He turned slowly, the light catching the sharp lines of his jaw, the intense blue of his eyes pinning me in place. "I was trying to protect you," he said, his tone steady but strained, as if every syllable were an exercise in restraint. "But the truth is... it's more complicated than I imagined."

"Complicated?" I scoffed, crossing my arms defensively. "My mother ran away from this man, and you think it's complicated? He's a monster, Luke! You don't just run from someone for no reason."

He sighed, dragging a hand through his tousled hair, the gesture speaking volumes about the turmoil within him. "No, it's not just about that. Henry is involved in things that go beyond what you can see. He's dangerous in ways you don't even understand, and your mother knew that. That's why she changed her name, left everything behind."

Each revelation hit me like a slap to the face, the stark reality of my mother's life unraveling before me. I had spent years painting her story with the soft brush of romanticism, imagining a love lost to time, a simple longing that had lingered in her heart. But now, the truth was shrouded in a darkness I hadn't anticipated. My heart raced as I struggled to grasp the implications.

"So what does that mean for me?" I asked, my voice trembling. "You said he's coming for me. Why?"

He stepped closer, the air between us thickening with unsaid fears and unfulfilled desires. "Because you're the last connection he has to your mother. He believes you know something, that you can lead him to her, to whatever secrets she took with her when she died." His words hung in the air like a storm cloud ready to burst, pressing down on my chest with a weight that made it hard to breathe.

"No, I don't know anything!" I felt the panic rise in my throat, a tightness that threatened to choke me. "I didn't even know he existed until you showed up!"

Luke's eyes softened, and he reached out, his fingers brushing against my arm, grounding me in the chaos of my thoughts. "I know. But the truth doesn't change the danger. Henry will come looking for you, and when he does, you need to be ready."

"Ready?" I echoed, a bitter laugh escaping my lips. "How do you prepare for a monster? You don't just wake up one day and decide you want to confront a ghost from your mother's past."

Luke's gaze held mine, the warmth of his touch sending a rush of adrenaline through me, igniting something deep within. "You're not alone in this. I'll help you. We'll figure it out together. You need to trust me."

Trust. The word felt foreign, clinging to my tongue like a sour taste. I wanted to believe him, wanted to grasp onto the hope that I wasn't navigating this storm alone. But doubt wormed its way through my thoughts. How could I trust someone who had kept such a monumental truth hidden from me? My heart warred with my mind, desire fighting against the instinct to push him away.

"I don't know if I can do this," I admitted, the weight of my fear clawing at my insides. "I don't even know who you really are. You're a stranger who suddenly appeared in my life, talking about my mother's secrets. What if you're not telling me everything?"

He took a step back, the light shifting around him as if reflecting the turmoil in his soul. "You're right; I'm not just a stranger. But I'm here because I care about you. What happened between me and your mother... it's complicated, but I want to protect you. That's all I've wanted since the moment I walked into Willow Creek."

I searched his face for sincerity, for a glimmer of the truth hidden beneath the layers of his guarded demeanor. There was something in his eyes, a flicker of vulnerability that made my heart race. This wasn't just a man hunting down a ghost; this was someone caught in the web of his own past, his feelings intertwining with mine in a way that made everything feel electric and terrifying.

"Okay," I said, the word slipping from my lips, heavy with uncertainty yet light with possibility. "What do we do next?"

Luke's expression shifted, determination flashing in those captivating blue depths. "We start by finding out everything we can about Henry. We need to understand what we're dealing with. And you need to be ready for whatever comes next."

A rush of adrenaline coursed through me, igniting the fire of resolve within. I was scared, yes, but the idea of confronting the past, of fighting against the shadows that had haunted my mother for so long, filled me with a strange sense of purpose. For the first time, I felt a spark of power over my own narrative, a chance to reclaim the story that had been shrouded in mystery for far too long.

The night deepened, wrapping Willow Creek in a shroud of darkness that felt almost suffocating. I could hear the distant hum of the river, its flow constant and relentless, a reminder that time moved forward even when my world felt suspended in uncertainty. Luke leaned against the wall, the tension radiating from him like heat from a fire, casting a flicker of shadows across his face. I could see the tightness around his mouth, the furrowed brow that hinted at a man burdened by secrets far heavier than mine.

"What do you know about him?" I asked, my voice barely above a whisper, as if speaking too loudly might shatter the fragile barrier of calm that surrounded us. "About Henry?"

He straightened, the change in posture signaling a shift in our conversation, the gravity of his expression deepening. "More than I wish I did. Henry's not just a name; he's a ghost that's haunted more than just your mother's past. He's involved in things that can't just be swept under the rug."

I leaned forward, driven by an urgency to understand. "What kind of things?"

"Things that involve money and power, corruption that seeps into every crevice of people's lives." Luke paused, the weight of his words palpable. "Your mother escaped, but she never really got away. There are people who won't let her go easily, and now that she's gone, they might think you're the next best lead."

The words stung, each one cutting deeper than the last. My mother had built her life on secrets, but to think that those secrets might not only have been a source of shame but also a source of danger felt like a betrayal. How many nights had I wondered about her past, fantasizing about a lost love, an unfulfilled romance? The truth was a bitter pill to swallow, the realization that her life had been a carefully constructed facade to shield me from something far more sinister.

"What do I do?" I asked, the tremor in my voice betraying the calm facade I struggled to maintain. "How can I fight against someone like that?"

Luke stepped closer, his warmth seeping into the cold space that had formed between us. "We prepare. We learn everything we can about him, what he wants, and why he wants it. But more importantly, we need to find a way to protect you."

"Protect me?" I scoffed, the absurdity of the notion hitting me like a wave. "How can you protect me from a ghost?"

He held my gaze, the intensity of his blue eyes captivating yet unnerving. "You're not just a victim in this, Claire. You have a strength that I've seen, even if you don't recognize it yet. You're not just your mother's daughter; you're your own person, and you have the power to reclaim your story."

A surge of defiance bubbled within me, igniting a spark I hadn't known I possessed. I had spent too long living in the shadows of my mother's choices, piecing together fragments of a life that had felt foreign and distant. If Henry was coming for me, I refused to cower in fear. I would stand my ground.

"What's the first step?" I asked, determination filling my voice.

"Tomorrow, we'll visit the archives at the old library. Your mother may have left behind records—anything that might give us a clue about Henry's past, his connections. It's not much, but it's a start."

"Okay," I agreed, the adrenaline pumping through me. "Let's do it."

As the adrenaline coursed through my veins, I felt a strange sense of exhilaration. I was finally stepping into the light of my own narrative, peeling back the layers of my mother's life and confronting the shadows that had haunted her. It was terrifying, but I couldn't deny the thrill of reclaiming my story.

The following morning dawned gray and overcast, the sky heavy with clouds that mirrored my mood. I met Luke at the library, my heart racing with anticipation and anxiety as I pushed open the heavy wooden doors. The scent of aged paper and polished wood greeted me, the atmosphere thick with the whispers of history.

Sunlight filtered through the tall windows, illuminating the dust motes that floated lazily in the air.

"Ready?" Luke asked, his voice low, almost reverent as we stepped into the stacks, surrounded by countless volumes, each one holding stories waiting to be uncovered.

"Ready as I'll ever be," I replied, trying to infuse confidence into my tone.

We scoured the archives, the hours slipping away as we delved into yellowed newspapers and brittle documents. My fingers traced the spines of forgotten books, and the weight of each one seemed to echo the burden of the secrets they held. We uncovered snippets about my mother—her life as a young woman in Willow Creek, the whispers of a passionate romance and subsequent heartbreak. Yet, each page seemed to end before the story truly began, a cliffhanger of her life leading to a silence that felt deafening.

Then, in the corner of the room, a worn leather-bound journal caught my eye. The cover was faded, the title long since illegible. My heart raced as I carefully pulled it from the shelf, the spine cracking as I opened it. The pages were filled with my mother's neat handwriting, the words flowing like a river, alive with the emotions of her youth.

As I read, the world around me faded away, leaving only her voice echoing in my mind. She wrote about her dreams, her fears, and, most hauntingly, about the man who had haunted her life—Henry. I could almost feel her presence beside me, guiding my hand as I turned each page, revealing a tapestry woven with both love and fear. The entries spoke of nights filled with laughter and joy, but they also hinted at an undercurrent of dread, of a shadow lurking in the corners of her mind.

"This is it," I whispered, barely able to breathe as I turned another page. "This is what I needed."

Luke leaned closer, his breath hitching as he caught a glimpse of my mother's life through her words. "What does it say?"

I continued reading, feeling a chill creep down my spine. Each line became a thread in the tangled web of her past, revealing a depth I had never fathomed. As I reached the end of an entry, a name caught my eye—Henry. A shiver raced through me, awakening the echoes of my mother's fears.

"I think... I think I know where he is," I said, my voice steadying as the weight of the revelation settled in my chest. "And I think we need to go there."

A quiet determination settled within me as I looked up from the journal, the weight of my mother's words heavy in the air. Luke's gaze was locked onto mine, a silent understanding passing between us. Whatever we were about to confront would not be easy, but in that moment, surrounded by the hushed whispers of the library, I felt an unyielding resolve to face the unknown head-on.

"Where do you think he is?" Luke asked, his voice steady but laced with urgency. The confidence in his tone was contagious, igniting the fire within me to push forward.

"The old mill," I replied, recalling a mention in one of my mother's entries, where she described a time when she and her friends used to gather at the crumbling structure on the outskirts of town. It had been a place of laughter and youthful abandon, but beneath the surface, it was a place filled with darker memories—the perfect hideout for secrets and shadows. "She wrote about it a lot, especially when she started feeling Henry's presence loom larger. I think it might have been where he cornered her."

Luke's expression shifted, the warmth in his eyes replaced by a steely resolve. "Then we need to go there. Now."

The mill loomed on the horizon as we drove, its silhouette cutting a stark figure against the stormy sky. The air grew thick with anticipation and something darker, a palpable tension that made the hairs on my arms stand on end. I gripped the edge of the seat, my heart pounding in time with the rhythm of the rain beginning to patter against the windshield. This was no longer just a quest for truth; it was a reckoning.

As we parked, the first droplets transformed into a downpour, drumming against the roof of the car like a warning. I stepped out into the cold, damp air, and the smell of wet earth enveloped me, mingling with the bittersweet scent of nostalgia that clung to the abandoned mill. The wooden beams, weathered and sagging, seemed to whisper tales of the past, each creak and groan echoing memories that I had yet to uncover.

"Are you sure about this?" Luke asked, his voice low, cautious.

"I have to be. If Henry is here, I need to face him. I need to understand."

We moved toward the entrance, the heavy door creaking open as if welcoming us into the ghosts of yesteryears. The interior was dim, the light filtering in through broken windows, casting elongated shadows that danced across the dusty floor. The remnants of machinery lay scattered, forgotten, their metal surfaces rusted and cold—a graveyard of forgotten dreams.

"Let's split up," Luke suggested, his eyes scanning the room. "We'll cover more ground that way."

"Okay," I agreed, though hesitation tinged my voice. I didn't want to be alone in this haunted space. "Just... be careful."

He nodded, a reassuring smile brushing his lips, before heading off toward the back of the mill. I felt the weight of the moment settle upon my shoulders, but I steeled myself, pushing the fear down deep. Each step deeper into the mill felt like stepping into my mother's past, each creak of the floor a reminder of the secrets that had shaped her life.

I ventured into a room that had once been vibrant with life but now lay in ruins. The walls were lined with fading photographs, remnants of the town's history, capturing moments of joy that felt worlds away from my current reality. As I stepped closer to one of the photos, a fleeting sense of recognition washed over me. There, among the laughing faces, stood my mother, youthful and carefree, an unguarded smile lighting up her face.

But behind her was a shadow I hadn't noticed before—a man with sharp features and a gaze that seemed to pierce through time, his presence lurking ominously behind my mother, a harbinger of the darkness that would one day chase her.

I shivered, a chill racing down my spine, and turned abruptly, the sensation of being watched settling like a cloak around my shoulders. I had to find Luke, to remind myself I wasn't alone. But as I moved through the rooms, the shadows grew thicker, the air heavier, as if the mill itself were aware of my presence, urging me to leave.

Suddenly, a sharp crash echoed from behind me, followed by the sound of muffled voices. My heart raced as I rushed toward the noise, my instincts screaming that something was wrong. I pushed through a doorway and into a small, dimly lit space. There, in the corner, Luke stood facing off against a figure I had only glimpsed in my mother's writings.

Henry.

The man's presence filled the room, an aura of menace surrounding him as he towered over Luke. His dark hair fell over his forehead, framing a face that was both striking and terrifying. There was a familiarity to him, a connection that felt deeply rooted in the stories my mother had shared with me, but now he stood before me as a living embodiment of the nightmares I had feared.

"Claire," he said, his voice smooth and laced with an unsettling charm, as if the darkness within him had been polished to a shine. "I wondered when you would show up. Your mother was always too clever for her own good."

"Stay away from her!" Luke shouted, stepping in front of me, a protective stance that made my heart swell with gratitude.

But Henry simply laughed, a sound devoid of warmth. "Protective little friend, are we? You have no idea what you're getting into, boy."

"Don't underestimate me," I said, surprising myself with the steadiness in my voice. "You may have haunted my mother's life, but you won't haunt mine."

The atmosphere crackled with tension, a standoff laden with history and pain. Henry's gaze flicked to me, a predatory gleam sparking in his eyes. "You think you can escape your mother's shadow? She ran from me for a reason, and now that she's gone, you're just a link to the past—a pawn in a game you can't possibly understand."

"You're wrong," I asserted, feeling the pulse of courage surge through me. "I am not my mother's pawn; I am my own person. Whatever darkness you brought into her life, I will not allow you to bring it into mine."

Luke took a step forward, ready to engage, but I held out my hand, grounding us both in that moment. I could feel the heartbeat of the mill, the ancient walls echoing with the weight of all the secrets they had witnessed, urging me to be the voice of strength I had finally found within myself.

Henry's eyes narrowed, the mask of charm slipping as anger flared within him. "You don't know what you're inviting. The past never truly dies, Claire. It waits patiently for the right moment to strike."

"And I'll be ready," I replied, refusing to back down.

With that, the air shifted, and I felt the balance of power begin to sway. I was no longer just my mother's daughter; I was carving my own path, confronting the specter of her past with a fierce resolve. I felt Luke's presence beside me, a silent promise that we were in this together.

The confrontation hung heavy in the air, charged with possibility and uncertainty. As Henry's figure loomed before us, the past clashed with the present, and the battle for my future began. Whatever the outcome, I was ready to face the storm.

Chapter 8: The Escape Plan

The air in Willow Creek hung thick with secrets, each whispering breeze weaving through the willows and rustling the leaves like a chorus of hidden truths. It was a town suspended in time, where the sun dipped below the horizon, casting golden hues over the faded clapboard houses, their porches sagging under the weight of history. I often wandered through the streets, feeling the warmth of nostalgia wrap around me like a cherished blanket, yet today, that warmth was a mere echo of comfort as I faced the uncertainty ahead.

Luke stood beside me, his presence both a balm and a burden. His dark hair tousled, his jaw set in a firm line, he exuded an intensity that made my heart race—not with desire, but with fear. His eyes, pools of determination, bore into me as if he could read the chaos churning within. "We need to go," he urged, his voice low but urgent, a stark contrast to the serene landscape around us. "Henry won't stop until he finds you."

I shivered at the mention of his name. Henry, with his calm exterior masking a tempestuous rage, was a specter I couldn't shake. He loomed over my life like a dark cloud, one that threatened to unleash a storm at any moment. In his presence, I felt the walls of my world closing in, the familiar sights of Willow Creek twisting into something suffocating and sinister. I clenched my fists, the edges of my palms biting into my skin as I fought against the rising tide of panic.

But how could I leave? The questions nagged at me like persistent gnats—buzzing incessantly, demanding answers that felt just out of reach. My mother's life, the life she had lived before me, was a tapestry woven with threads of deception and regret. I needed to uncover those threads, to understand the choices she made, the shadows she chased. Leaving now felt like abandoning a part of myself, a part that held the key to unlocking the truth.

Luke leaned closer, his breath warm against my ear. "We can figure it out later. Just trust me. I know a way. A place. It's safe." His words wrapped around my heart, tugging at the fragments of my trust still clinging to him like stubborn ivy. The thrill of escape sparkled in his eyes, promising freedom, but the cost weighed heavily on my conscience.

A small town like ours didn't just fade from memory; it etched itself into the minds of its inhabitants, a bittersweet mural of shared experiences. I thought of my friends, the bakery where Mrs. Lindley crafted her cinnamon rolls, the small library bursting with tales of adventure, and the park where laughter floated like dandelion seeds on a summer breeze. Each place carried a piece of me, a moment captured in time, and to walk away now felt like severing ties with my very soul.

"I can't just leave," I finally whispered, my voice trembling. "There are things I need to know. About her, about everything. What if I never get the chance again?"

Luke's expression softened for just a moment, a flicker of understanding crossing his face before the urgency snapped back into place. "And what if Henry finds you first? You'll have no chance to learn anything, no chance to do anything but run." The frustration in his tone twisted something inside me, a knot of fear and longing. He was right; the clock was ticking, and every second felt like a breath stolen from my lungs.

I turned to the expanse of the town, the setting sun painting the sky in hues of orange and purple, a farewell kiss to the day. "What's your plan?" I asked, my curiosity igniting. I needed to know, needed to believe that escaping wasn't just a fantasy, but a viable path.

"There's an old road, one that leads to the edge of town. Most people forget about it. We can take my truck—load it up with supplies and just go." His gaze drifted to the horizon, to the possibility of a new beginning. "No one will be looking for us. Not right away."

The thought of freedom washed over me, but with it came a swell of guilt. What about my mother's memory? The unanswered questions that haunted my dreams? "What if I come back?" I found myself asking, the words slipping out before I could catch them.

Luke turned to me, surprise mingling with frustration in his eyes. "Come back? Why would you want to? This place holds nothing but pain for you now."

"But it's part of me," I insisted, my heart racing with a mix of desperation and defiance. "I can't just erase it. I need to understand."

His shoulders slumped slightly, as if the weight of my indecision was a physical thing pressing against him. "Then let's do it together. We'll find the answers, but first, we need to get out of here."

The determination in his voice ignited a flicker of hope within me, and I felt the icy grip of fear begin to loosen. Maybe, just maybe, I could escape the chains binding me to my past while still pursuing the truth. As I looked into his eyes, I recognized a spark of resolve that mirrored my own—a shared desire to break free from the confines of our lives, to redefine ourselves beyond the shadows that lingered.

Taking a deep breath, I nodded. "Okay. Let's do this." My heart raced with each word, a thrilling mix of fear and exhilaration swirling within me. The prospect of an adventure, of leaving behind everything I had ever known, was intoxicating.

Together, we turned toward the road that would lead us out of Willow Creek, a path shrouded in mystery and the promise of new beginnings. With every step, I felt the weight of my past begin to shift, like the first light of dawn breaking over the horizon, illuminating the way ahead. The journey wouldn't be easy, and the questions would still linger, but perhaps in the act of leaving, I could find a way to discover who I truly was beyond the confines of my mother's legacy.

And so, hand in hand, we walked toward the unknown, the twilight enveloping us in its embrace, the promise of a new chapter shimmering just beyond the horizon.

The weight of impending choices bore down on me as we navigated the familiar streets, each footfall echoing with a sense of finality. The sun sank lower, its rays filtering through the trees like liquid gold, casting a warm glow on the pavement, yet every flicker of light felt cold against my skin. Luke's hand brushed mine, a gentle reminder of our shared resolve, but my thoughts were tangled in the shadows of uncertainty.

We veered onto the forgotten road, a narrow path lined with wildflowers that had long since claimed their territory, unfurling like the bright strokes of an artist's brush. The scent of earth and blooming honeysuckle enveloped us, mingling with the distant hum of cicadas, creating an atmosphere of peaceful rebellion. It felt as if this road, overgrown and neglected, held secrets of its own, just waiting to be unearthed.

"I used to come down here as a kid," Luke remarked, his voice a soft murmur against the backdrop of nature. "It was like my secret world, a place to escape." He paused, glancing at me, his expression a mixture of nostalgia and urgency. "I thought I'd never need it again."

"Do you think it's safe?" I asked, a tinge of skepticism creeping into my tone. The road twisted ahead, shrouded in dense trees that seemed to lean closer as if eavesdropping on our conversation.

He shrugged, a casual gesture that masked the tension simmering beneath the surface. "Safer than anywhere else right now. We'll take my truck and head out toward the mountains. No one will think to look for us there."

The thought of being tucked away in the embrace of the mountains filled me with a mixture of excitement and dread. Would it really be an escape, or just another chapter of running? Each step on this path felt like a gamble, the stakes higher than they had ever been before. I could feel the familiar tug of Willow Creek behind me, its memories both bitter and sweet.

As we approached the rusted pickup parked at the edge of the woods, I noticed the way the vehicle leaned slightly to one side, as if tired from years of neglect. It looked like it had stories of its own, tales etched in the chipped paint and faded interior, just waiting to be shared. Luke opened the door with a creak that echoed in the stillness, inviting me into this world of uncertainty and possibility.

I slid into the worn leather seat, feeling the warmth of the sun-drenched material seep into my skin. "So, what's next?" I asked, the questions swirling in my mind like leaves caught in a whirlwind. "How do we start fresh? How do we even know where to go?"

Luke leaned back, his fingers drumming lightly on the steering wheel, his brow furrowed in thought. "We just drive. Find a small town, somewhere off the map. We'll figure it out as we go." The confidence in his voice was both reassuring and disconcerting; the lack of a clear plan left an unsettling flutter in my stomach.

I couldn't help but think of the life I would be leaving behind—the laughter with friends, the warmth of summer evenings spent sipping lemonade on porches, the comforting routines that had formed the fabric of my existence. Yet, beneath it all lay the truth of my mother's life, the tangled web of lies that had ensnared me, threatening to drag me down if I didn't act.

With a deep breath, I nodded, surrendering to the possibility of adventure, however daunting it felt. "Okay, let's go."

As we pulled away from the familiarity of Willow Creek, a strange sensation washed over me—a blend of fear, excitement, and hope. The town receded in the rearview mirror, its contours blurring into a watercolor painting as we sped toward the unknown. With every mile, the weight of the past began to lift, replaced by the invigorating thrill of freedom.

The road opened up before us, a ribbon of asphalt stretching toward the horizon, where the sky melded into the deepening hues of twilight. I stole glances at Luke, watching him navigate the curves with a steady hand and an intensity that mesmerized me. There was a quiet strength in him, a willingness to dive into the chaos with me, and for the first time, I felt a flicker of trust rekindling amidst the ruins of betrayal.

"Have you thought about what you'll do once we're gone?" he asked, his voice breaking the comfortable silence that had settled around us.

"I don't know," I admitted, the honesty surprising even myself. "I've always wanted to be a writer, but I never thought I'd actually get to try. I always felt like I was waiting for something to change, for my life to give me permission to chase that dream."

Luke nodded, his expression thoughtful. "Maybe this is that chance. A blank page, just waiting for you to fill it."

The thought lit a spark within me, the idea of crafting my own narrative, untethered from the past. I imagined sitting in a cozy café in some small town, sipping coffee as I scribbled my thoughts onto paper, weaving stories from the threads of my experiences. The notion danced tantalizingly close, like a mirage shimmering in the distance, yet I hesitated, still tethered to the weight of unresolved questions.

"What about you?" I asked, curious about the layers of his own story. "What's waiting for you out there?"

He glanced at me, a flicker of something deep within his eyes—maybe vulnerability, maybe ambition. "I've always wanted to travel. See the country, meet new people. I never fit in here. But..." His voice trailed off, and I sensed a battle waging within him, an internal struggle he wasn't ready to share.

"But?" I prodded gently, the intimacy of the moment coaxing him to open up.

"But I thought I'd always be here, stuck in this cycle. Helping my father with the farm, living the same day over and over." He chuckled softly, the sound both sad and hopeful. "I guess this is my way of breaking free."

The connection between us deepened, woven together by shared dreams and the desire for something more. I realized that our paths had intertwined in ways I hadn't fully comprehended until now. We were both escaping—escaping the weight of expectations, the shadows of our pasts—and in doing so, forging a new reality.

As we drove deeper into the night, the stars began to sprinkle across the sky, shimmering like scattered diamonds on a dark velvet canvas. The world outside the truck transformed, each passing mile unveiling a landscape rich with possibility. Fields of wild grass stretched out on either side, illuminated by the moonlight, while the scent of fresh earth mingled with the crispness of night air.

For the first time in a long while, I felt a sense of exhilaration swell within me, a thrill at the thought of what lay ahead. With every turn of the wheels, I could feel the shackles of the past loosening, replaced by the intoxicating freedom of choice.

Together, we raced toward a future unwritten, the open road beckoning us forward—a promise of new beginnings, and the chance to redefine who we were meant to be. With Luke by my side, I felt brave enough to confront whatever came next, ready to write my own story, one that would finally be mine alone.

The miles unraveled behind us like a spool of thread, each rotation of the tires marking a significant shift in my reality. The familiar sights of Willow Creek melted away into the night, swallowed by the dark embrace of towering trees and the whisper of the wind weaving through their branches. The deeper we ventured into the heart of the countryside, the more the moonlight danced upon the landscape, illuminating our path with an ethereal glow that felt almost surreal.

As we drove, I turned my attention to the details that surrounded us—the way the distant hills rose and fell like the gentle waves of an ocean, the smell of damp earth and wildflowers wafting in through the cracked window. It was a scent steeped in promise, carrying with it the hopes of countless wanderers who had sought refuge in the embrace of nature. I leaned back in the seat, letting the sensation wash over me, embracing the warmth of this unexpected adventure.

"Where do you think we'll end up?" I asked, the question hanging in the air, filled with the weight of our uncertain futures.

Luke glanced over, his expression thoughtful. "Maybe a place where no one knows our names. Somewhere we can breathe without the past suffocating us." His words struck a chord within me, resonating with the very essence of what I craved. Freedom, yes, but also the chance to rebuild, to redefine what home meant.

He turned the truck onto a gravel road, the tires crunching against the stones, sending a spray of dust dancing into the night. I watched as the world transformed, the trees thinning to reveal a small clearing adorned with fireflies, their flickering lights twinkling like stars fallen to Earth. In that moment, I could almost envision a life where I could pause, breathe deeply, and let the chaos of my life dissolve into the ether.

"We could stop here for a moment," Luke suggested, pulling to a halt. He turned off the engine, and the world fell silent around us, save for the soft hum of nature awakening to the night.

I stepped out of the truck, my feet sinking into the cool grass, the earth firm beneath me as I took a deep breath. The air was crisp, infused with the sweetness of blooming jasmine, and I felt a surge of exhilaration mixed with vulnerability. "What if we never go back?" I mused, the weight of my words settling in the air between us.

Luke leaned against the side of the truck, his silhouette framed by the glow of the fireflies, his expression contemplative. "What if we don't need to? What if we're finally free to be whoever we want?" His voice was low, almost conspiratorial, as if sharing a precious secret.

The prospect of freedom felt intoxicating, yet fear lurked in the corners of my mind, whispering caution. "And who would that be? What if we don't know how to be anyone else?"

His gaze met mine, the intensity of his blue eyes grounding me. "We figure it out together. One step at a time."

As the fireflies danced around us, I felt a sense of clarity begin to bloom amidst the uncertainty. In this moment, under the canopy of stars, I realized that I didn't have to have all the answers. The journey itself could be a revelation, a chance to peel back the layers of who I was meant to be.

With a newfound resolve, I took a step closer to him, the air between us crackling with an unspoken connection. "Okay, let's do this. Let's be whoever we want to be."

The thrill of adventure surged through me as I climbed back into the truck, my heart racing with the anticipation of what lay ahead. Luke slid into the driver's seat, a smile breaking across his face, illuminating the shadows that had once loomed large in my heart.

As we resumed our journey, the road ahead began to unfold like the pages of an unwritten story, ripe with possibility. With every mile, I felt the burdens of my past growing lighter, the haunting specters of my mother's life fading into the background.

We traveled deeper into the night, the moon hanging low and full, casting silver beams across the landscape. The world transformed around us; lush fields gave way to rocky outcrops, the scent of pine mingling with the sweet floral notes that clung to the evening air.

After what felt like hours, we finally reached the foot of a mountain range, the jagged peaks towering above us like ancient sentinels. I could feel the air shift, charged with a sense of mystery and awe. "This is it," Luke said, his voice tinged with excitement. "This is where we start over."

I stepped out of the truck again, feeling the cool mountain air caress my skin. The vastness of the landscape stretched before us, a wilderness untouched and free, a stark contrast to the confines of Willow Creek. The night was alive with the sounds of nature, the rustle of leaves, the distant call of an owl, and the faint trickle of a nearby stream.

"This feels like a dream," I murmured, taking a moment to soak it all in. It was beautiful and wild, the kind of beauty that made my heart ache with longing—a longing for freedom, for authenticity, for life unchained.

Luke grinned, the joy radiating from him infectious. "Let's find a place to set up camp. We can figure out our next move in the morning."

As we trekked a little further into the woods, I spotted a clearing adorned with soft moss and sheltered by towering evergreens, a perfect spot to lay our heads for the night. We quickly unloaded our gear, setting up a modest campfire that flickered to life, its warm glow chasing away the shadows that crept along the forest floor.

As the fire crackled, I felt a sense of camaraderie grow between us, a bond forged in the flames of shared adventure and mutual reliance. We roasted marshmallows, laughing at the sticky sweetness and the absurdity of it all—two souls, bound by circumstance, embarking on a journey into the great unknown.

"Tomorrow, we'll explore the area," Luke suggested, his eyes dancing with enthusiasm. "There are small towns not far from here—places where we can lay low, where no one knows our names."

The prospect thrilled me. I could imagine strolling through a quaint village, feeling the warm sun on my face, the weight of my past slipping further from my grasp. "And who knows?" I said, allowing myself to dream. "Maybe we'll even find a place to settle down."

The thought lingered in the air, shimmering like the stars overhead, brightening the space between us with possibility. "I'd like that," he replied softly, his gaze steady. "Somewhere we can create new memories, find new beginnings."

As the night deepened and the stars twinkled above, I felt an unshakeable sense of hope settling in my heart. It was a fragile thing, yet undeniably potent—a promise that tomorrow held potential beyond our wildest dreams.

Underneath the vast sky, with Luke beside me and a world of possibilities stretching out before us, I felt, for the first time in years, a genuine smile break across my face. Maybe this was what it meant to be free—an opportunity to step into the unknown, to embrace the wildness of life and to find my place within it.

In the heart of the wilderness, I finally felt like I was home.

Chapter 9: The Truth About Henry

The sun hung low in the sky, casting a golden hue over the sprawling fields that surrounded my quaint little house in Willow Creek. The air was thick with the scent of freshly mown grass and the sweet notes of honeysuckle that clung to the fence posts, a delightful contrast to the heavy weight of the moment. I had spent countless evenings here, lounging on the porch swing, daydreaming of the life I would build. But now, with the horizon painted in shades of orange and pink, I felt the sharp edges of reality pierce my reverie.

There he stood, Henry, a figure carved from shadows, lurking just beyond the edge of my world. His presence was unsettling, like a storm cloud threatening to break overhead. I could hardly believe my eyes as I blinked against the sun's glare, hoping that this apparition would vanish into the ether. But he remained, tall and imposing, with his tousled dark hair catching the wind like an errant whisper. My heart raced, an erratic drumbeat echoing the confusion and dread swirling within me.

"Henry," I finally managed, the name tasting foreign on my tongue, heavy with unspoken words. He stepped forward, each movement deliberate, like a predator stalking its prey. My pulse quickened, not from fear alone, but from the tangled emotions that had been buried since he had vanished from my life. The boy I once knew had morphed into this enigmatic man, and the chasm of time stretched between us like an unbridgeable gulf.

"I didn't think you'd come back," I said, my voice wavering slightly, betraying the uncertainty that gnawed at my insides. He stopped a few feet away, and I noticed the vulnerability in his deep-set eyes. They glimmered with a softness I had never expected to see in someone who had once exuded such intensity. It was almost comforting, yet the unease lingered, like the taste of metal after a summer storm.

"I didn't want to," he replied, his voice low and gravelly, wrapping around the words like smoke. "But there are things we need to discuss. Things you deserve to know." The atmosphere thickened with tension, charged like the air before a lightning strike. I took a step back, feeling the wooden railing bite into my palm as I gripped it tightly, grounding myself against the turbulence of emotions he stirred within me.

"Things? What things?" I demanded, the bravado laced with a hint of desperation. I needed answers—answers that felt as elusive as fireflies on a summer night. "You left me without a word, Henry. Why should I trust you now?" The words came tumbling out, each one wrapped in the pain of abandonment.

"I know I hurt you," he said, and there was a sincerity in his tone that made me hesitate. "But this isn't about us. Not anymore. It's about your mother." The mention of her name was like a knife to my heart, slicing through layers of grief that I had tried so hard to manage. "She left something behind, something that's connected to me. Something important."

I stood frozen, caught between the past and the present, trying to piece together what he was saying. The sun dipped lower, casting long shadows that danced around us, amplifying the urgency of his words. "What are you talking about?" I asked, my voice barely above a whisper, the weight of grief and longing tightening around my chest.

Henry took a breath, and the vulnerability returned to his eyes, mingling with a resolve that made me question the choices I had made since he disappeared. "Your mother's legacy isn't just memories. It's a secret she took to her grave—something she guarded fiercely." His words hung in the air, heavy with the promise of revelation, yet shrouded in the mystery that had always surrounded my mother.

A shiver raced down my spine. My mother had always been a fortress of secrets, and her death had left me standing before its walls, desperately trying to understand the person I had lost. "What secret? What does it have to do with you?" I pressed, my mind racing, connecting dots that had long seemed disconnected.

"Everything," he said, stepping closer, the intensity of his gaze unwavering. "It has everything to do with me. She knew things about my past—things that would change everything if they were uncovered. I didn't come back for revenge or anything twisted like that. I came because it's time for the truth to be revealed. We can't move forward without understanding the past."

His confession struck a chord deep within me, resonating with the unfulfilled need for closure, for answers that had been withheld for too long. The world around us blurred momentarily, and I felt the tug of nostalgia, memories flooding my senses—Henry's laughter echoing through sunlit afternoons, our shared dreams whispering in the evening breeze.

And yet, the stakes had never been higher. My heart raced as I grappled with the implications of his words. Trust was a fragile thread, and I felt it fraying between us. I turned my gaze to the horizon, the last rays of sunlight glinting off the fields, reminding me of everything I had once held dear. "Why should I trust you, Henry? After all this time?"

His expression softened, a flicker of regret in his eyes. "Because I'm here now, and I want to help you uncover the truth. I owe it to your mother—and to you." Each word fell heavily, the weight of history hanging between us like a taut wire, ready to snap under the pressure of secrets waiting to be unveiled.

As the sun finally dipped below the horizon, I found myself at a crossroads. Trusting him could mean unraveling the tapestry of lies woven around my mother's legacy, but it also meant reopening wounds that had barely begun to heal.

I stood there, rooted in place, my heart racing in my chest like a wild animal trying to escape. The familiar, sun-drenched yard suddenly felt like a stage, the air thick with unspoken words, tension crackling around us. Henry's presence was an unsettling mix of nostalgia and fear, the remnants of our past colliding with the jagged edges of my current reality. His features were softer than I remembered, the sharp lines of his face softened by time and a vulnerability that caught me off guard. It was a stark contrast to the dangerous man I had been warned about, leaving me unsure of the enemy standing before me.

He took a step closer, and I instinctively stepped back, my pulse quickening further. "I didn't come to hurt you," he said, his voice low and steady, yet it trembled with an emotion that seemed to ripple through the air. "I need to explain."

I watched him closely, analyzing every nuance of his expression, every twitch of his lips. I wanted to believe him, to shake off the fears that clung to me like a heavy fog. But the words Luke had spoken echoed in my mind, a chorus of warnings about Henry's capacity for manipulation and deceit. "Explain what?" I managed, the sharpness of my tone a futile attempt to shield myself from the reality of this unexpected confrontation.

"Your mother," he replied, the weight of his words hanging between us. "There's so much you don't know about her. About what she left behind." His gaze fell to the ground as if the very earth bore the burden of our past. "I didn't want to bring this to you, but I have no choice."

I crossed my arms defensively, my resolve hardening. "Why should I trust you? You vanished without a trace, Henry. You left us, and now you want to waltz back into my life like nothing happened?"

"Because you need to know the truth," he insisted, lifting his gaze to meet mine. "The truth about your mother's legacy. It's not just about her. It's about you—about what she hoped for you, and what it means for the future."

The air between us crackled, charged with history and a thousand unsaid things. I could feel my skepticism warring with a flicker of curiosity. My mother had always been a woman of secrets, a guardian of stories that danced just out of reach. I had spent years piecing together her life, but every revelation felt like a drop in a vast ocean of uncertainty. What more could Henry possibly know?

"Tell me," I said, my voice barely a whisper, caught somewhere between fear and intrigue. "What are you talking about?"

Henry took a deep breath, as if steeling himself for a plunge into deep waters. "Your mother wasn't just a teacher, a simple woman in a small town. She was part of something much larger—a movement that sought to protect knowledge, to keep powerful truths from falling into the wrong hands. There's a reason she was so adamant about keeping her past hidden."

As he spoke, a thousand memories flickered through my mind—the nights I had spent sifting through old boxes, the cryptic notes she had left, the stories whispered in hushed tones. Each piece suddenly felt like a breadcrumb leading to a hidden path, and for the first time, I felt the contours of that path shaping into something tangible.

"I still don't understand," I replied, shaking my head. "What does that have to do with me?"

"Because you're her daughter," he said, urgency rising in his voice. "You've inherited her legacy, and there are people who will stop at nothing to obtain it. You're in danger, and I can help you, but we need to act fast. There's a reason I came back, and it's not just to rekindle the past."

My thoughts spiraled. The idea that my mother had been part of something significant was both exhilarating and terrifying. "What are you talking about? What kind of danger?"

He hesitated, a shadow passing over his features. "Those who seek to control what your mother protected will come for you. They'll try to manipulate you, to turn you into a pawn in their game. But you can't let them."

As I absorbed his words, I felt the weight of responsibility settle on my shoulders. The thought of being caught in a web of intrigue and danger was overwhelming, but the thought of losing the only legacy my mother had left me was unbearable. "What do I need to do?"

Henry's eyes darkened with a mix of determination and sorrow. "First, you need to trust me. I know it's a lot to ask, but I promise I won't let anything happen to you. You need to be prepared to fight back. This isn't just about knowing the truth; it's about taking control of your life, your future."

The flickering light of hope and dread danced in my chest as I considered my options. The world I had known was shifting beneath me, and I felt a strange thrill at the thought of reclaiming my mother's legacy. Perhaps in this chaos, I would find the answers I had been seeking.

"I'll do it," I said, my voice steady and resolute. "But I need to know everything. I need to understand what I'm fighting for."

Henry nodded, his expression a mixture of pride and something deeper, a flicker of regret perhaps. "Then let's start from the beginning. There's so much at stake, and you deserve to know the truth."

As he began to recount the threads of my mother's story, weaving a tapestry of bravery and sacrifice, I felt the air around us shift once again. This wasn't just about Henry and me anymore; it was about reclaiming my mother's legacy and confronting the shadows that had lingered for far too long. And for the first time in years, I felt the warmth of resolve wash over me, illuminating a path I never expected to tread.

The sun hung low in the sky, casting long shadows across the grass as the remnants of afternoon warmth clung to the air. With each passing moment, the weight of Henry's revelation settled deeper within me, a heavy cloak woven from threads of fear and fascination. I found myself caught in a delicate dance of emotions, trying to balance my trepidation about Henry's intentions with an insatiable curiosity about my mother's hidden life. The unease that had settled in my gut gnawed at me, yet a flicker of excitement ignited my spirit. Perhaps this was the moment I had long yearned for, a chance to uncover the mysteries that had defined my mother's existence and, by extension, my own.

Henry gestured for me to follow him, leading me away from the safety of my porch and into the shadowy embrace of the trees that lined the perimeter of my yard. As we ventured deeper into the thicket, the world around us morphed into something more ethereal, the rustling leaves whispering secrets I had yet to understand. Each step felt both familiar and foreign, as if I was tracing the footsteps of my mother, unraveling the stories buried beneath the surface of our mundane lives.

"Here," he said, stopping beneath the sprawling branches of an ancient oak, its gnarled limbs stretching like the arms of a guardian. "This is where she used to come."

The ground was strewn with fallen leaves, their earthy scent mingling with the cool breeze. I knelt down, brushing my fingers across the brittle remnants of the past. It struck me that this place, this sanctuary, was steeped in memories—my mother's laughter, her whispered dreams, and perhaps even her fears. "What did she find here?" I asked, my voice barely a whisper as if speaking too loudly might shatter the fragile atmosphere.

Henry's gaze softened, a flicker of nostalgia dancing in his eyes. "This was her refuge, a place where she could think and write. She had ambitions beyond what she shared with you." He reached into his jacket pocket and pulled out a small, weathered journal, the cover embossed with a faded emblem I couldn't quite make out. "She entrusted me with this before she—before she passed. It holds her thoughts, her ideas about the legacy she left behind."

My heart raced as he handed me the journal, the worn leather cool against my fingertips. As I held it, I felt a surge of connection to my mother, a bridge spanning the gap that time and silence had forged between us. "What kind of ideas?" I pressed, my curiosity burgeoning with each passing second.

"Your mother believed in the power of knowledge," Henry replied, his voice heavy with reverence. "She thought that information could change lives, empower the disenfranchised, and spark revolutions. She wrote about a network—people who shared her vision, protecting knowledge from those who would misuse it." He paused, his gaze turning serious. "But there were others who wanted to control that knowledge for their own gain. That's where the danger lies."

As I leafed through the journal, snippets of my mother's elegant handwriting leaped from the pages, revealing fragments of her thoughts, ideas that vibrated with a sense of urgency. Her words echoed with passion, weaving tales of truth and justice that ignited a fire in my belly. "What happened to this network?" I asked, desperate for clarity.

"They scattered," he explained, a hint of regret lacing his voice. "After your mother's passing, those who were involved became wary, fearing that they might become targets. But some stayed behind, lurking in the shadows, waiting for the right moment to seize what they believe is rightfully theirs."

A chill ran down my spine as I processed the implications of his words. "And they're after me? Because of what she left behind?"

Henry nodded, his expression grave. "Exactly. You are now a key player in this game, whether you want to be or not. They'll see you as a threat to their ambitions, and they won't hesitate to do whatever it takes to neutralize that threat."

The weight of responsibility pressed heavily upon me, yet alongside it was an undeniable thrill. I had always felt like a mere spectator in my own life, but now I stood at the precipice of something extraordinary. "What do we do next?" I asked, determination rising within me like a tidal wave.

"We need to gather the remaining members of her network," he said, his eyes sparking with renewed purpose. "They're scattered, but they're still out there. We need to find them, piece together what your mother left behind, and fortify ourselves against those who wish to silence us."

As Henry spoke, the fog of uncertainty began to clear, revealing a path laden with challenges but also hope. I could see it vividly—an adventure waiting to unfold, filled with allies and adversaries, mystery and revelation. "But how do we find them?" I pressed, my mind racing with possibilities.

"Your mother left clues," he replied, a knowing smile creeping onto his lips. "There are places she frequented, individuals she trusted. We'll have to dig deeper into her past and uncover the hidden ties that will lead us to them."

With that, our plan took shape, a fragile yet exhilarating outline of the journey ahead. I felt a mixture of excitement and trepidation, each heartbeat echoing in sync with the resolve forming within me. This wasn't just about uncovering the truth of my mother's legacy anymore; it was about reclaiming my narrative, asserting my place in a story that had been written long before I understood its significance.

As the evening sky deepened into twilight, painting the world in hues of indigo and violet, I knew we were standing at the crossroads of destiny. Henry, once a figure shrouded in danger, was now a crucial ally, and together we would navigate the complexities of the past to forge a future imbued with purpose. With the journal clutched tightly in my hands, I felt the pulse of my mother's legacy coursing through me, awakening a fire I hadn't known existed. And as darkness descended around us, I found solace in the knowledge that the quest for truth had only just begun.

Chapter 10: A City in Ruins

The sun dipped low on the horizon, casting an orange hue that wrapped around the towering glass structures like a warm embrace. Yet, that warmth never reached me. The streets, once bustling with laughter and life, now felt suffocatingly quiet, as if the city itself were holding its breath. The scent of rain lingered in the air, mingling with the bittersweet aroma of fried food wafting from a nearby vendor, a stark reminder of the normalcy that had slipped through my fingers. I glanced at Luke, his handsome face lined with concern, and wondered what comfort he could offer when I was drowning in uncertainty.

"Are you okay?" His voice was a gentle murmur, a stark contrast to the chaos swirling in my mind. I wanted to nod, to assure him that I was fine, but the truth was lodged in my throat, a heavy stone I couldn't swallow. Instead, I offered a half-hearted smile, one that didn't quite reach my eyes. Luke's concern deepened, his brow furrowing as he studied me, searching for answers in the depths of my turmoil.

I turned my gaze back to the skyline, each building a sentinel of memories I couldn't bear to revisit. The Willis Tower stood tall, its once-majestic silhouette now a haunting reminder of a life that seemed like someone else's story. I had spent countless nights dreaming of success, standing in its shadow, yearning for the power that came with corporate ambition. But those dreams had crumbled into dust, buried beneath the weight of grief and betrayal.

"Let's get something to eat," Luke suggested, trying to coax me into the present. "I hear there's a great little pizza place around the corner."

I forced my feet to move, each step heavier than the last, the cobblestones beneath me rough against my soles. As we wandered through the labyrinth of buildings, the flickering neon lights overhead danced like fireflies, casting long shadows that seemed to twist and curl around us. My heart ached with longing for the life I had known—the laughter of friends over shared meals, the thrill of promotions, the simple joy of being seen and valued.

But here, amidst the ruins of my past, I felt like a ghost haunting a memory that had long since faded. The laughter I had once taken for granted was now a distant echo, haunting the spaces between us. I turned to Luke, desperate to cling to something solid. "What do you think we'll find here?" I asked, my voice barely above a whisper.

"I don't know," he admitted, his eyes searching mine. "But it's a chance to start over. A chance to find some peace." His words held a promise, but the shadows lurking behind his eyes suggested there was more at play than he was willing to share.

As we rounded a corner, the bustling atmosphere shifted. The pizza place came into view, its cozy warmth spilling out onto the street like an invitation. The sound of laughter and clinking glasses beckoned us, offering a glimpse of normalcy. The rich scent of tomato sauce mingled with the yeasty aroma of freshly baked crust, drawing me closer despite my reluctance.

Inside, the dim lighting wrapped around us like a comforting blanket. The walls were adorned with faded photographs of old Chicago—images of laughter, of life, and of resilience. I felt a flicker of nostalgia, a reminder that even the most shattered places could be stitched together with threads of hope. We found a small table in the corner, the wooden surface worn smooth by years of patrons sharing stories and dreams. As I slid into my seat, I caught a glimpse of my reflection in the window—eyes weary, shoulders heavy with the weight of the world.

"Two slices of your finest, please," Luke ordered, his voice carrying a warmth I desperately craved. I watched him as he spoke with the waitress, a familiar ease in his demeanor that made my heart ache. I wanted that ease. I wanted to trust him. Yet, the shadows of his past loomed large in my mind, creating a barrier I couldn't quite breach.

When the pizza arrived, steam curling up from the cheese like tendrils of a forgotten dream, I hesitated. Each slice looked perfect—golden brown crust, glistening with a sheen of olive oil, melted cheese stretching between us like a bridge over troubled waters. I took a bite, and the flavors exploded in my mouth, a symphony of tangy tomato, rich cheese, and herbs that transported me back to simpler days. I closed my eyes, savoring the moment, but the joy was bittersweet, tangled with memories of laughter shared with my mother over slices just like these.

"What's wrong?" Luke's voice cut through the haze, and I opened my eyes to find him watching me intently, concern etched on his face.

"I just... it feels like a lifetime ago," I admitted, the words spilling out before I could stop them. "My mom and I used to come to places like this. It was our thing."

"I'm sorry," he said softly, reaching across the table to take my hand. His warmth enveloped me, a brief flicker of solace against the coldness that clung to my heart.

I looked into his eyes, searching for the truth hidden beneath the surface. "Do you ever feel like you're running from something? Like you're always just one step behind?"

Luke's expression shifted, shadows passing over his features, and for a moment, I saw the flicker of something unspoken. "Yeah," he replied, his voice barely a whisper. "All the time."

His honesty struck a chord deep within me, and I found myself wanting to draw closer, to peel away the layers that separated us. In that moment, as the city pulsed around us, I realized we were both lost souls trying to find our way through the ruins, each with our own burdens to bear. The weight of the past lingered, but perhaps together we could navigate the remnants and discover a path toward something new.

With our half-eaten pizza resting forgotten on the table, I found myself leaning into Luke's presence, the warmth radiating from his hand anchoring me against the onslaught of memories. He watched me, waiting for the storm of emotions to subside, and in his gaze, I sensed a sincerity that both comforted and terrified me. Here, in this city of echoes, our shared silence grew heavy, the unspoken words hanging between us like the smoke curling from the pizza oven, thick and tangible.

I took a breath, filling my lungs with the scent of baked dough and bubbling cheese, willing the air to cleanse the remnants of sorrow that clung to me. "Do you think we'll ever escape our pasts?" I asked, my voice barely above a whisper, barely daring to disturb the fragile peace that surrounded us.

Luke considered my question, his expression shifting into something deeper, more contemplative. "I think it's less about escaping and more about learning to live with it," he said. "We all carry pieces of our pasts with us, like scars. They shape us, but they don't have to define us."

His words resonated within me, reverberating against the walls of my heart, a truth that felt both liberating and suffocating. I wanted to believe that the past could fade, but each memory was a ghost that haunted my every step, trailing behind me like a wayward shadow.

A sharp laugh erupted from the table next to us, pulling me from my reverie. A group of friends, all animated and full of life, shared stories and laughter, their joy infectious. I couldn't help but smile, a genuine flicker igniting within me as I observed their camaraderie. Moments like this reminded me of the light that once filled my life, before grief dimmed it.

Luke followed my gaze, and a smile broke across his face, brightening his features. "See? There's still life in this city, even if it feels broken."

"Life, yes. But is it good?" I couldn't help but challenge him, the cynic in me rising.

"Good, bad, it all depends on how you look at it," he replied, his eyes twinkling with mischief. "The beauty is in the chaos, in the unpredictable nature of it all. Like pizza, you never know what you're going to get with each slice."

I chuckled, appreciating the absurdity of his metaphor. "Are you comparing life to pizza?"

"Why not? Everyone loves pizza, even if it's sometimes a bit messy."

The warmth of his laughter wrapped around me, and for a moment, I allowed myself to forget the shadows lurking at the edges of my mind. As we chatted, the atmosphere shifted subtly, an unspoken understanding weaving between us. Beneath the layers of grief and uncertainty, I sensed a flicker of hope. Perhaps there was a way to carve out a space for myself here in this city, despite the ruins.

After finishing our meal, Luke suggested we take a walk along the river. The sun had begun its descent, casting a warm golden glow over the water, transforming the Chicago River into a glimmering ribbon of light. I hesitated for a moment, the thought of immersing myself in the vibrant chaos of the city both enticing and daunting. But the spark in Luke's eyes urged me on, and I found myself nodding in agreement.

We strolled along the riverwalk, the rhythmic sound of water lapping against the shore a soothing backdrop to our conversation. The city began to come alive as twilight descended, the skyline illuminated by a tapestry of twinkling lights. Street performers dotted the pathway, their music and energy mingling with the laughter of passersby. It was a reminder that life, in all its imperfections, continued to flourish.

"What did you love most about the city before?" Luke asked, curiosity dancing in his eyes.

I thought for a moment, the memories flooding back—frozen lakes in winter, the vibrant street art that transformed drab buildings into canvases of color, the rich aroma of coffee wafting from corner cafes. "It was the people, really. The sense of community. Even in a city this big, I always felt connected."

"Community is a powerful thing," he mused, glancing around as if searching for something more. "It's what makes a place feel like home."

The word "home" settled in my chest like a warm ember, igniting a flicker of longing. The concept felt distant, elusive—a whisper of something I had lost along with my mother. But as I looked at Luke, a man forged in the fires of his own struggles, I felt the beginnings of something new, something I wasn't quite ready to name yet.

We continued walking, and as we passed the iconic Marina City, the cylindrical towers rising majestically above us, I felt the familiar tug of nostalgia. Memories of rushing past these buildings, my heart full of ambition and dreams, echoed in my mind. I had once believed in a future painted with success, each step on the pavement a stride toward destiny.

"How about you? What makes you feel at home?" I asked, genuinely curious about the layers beneath his handsome exterior.

Luke paused, his gaze fixed on the river, lost in thought. "I think it's the moments that catch you off guard. Like this," he gestured broadly to the scene around us, "the unexpected beauty in chaos. I've seen things, experienced things that could break a person, but there's also resilience in those moments."

"Like finding joy in pizza?" I teased, nudging his arm playfully.

"Exactly!" he laughed, the sound like music to my ears, and for a fleeting moment, the heaviness in my heart lifted.

As the stars began to twinkle overhead, I found myself yearning for connection, for the kind of companionship that could weather storms. I was scared, terrified of the implications, but there was a bond forming, one forged in shared vulnerability and unspoken truths.

Underneath the vast expanse of the night sky, I took a deep breath, feeling the cool air wash over me. Perhaps in this city of ruins, amid the chaos of our intertwined stories, we could find a way to rebuild—brick by brick, moment by moment.

The rhythm of the city pulsed around us as we strolled along the river, the sound of laughter and conversation swirling in the air like a gentle breeze. I watched the water shimmer under the streetlights, the reflections dancing and twisting, creating a kaleidoscope of colors that momentarily distracted me from my turbulent thoughts. It was easy to lose myself in the charm of Chicago, the way the city breathed life into its inhabitants, drawing them into its chaotic embrace. I couldn't help but wonder if I, too, could be swept away by its charm.

As we walked further, the architecture began to shift from the sleek modernity of the downtown skyscrapers to the more eclectic styles of the neighborhoods. Brick buildings, their facades rich with character, stood proudly against the backdrop of the glistening river. Each seemed to tell a story, whispering secrets of the past to anyone who would listen. I found myself drawn to a particularly vibrant mural adorning a nearby wall, bursting with colors that told tales of struggle and triumph. Art had a way of capturing emotions too complex for words, and in that moment, I felt a flicker of kinship with the artist, a shared understanding of what it meant to confront pain.

"Do you ever wonder about the stories behind these murals?" I asked Luke, gesturing toward the artwork. "What inspired the artist to create something so raw and beautiful?"

He looked at the mural, then back at me, a thoughtful expression crossing his face. "Every story is a piece of someone's journey. Maybe they found solace in creating it, just like you might find in expressing your own story. The beauty of art is that it connects us in ways we can't always articulate."

His words lingered, wrapping around my heart like a gentle hug, and I considered how art could serve as a refuge for the wounded. I had spent so much time locked inside my grief, convinced that vulnerability was a weakness. Yet here, amidst the crumbling remnants of my life, I felt the urge to embrace that vulnerability, to allow the pain to transform into something beautiful.

As we continued along the river, the sun dipped lower in the sky, painting the horizon in hues of lavender and rose. I could see the iconic bridges arching gracefully over the water, their silhouettes outlined against the fading light. I was suddenly overwhelmed by a desire to create my own piece of art, to capture this moment in a way that echoed the vividness of my emotions.

"Let's take a picture," I said impulsively, pulling my phone from my pocket. Luke raised an eyebrow, a smile breaking across his face as he obliged, standing beside me with the skyline as our backdrop.

"Say 'Chicago!'" he teased, striking a goofy pose that sent a giggle spilling from my lips. It felt good to laugh, the sound echoing off the buildings and intertwining with the distant music of a street performer strumming a guitar.

As the camera clicked, freezing the moment in time, I felt a sense of freedom wash over me. This city, this ruined yet resilient landscape, was a part of my journey now—a canvas waiting for my brush strokes, for the story I had yet to tell.

When the photo was taken, we resumed our walk, the conversation ebbing and flowing like the tide. I wanted to ask Luke about his past, about the darkness he carried, but the thought lingered uneasily on the edge of my mind, a question I hesitated to voice. It felt too personal, too fragile, as if probing too deeply might shatter the moment we had created together.

Instead, I found myself sharing snippets of my life—stories about my mother and the little things that made her so extraordinary. I spoke of her laughter, her love for Sunday brunches filled with pancakes and syrup, and her passion for life that spilled into every corner of our home. Luke listened intently, a soft smile playing on his lips, and I felt a warmth blossoming within me, a sense of connection growing between us.

"I wish I could have met her," he said finally, sincerity woven into his words. "She sounds like an incredible woman."

"She was," I replied, my voice thick with nostalgia. "She taught me to find beauty in the chaos, to embrace every moment. I just wish I had more time with her."

Luke's expression shifted, a flicker of something unspoken passing between us. "We don't always get to choose how much time we have, but we can choose what to do with the time we're given," he said, his voice low and earnest.

The weight of his words sank in, resonating with the struggles we both faced. Perhaps we were not defined solely by our pasts, but rather by how we chose to move forward, to weave the strands of our experiences into something new. I glanced at Luke, noticing the way the fading light danced in his eyes, and I felt a flicker of hope stirring within me—a fragile ember that had been reignited against all odds.

As we continued walking, I noticed the city had transformed into a tapestry of light, the storefronts aglow with vibrant hues. The laughter of children mingled with the sounds of music, creating a symphony of life that wrapped around us. It was intoxicating, and for the first time in a long while, I felt a sense of belonging, a whisper of home in a city that had once felt so foreign.

"Do you want to grab a drink?" Luke asked as we approached a lively bar with a patio overlooking the river, the atmosphere buzzing with energy.

I hesitated, the ghost of my past nudging at the edges of my thoughts. But the spark of connection I felt with him urged me forward. "Sure," I replied, my heart racing with the thrill of spontaneity.

We settled onto the patio, surrounded by laughter and clinking glasses, the world feeling simultaneously vast and intimate. As we sipped our drinks, I felt the walls I had built around my heart beginning to crumble. Luke's presence was a balm, soothing the raw edges of my grief while gently coaxing me into the light.

The conversation flowed easily, each moment layered with meaning and laughter. I felt lighter, the shadows receding as we shared stories about our favorite places in the city, our dreams for the future, and our fears that had chased us into the night. I began to understand that my life was not a series of shattered pieces, but rather a mosaic of experiences, and each interaction with Luke was a vibrant tile waiting to be added to my story.

As the night deepened, I looked out over the water, the moon casting a silvery sheen across its surface. I realized that while my journey was still marred by loss, I had the power to redefine it, to reshape my narrative. In that moment, I made a silent vow to embrace whatever came next—to step into the chaos of this city, to forge connections that would anchor me, and to allow the beauty of the present to drown out the ghosts of my past.

With Luke by my side, the city felt alive again—a world of possibilities waiting to be explored, and for the first time, I was ready to take that leap.

Chapter 11: The Things We Bury

The wind whispered through the trees, sending a shiver down my spine as I traced my fingers over the cold, rough surface of the gravestone. It was a stark reminder of life's transience, the finality of it all echoing in the spaces between my thoughts. Each letter carved into the granite was a punctuation mark in the narrative of a life once lived, a life that had gone silent long before its time. I felt the urge to kneel, to place my palm flat against the stone as if by some act of devotion, I could somehow conjure the spirit of this stranger back to the world of the living, if only for a moment.

Willow Creek wasn't just a town; it was an intricate tapestry woven from the threads of memory and loss. The cemetery stood as a silent witness to the stories that had unfolded here—stories of love and heartbreak, of families torn apart and dreams dashed like fragile glass against the jagged rocks of reality. I was but a visitor in this vast narrative, an interloper seeking solace in a place thick with echoes of the past. I inhaled deeply, the air filled with the scent of damp earth and wilting flowers, a bittersweet reminder of both life and death.

Luke's presence anchored me, though his silence often felt like a chasm separating us. He was a curious contradiction—a man with laughter dancing in his eyes yet shadows lurking in the corners of his soul. Sometimes, I found it hard to reconcile the two sides of him, as if he were the embodiment of all my uncertainties wrapped up in one captivating figure. I turned slightly, catching his profile against the backdrop of gravestones that jutted like sentinels into the sky. The wind tousled his hair, and for a brief moment, he looked almost vulnerable—an unexpected crack in the armor he wore so effortlessly.

"Are you okay?" I asked, my voice barely above a whisper, hoping to bridge the distance that had formed between us since our arrival. He looked over, those deep-set eyes revealing nothing, yet somehow everything. I could sense the weight he carried, the burdens he bore quietly, and it made my heart ache for him.

He shrugged, a simple gesture that belied the turmoil roiling beneath the surface. "Just thinking," he replied, his tone nonchalant yet laden with the unspoken. I nodded, not wanting to press him further. We had both come to this place seeking something—answers, understanding, closure—yet here we were, wrapped in our own private worlds, struggling to navigate the murky waters of our emotions.

The sun dipped lower in the sky, casting long shadows across the grass, the world around us bathed in a soft golden light. It was beautiful in a haunting sort of way, the vibrant colors mingling with the gray stone and lush greenery, a juxtaposition of life and death that felt almost poetic. I closed my eyes for a moment, allowing the warmth to wash over me, reminding me that even in the darkest of places, light could still seep through the cracks.

I thought about my mother and the secrets she had woven into the fabric of our lives. The memories were like ghosts, haunting me in my dreams, pulling at the edges of my consciousness when I least expected it. What had she been hiding? What had she buried beneath the veneer of her carefully curated existence? The questions spiraled through my mind, an endless loop of doubt and desire for truth. I had spent so long running from these revelations, hiding behind the facade I had built. But now, in this cemetery that felt like a portal to the past, I knew I couldn't run any longer.

My thoughts were interrupted as Luke shifted beside me, breaking the spell of introspection. "You know," he began, his voice steady, "I never understood why people come to places like this." He gestured to the grave markers, the names and dates telling tales of lives cut short. "It always felt like a reminder of what's gone, not what's left."

I turned to him, intrigued. "But isn't that the point? To remember? To acknowledge the stories that came before us?" The words flowed freely, as if I were pulling from a wellspring of emotions I had kept bottled up for far too long. "We can't move forward unless we understand where we came from."

He considered my words, a flicker of something in his eyes—curiosity, perhaps, or a hint of understanding. "Maybe," he replied slowly, "but sometimes I think it's easier to forget." The vulnerability in his admission caught me off guard. I had expected bravado, a mask of indifference, but here he was, peeling back layers I hadn't even realized existed.

The shadows stretched and shifted as the sun continued its descent, the warmth giving way to the cool embrace of dusk. I could feel the chill creeping in, wrapping around me like a shroud, and I shivered involuntarily. Luke shifted closer, his warmth radiating against the encroaching cold, an unspoken promise of solidarity. In that moment, standing in the fading light with the weight of our histories hanging in the air, I felt an unshakeable connection form between us—a thread binding our stories together, weaving us into the larger narrative of this town and its secrets.

As we lingered there, I knew this wasn't just a moment in time; it was the beginning of something new. Together, we would uncover the layers of our pasts, peeling back the masks we wore until we reached the heart of the truths that lay buried within. I glanced back at the gravestone, the name etched in stone serving as a reminder that every story deserved to be told, even those that had been silenced.

In the midst of that silence, beneath the canopy of trees that swayed gently in the twilight breeze, I felt a flicker of hope ignite within me. I wasn't alone in this journey; I had Luke by my side. And perhaps, just perhaps, we could find the answers we sought together, bringing light to the shadows that had haunted us for so long.

The air shifted as nightfall crept in, draping the cemetery in a blanket of soft shadows. The vibrant colors of the sunset faded, leaving only hints of pink and gold peeking through the branches, like ghosts of warmth unwilling to fully surrender to the darkness. I turned my back to the grave, the weight of the stone a constant presence in my mind. It felt like an anchor, tethering me to a reality I had long avoided.

"Let's get out of here," I suggested, my voice wavering slightly as I attempted to inject levity into the moment. I didn't want to wallow in the somber air, even though the cemetery had opened a floodgate of emotion I hadn't anticipated. Luke stepped forward, his footsteps muted on the grass, and as he moved beside me, I could feel the pulse of unspoken words thrumming in the space between us.

"Where to?" he asked, glancing down the path that wound through the gravestones, each one a reminder of life's inevitable end. He seemed to contemplate every direction and every decision with a seriousness that belied his youthful appearance. His dark hair, tousled from the wind, framed his face, highlighting the intensity in his gaze.

"Anywhere but here," I replied, feeling the urgency of my own words. I needed to escape the weight of what I had just confronted. As we walked side by side, the stones receded behind us, and the world opened up, offering a glimpse of life beyond the finality of death.

The streets of Willow Creek were alive with flickering lights and the distant sounds of laughter spilling from nearby cafes. The familiar scent of roasted coffee and freshly baked pastries drifted through the air, wrapping around me like a comforting embrace. It was a stark contrast to the silence of the cemetery, a vibrant reminder of the living tapestry of human experience just beyond the gates. I caught myself smiling as we approached a small café tucked into a corner, its windows glowing warmly against the encroaching night.

"Let's stop in there," I suggested, pointing to the inviting space. The place was a small sanctuary, its wooden façade adorned with hanging plants that danced lightly in the breeze, and I could already envision the cozy atmosphere inside—the gentle hum of conversation, the clink of porcelain cups, and the aromatic steam curling from freshly brewed coffee.

Luke hesitated for just a moment, but then nodded, a hint of a smile tugging at his lips as we stepped inside. The café was a haven of warmth, with low-hanging lights casting a golden glow across the small tables scattered throughout. I breathed in the rich aroma of coffee mingling with the sweetness of pastries, and for a fleeting moment, the weight of my worries lifted.

We settled into a corner booth, the plush seats inviting us to sink in and relax. I glanced at the menu, but the choices blurred together as my mind wandered back to the graveyard. I fumbled with my phone, scrolling through images of my mother from happier times. There she was, smiling brightly, her laughter a melody I could almost hear echoing in my mind. I longed for those moments, the carefree days before everything had changed.

"What are you looking at?" Luke asked, his voice breaking through my reverie. I looked up, my heart racing slightly at the thought of sharing these fragments of my life with him. The vulnerability that comes with exposing one's past is both terrifying and exhilarating.

"Just some old pictures," I admitted, holding the phone out for him to see. "My mom, back when she was... happier." I swallowed hard, the lump in my throat threatening to choke me.

He leaned in closer, studying the image with a thoughtful expression. "She looks like she had a light about her," he said softly, his tone respectful. "What happened?"

The question hung in the air like a weight, and I felt the familiar wave of grief crash over me. "I don't really know," I confessed, my voice barely above a whisper. "She became someone else, a shadow of the person in these pictures. Maybe it was just life catching up to her, or maybe... maybe it was more than that." I drew in a deep breath, gathering the courage to continue. "I never really understood it until now."

Luke regarded me with a quiet intensity, as if he were peeling back the layers of my guarded heart, and I felt a strange mix of comfort and trepidation. "We're all just trying to figure it out, aren't we?" he replied, a hint of sincerity weaving through his words. "Sometimes the light fades, but that doesn't mean it's gone forever."

His insight struck a chord within me. I had been running from the shadows for so long that I had forgotten to look for the light. In that small café, with the warmth enveloping us and the faint sound of laughter swirling around, I felt the possibility of healing begin to stir.

Our drinks arrived—steaming mugs of coffee adorned with delicate foam art—and we settled into a comfortable rhythm, sipping and sharing small anecdotes about our lives. With each laugh and gentle tease, the walls I had built around my heart began to crumble. I learned that Luke had grown up in a different town, one filled with its own ghosts and stories. His family, too, had been shaped by loss, a shared understanding of grief connecting us in an unspoken bond.

"Did you ever go back?" I asked, curiosity piquing as I leaned in closer. "To confront whatever it was you left behind?"

He paused, his expression growing contemplative. "Not yet. I'm not sure if I'm ready," he admitted, vulnerability shining through his bravado. "But maybe one day I will. We can't bury everything forever, right?"

The notion resonated deeply, echoing in my heart as I recognized that we were both on the cusp of uncovering the truths we had buried so deeply. In this shared moment, the flickering lights above us casting a soft glow on our faces, I realized that perhaps together we could navigate the shadows and find our way back to the light.

As we finished our coffee, the conversation flowed like the river running through Willow Creek, moving effortlessly and yet with an undercurrent of tension—an acknowledgment of the uncharted territories we both faced. With every story shared, I felt a little less alone, a little more empowered to face whatever lay ahead. The secrets we carried might weigh heavily on our souls, but in the embrace of newfound companionship, I sensed the possibility of letting go.

With the café slowly emptying around us, I could feel the night settling in, but instead of the familiar fear that often accompanied the dark, there was a spark of hope igniting within me. I glanced at Luke, his eyes alight with a mix of mischief and sincerity, and for the first time in a long time, I dared to believe that we could both step into the light, leaving behind the burdens of the past to forge a path forward—together.

The café's ambiance settled around us, a cocoon of warmth and familiar scents, creating a sanctuary from the world outside. Each sip of coffee brought with it a wave of comfort, coaxing forth a sense of belonging I hadn't realized I craved. I felt like I was peeling back layers, revealing not only pieces of my past but also discovering parts of myself I had long thought lost.

Luke leaned back, his fingers tracing the rim of his cup, a contemplative look overtaking his features. "You know," he began, his voice low and rich like the coffee we drank, "I think we bury more than just memories. Sometimes, we bury the people we want to become."

His words hung in the air like a delicate thread, weaving an intricate connection between us. I pondered this notion as I glanced out the window, where the city thrummed with life just beyond our little oasis. Cars whizzed by, their headlights cutting through the dimming light, casting fleeting shadows that danced on the pavement. The world outside was vibrant and chaotic, a stark contrast to the hushed introspection we shared within the café's cozy walls.

"What if I don't know who I want to become?" I admitted, a hint of vulnerability slipping through my carefully crafted facade. The admission felt like a pebble dropped into a still pond, creating ripples that reached far beyond the surface. I could feel the weight of my own uncertainty settling over me, pressing down like a heavy fog.

"You will," he assured me, his tone unwavering. "It takes time to sift through everything we carry." He shifted closer, his earnest gaze never leaving mine. "You just have to be willing to look."

In that moment, a quiet resolve bloomed within me. I had been so consumed by my past—by the ghosts that haunted me and the shadows that threatened to swallow me whole—that I had forgotten to envision a future. I nodded slowly, contemplating the journey ahead, the road littered with both challenges and the potential for rebirth.

As if sensing my thoughts, Luke leaned forward, excitement lighting up his features. "Let's take a walk after this. I want to show you something."

"Okay," I replied, intrigued. A part of me felt exhilarated at the idea of an adventure, the unknown beckoning like a siren's call. After paying the bill, we stepped out into the cool night air, the breeze swirling around us, carrying with it the fragrance of blossoming jasmine from nearby gardens.

We walked side by side, our footsteps echoing against the pavement, the city alive with sounds and sensations. The streets were lined with charming brick buildings that exuded history, their façades worn yet resilient, just like the stories they held. Each block we traversed felt like a piece of a larger puzzle, revealing the tapestry of life in Willow Creek—where laughter mingled with sorrow, where memories intertwined with dreams.

"Here it is," Luke said, stopping abruptly and gesturing toward a small park nestled between two buildings. It was almost hidden, the entrance marked by arching trees that framed a path leading to a stone bench bathed in moonlight. The serenity of the park was a stark contrast to the bustling city surrounding it, a secret haven waiting to be discovered.

As we stepped inside, the atmosphere shifted. The sounds of the city faded away, replaced by the rustling leaves and the gentle crooning of distant frogs. I felt as if I had entered another realm, one where the weight of the world could be momentarily forgotten. The moon hung low in the sky, casting silvery beams that danced across the grass, creating a magical landscape that stirred something deep within me.

"Why do you love this place?" I asked, curiosity piquing as I observed the serene beauty around us.

Luke smiled, a soft, genuine smile that reached his eyes. "It's where I come to think, to breathe," he confessed. "When everything feels too heavy, I can just sit here and let it all wash away."

I could see the peace this place afforded him, the way his shoulders relaxed as he spoke. I took a seat on the bench, its cool stone grounding me as I inhaled the fragrant air. "What do you think about?" I pressed, eager to understand the man beside me, to peel back the layers that concealed his heart.

He sat beside me, the warmth of his body radiating against the cool night air. "About life, mostly," he said, his voice thoughtful. "About what's real and what's not. About the things we hide."

His honesty was refreshing, and it urged me to confront my own truth. I felt the urge to share my fears, to expose the raw edges of my soul. "I've hidden so much from myself, from everyone," I murmured, the words escaping me before I could stop them. "I feel like I'm drowning in the expectations of others, and in my own doubts."

Luke turned to me, his gaze piercing yet gentle. "You don't have to drown. You can learn to swim."

The determination in his voice ignited a flicker of hope within me. Perhaps this was the moment I had been waiting for—the catalyst to ignite my transformation. I had buried so much, but now, perhaps it was time to unearth those hidden treasures.

"Tell me more about your past," I urged, eager to shift the focus onto him, to dive into the stories that had shaped his own journey. "What have you buried?"

He hesitated, the vulnerability flashing across his features before he composed himself. "My family, like yours, has its share of struggles. My father..." His voice trailed off, and I could sense the gravity of what he was about to reveal. "He was a good man, but the world chewed him up and spat him out. I watched him become a shadow of who he once was."

The confession hung heavily between us, and I felt an overwhelming sense of empathy. "I'm sorry," I whispered, the weight of his words resonating deeply within me. "That must have been incredibly hard."

Luke nodded, a wistful smile touching his lips. "It was. But it taught me resilience. I learned to find light even in the darkest places. And now..." He paused, his eyes sparkling with determination. "Now I want to help others find their light too."

In that moment, I felt a surge of connection—a bond formed not just by our shared experiences of loss, but by the hope that flickered between us like the stars dotting the night sky.

As we sat there, the world fading into a quiet hum around us, I felt a newfound strength within me. The things I had buried could rise again, not as burdens but as the very foundation upon which I would build my future. I glanced at Luke, the man who had become my unexpected confidant, and saw in him not only a reflection of my struggles but also a beacon of hope.

"Thank you for sharing that with me," I said, my voice steady, my heart lighter. "I think we both have some digging to do."

With a knowing smile, he nodded, our eyes locking in a moment of unspoken understanding. Together, we could uncover the treasures hidden beneath the rubble of our pasts, revealing the beauty that awaited us on the other side. The journey wouldn't be easy, but with each step forward, I felt the darkness retreating, replaced by the burgeoning light of possibility.

As we sat in the tranquil park, the moon rising higher in the sky, I knew we were embarking on a path that would redefine us both. We were no longer defined solely by what we had lost; we were ready to embrace what could still be found. And in that shared moment of vulnerability, I felt more alive than ever, ready to uncover the things we had buried and discover the truth that lay waiting just beneath the surface.

Chapter 12: A Flicker of Hope

The city loomed outside my window, a sprawling mass of glass and concrete that seemed almost alive, pulsing with energy and ambition. I could hear the honking of taxis, the chatter of people rushing past, and the distant sound of a saxophonist playing a mournful tune on the corner of State and Madison. There was something poetic about the chaos, a beautiful disarray that felt like home, yet today, I found it suffocating. I was tangled in thoughts that echoed louder than the cacophony outside, each one a haunting reminder of my past.

The photograph rested in my palm, a frail piece of history, and I traced the edges with my fingertips, as if I could unearth secrets embedded within its fibers. My mother's laughter was frozen in time, a vibrant burst against the sepia backdrop that seemed to whisper stories of joy and regret. There was a light in her eyes that sparked a longing in me, a desire to understand the woman who had shaped so much of my life yet remained an enigma. Who was this man, this stranger whose presence seemed to ignite a flicker of warmth in her heart?

I closed my eyes, imagining the summer days she must have spent with him. I could almost hear the rustle of leaves in the park where they might have strolled, the golden rays of the sun filtering through the branches, casting playful shadows on their faces. In my mind's eye, they laughed as they shared secrets beneath the sprawling oak trees, their youthful exuberance a stark contrast to the burdens of adulthood that lay ahead of them. The image faded, replaced by the stark reality of my cramped apartment, its walls closing in as if mirroring my growing sense of unease.

Luke returned shortly, the air around him charged with an electric tension that sent shivers down my spine. His eyes flickered to the photograph, and in that moment, I could see the walls he had built around himself start to tremble. "You okay?" I asked, my voice a soft thread woven with concern. He hesitated, his lips curling slightly, but I could tell the smile didn't reach his eyes.

"Just...thinking," he murmured, averting his gaze as he leaned against the kitchen counter, the cool marble a stark contrast to the heat radiating from my uncertainty. I placed the photograph on the table, the image of my mother and the stranger glaring at us both, demanding answers that seemed elusive. "What do you know about him?" I asked, my heart racing as I tried to navigate the precarious balance between trust and suspicion.

Luke took a deep breath, his expression a blend of contemplation and regret, as if he were trying to untangle the threads of his own memories. "Henry was...he was a part of your mother's life before you. A complicated part." The hesitation in his voice made my stomach twist uncomfortably. Complicated was a word that danced around so many truths, but what truths lay hidden behind it?

"Did she love him?" I pressed, unable to quell the urgency in my tone. The atmosphere between us thickened, and I could sense the weight of the moment—a shared vulnerability that could either strengthen our bond or shatter it entirely.

Luke shifted, the tension in his shoulders betraying his calm facade. "I think she did," he replied slowly, each word deliberate, as if he were constructing a fragile bridge between us. "But it was more than that. There was fear, too."

Fear. The word hung in the air like a ghost, haunting me with the specter of unanswered questions. I could see it in my mother's eyes, the sparkle of joy shadowed by something darker. I took a step closer to Luke, my heart hammering in my chest. "What happened to him? Why did he leave?"

He hesitated, and in that silence, I felt the chasm widening between us, a rift of unspoken truths and half-remembered stories. "It's not my place to say," he finally replied, his voice barely above a whisper. I could feel the pulse of my disappointment mingling with the frustration of being left in the dark, the photograph a constant reminder of the secrets that seemed to enshroud my mother's past like a thick fog.

I sighed, the weight of the conversation settling heavily on my shoulders. "I just want to understand," I admitted, my voice trembling slightly as I reached for the photograph again. "To know the woman she was before she became my mother."

Luke stepped forward, his brow furrowed with concern. "You're not alone in this," he assured me, his hand reaching out to grasp mine, warm and reassuring. But even as he spoke, a flicker of doubt ignited within me, a quiet voice questioning how well I truly knew him.

In that moment, the vibrant city outside felt like a distant dream, a world that continued to spin while I stood frozen in time, caught between my mother's forgotten laughter and the uncertain shadows lurking in Luke's eyes. I needed answers, and with each passing moment, it became increasingly clear that unraveling the truth would require more than just a few questions and a photo. It would demand courage, resilience, and perhaps a willingness to confront the darker corners of my family's history—those hidden secrets that could either bind us together or tear us apart.

As I gazed out the window at the bustling street below, I felt the first flicker of hope amidst the uncertainty, a spark igniting within me. I would not allow fear to dictate my path. I would chase the echoes of my mother's past and confront the shadows that lingered between us, even if it meant unearthing truths I might not be ready to face.

The city pulsed with life beneath my window, yet I remained ensnared in a labyrinth of my thoughts, grappling with the weight of the photograph and the implications of Luke's silence. It felt as if the air around me crackled with tension, each moment stretching thin like a taut wire ready to snap. I could almost hear the low hum of anticipation echoing through the streets, a melody played just for me, urging me to step out, to confront the chaos outside instead of allowing it to swirl within my mind.

With a deep breath, I decided I could no longer hide behind the confines of my apartment. I slipped into a pair of worn jeans and a cozy sweater, the fabric soft against my skin, offering a strange sense of comfort. The streets of Chicago awaited me, alive and chaotic, and I needed to lose myself in their rhythm. I stepped outside, the brisk air wrapping around me like a cool embrace, shaking off the remnants of doubt that had clung to me like a shadow.

The scent of roasted coffee beans wafted through the air as I passed a local café, and I felt a magnetic pull toward it. The warmth inside was a welcome relief from the chill, and I ordered a steaming cup of black coffee, watching as the barista expertly maneuvered around the small counter, crafting the perfect frothy latte for a customer. I found a spot by the window, my eyes drifting to the bustling street as people hurried past, their faces a tapestry of stories and emotions, each one a flicker of life in the grand narrative unfolding around us.

As I sipped my coffee, the rich flavor grounding me, I couldn't help but wonder about the lives I glimpsed outside. Did they harbor secrets like mine? Did they, too, carry photographs that held unspoken truths? In that moment, I felt an undeniable kinship with the strangers who brushed shoulders with one another, their lives intertwined in ways they might never fully understand. I closed my eyes, imagining their tales, until my thoughts wandered back to Luke, his reaction lingering like a ghost in my mind.

I took another sip, the warmth igniting a spark of determination within me. If Luke wouldn't share what he knew, I would find my own answers. With a newfound resolve, I pulled out my phone and began to search for anything related to Henry, desperate to grasp even the faintest thread that could lead me to the truth. My fingers flew across the screen, the soft clicking sound a reminder that I was actively seeking, moving toward a resolution rather than lingering in uncertainty.

Hours slipped away as I delved into online archives, sifting through old newspapers and obituaries, my heart racing with each new lead. I stumbled upon snippets of articles about a man named Henry Sullivan, a local musician whose star had flickered brightly in the Chicago scene before mysteriously fading into obscurity. The words leaped off the page: "haunting melodies," "tragic past," and "unfulfilled potential." My heart ached for the man my mother had once loved, a name that now felt both foreign and intimate, like an unfinished melody lingering in the back of my mind.

With every new detail I uncovered, the photograph became more than a relic; it transformed into a key, unlocking pieces of a past I was desperate to understand. I learned about the vibrant clubs where Henry had played, the very establishments I had often passed without a second thought. As dusk fell, the city glowed, the neon lights flickering to life as if each one had a story to tell, and I felt drawn to the heart of that world.

I decided then: I would visit one of those clubs. It was reckless, perhaps, but a thrill ignited within me. I wanted to feel the pulse of the music that once enveloped my mother and Henry, to immerse myself in the history that lingered in the shadows. I slipped on my leather jacket, feeling an unexpected surge of confidence as I stepped back onto the streets.

The club was tucked away on a side street, its entrance framed by a red door that looked worn yet inviting. The music thumped against the walls, vibrant and alive, wrapping around me like a familiar embrace. I stepped inside, and the atmosphere shifted, a sensory overload of voices, laughter, and melodies swirling together. The dimly lit room was filled with the scent of whiskey and the warmth of camaraderie, a tapestry of humanity woven together by the universal language of music.

I found a spot at the bar, the wooden surface cool beneath my fingertips as I took in the scene. A band played on a small stage, their passion palpable as they poured their souls into every note. My heart raced as I scanned the room, searching for any remnants of Henry's presence in the faces that surrounded me. It was as if I was looking for a ghost in a sea of memories, each face blurring into the next, until I finally caught sight of a couple swaying together, lost in their own world.

They were so absorbed in their dance that they seemed untouched by the reality around them, a perfect picture of joy. In that moment, I felt a pang of longing—an aching desire for the kind of connection they shared. But it wasn't just a longing for love; it was a yearning for understanding, for the pieces of my own life to fall into place.

I ordered a drink and watched as the band played on, their music carrying me away, the rhythm pulsing in time with my heartbeat. With each passing moment, I felt the flicker of hope growing stronger, illuminating the path before me. I was not merely a spectator in this world; I was a part of it, intertwined with the lives that unfolded in the shadows of the stage.

As the evening wore on and the crowd ebbed and flowed, I felt an undeniable sense of clarity settling over me. I was here to find answers, to confront the past, and in doing so, I might just uncover a deeper connection not only to my mother but also to myself. In the vibrant chaos of the club, I realized that even in the darkest corners of uncertainty, there exists a flicker of hope—a beacon guiding us through the labyrinth of our lives, urging us to keep moving forward, no matter the obstacles we face.

The music thrummed through the club like a heartbeat, enveloping me in its warm embrace as I leaned against the bar, letting the notes wash over me. My drink sat untouched for the moment, the glass slick with condensation, as I let myself be carried away by the rhythm. The band played on, pouring their souls into every riff, and I felt an inexplicable connection to the melodies that resonated deep within my chest. Each chord seemed to pulse in sync with my own heartbeat, a reminder of the life I was striving to uncover.

As the night unfolded, the light from the stage flickered like fireflies, casting shadows across the faces of the crowd. I watched couples dance, swaying in a world that felt both foreign and achingly familiar. Their laughter rang out, mingling with the music, creating a tapestry of joy and sorrow woven together in the smoky haze. It was intoxicating—every moment was a story unfolding, and I was but a spectator caught in the web of their lives.

Then I saw her. A woman with fiery red hair, her curls cascading down her back like molten lava, dancing with abandon in the corner of the room. There was something about her that drew me in—an infectious energy radiated from her as she spun, her laughter slicing through the noise like a sharp note rising above a symphony. I couldn't help but smile, caught up in her uninhibited joy, and as if sensing my gaze, she turned and met my eyes.

For a fleeting second, everything around us blurred, and it was just the two of us in a bubble of shared understanding. She raised her glass in a playful toast, and I found myself mirroring her movement, laughter bubbling up inside me. Encouraged by her warmth, I pushed off the bar and wove my way through the crowd, the music pulling me closer to her like a siren's call.

"Join me!" she shouted above the din, her voice vibrant and inviting. Without hesitation, I plunged into the sea of bodies, swaying with the rhythm as I felt an exhilarating sense of freedom wash over me. We danced like no one was watching, losing ourselves in the moment, the worries of the outside world slipping away as we moved in sync with the music.

"I'm Claire!" she shouted, her eyes sparkling with mischief. "What's your story?"

"Just trying to figure it all out," I replied, caught off guard by the honesty in my words. It felt liberating to share a glimpse of my journey with a stranger who seemed to embody the essence of life itself—unapologetically alive.

Claire grinned, her laughter infectious. "Aren't we all? This city has a way of hiding things, but if you dig deep enough, you'll find gems beneath the surface." She gestured around us, the people, the lights, the music—it all seemed to shimmer with potential.

"Speaking of gems, do you know anything about the old music scene here?" I ventured, curiosity piquing as I recalled the name Henry Sullivan and the snippets I had unearthed earlier.

Her expression shifted, becoming more serious, though her eyes sparkled with intrigue. "Henry? The musician? I've heard whispers, stories passed down from the old-timers. He had a presence that could light up a room. Tragic, really."

"Tragic?" I echoed, leaning in, eager to catch every word.

"He loved fiercely, but life didn't love him back. They say he lost everything in a blink—his music, his dreams, and maybe even his heart. But oh, when he played? It was as if the world stopped to listen." Her words danced around me, painting a picture of the man who had once held my mother's heart.

"Do you know where I can find any of his old recordings?" I pressed, a spark igniting within me as I envisioned unearthing the music that had once filled my mother's life with joy.

"I might have a lead or two," she said, her brow furrowing in thought. "But you'll have to prove your dedication first."

"Prove my dedication?" I chuckled, intrigued.

"Come with me to an open mic night next week at a spot called The Blue Note. It's where musicians gather to share their souls. You'll hear stories there—some that might lead you right to Henry."

The prospect excited me, and I felt the thread of fate weaving us together in this shared journey. "Count me in," I replied, my heart racing at the possibility of uncovering more about the man who had slipped through my mother's fingers like sand.

The evening flowed, a cascade of laughter and camaraderie, and I reveled in the connection I had forged with Claire. She shared tales of her own journey through the city, a winding path of dreams and disappointments that mirrored my own struggles. There was something liberating about being vulnerable with a stranger, about embracing the fleeting moments that could change everything.

As the night wore on, the band's final song echoed through the club, a bittersweet melody that stirred something deep within me. I took a deep breath, the air thick with possibility, and glanced at Claire, who was now animatedly discussing her plans to take on the world. The thrill of our newfound friendship mingled with the anticipation of what lay ahead.

When the last notes faded and the crowd began to disperse, I felt a pang of reluctance at the thought of leaving this vibrant world behind. "Will you be there at The Blue Note?" I asked, hoping for the chance to reconnect.

"Absolutely! I'll save you a seat up front," Claire replied, a wide grin illuminating her face.

As we exchanged numbers, I felt a strange sense of hope unfurling within me. The photograph, Henry, and the secrets of my mother's past were no longer just fragments of a story—they were threads weaving into a greater narrative, one that encompassed friendship, music, and the pursuit of truth.

Stepping back into the cool night air, I felt invigorated, the city alive with the promise of new beginnings. I had embarked on a quest—not just to discover the past, but to embrace the potential of my future. Each step I took was a heartbeat, a beat that echoed the rhythm of the music I had just experienced, propelling me forward into the unknown.

I would find Henry. I would piece together the fragments of my mother's life. And maybe, just maybe, I would find a little piece of myself along the way.

Chapter 13: The Man in the Shadows

The door finally clicked open, and I stepped into the familiar chaos of our apartment. A vibrant tapestry of mismatched furniture and half-finished art projects littered the space, a testament to our shared ambition and the dreams we'd once painted with broad strokes of enthusiasm. As I closed the door behind me, the solid thud resonated in my ears, grounding me against the storm of uncertainty swirling within. The rich scent of old wood mingled with the faint aroma of paint and something else—an undercurrent of impending change that made me shiver despite the warmth of the room.

I tossed my keys into the bowl on the table, a routine action that somehow felt monumental in the wake of the evening's events. My eyes darted around the room, searching for something to anchor me, some reassuring sign that everything was still normal. Luke's guitar leaned against the wall, a silent witness to our many evenings filled with laughter and music, a stark contrast to the chill creeping up my spine.

An uneasy energy lingered in the air, prickling my skin. I crossed to the window, peering out at the street below, half-expecting to see that man lurking in the shadows again. But the street was empty, bathed in the soft glow of streetlights, illuminating the sidewalk like a stage awaiting its actors. I leaned closer, my breath fogging the glass as I searched for something that wasn't there—something tangible to hold onto in this moment of disquiet.

What was it about him that had triggered the memories of Henry, of that fair in Willow Creek? The same rush of excitement mixed with dread surged through me, a reminder of a past I thought I had escaped. I shut my eyes, trying to block out the swirl of thoughts, but they danced behind my eyelids like flickering fireflies.

A sharp knock on the door jolted me back to reality, and I startled, nearly losing my balance as I turned away from the window.

My heart raced as I approached the door, hesitation weighing heavy in my chest. It was too soon for Luke to be home. Who else could it be? I took a deep breath, steadying myself, and opened the door to reveal my best friend, Clara, her vibrant energy spilling into the dim light of the apartment.

"Hey! I brought snacks!" she announced, her infectious enthusiasm filling the room like sunshine. She stepped inside, kicking off her shoes and shaking off the chill from the outside air, her golden hair swinging like a banner behind her.

"Clara, you scared me," I admitted, letting the door swing closed behind her. "What are you doing here?"

"I was in the neighborhood," she said, her eyes sparkling with mischief. "And I figured you could use a distraction. You look like you've seen a ghost."

I laughed, though the sound felt strained, as I gestured for her to take a seat on the worn couch that had been the backdrop to countless late-night conversations and shared secrets. "You could say that. Just... a strange encounter on my way home."

Clara's brows furrowed as she settled next to me, the cushions sinking beneath her weight. "What happened? Was it someone weird? Please tell me you didn't get approached by a street magician or something."

"No," I replied, forcing a lightness I didn't feel. "Just a guy leaning against a lamppost. He was watching me, and it gave me the creeps."

She leaned closer, her expression shifting from playful to serious in an instant. "Did you recognize him?"

"No," I said, shaking my head. "But he felt... familiar. Like a memory I couldn't quite grasp."

Clara reached for the bag of chips she had brought, tearing it open with a flourish. "You know how this city is. It's full of characters. Maybe he's just some random guy." She crunched a chip, her focus on me unwavering. "Or maybe it's just your imagination playing tricks."

I nodded, but unease coiled within me. The shadow of that man lingered in my thoughts, weaving itself into the fabric of my mind like a thread of darkness that refused to be severed. I was about to respond when I heard the familiar sound of the key turning in the lock, and my heart leapt with a mix of relief and apprehension.

Luke stepped in, his face lighting up with surprise as he spotted Clara. "Hey! What's going on?"

"Snacks and girl talk," Clara announced with a grin, her playful demeanor easily cutting through the tension that hung in the air.

Luke's gaze shifted to me, searching for something unspoken. "You okay?"

"Yeah, I'm fine," I lied, my smile faltering slightly. He stepped closer, and for a brief moment, the distance that had been growing between us seemed to shrink. But then the moment passed, and the familiar gap returned, an unbridgeable chasm formed by unsaid words and unresolved feelings.

"Let's eat," Clara suggested, her voice brightening the atmosphere as she nudged the chip bag toward Luke. "I brought your favorite."

As the three of us sat together, a semblance of normalcy enveloped us. The laughter and chatter filled the room, but beneath it all, the shadow of the man loomed in the corners of my mind, refusing to be ignored.

The evening unfolded with familiar ease, Clara's energy dancing through the room, but every laugh echoed with the weight of unspoken fears. I could feel the distance between Luke and me stretching again, the threads of connection fraying at the edges, as I remained haunted by the memory of that man in the shadows, his presence tethering me to something I had yet to understand.

The chatter between Clara and Luke provided a comforting backdrop, a balm for my frayed nerves, yet I could feel the undercurrent of anxiety swirling around me like a thick fog. I picked at the chips Clara had brought, my mind a million miles away, chasing shadows that danced just beyond my reach. The laughter felt strangely hollow, and every joke shared felt like a mask concealing the truth. I forced myself to smile, but it felt more like a twitch of the lips than genuine happiness.

Clara, ever perceptive, paused mid-laugh, her gaze shifting to me with an intensity that made me shift uncomfortably in my seat. "You're not really here, are you?" she asked, her tone shifting to a gentle concern that pierced through the evening's lightheartedness.

I glanced between her and Luke, their faces illuminated by the soft glow of the overhead lights. "I'm just... tired," I managed to reply, not wanting to unravel the threads of this evening. I couldn't burden them with the weight of my fears, not when they were so effortlessly lost in laughter, as if the world outside our apartment didn't exist.

"Long day at work?" Luke probed, his brows knit in that familiar way that told me he was concerned, genuinely invested in how I was feeling.

"Something like that," I said, avoiding his gaze. My thoughts flickered back to the man in the shadows, that unsettling familiarity still gnawing at me. It was as if he had slipped into my life uninvited, carrying whispers of memories long buried.

The conversation shifted back to the mundane, Clara detailing her latest escapades at her job in advertising, where every day felt like a whirlwind of creativity and chaos. I watched her animated gestures and felt a pang of longing for that sense of purpose she seemed to embody effortlessly. I had once been that person—the passionate dreamer crafting vibrant stories. Now I felt like a ghost, hovering on the outskirts of my own life, trying desperately to remember the vibrant hues of my aspirations.

"Let's do something fun this weekend!" Clara suggested, her enthusiasm bubbling over as she crunched another chip, the sound a stark reminder of my own silence. "Maybe a road trip? Or we could hit up that new karaoke bar downtown!"

Luke's face lit up at the mention of karaoke, his competitive spirit flaring to life. "I'm in! Just wait until you hear me sing. It'll be a showstopper."

I forced a smile, but inside I felt torn. A weekend escape could be just what I needed, a chance to breathe and break away from the heaviness that had settled in my chest. Yet, the shadow of that man loomed larger than my fleeting moments of joy, threatening to darken the laughter shared in our cozy apartment.

As the evening stretched on, I found myself retreating further into my thoughts, the laughter around me fading into a distant hum. I excused myself under the pretext of needing a glass of water, escaping to the small kitchen that felt like a refuge from the tumult of my emotions. The dim light flickered as I poured water into a glass, watching the liquid swirl like the confusion in my mind.

The coolness of the water felt refreshing against my parched throat, a momentary distraction. I leaned against the counter, eyes drawn to the window, where the city unfolded like a living tapestry beneath the stars. The lights flickered like fireflies, illuminating the streets with a warm, inviting glow. Yet, even this beauty couldn't drown out the chill that had settled in my bones.

What was it about that man? I pressed my forehead against the cool glass, my breath fogging the surface as I tried to piece together the fragments of my memories. A name danced just beyond the reach of my consciousness, an echo of familiarity that clawed at the edges of my mind. I closed my eyes, summoning images of my past—the fairgrounds, laughter, cotton candy melting in the summer heat—but each recollection slipped through my fingers like grains of sand.

"Hey, you okay?" Luke's voice cut through my reverie, warm and grounding. I turned, forcing a smile as he leaned against the doorframe, his concern palpable.

"Yeah, just... needed a moment."

He stepped closer, his hands sliding into his pockets as he regarded me with those piercing eyes that had once made me feel safe. "You've been quiet tonight. If something's bothering you, you can talk to me, you know."

I wanted to let him in, to share the turmoil swirling in my heart, but the words felt lodged in my throat, stuck like a ball of yarn unraveling too quickly. "It's nothing," I said, the familiar lie rolling off my tongue. "Really. Just a bit of stress from work."

His expression shifted slightly, a mix of understanding and disappointment flickering across his face. "Alright, but just know I'm here if you need me."

"I know," I replied softly, my heart tightening at the distance I felt between us. We had been through so much together, yet at that moment, it felt as if we were two ships passing in the night, tethered by memories but adrift in our own oceans of solitude.

As he returned to Clara, I couldn't shake the sense of impending change. That man, whoever he was, had invaded my thoughts like an uninvited guest, and I knew I had to confront this feeling that clung to me like a second skin. I took a deep breath, steeling myself for whatever lay ahead.

Later that night, after Clara had left and the echoes of laughter faded into the walls, I lay awake in bed, staring at the ceiling, my thoughts a cacophony of doubt and dread. The shadows danced in the corners of the room, mimicking the man from earlier, his presence lingering like a ghost that refused to be exorcised.

I needed answers, but what questions could I even ask? My mind spun in circles, seeking clarity in the chaos, yearning for the light that had once filled my life. The city beyond my window buzzed with life, but within these four walls, I felt trapped in a web of uncertainty.

Sleep eluded me as I listened to the soft sounds of the city—the distant hum of traffic, the occasional siren wailing like a mournful song. The night stretched on, each tick of the clock amplifying my restlessness, and I finally sat up, determination coursing through me like a river breaking free from its dam.

I would find that man, confront whatever shadows he cast over my past. It was time to face the fears that had been gnawing at me, to reclaim the pieces of myself that felt lost in the fog. And in doing so, perhaps I could illuminate the path ahead, guiding me back to the vibrant life I had nearly forgotten.

A sliver of moonlight filtered through the window, illuminating the room in a soft glow as I lay awake, the events of the evening swirling in my mind like autumn leaves caught in a brisk wind. I pushed myself up and glanced at the clock—2:17 AM—each tick of the second hand echoing like a drumbeat in my head. The vibrant city outside continued its nightly dance, oblivious to the turmoil within my own heart.

I swung my legs over the edge of the bed, letting my feet dangle for a moment before planting them firmly on the cool wooden floor. The chill reverberated through my body, waking me further. A quick glance around our cluttered living room reassured me I was still in familiar territory—art supplies scattered across the coffee table, half-finished paintings leaning against the walls, remnants of our dreams whispering in the corners. This was my sanctuary, and yet, the familiarity felt oddly foreign now. I needed to clear my head.

After dressing in a cozy oversized sweater that smelled faintly of Luke's cologne, I slipped on my boots and stepped outside into the brisk night air. The coolness enveloped me, invigorating my senses and urging me forward. The streets were quieter now, the laughter and chatter of the day replaced by the occasional rustle of leaves or distant car horns, creating a symphony of solitude that echoed my inner turmoil.

As I walked, I replayed the scene from earlier. The man's gaze had been penetrating, a mix of curiosity and something darker that hinted at unspoken secrets. Who was he? Why did he feel like a phantom from my past, a shadow cast by memories I had thought buried? The questions swirled around me like the wind tugging at my hair, refusing to settle.

The rhythm of my footsteps became my mantra as I turned down familiar streets, each corner a snapshot of my life in Chicago. The dimly lit coffee shop on the corner was still open, a beacon of warmth and caffeine in the darkness. I hesitated, the scent of roasted beans and pastries wafting through the door, and decided to step inside, hoping the comforting atmosphere would soothe my racing thoughts.

The café was nearly empty, save for a couple nestled in a corner booth, whispering sweet nothings over steaming cups, and an elderly man hunched over a newspaper, his brows knitted in concentration. I approached the counter, greeted by the barista's warm smile that seemed to slice through the chilly air.

"What can I get for you?" she asked, her voice melodic, a soft anchor in the night.

"I'll have a chai latte, please," I replied, grateful for the simple pleasure.

As she prepared my drink, I settled into a corner table, my fingers tracing the rim of my cup once it was handed to me. I took a moment to breathe in the sweet, spicy aroma, letting it ground me. I watched the steam curl into the air like wisps of my thoughts, and for a fleeting moment, the world around me faded, the warmth of the café enveloping me.

Yet, the man's image flickered in my mind, igniting a flame of determination. I would find out who he was. I wouldn't let this shadow follow me unchallenged. My heart raced at the thought, a mix of excitement and dread coursing through me.

After finishing my drink, I stood and wandered outside, the chill wrapping around me again as I stepped into the night. The streets were still quiet, the city's pulse a low thrum beneath my feet. As I strolled, I contemplated where I could go for answers. My thoughts turned to the fairgrounds where Henry and I had spent countless nights, wrapped in the warmth of cotton candy and laughter, unaware of the shadows looming on the horizon.

The thought propelled me forward. I could return to Willow Creek, the very site where my past had begun to intertwine with my present. I could confront those memories head-on, dissect the feelings of nostalgia and dread until the roots of this familiarity were unearthed. The fairground held secrets of its own, remnants of who I was before Chicago had beckoned me with promises of dreams fulfilled.

As the city melted into the background behind me, the horizon slowly lit up with the first hints of dawn, painting the sky in hues of lavender and gold. The drive to Willow Creek felt different this time, the air thick with expectation and uncertainty. I passed familiar landmarks—the diner where Luke and I had shared our first meal, the little bookstore where we lost track of time wandering through dusty shelves. Each stop along the way pulled me deeper into the tapestry of memories woven with laughter and heartbreak.

Upon arriving at the fairgrounds, I felt an odd mix of nostalgia and trepidation. The faded lights of the rides still stood tall, albeit dimmed by time. I parked the car and stepped out, the gravel crunching beneath my boots, sending echoes into the stillness. The air was sweet with the remnants of past summer nights, a concoction of popcorn and fried dough lingering like a ghost.

I wandered through the grounds, the memories flooding back—the exhilaration of spinning on the Ferris wheel, the sweet taste of candy apples, the sound of laughter ringing through the air. It felt like a different world, a chapter long closed yet somehow still vivid. Each step pulled me deeper into that realm, and as I explored, I felt a tug at my heart, a whisper of who I once was, untouched by the shadows that now haunted me.

I paused near the old carousel, its paint peeling but still beautiful in its weathered charm. As I traced the edges of one of the horses, a chill danced down my spine. It was here, in this very spot, that I had first glimpsed Henry's magnetic charm. The memory flooded my mind: the way he had laughed, the sparkle in his eyes, how easily he had filled the empty spaces in my heart.

But there was another memory lurking beneath, one I had tried to suppress. I took a deep breath, forcing myself to confront it, to not shy away from the shadows that clung to this place. It was a late summer evening, the golden light casting long shadows on the ground, laughter floating through the air. I had seen something, a glimpse of something I wasn't meant to witness. My heart thudded as I recalled the argument, the desperation in voices raised, secrets unveiled in the backdrop of carefree joy.

"Why didn't you tell me?" I had overheard someone say, the pain palpable even through the veil of time.

As the echoes of that moment crashed against me, I turned abruptly, feeling the weight of the past pressing heavily upon my shoulders. The faintest rustle from the shadows caught my attention, and I whipped around, instinctually reaching for the invisible tether that connected me to my fears.

And there he was—the man from the lamppost—standing at the edge of the fairgrounds, his silhouette framed against the morning light. My heart raced, a mix of fear and recognition as I stepped forward.

"Who are you?" I called out, my voice trembling but determined.

His gaze met mine, and in that moment, the world around us faded, leaving only the two of us suspended in the stillness. "I've been waiting for you," he replied, his voice low and smooth like velvet.

With that single phrase, the shadows that had loomed over me began to unravel, threads of the past weaving into the present as I prepared to face whatever secrets lay ahead.

Chapter 14: The Breaking Point

The night pressed against the window, thick and heavy, with the kind of darkness that swallows sound and thought. I paced our modest living room, the rhythmic crunch of my footsteps echoing against the polished wooden floorboards. Outside, the Chicago skyline loomed, a jagged silhouette of steel and glass, punctuated by the occasional glow of a streetlamp, a distant reminder of the city's pulse that felt so far removed from the turmoil swirling within me.

Luke had always been my anchor, his laughter a warm balm against the icy winds of uncertainty that threatened to engulf me. But tonight, the laughter felt like a ghost, haunting the corners of my mind as I replayed our earlier conversations, the subtle shifts in his demeanor like a warning sign blinking in the recesses of my thoughts. The moment he walked through that door, a chill swept through me, wrapping around my heart and squeezing until it hurt.

The air was thick with unspoken words, each second stretching into a taut wire of tension that could snap at any moment. I could see the way his shoulders were hunched, as if bearing the weight of secrets he had no intention of sharing. My heart raced, an erratic drumbeat against the backdrop of our silence. I took a deep breath, the familiar scent of him mingled with the faint aroma of the Italian takeout he had brought home—linguine with clam sauce, my favorite, a feeble attempt at normalcy. But the meal sat untouched on the coffee table, a stark reminder of the conversation we had avoided.

"Luke," I finally broke the silence, the sound of his name feeling heavy on my tongue. "We need to talk about the photograph."

He shifted, the muscle in his jaw tensing as he avoided my gaze. The photograph had been an accident—a misplaced memory from a night I'd rather forget. Yet the man in that photograph haunted my thoughts, a dark specter lingering just out of reach, teasing me with questions that gnawed at my insides. Why hadn't he told me? The answer was there, lurking in the shadows, but Luke's reluctance to share felt like a betrayal.

"I thought we agreed to leave the past behind us," he replied, his voice barely above a whisper, each word laced with an urgency that did little to mask the evasiveness. I could hear the frustration threading through his tone, like a frayed rope nearing its breaking point.

"Agreed?" I countered, the incredulity spilling out. "You think this is about agreements? This is about trust, Luke! You were in that photograph with him, and yet here we are, pretending everything is fine?"

He flinched at my words, and the sight sent a flicker of regret through me, but it was drowned out by the swell of anger. I had fought too hard to rebuild our lives, to stitch together the torn fabric of our relationship after the chaos that had once consumed us. And now, standing at the edge of this new abyss, I realized how fragile our truce really was.

"Trust?" he echoed, the word hanging heavily in the air between us. "What do you know about trust? You don't even know why I—"

"Why you what?" I interjected, my voice rising. "Why you kept secrets? Why you thought it was okay to hide parts of your life from me? It's not just about that photograph, Luke. It's about everything!"

The fight erupted, words cascading into a symphony of accusations and half-formed explanations, the kind of emotional maelstrom that leaves you gasping for air. Each word flung between us felt like a dagger, sharp and unforgiving. I could see the hurt in his eyes, and yet, it barely tempered my resolve. I needed to unearth the truth, needed to rip away the layers he had so carefully constructed around himself.

"I'm trying to protect you," he insisted, desperation creeping into his voice, yet the sincerity I once cherished felt like a shadow slipping through my fingers.

"Protect me?" I laughed, a bitter sound that echoed in the otherwise quiet room. "Or protect yourself? Because you're terrified of what I might think if I knew the truth?"

Silence enveloped us again, thicker than before, wrapping around our throats and stifling our breaths. I could see the flicker of guilt in his eyes, a tiny crack in the facade he had built. But I wasn't here to soothe his conscience; I needed answers, even if they cut like glass.

"I don't want to be with someone who can't be honest with me," I said, my voice steady despite the turmoil roiling within. "I deserve to know who I'm with, Luke. You can't keep me in the dark forever."

A moment passed, heavy and electric, charged with the weight of our shared history and unspoken fears. The soft hum of the city outside felt almost foreign now, a distant echo to our intimate battleground. His eyes searched mine, and I could see the turmoil reflecting back, a storm of emotions I had never seen before.

"I thought you'd understand," he finally admitted, his voice breaking, the vulnerability in his tone disarming. "I thought I was doing the right thing."

"Right for whom?" I shot back, but my words lacked their earlier bite. The façade he had constructed around himself seemed to be crumbling, and I wondered if there was more to this than just the photograph.

As the silence stretched between us, I felt the realization dawning—a bitter sweetness that lingered on my tongue. The night was still, yet the storm within me brewed louder than ever. Secrets have a way of festering, of growing into monsters in the dark, and I was tired of being scared. Tired of being left in the shadows of his past.

In that moment, I made a choice. The photograph, the lies, the fear—they could no longer bind us. We were standing on the precipice, a fragile ledge that could crumble beneath the weight of our unsaid truths. I stepped closer, my heart racing, not knowing if I was heading toward salvation or destruction. But the one thing I did know was that whatever lay ahead, I had to confront it head-on.

"Tell me everything, Luke," I urged, my voice barely above a whisper, trembling with the intensity of my need to know. "No more hiding."

And as the words hung in the air, an electric charge coursing through the room, I felt the fragile threads of our relationship straining, pulling, threatening to snap. But within that tension lay the possibility of rebirth, of uncovering the truth that had remained shrouded in darkness for far too long.

The air thickened between us, a palpable force pressing down like a storm cloud ready to unleash its fury. I stood there, rooted in place, watching as he turned away, his back to me, shoulders taut with unshed tension. The faint sounds of the city outside faded into a dull hum, overshadowed by the turmoil swirling within our four walls. I wanted to reach out, to close the distance that felt like a chasm, but my feet were encased in ice, anchored by the gravity of our unresolved conflict.

The shadows in the room danced as the lone lamp flickered overhead, casting elongated shapes on the walls that reminded me of the silhouettes of our past—the moments filled with laughter and warmth now tinged with an unsettling chill. I felt like an outsider in my own home, a stranger peering through the window at a life that had once felt so secure.

"Why won't you just tell me?" I finally broke the silence, my voice trembling with the weight of unspoken fears. "Whatever it is, I can handle it."

He turned slightly, enough for me to catch the flash of pain in his eyes. "You don't know what you're asking, Claire," he replied, each word laced with a blend of desperation and caution, as if the mere act of speaking would unravel everything he had tried so hard to protect.

"Try me," I insisted, my heart pounding like a war drum. "This isn't just about the photograph anymore. It's about us, about trust. If you keep pushing me away, you're going to lose me."

The silence stretched again, heavy and charged, as I watched the conflict play out on his face. There was a flicker of something—fear, perhaps?—and I realized how vulnerable he must feel in that moment. Beneath the bravado, beneath the secrets, was a man grappling with demons I had yet to understand.

"You think I want to lose you?" he whispered, and in that moment, the anger that had coursed through me began to ebb, replaced by something softer, something that made my heart ache. "I'm trying to keep you safe, Claire. I can't explain everything, not yet."

"Then what am I supposed to do with that?" I shot back, frustration lacing my voice, but there was a tremor beneath my resolve, a crack in the fortress of my anger. "How can I trust you if you won't let me in?"

He turned fully now, and I could see the battle waging within him, the internal war that raged just beneath the surface. "It's complicated," he said, his voice dropping to a near whisper, laden with an urgency that suggested there was much more at stake than I could fathom. "I made mistakes, Claire. Dangerous ones."

The words hung in the air like a dark cloud, threatening to unleash a tempest. I felt a chill run down my spine, my instincts flaring to life as I began to grasp the enormity of his confession. "Mistakes? What kind of mistakes?"

He took a step closer, the gap between us narrowing, the tension now a taut wire stretched to its limit. "I was involved with people who... they're not like us. They operate in shadows, Claire, and I thought I could walk away. I thought I could protect you by staying silent."

The revelation struck me like a bolt of lightning, illuminating the depths of his fears and my own. My mind raced, grappling with the implications of his words. "You mean to tell me you were mixed up in something illegal?"

He nodded slowly, the weight of the truth pressing down upon him like an anvil. "It's more than that. I got in over my head, and now I don't know how to get out without putting you at risk."

I felt the ground shift beneath me, the world tilting on its axis. I had thought I knew him, thought our love was a fortress against the storms of the past. Yet here we stood, teetering on the edge of an abyss that threatened to swallow us whole. "And you thought hiding it from me was the answer?" I asked, my voice rising again, tinged with disbelief. "You've kept me in the dark while you dealt with your mess?"

"It was never about you!" he shouted suddenly, the frustration boiling over. "I thought I was protecting you! I thought I could spare you from the fallout, from the danger that comes with knowing."

"Knowing what?" My heart raced as the pieces began to fit together, painting a picture more sinister than I had ever imagined. "That you were lying to me? That you were willing to let me live in ignorance while you played with fire?"

His eyes blazed with an intensity I had never seen before, a mixture of fear and regret swirling together like a tempest. "I never wanted to put you in this position, Claire. I thought I could handle it, but it's spiraled out of control. I'm scared of what will happen if I tell you everything."

"And I'm scared of what will happen if you don't." The words slipped out before I could catch them, and suddenly, I felt as though we were on the precipice of something monumental—a revelation, a reckoning that could either bind us closer together or tear us apart.

He closed his eyes for a moment, breathing deeply, the tension radiating from him palpable as I watched the storm of emotions flicker across his face. "You have to believe me when I say that I love you," he finally said, his voice raw and earnest. "That's why I did this. I thought I could shield you from the darkness. But I see now that I've only succeeded in creating a void between us."

"Love isn't about keeping secrets," I replied, my voice steadier now, a whisper of determination rising within me. "Love is about sharing everything—the light and the dark. If we can't do that, then what do we have?"

His gaze met mine, and in that moment, the world around us faded away, leaving just the two of us standing on that precarious edge. I could see the fear in his eyes, a flicker of vulnerability that resonated deep within me. And as I stood there, grappling with the weight of his secrets, I realized that our love had the power to weather any storm, as long as we faced it together.

"Then let's face it," he said, his voice firm, a sense of resolve crystallizing between us. "I'll tell you everything. No more shadows. No more lies."

The warmth of his words wrapped around me like a comforting embrace, infusing me with a renewed sense of hope. Together, we would dismantle the walls that had sprung up between us, brick by brick, and illuminate the darkness that threatened to engulf our love. It was a risk, but one I was willing to take. With every moment that passed, I felt the embers of our connection ignite, ready to blaze a path forward through the uncertainty that lay ahead.

As the night deepened, the city outside our window transformed into a glittering tapestry, lights twinkling against the velvety backdrop of darkness. But within the confines of our apartment, shadows loomed larger, filled with the weight of unsaid words and uncharted territories of our relationship. I found myself ensnared in a tumultuous web of emotions—fear, anger, love—each thread pulling me in conflicting directions.

I crossed the room to the kitchen, the familiar scent of garlic and herbs lingering from the meal Luke had prepared earlier that evening, a faint reminder of the man I thought I knew. I opened the fridge, staring blankly at its contents, searching for something to steady my racing heart. A bottle of wine caught my eye, a half-empty remnant from our last celebration, an evening marred only by the specter of the secrets that now stood between us. I poured myself a glass, the rich crimson liquid swirling as if echoing the tempest within me.

The sound of Luke's footsteps echoed in the hallway, drawing me back to the present. I turned to face him, my heart pounding against my ribcage, both of us caught in a moment suspended in time. His expression had softened slightly, a mix of regret and resolve. "I'll tell you everything," he said, his voice steady but strained, each syllable resonating with a sincerity that pierced the air between us.

"Then start talking," I urged, taking a sip of the wine to steady my nerves, its warmth cascading down my throat like a soothing balm. "What do I need to know?"

He ran a hand through his hair, a gesture I recognized as a sign of his anxiety. "It all began a few months ago," he started, the weight of his confession palpable in the space between us. "I was approached by a guy named Ethan. At first, it seemed harmless—just some side work to help with a few tech projects. But I didn't realize the extent of what I was getting into."

My breath caught in my throat as he spoke, each word a brick falling from the wall of my understanding. "Ethan was involved with some shady people. He didn't mention it at first, and I thought I was just helping him with data analysis and a couple of marketing strategies."

His gaze shifted to the window, where the city lights twinkled like stars in a universe of uncertainty. "But as things progressed, I started to see the cracks. It wasn't just tech work; it was laundering money, Claire. I didn't want to believe it, but the deeper I got, the more entangled I became. I was scared, and I thought if I distanced myself, I could protect you. But leaving was never an option without consequences."

My heart sank as the gravity of his situation settled around us, an oppressive fog that stifled the air. I moved closer, my fingers brushing against the counter as I sought to ground myself in the reality of his words. "What do you mean, consequences?"

"I made some enemies, Claire. People who don't take kindly to being crossed." His eyes darkened, reflecting the seriousness of his situation. "That photograph you saw—it wasn't just an old friend. He's part of this world, and when I cut ties, I put you in danger."

Panic surged through me, a rush of adrenaline that left my thoughts scattered like leaves in a storm. "So, what are we supposed to do? Live in fear? This isn't just about you anymore, Luke. It's about us. It's about our future!"

His face tightened, the strain of the moment evident in every line etched upon his brow. "I don't want to drag you into this, but I need your help to untangle myself from it. I need you to understand that I never wanted any of this."

I felt the heat of his plea, the urgency of his situation igniting a flame of determination within me. "Then we'll face it together. I won't let you shoulder this alone. But we need a plan."

Luke nodded, and for the first time since his arrival, I saw a flicker of hope in his eyes. "I've been gathering information. There are safe houses, ways to get me out of sight until things blow over. But I need to be cautious. I don't want to put you at risk."

"Too late for that," I shot back, surprising myself with the firmness in my voice. "You already have. We're in this together now, whether you like it or not."

The tension between us shifted, the air crackling with a new energy. I could see him processing my words, the realization settling in that I wasn't going to back down. The vulnerability that had haunted him began to transform into something resembling resolve, a bond forged in the fires of shared peril.

"Okay," he said finally, his voice low and steady. "But I need to know you're ready for this. It's going to be dangerous. They won't take kindly to me walking away."

"Then we'll walk together," I said firmly, the weight of his hand meeting mine across the counter, the warmth of his touch igniting the fierce protectiveness I felt. "No more secrets, no more hiding. Whatever comes our way, we'll face it side by side."

He searched my eyes, a mix of disbelief and gratitude flashing across his features. "You're braver than I ever realized."

"I learned from the best," I quipped, attempting to lighten the atmosphere, but underneath the playful facade lay an unyielding determination.

We spent the next few hours strategizing, every whisper and glance echoing the gravity of our situation. I jotted down notes, my hands trembling slightly as I wrote down names and potential allies Luke had mentioned. Together, we mapped out a plan, a fragile outline of what could be our salvation. Each detail felt monumental, a step toward reclaiming our lives from the shadows that had threatened to consume us.

As dawn broke, casting a pale light over the city, I felt a sense of resolve settle in my chest. The shadows of uncertainty still loomed, but they felt less daunting now, transformed by our shared commitment to face whatever lay ahead. We were no longer just a couple navigating the complexities of love; we were partners in a battle that would test the very foundation of our relationship.

The first rays of sunlight streamed through the window, illuminating the room in a soft golden hue, revealing the scattered remnants of our late-night strategy session. I glanced at Luke, who stood by the window, his silhouette etched against the light, a warrior ready to face his demons.

"Whatever happens next," I said softly, stepping beside him, "we'll do it together."

He turned to me, his expression filled with a mixture of gratitude and resolve, a promise of loyalty woven into the fabric of his gaze. "Together," he echoed, and in that moment, the world outside faded away, leaving just the two of us, poised to face the challenges ahead.

And as the first light of day spilled into our lives, I knew we would rise, not merely to survive but to reclaim our story, forging a path illuminated by truth, love, and an unbreakable bond forged in the fires of adversity.

Chapter 15: The Secret I Never Knew

The letter crackled softly in my hands, each fold and crease a testament to time's relentless passage. As I sat cross-legged on the floor of my cramped apartment, the scent of dust mingling with the lingering aroma of last night's takeout, I traced my fingers over the cursive letters, each stroke imbued with the weight of a history I had never fully grasped. The dim light from the single window cast a golden hue across the faded pages, illuminating the words that felt like a haunting melody, echoing through the corridors of my heart.

"I loved him once," my mother's handwriting danced across the paper, her words vivid yet shadowed by an undeniable sorrow. "Before the darkness enveloped us, Henry was laughter and light, a gentle storm that swept me off my feet. But secrets have a way of unraveling love, revealing the jagged edges beneath the polished surface."

With every line I read, a kaleidoscope of emotions swirled within me. I could almost hear her voice, soft yet quivering with emotion, as she spoke of the man who had been a phantom in my life. The wind whistled through the narrow streets outside, a mournful tune that resonated with the turmoil in my chest. Henry. I had known that name only in fleeting moments, whispers of a past that never truly belonged to me.

As I delved deeper into her words, the scenery around me faded into a backdrop, replaced by the vivid imagery of my mother's memories. I could almost see her, young and wild, with laughter in her eyes that mirrored the blue skies of a summer day in Seattle. She described a picnic by the lake, where the sun glistened on the water like a thousand diamonds, and the air was thick with the sweet scent of blooming wildflowers. "He made me feel like I could conquer the world," she wrote, the ink smudged slightly, as if her tears had mingled with the memories.

In that moment, I understood that the stories she had never shared were woven with threads of hope and despair, each detail a brushstroke painting the portrait of her love for Henry. Yet, with every stroke, the darkness loomed, lurking just beyond the periphery, a silent predator waiting to consume their fragile happiness.

"It wasn't long before I discovered the truth," she continued, her pen seemingly trembling with the weight of the confession. "Henry wasn't just my lover; he was a man bound by chains of his own making, entangled in a web of deceit and despair. By the time I realized he was more shadow than substance, I was already carrying you."

The revelation struck me again, a visceral punch that knocked the wind out of my lungs. I had always thought of my origins as a simple tale, a straightforward narrative of a mother raising her daughter alone. But now, the intricate layers of my lineage unfurled before me, revealing a father I had never known, a legacy steeped in secrets. My heart raced, thoughts spiraling like autumn leaves caught in a gust of wind.

"Knowing I was pregnant changed everything," she wrote, her words now heavier with regret. "I felt a fierce love for you, but I was also terrified. The thought of bringing you into a world where I had been deceived—where love could turn toxic—was unbearable. I had to protect you from the truth, from the man who had woven lies into the very fabric of our lives."

In that moment, my heart ached for her. I envisioned her standing on the precipice of uncertainty, a young woman brimming with dreams, suddenly shackled by the weight of responsibility. My mother, a warrior cloaked in tenderness, had made a choice that would reverberate through the years, shielding me from the dark undercurrents of our family history.

As the letter continued to unravel the tapestry of our past, I felt myself being pulled deeper into the story. She wrote of Henry's eventual disappearance, how he had vanished like smoke in the wind, leaving behind only echoes of his laughter and the remnants of shattered dreams. "I wanted to believe he could change," she confessed, the pain seeping through the ink. "But I learned that some storms are meant to pass, not to stay."

Each word resonated within me, echoing the struggles I had faced in my own relationships. The ghosts of past loves haunted me, shadows lurking in the corners of my mind. Had I inherited this propensity for love entangled in darkness? Was my fate destined to mirror hers, to find solace in men who wore masks that concealed their true selves?

The sunlight began to fade outside, casting long shadows across my apartment, and I felt a sense of urgency to uncover more of this tangled legacy. There had to be more to the story, more hidden truths buried beneath layers of time and pain. As I tucked the letter back into the box, a sense of determination ignited within me. I wouldn't be a passive observer in my own life, merely accepting the burdens of the past. I needed to know who Henry truly was and how his choices had shaped the contours of my existence.

I rose to my feet, the world outside my window bathed in hues of orange and pink, the horizon a canvas of possibilities. The city pulsed with life, the streets teeming with stories waiting to be uncovered. I could feel the thrum of adventure coursing through me, the promise of discovery igniting my spirit. Perhaps, just perhaps, the secret I never knew held the key to understanding not only my past but my future as well.

The revelation wrapped itself around my heart like ivy on an old oak, both beautiful and suffocating. The words danced in my mind, blurring the lines between the past and the present. I stared out the window, where the city lay sprawled before me, bathed in the golden hues of the setting sun. Each face that passed on the sidewalk seemed imbued with stories, some mundane, others extraordinary, yet all strangers to the weight I carried within me. I felt a familiar yearning tug at my heart—a need to understand, to connect, to seek out the roots that had been hidden from me for so long.

As night fell, I grabbed my jacket, the fabric familiar and comforting against the chill that crept into the air. I stepped into the bustling streets of Seattle, the vibrant city alive with energy, the sounds of laughter and conversation weaving together into a tapestry of life. The scent of roasting coffee and freshly baked pastries wafted through the air, beckoning me toward my favorite café. I pushed open the door, and the warm glow enveloped me like a long-lost friend.

I found a small table by the window, the ambiance cozy and inviting, with the barista behind the counter moving with an effortless grace that reminded me of dancers I had watched twirl in local theaters. As I settled in, I pulled the letter from my bag, the words illuminated by the soft glow of a nearby lamp. I needed to absorb every detail, to unravel the mystery of my father, the man whose existence was now woven into the fabric of my identity.

With a steaming mug of coffee in hand, I dove back into the letter, my mother's voice guiding me through a labyrinth of emotions. She wrote of the days when love felt like an unbreakable bond, an eternal promise. "Henry had a charm that drew me in," she recalled, "with eyes like the stormy sea and a smile that made my heart race." The vivid imagery made me feel as though I were standing in the rain, the world glistening around me, experiencing her passion firsthand. Yet, just beneath that enchanting surface lay the murky waters of betrayal and deception.

The narrative shifted as she detailed the darkness that seeped into their lives, like ink bleeding through the pages of a cherished book. "He was involved in things I didn't understand," she confessed, her pen trembling with the weight of her admission. "The glimmer of danger that once thrilled me became a shadow, an omen of despair. I didn't see it until it was too late." Each word pulsed with urgency, as if she wanted to reach out across the years and warn me, to shield me from repeating her mistakes.

I could almost feel the despair radiating from her, the way it must have felt to grapple with the realization that the man she loved was a stranger beneath the layers of charm and charisma. It wasn't just a tale of love gone wrong; it was a profound lesson about trust and the intricate web we weave with those we hold dear. I took a deep breath, a sense of clarity washing over me. Perhaps my mother's journey was not just hers but a cautionary tale meant to guide me through my own choices.

The café buzzed with conversation, but my world narrowed to the letter in my hands. I felt a kinship with her, an unbreakable bond that transcended the barriers of time and death. She had fought for me, for the future she envisioned, even when the man she once adored spiraled into chaos. "When I learned I was pregnant," she wrote, "it was as if a new light pierced through the darkness. I knew then that I had to forge a different path, one that would lead you away from the storm."

The power of her love enveloped me, filling the hollow spaces I had carried for so long. My eyes welled with tears as I envisioned her, alone in that tiny apartment, cradling the knowledge of her past while nurturing dreams for a child she had yet to hold. It struck me then how brave she had been, how fiercely she had fought against the tides of her own making.

With newfound determination, I tucked the letter back into my bag and made my way outside, the cool night air refreshing against my skin. Seattle was a city that thrived on contrasts—the serene beauty of the water against the towering skyscrapers, the laughter of friends mingling with the solitude of strangers. Each step I took felt purposeful, leading me toward the answers I craved.

I wandered the streets, the glimmering lights reflecting in the puddles that had formed after a recent rain. My thoughts drifted to Henry. What kind of man was he? Did he even know I existed? Would he want to know me if he did? The questions spun around my mind like autumn leaves caught in a breeze, swirling and tumbling, each carrying a weight of possibility.

As I approached the waterfront, I felt an inexplicable pull toward the pier. The air was alive with the sounds of laughter and music, the distant thrum of a street performer's guitar mingling with the waves lapping against the docks. It was a place where dreams could materialize, where the horizon whispered promises of what could be. I took a seat on a weathered bench, the wood cool beneath me, and gazed out at the shimmering water, my heart racing with anticipation.

Just then, a voice broke through my reverie. "Beautiful night, isn't it?" I turned to see a stranger—a young man with tousled hair and a warm smile that instantly felt familiar. His eyes sparkled with mischief, as if he were harboring secrets of his own.

"It is," I replied, my voice soft but steady, the kind of quiet strength that felt new yet comforting.

"I come here often to think," he said, his gaze drifting over the water. "It's the perfect escape from the chaos."

I studied him, drawn to the sincerity in his demeanor. "What do you think about?" I asked, curiosity bubbling to the surface.

"Life, mostly," he shrugged, his smile widening. "The paths we take, the people we meet, the stories we carry. It's all connected somehow, don't you think?"

His words resonated with me, weaving seamlessly into the fabric of my own thoughts. "I suppose it is," I said, feeling a spark of connection with this stranger beneath the stars.

In that moment, I realized that I was not alone in my search for understanding. The world was full of stories, and perhaps this chance encounter was just another thread in the intricate tapestry of my life. I smiled back, feeling the weight of my mother's love encircle me like an embrace. The journey ahead might be fraught with uncertainty, but I was ready to uncover the truth, to seek out my father, and to embrace the secrets that had shaped my existence.

The sensation of the night air wrapped around me like a comforting blanket, but my mind felt as if it were teetering on the precipice of chaos. I had always imagined my family tree as a simple structure: roots reaching into the past and branches spreading toward the future. Now, it appeared more like a tangled vine, knotted and twisted, hiding secrets that could either bloom into something beautiful or choke the life out of everything I had known. As the lights of Seattle flickered around me like stars falling from the sky, I could not help but wonder about the man whose existence had been shrouded in mystery and shadows.

The stranger seated beside me had drifted into my thoughts, and I turned to him, curiosity igniting the atmosphere between us. "What about you? What do you carry in your story?" I asked, my voice barely above the whispers of the wind.

He met my gaze, an intensity sparking in his eyes. "Ah, well, my story is still being written, but I can tell you it's a bit of a rollercoaster," he replied with a wry smile, his charm infectious. "Family, love, loss—all the good stuff. I think we all have those chapters, don't we?"

I nodded, feeling a strange kinship with this kindred spirit. "You could say that. I just uncovered a whole new chapter I didn't even know existed."

His eyebrows lifted, intrigue painted across his face. "Do tell."

I hesitated, unsure of how much to reveal to this stranger whose laughter seemed to melt away the chill of the evening. But something in the way he leaned forward, genuinely interested, encouraged me to share. "I found a letter from my mother. She wrote about my father, a man I've never known but who somehow haunts our past."

His expression shifted, a blend of empathy and understanding washing over him. "That sounds heavy. But isn't it incredible that you have a tangible connection to him? Even if it's complex, it's still a piece of you."

There was truth in his words, a realization that settled like warmth within me. "Yes, I suppose. But it's also unsettling. I've spent my life believing one story, and now it feels like I'm rewriting everything."

"Rewriting can be good," he said, the corners of his mouth curling into a soft smile. "It's a chance to take control of your narrative. You can choose which pieces to keep and which to change."

As I absorbed his encouragement, the weight on my heart lifted slightly, transforming into a flicker of hope. The night unfolded around us, filled with laughter, music, and the gentle lull of waves kissing the shore. The strangers who passed seemed like characters in an unwritten tale, each with their own secrets and stories waiting to be shared.

"Do you want to find him?" he asked, his voice a gentle nudge, as if sensing the tumult within me.

I pondered for a moment, the question heavy with implications. "I think I need to," I admitted, my voice steady. "To understand who I am, I have to understand where I come from."

"Then let's find him," he declared, a spark of adventure igniting in his gaze. "Life's too short for half-measures."

The boldness of his words resonated with me, igniting a daring spirit that had been dormant for far too long. Perhaps this journey would lead me to more than just answers; it might reshape my understanding of love, family, and identity.

The next few days transformed into a whirlwind of research and discovery. The internet became both my ally and my adversary as I scoured databases and public records, piecing together fragments of my father's life. Seattle's history felt intertwined with my own—each street corner, every faded sign, whispering tales of love lost and dreams unfulfilled. I felt like a detective on the hunt, tracing the footsteps of a man whose absence had shaped so much of my existence.

The stranger from the pier, whom I learned was named Sam, became my partner in this exploration. With his easy laughter and unrelenting optimism, he infused the mundane with an electrifying energy that made every step forward feel significant. Together, we navigated the labyrinth of my family's history, uncovering hints of Henry's life—a childhood spent in the Pacific Northwest, dreams of becoming a painter, a flash of trouble that seemed to shadow him wherever he went.

One afternoon, while sifting through public records at the local library, I stumbled upon a file that sent my heart racing. Henry had lived in a modest home on the outskirts of the city, a place not far from where my mother had once found solace. My fingers trembled as I traced the ink of his name on the yellowed paper, and a sense of inevitability washed over me.

"I think I'm ready," I whispered to Sam, who had been reviewing nearby documents. "I want to go there."

"Let's do it," he said, his enthusiasm contagious. "Adventure awaits!"

That evening, as the sun dipped below the horizon, we drove toward Henry's last known address, the anticipation crackling in the air between us. The streets transformed from the bustling city to a quieter, more intimate setting, where the trees stood like ancient sentinels guarding forgotten secrets.

When we arrived, the house loomed before us—a small, unassuming structure cloaked in shadows, its once-vibrant paint now faded and peeling. It had an air of melancholy, a ghost of its former self, yet it felt alive with memories waiting to be unearthed. The neighborhood was eerily silent, save for the distant rustle of leaves and the occasional hoot of an owl, as if the world was holding its breath in anticipation of what might unfold.

"Are you ready?" Sam asked, his eyes sparkling with excitement.

I nodded, swallowing the lump in my throat. "I think so."

With cautious steps, we approached the front door, my heart pounding like a drum in my chest. I lifted my hand to knock, but before I could make contact, the door creaked open, revealing a figure silhouetted against the warm glow of a lamp inside.

The moment felt surreal, a collision of past and present. The man standing before me had a resemblance to the man in the photograph, the very image I had imagined since childhood. Henry. His eyes, deep and stormy, reflected a lifetime of stories untold.

"Can I help you?" he asked, his voice a gravelly whisper that sent a shiver down my spine.

My breath caught in my throat as the enormity of the moment settled upon me like a heavy cloak. "Are you Henry?" I managed to say, my voice trembling.

"Yes," he replied, his gaze sharp and penetrating. "Who are you?"

In that fleeting second, the world narrowed to a singular point—the man who had been nothing more than a ghost in my life stood before me, and I was no longer just the daughter of a woman who had loved him. I was the living proof of that love, the tangible echo of a history that had finally come home.

"I'm your daughter," I whispered, the words floating into the space between us, bridging the chasm of years and choices, of love and loss.

His expression shifted, confusion flickering across his features, and for a moment, the weight of our shared past hung in the air, a fragile thread binding us together. In that instant, I knew this was only the beginning of a story I was meant to write—a narrative rich with the complexities of love, forgiveness, and the journey toward understanding oneself. And as I stood there, hand poised to embrace the unknown, I felt an undeniable connection to this man, my father, and the legacy that would define us both.

Chapter 16: Running From the Past

The asphalt rolled beneath us, a black ribbon of escape winding through the heart of America, glimmering under the early morning sun like a promise whispered in the hush of dawn. I leaned back in the passenger seat, my fingers brushing the cold glass of the window, watching as the city of Chicago faded into a hazy outline of steel and glass, a distant memory consumed by the horizon. Each mile we traveled felt like peeling back layers of my life, revealing the raw, tender flesh of who I once was—a woman cloaked in shadows, now stumbling toward the light.

Luke's presence beside me was both a comfort and a torment. The man who had swept into my life like a summer storm, igniting something deep within me that I thought had long been extinguished, now seemed a stranger. His eyes, usually warm and inviting, were steely and focused, and the weight of unsaid words hung heavily between us. I could see the tension in his clenched jaw, the tightness in his grip on the wheel, a reflection of my own turmoil. The last thing I wanted was to add to the burden he bore, but silence had never been our friend, and as the miles ticked away, the space between us widened, filled with uncertainty and unrelenting questions.

The scenery outside morphed from the gray monotony of the city to rolling fields of gold and emerald, dotted with wildflowers that swayed in the gentle breeze. The vastness of it all—a canvas painted in sunlit hues—stirred something deep within me. I had grown up in these lands, chasing fireflies in the evening dusk and dreaming of distant places under a canopy of stars. Now, the mountains loomed ahead, majestic and daunting, a siren call to my restless spirit. The closer we got, the more I felt the pull of their ancient strength, a promise of refuge and anonymity.

"Do you think he'll find us?" I finally broke the silence, my voice barely rising above the hum of the engine. The question hung in the air, heavy and suffocating. I needed to know if I was still running, or if there was a chance to hide from my demons.

Luke's grip on the wheel tightened further. "Not if we keep moving." His words were clipped, each syllable a reminder of the storm brewing inside him. I wanted to reach out, to touch his arm, to remind him that we were in this together, but the wall between us felt insurmountable, built on the revelations of the past few days—the letter, the truth about Henry, and everything I had hidden even from myself.

We stopped at a roadside diner, a relic from a bygone era, its neon sign flickering like a beacon of hope in the twilight. The moment we stepped inside, the smell of sizzling bacon and freshly brewed coffee enveloped us like a warm embrace. The diner was a collage of memories—checkerboard tiles, vinyl booths, and the clatter of cutlery that echoed the laughter and heartache of countless patrons.

As I slid into a booth, I could feel the weight of Luke's gaze on me, searching, questioning. I looked down at the menu, my fingers tracing the laminated edges, but the words blurred together in a haze of worry and longing. "I'll have the pancakes," I finally said, my voice steady despite the turmoil inside. "And coffee. Black."

"Same," Luke replied, the edge in his tone softening just a fraction.

The waitress, a woman with bright pink hair and a smile that felt like home, poured us each a steaming cup. "You two on a road trip?" she asked, her eyes sparkling with curiosity.

I shared a fleeting glance with Luke, and the brief connection felt like a tether in the chaos swirling around us. "Something like that," I answered, a hint of a smile breaking through my uncertainty.

"Best pancakes in the state," she assured us, before bustling off to fulfill our order. I watched her go, admiring the ease with which she navigated the crowded diner. It was a reminder of normalcy, of moments untainted by the shadows that clung to me. But then, as quickly as it had appeared, that sense of comfort evaporated, replaced by the gnawing realization that my past was not so easily left behind.

Luke took a sip of his coffee, his expression contemplative. "You know we can't keep running forever."

I nodded, knowing he was right but unwilling to face the truth of it. "I'm not ready to stop yet," I admitted, the vulnerability spilling out before I could rein it in. The thought of standing still, of confronting Henry and the tangled web of my past, was terrifying.

His eyes softened for a moment, and I caught a glimpse of the man I had fallen for—the one who had held my hand during sleepless nights, who had danced with me in the kitchen as the rain pattered against the windows. But those moments felt like echoes of a time that was slipping away, fading under the weight of what lay ahead.

The waitress returned with our plates, steam rising like tendrils of warmth. The pancakes were fluffy and golden, the syrup glistening like liquid gold. As I took a bite, the sweetness enveloped my senses, grounding me in this moment, even as my heart raced with the knowledge of the storm gathering on the horizon.

"Let's just enjoy this for now," Luke said, a faint smile finally breaking through the storm clouds of his expression. It felt like a small victory, a moment of peace amidst the chaos, and I clung to it, desperate for a respite from the weight of our reality.

But even as I savored the warmth of the pancakes and the camaraderie of our quiet moments, I couldn't shake the feeling that we were mere travelers in a land where time no longer flowed the same. We were lost in the liminal space between what was and what might be, and as the sun dipped lower in the sky, casting a golden glow across the diner, I realized that the road ahead was as uncertain as my own heart—forever chasing the promise of freedom, yet bound to the ghosts that lingered in my shadow.

The moments stretched as we finished our meal, each tick of the clock echoing the pulse of my anxiety. I could see the glint of the diner's neon sign reflecting in the windows, a fading promise of safety. As I pushed my plate away, half-finished, the weight of what lay ahead settled heavily on my chest. I could almost hear the whispers of my past—distant and haunting—reminding me of the choices that had led me here.

Luke's gaze flickered toward me, his brow furrowed in thought, and for a heartbeat, I saw the man I'd fallen for beneath the layers of worry. He reached for my hand, his fingers brushing against mine, sending a shiver of warmth through me, a fleeting reminder of what we could be if the shadows would just recede. "What's on your mind?" he asked, his voice a gentle nudge through the haze of my thoughts.

"Just...thinking about the road ahead," I replied, trying to keep my tone light. "And how long we can keep this up."

His fingers tightened around mine, grounding me amidst the swirl of uncertainty. "We'll figure it out. Together." The promise hung between us, both a reassurance and a challenge. The truth was, I was terrified of what together might mean. Could we really navigate the storm swirling in our lives without getting lost in the chaos?

As we left the diner, the sun hung low in the sky, casting long shadows that stretched across the parking lot. The mountains loomed in the distance, majestic and unyielding, a reminder of the beauty that lay beyond the darkness. The thought of reaching those peaks, of feeling the cool air on my skin and the earth beneath my feet, ignited a flicker of hope within me.

The car roared to life, the engine a comforting growl as we merged back onto the highway. I watched the landscape shift from flat farmland to rolling hills, the world outside a vibrant tapestry of colors. The rhythm of the road beneath us felt almost hypnotic, and as we drove, the silence transformed from suffocating to contemplative, allowing space for unspoken thoughts to settle between us.

"I used to dream about escaping to the mountains," I admitted after a long stretch of quiet, my voice barely above a whisper. "I thought maybe one day I'd find a little cabin by a lake, somewhere I could disappear and start over."

Luke turned his head slightly, a hint of surprise in his eyes. "Is that what you want?"

I paused, the question hanging in the air like the dust motes swirling in the light. Did I want to disappear? Or did I want to confront the ghosts that haunted me? "I don't know anymore. I just feel...torn. Like I'm two people battling for control."

He nodded, understanding etched into his features. "I get that. But you're not alone in this fight." His voice was steady, a rock in the tumult of my emotions. I wanted to believe him. I wanted to believe that together, we could navigate the winding paths of our pasts, but the fear of losing him loomed just as large as the shadows I was running from.

The mountains beckoned closer as we drove, their peaks dusted with snow even in the warm embrace of spring. I imagined the fresh air filling my lungs, the scent of pine and earth mingling in a sweet symphony. I craved that clarity, a chance to breathe freely, away from the memories that clung to me like a second skin. The landscape shifted again, revealing towering trees standing sentinel over the winding road, their branches swaying gently in the breeze.

As we entered a small town nestled at the foot of the mountains, I felt a strange sense of familiarity wash over me, as though I had stumbled upon a piece of my childhood. The quaint shops with their colorful awnings lined the street, each one a little universe of its own, bursting with charm and life. A small bakery caught my eye, the scent of freshly baked bread wafting through the air, drawing me in like a moth to a flame.

"Let's stop there," I said, the words tumbling out before I could second-guess myself. Luke raised an eyebrow but didn't protest. As we parked and stepped into the warmth of the bakery, the bell above the door chimed softly, welcoming us into this cozy haven. The walls were adorned with whimsical artwork, and the shelves were stocked with treats that seemed to dance in the light.

I could feel the tension in my shoulders begin to ease as I took in the vibrant atmosphere. The owner, a sprightly woman with flour-dusted hands and a contagious smile, greeted us like old friends. "What can I get for you?" she asked, her voice as sweet as the pastries lining the display.

"Two croissants and a couple of those cinnamon rolls, please," I replied, my mouth watering at the thought of the warm, buttery pastry melting on my tongue.

"Excellent choice! You won't regret it," she beamed, bustling away to fill our order. I turned to Luke, who was watching me with a hint of amusement. "What?" I asked, feigning innocence.

"You just lit up like a kid in a candy store," he chuckled, his smile breaking through the heaviness that had settled between us.

"Can you blame me?" I replied, trying to suppress my laughter. "I mean, look at this place! It's magical."

His laughter faded, but the warmth in his eyes remained. "Yeah, it is."

The owner returned with our treats, presenting them with a flourish. I took a moment to admire the cinnamon rolls, their swirls glistening with icing, each one a promise of indulgence. As we settled at a small table by the window, I took a bite of my croissant, the flaky layers melting in my mouth, a taste of happiness that seemed to chase the shadows away.

"I've always loved small towns," I mused, savoring the moment. "They have a way of making you feel connected, even when you're running away from everything."

Luke nodded, his expression thoughtful. "Maybe this is what we need—a little time to breathe, to gather ourselves before we decide what's next."

For the first time in days, I felt a flicker of hope—a tiny ember igniting within me. The world outside the window was alive with possibility, and though the shadows of my past loomed large, I was beginning to believe that perhaps, just perhaps, I could reclaim my story. As we sat together in that small bakery, the warmth of the cinnamon rolls and the sweet laughter shared between us felt like a tentative step toward something new.

In that moment, I chose to focus on the light, allowing it to guide me as we ventured into the unknown, ready to embrace whatever came next, hand in hand with the man who still held a piece of my heart.

The smell of cinnamon wafted around us like a warm embrace as we savored our pastries. Each bite of the cinnamon roll sent waves of sweetness through me, softening the edges of my anxiety, if only for a moment. I could see Luke watching me, the corner of his mouth twitching in a smile that I desperately wanted to return. But even as I indulged in the simple pleasure of the food, my mind churned with the complexities of our situation, a whirlwind of emotions just beneath the surface.

The bakery felt like a portal to another world—one where time slowed down, and the worries of life faded into the background. Through the window, I could see children laughing as they chased each other down the street, their voices ringing like music against the backdrop of quaint storefronts adorned with flowers and bright awnings. It was the kind of scene you would see in a painting, framed with nostalgia and innocence. I longed to be one of those carefree souls, blissfully unaware of the storm clouds gathering on the horizon.

"Do you think we can stay here for a while?" I asked, the question tumbling out before I could think twice. "Just...enough time to catch our breath?"

Luke leaned back, considering my request. "We could. But we need to be cautious." His voice was low, the gravity of our situation creeping back into our conversation like an unwelcome guest. "Henry won't stop until he finds you, and the longer we linger, the more time he has to catch up."

I swallowed hard, the weight of his words settling into my chest. I wanted to argue, to cling to the hope that maybe this could be our sanctuary, if only for a little while. But I couldn't ignore the truth that hovered around us like a dark cloud, ominous and relentless. "I know," I finally murmured, the brightness of the bakery dimming just a little as reality seeped back in.

The warmth of the pastries and the laughter of strangers couldn't shield us from the reality of our predicament. After finishing our treats, we stepped back out into the crisp air, a chill biting at our skin. The sun had dipped lower in the sky, casting long shadows that stretched toward us, as if eager to reclaim their territory.

As we wandered down the street, the charm of the town enveloped me, and for a fleeting moment, I allowed myself to imagine a different life. A life where I wasn't running, where I could walk hand-in-hand with Luke, exploring art galleries, sipping coffee in little cafés, and laughing with the ease that once felt so natural between us.

"What do you think?" Luke asked suddenly, snapping me from my reverie.

"About what?" I replied, my heart racing slightly as I tried to catch up to the conversation.

"I saw a place for rent just up the street," he said, nodding toward a quaint cottage with a small garden bursting with spring flowers. "Could be a perfect little hideaway for a while."

I looked at the cottage, its whitewashed walls and inviting porch adorned with potted plants, and felt a flicker of hope. It looked so peaceful, a stark contrast to the chaos that had defined my life for far too long. "It does look charming," I admitted, a tentative smile breaking through the fog of worry.

"But it's not just about charm," he said, his expression serious again. "We need to think about safety. We can't let our guard down."

I nodded, feeling the weight of his words but also the pull of possibility that tugged at my heart. "What if we did rent it? Just for a few days?"

Luke studied me, his eyes searching for something—an affirmation, perhaps, or a flicker of determination. "We could. But only if you promise to stay aware."

The thought of retreating into that cottage, of cocooning ourselves in a world far removed from the one we were fleeing, was almost intoxicating. "I promise," I replied, my voice steadier than I felt. "But I need to feel safe too. I need...a space to breathe."

With a reluctant nod, Luke agreed, and we approached the cottage, the path lined with colorful wildflowers and fragrant herbs that danced gently in the breeze. The moment we stepped onto the porch, the creaky wooden boards whispered secrets of the past, and the air around us seemed to sigh in relief as we crossed the threshold.

Inside, the cottage was a delightful blend of rustic charm and cozy warmth. Sunlight streamed through the windows, illuminating the wooden beams and the inviting living room adorned with plush furniture. It felt like stepping into a dream—a sanctuary where the outside world couldn't reach us, if only for a little while.

As we explored, I could feel the tension between us easing, the walls that had grown so formidable slowly starting to crumble. We moved through the small kitchen, where a potbelly stove sat, promising warmth against the cool mountain nights. The bedroom was bright and airy, with a window that offered a breathtaking view of the mountains framed in lush greenery.

"This could really be our place for now," I murmured, leaning against the doorframe, the sensation of safety wrapping around me like a soft blanket.

Luke walked over, his expression shifting from serious to hopeful. "Yeah, it could be." He paused, his gaze drifting out the window. "If we stay here, we'll need to get creative about keeping a low profile."

The words lingered in the air, a reminder of the ever-looming threat of Henry. I felt a wave of determination wash over me. "Then let's do it," I said, feeling the fire ignite within me. "We'll make it work. We'll figure this out together."

He turned to me, a spark of admiration flashing in his eyes. "Together," he echoed, a slow smile spreading across his face.

We spent the next hour arranging our temporary haven, filling the space with little touches that made it feel more like home. We fluffed pillows, unpacked a few essentials, and even lit a few candles that flickered cheerfully against the walls, casting dancing shadows that added warmth to the air.

As night began to fall, the sky transformed into a canvas of pinks and oranges, the sun dipping behind the mountains. We settled on the porch, side by side, watching as the world around us shifted into a tranquil hush. The chirping of crickets began to play their nocturnal symphony, and the first stars appeared, twinkling like distant memories, each one a reminder of hope, of dreams yet to be realized.

"I can't believe we actually did this," I said, glancing at Luke, whose profile was outlined against the twilight.

"We needed it," he replied, his voice low and soothing. "And we deserve to breathe."

I leaned into him, seeking comfort in his presence as the night wrapped around us. "I'm scared," I admitted, vulnerability creeping back into my voice. "But I'm also relieved."

"Scared is okay," he reassured me, wrapping his arm around my shoulders. "It means you're still alive, still fighting. And I'll be right here beside you every step of the way."

In that moment, beneath the blanket of stars, I felt a shift within me—a flicker of courage ignited by his words. I realized that I wasn't just running away from my past; I was also running toward something new, something worth fighting for. As the cool night air brushed against my skin, I breathed deeply, allowing the scents of pine and earth to fill my lungs, grounding me in this moment of newfound hope.

With Luke beside me, I could face whatever lay ahead, no longer just a woman running from her past, but one stepping boldly into a future that was finally starting to feel like mine.

Chapter 17: The Mountains

The cabin stood resilient against the backdrop of the Rockies, its weathered wooden beams exuding an earthy scent, mingling with the crisp mountain air. Pine trees formed a protective barrier around us, their tall, slender trunks reaching up to the brilliant blue sky, which felt impossibly vast, like a promise we dared to embrace. Mornings unfolded with the soft glow of dawn filtering through the sheer curtains, casting delicate patterns on the worn wooden floorboards. The sunlight danced like a playful spirit, but my heart remained heavy, tethered to the past in a way I couldn't quite shake.

Luke moved through the space with a quiet grace, his tall frame contrasting against the snug corners of the cabin. There was an elegance in the way he chopped wood, each swing of the axe both precise and purposeful. The rhythmic thud echoed through the silence, a steady heartbeat that was both soothing and suffocating. I often found myself lost in thought as I watched him, the way his muscles tensed with each movement, glistening under the gentle embrace of sweat. But the sight of him, usually so grounding, stirred something in me that felt dangerously close to longing.

Evenings were our sanctuary, moments carved out of the mundane where laughter and warmth mingled with the crackling of the fireplace. We would sit side by side, sipping on mugs of hot cocoa, the rich chocolate a balm against the cold that seeped in through the cracks. Yet, as I curled into the frayed quilt, the blanket of comfort only heightened the distance I felt between us. The flickering flames painted our faces in shades of orange and gold, casting shadows that danced across the walls, but my heart felt like an unwelcome guest at this intimate gathering, weighed down by unspoken words.

The lake nearby reflected the rugged beauty of the mountains, its surface shimmering like scattered diamonds under the sun. I often took long walks, my boots crunching against the gravel as I followed the trail winding through the dense forest. The scent of pine was intoxicating, filling my lungs with the essence of nature, yet it did little to quell the storm brewing inside me. I wandered alone, hoping the serenity of the landscape would ease my mind, but the rustling leaves and distant calls of birds became a backdrop to my spiraling thoughts.

Trust was a fragile thread, frayed and worn, and I wasn't sure how to mend it. Each time I glanced at Luke, I saw not just the man I loved but also the ghosts of our past, taunting me with reminders of the betrayal that had broken us. We had built a fragile sanctuary in this isolated haven, but the walls felt insurmountable, the chasm between us deepening with each passing day.

Luke, too, bore the marks of our struggles. His laughter, once infectious, now felt like an echo, fading into the quiet. There were moments, brief and fleeting, when his gaze would linger on me, revealing a glimmer of vulnerability beneath his stoic facade. In those moments, I wanted to reach out, to bridge the gap that felt like a yawning chasm. But doubt held me back, a cruel hand gripping my heart. What if the trust we sought to rebuild was an illusion, just another mirage in the vast desert of our hearts?

One afternoon, the weight of silence became unbearable, and I found myself at the lake's edge, the water lapping gently against the shore. I knelt, tracing patterns in the soft mud, my fingers sinking into the earth as if I could unearth the roots of my turmoil. The sky was a canvas of deep blues and greens, swirling together in an otherworldly dance, and for a brief moment, I lost myself in the beauty of it all.

"Hey," Luke's voice broke through the stillness, a warm baritone that wrapped around me like a soft blanket. He approached cautiously, as if stepping into a sacred space. "What are you thinking about?"

I looked up, his silhouette framed against the backdrop of the mountains, and I struggled to articulate the turmoil within. "Just... everything," I finally managed, my voice barely above a whisper. "It's hard to let go of what happened."

His eyes, once so full of mischief and light, darkened with understanding. "I know. I wish I could take it all back. I hate what I did to us."

I nodded, the lump in my throat constricting. "But can we ever get back to what we had? Or are we just pretending?"

The question hung heavy in the air, and I watched as his expression shifted, a flicker of pain crossing his features. He knelt beside me, the cool water splashing against his jeans. "I don't want to pretend. I want to fight for us."

The sincerity in his voice sent a shiver through me, igniting a spark of hope that was quickly doused by my skepticism. "What does that even look like? Can we just erase the past?"

He reached for my hand, his grip firm yet gentle. "No, we can't erase it. But we can learn from it. I want to build something new, brick by brick, even if it takes a lifetime."

In that moment, I realized the enormity of what we were facing, the immense challenge of transforming hurt into healing. The mountains stood resolutely behind us, timeless witnesses to our struggles, and I couldn't help but wonder if they, too, understood the weight of love and trust. The path ahead was fraught with uncertainty, but as I looked into Luke's eyes, I saw a flicker of the boy I fell in love with, buried beneath layers of pain and regret.

The sun began its descent, casting long shadows across the water, and as we sat there, hands intertwined, I felt the first real warmth of connection in what felt like an eternity. The mountains loomed, grand and unyielding, but perhaps they were also a testament to resilience. And with every heartbeat, I hoped we could find our way back to the light.

The nights were an orchestra of whispers—the wind rustling through the trees, the distant call of an owl, and the crackling of the fire that flickered valiantly against the encroaching darkness. Each sound seemed to resonate deep within me, a reminder that our isolation was both a blessing and a curse. I would lay awake on those long, quiet nights, staring at the beams above, tracing the knots in the wood with my eyes as if they held the secrets to our survival. The shadows danced around us, uninvited guests at our evening gatherings, fueling a sense of disquiet that crept beneath my skin.

One particular evening, after a day spent hiking the rugged trails, I caught Luke staring into the fire, his expression a mix of contemplation and weariness. The embers glowed like tiny stars, illuminating his face and casting a flicker of light on the worry lines etched on his brow. I had grown accustomed to this look, one that spoke of unspoken fears and regrets—an unyielding echo of the decisions we had made.

"Do you remember the first time we came here?" I asked, my voice soft as I settled beside him on the worn sofa, its fabric frayed but inviting.

He turned to me, surprise flickering in his eyes. "You mean the trip with everyone?"

"Yeah," I nodded, a smile creeping onto my face. "We were so reckless. Climbing cliffs, racing to the top of that hill to see the sunset."

He chuckled, the sound low and warm. "And you almost slipped and took a dive into the lake. I swear, my heart nearly stopped."

"Because you were too busy trying to impress me, trying to look cool," I teased, nudging him playfully.

"I still wanted to look cool." He shrugged, but the grin on his face revealed a softer side that I cherished.

For a moment, we were simply two people reliving memories, suspended in a time before the weight of our realities crushed us. I felt the laughter between us spark something I hadn't realized was flickering—an ember of hope that maybe, just maybe, we could return to that carefree essence, even if only for a moment.

As the fire dwindled, I noticed a shift in the air, a charge that hummed just beneath the surface. It was the kind of tension that whispered promises of uncharted territory, a reminder that intimacy was still within reach if we were brave enough to grasp it. I leaned closer, the warmth of his body beckoning me like a moth to a flame, our proximity igniting a long-buried yearning.

"Can I ask you something?" I hesitated, the weight of my question hanging between us like the heavy silence that had dominated our days.

"Anything," he replied, his gaze unwavering, an invitation wrapped in sincerity.

"Do you think we'll ever really be able to let go of the past?"

The flicker of the fire reflected the tumult of emotions in his eyes, a swirling storm of vulnerability and resolve. "I don't know. It haunts me. But I believe we can learn to live with it. We have to try."

I nodded, the weight of his words resonating deep within me. The past was a relentless tide, and with each wave, I felt the sand beneath my feet erode. But standing beside him, there was also a flicker of resilience, a promise that together we could forge a new path. The mountains outside seemed to loom larger in that moment, silent guardians of our journey, reminding me that they had weathered storms far greater than ours.

With dawn came an entirely different hue, the soft light breaking through the trees like a lover's caress. I slipped out of bed, careful not to wake Luke, and made my way outside. The air was crisp, invigorating, and I inhaled deeply, feeling the chill awaken my senses. Mist curled over the lake, transforming the surface into a shimmering mirror that reflected the awakening sky.

As I stood there, lost in the beauty, I sensed a presence beside me. I turned to find Luke, his hair tousled and a sleepy grin illuminating his face. "You're up early," he murmured, his voice husky with sleep.

"I couldn't resist. It's beautiful out here," I replied, gesturing toward the lake, where the sun broke free from its slumber, casting a golden glow over the water.

He stepped closer, wrapping his arms around me from behind, and I leaned into him, allowing the warmth of his body to seep into my skin. Together, we watched as the mist began to dissipate, revealing the lake's tranquil depths. "It feels like a new beginning," he whispered, and I couldn't help but agree.

That day, we decided to explore the trails that wound through the dense forest, our feet crunching against the carpet of leaves and twigs. The air was alive with the sounds of nature—birds chirping, the rustle of critters in the underbrush, and the distant rush of a stream. As we hiked deeper into the woods, I found myself sharing pieces of my heart that I had kept locked away for too long.

"I used to come here every summer as a kid," I admitted, glancing at him as we maneuvered over a fallen log. "It was my escape. I'd pretend I was in a different world, away from everything."

Luke nodded, his eyes focused on the path ahead, but I could see the way his expression shifted, revealing the boy who had been forced to grow up too fast. "I never had that," he said, a hint of sadness lacing his words. "It was always about survival for me."

We paused at a clearing, the sun filtering through the branches and casting dappled shadows across the forest floor. The beauty of the scene was overwhelming, and I could see the struggle within him, battling the darkness of his past against the light of our present. "But you're here now," I said gently, stepping closer, searching for his eyes. "You've fought for this. For us."

The connection between us pulsed with an intensity I hadn't felt in weeks. It was as if the very earth beneath our feet thrummed with the possibilities that lay ahead.

"Yeah," he said, finally meeting my gaze, and I could see the determination etched into his features. "I don't want to let it go to waste. I want to be better, for you—for us."

The mountains rose majestically around us, silent witnesses to our struggles and triumphs. I felt a profound sense of belonging in that moment, standing beside him amidst the wild beauty of the Rockies. Whatever lay ahead, I knew we would face it together, with the strength we had forged in the fires of our past. The journey wasn't over, but perhaps, just perhaps, we had found our way back to each other, one step at a time.

The tranquility of the cabin masked the turbulence that lay beneath the surface, a fragile façade that flickered like the flames in our hearth. One morning, as the sun bathed the mountains in a golden hue, I stood on the porch, the wooden planks cool beneath my bare feet. I closed my eyes, breathing in the crisp mountain air, allowing it to fill my lungs with the promise of renewal. Yet, even in the embrace of nature, my heart felt heavy, as if it carried the weight of unshed tears.

I turned to see Luke emerging from the cabin, his tousled hair catching the light, creating an ethereal halo that made him appear almost otherworldly. The sight of him stirred something deep within me, a mix of affection and sorrow. He approached with a mug of coffee in hand, the steam curling upwards like a whisper of hope.

"Thought you might need this," he said, his voice rough with sleep yet laced with warmth. I accepted the mug, our fingers brushing against each other—a fleeting touch that sent a spark coursing through me.

"Thanks," I replied, taking a sip and savoring the rich flavor, the bitterness balancing the sweetness of the moment.

We stood side by side, the mountains rising majestically around us, their ancient presence a reminder of the storms we faced and the calm that could follow. But I could sense the heaviness in Luke's silence, the way his gaze drifted toward the horizon as if searching for answers in the endless expanse of sky and peak.

"Are you okay?" I ventured, breaking the stillness that enveloped us.

He hesitated, the weight of his unspoken thoughts pressing down on him. "Just thinking about how we got here," he finally said, his brow furrowing slightly. "How easy it is to lose sight of what really matters."

I nodded, feeling the truth of his words resonate in my chest. "We've been through a lot. It's hard to let go."

His gaze shifted to me, and I saw the vulnerability in his eyes, a glimpse of the man who had fought so fiercely to keep us together. "I know I messed up. I know I hurt you."

The admission hung in the air, palpable and raw. "You did, Luke. But I want to understand why."

His shoulders slumped slightly, the weight of regret hanging heavy on him. "It's complicated. I let my past dictate my present, and I didn't think about how it would affect you."

Silence enveloped us once more, and I could feel the walls we had built around our hearts begin to tremble. Perhaps it was the mountains witnessing our struggle, or perhaps it was the love that still flickered between us, but I sensed a shift, a faint glimmer of possibility that dared to break through the darkness.

As the days wore on, we ventured deeper into the wilderness, the trails becoming our sanctuary, a place where we could lose ourselves among the whispering trees and the rushing streams. Each step we took together felt like a new chapter in our story, a deliberate move toward healing.

One afternoon, while wandering along a particularly scenic path, we stumbled upon a secluded waterfall. The water cascaded down the rocks in a shimmering veil, the sound a soothing symphony that drowned out our worries. Luke's eyes lit up with excitement, and for a moment, he was the carefree boy I had first fallen in love with.

"Let's swim!" he exclaimed, already shedding his clothes as he dashed toward the water.

I hesitated, laughter bubbling up inside me as I watched him. "You're crazy!"

"Come on! It's perfect!"

His enthusiasm was infectious, and before I knew it, I had joined him, the cool water enveloping me in an embrace that felt both shocking and exhilarating. The cascade of the waterfall created a mist that kissed my skin, refreshing and invigorating.

We splashed and laughed like children, the weight of our past momentarily forgotten. I felt the tension between us dissolve with every wave, every ripple of water that crashed around us. Luke's laughter rang out, mingling with the sounds of nature, and I realized that in this moment, we were free.

Eventually, we pulled ourselves out of the water, breathless and exhilarated, our hearts racing in tandem. As we lay on the sun-warmed rocks, the water glistening on our skin, I turned to Luke, my heart swelling with a mixture of gratitude and longing.

"Do you think we can really move forward?" I asked, my voice barely above a whisper.

He turned to face me, his expression serious yet tender. "I want to. I want to fight for us. But it's going to take time."

"Time and trust," I echoed, the weight of those words settling between us like an unspoken vow.

Days turned into weeks as we continued our journey of rediscovery, the mountains bearing witness to our healing. The simple act of cooking together in the cabin transformed into a dance of laughter and shared stories, our voices intertwining like the aromas of herbs and spices wafting through the air. We learned to navigate our scars, using them as stepping stones rather than stumbling blocks.

One evening, as we sat by the fire, I took a deep breath, the crackling flames casting flickering shadows on the walls. "Luke, I want to talk about Henry," I said, my heart racing at the prospect of revisiting the very thing that had almost torn us apart.

His expression hardened, but I could see a flicker of understanding behind his eyes. "Okay," he replied cautiously.

"I don't want to live in fear anymore," I confessed. "Fear of what could happen if we confront the past. I want us to be honest, to lay everything bare. If we're going to move forward, we have to face it together."

He took a moment, the firelight reflecting the turmoil within him. "You're right. I've been avoiding it, thinking if I didn't talk about it, it would somehow go away."

The admission hung in the air, and I felt the weight of our shared pain begin to lift, like the clouds parting after a storm. "It won't go away, but we can work through it. Together."

As we delved into the depths of our hearts that night, peeling back the layers of hurt and betrayal, I realized that the mountains were not just a backdrop to our story but a reflection of our journey. Each peak we faced was a challenge, and each valley was a lesson learned.

Underneath the vast, star-studded sky, we shared our fears, our hopes, and our dreams, weaving them into a tapestry that felt both fragile and strong. The past would always be a part of us, but it no longer had to define us. The cabin became our sanctuary, a place where we could create new memories, filled with laughter and love.

And as the sun rose over the Rockies each morning, I knew that with each new day, we were reclaiming our narrative, one step at a time. The mountains stood tall around us, ancient guardians of our love story, reminding us that even the most tumultuous paths could lead to the most breathtaking vistas. In the heart of the wilderness, we found not only ourselves but each other again.

Chapter 18: The Call

The night unfolded like a silken sheet, its dark expanse dotted with pinpricks of distant stars, each one a silent witness to my solitude. The cabin stood sentinel against the vast wilderness, its weathered wood siding absorbing the chill of the night air, wrapping me in an embrace that felt both comforting and suffocating. I leaned against the window frame, the cool glass biting at my skin, as I gazed out into the surrounding forest. The trees whispered secrets to one another, their branches swaying gently in the breeze, as if sharing tales of the past and the quiet hopes of what lay ahead.

With Luke gone into town to gather supplies, I had settled into the stillness, letting my thoughts drift like the leaves that danced in the moonlight. I often cherished these moments alone, a chance to reflect on the life I had carved out here, far from the tumult of my past. I had thought I was free, that the ghosts of my childhood had finally receded into the shadows. But the shrill ring of the phone shattered the calm, its sound slicing through the tranquility like a knife.

A shiver ran down my spine as I approached the old rotary phone, its vintage charm feeling oddly out of place in my otherwise modern life. The caller ID displayed an unfamiliar number, an unwelcome herald of uncertainty. Against my better judgment, I picked up the receiver, the weight of it heavy in my palm. My heart raced, pounding like a drum, as I pressed it to my ear.

"Hello?" I said, my voice a fragile whisper in the stillness.

Silence stretched out, pregnant with expectation, before a voice emerged from the other end, one that made my breath hitch in my throat. It was deep and rough, tinged with the gravel of years gone by. It was my father—Henry. A flood of memories surged forward, both tender and painful. I had long since learned to keep that name tucked away in a dark corner of my mind, a relic of a life I had fought hard to escape.

"I'm close, Ellie," he said, the words hanging between us like a storm cloud. "I've been looking for you."

His tone was both familiar and foreign, wrapped in an urgency that sent a jolt of unease through me. "Why now?" I managed to ask, though part of me wanted to hang up and retreat into the safety of my solitude.

"Because there's something you need to know," he continued, his voice dropping to a conspiratorial whisper that sent goosebumps skittering across my skin. "Something your mother kept hidden. Something only you can find."

I clenched my jaw, every instinct screaming at me to deny him, to reject this intrusion into my life. Memories of my mother's frantic whispers, her warnings, and the way she had pulled me close when shadows loomed too large flooded my mind. She had spoken of Henry with a mixture of fear and resolve, weaving a tapestry of caution that had kept me on edge. "What do you want from me?" I demanded, trying to sound braver than I felt.

"Your mother's secret," he replied, the words dripping with a hunger I couldn't quite place. "I know she left something for you. A map, a key—something that leads to the truth. I need you to help me find it."

A frigid wind howled outside, and I wrapped my arms around myself, suddenly feeling exposed and vulnerable. The walls of the cabin, once a fortress against the world, now felt like a cage. "You don't get to just waltz back into my life and demand anything," I snapped, channeling my fear into anger. "You made your choices."

"I didn't have a choice," he shot back, the desperation in his voice cracking like thunder. "I've been trying to make things right, Ellie. But time is running out. Please, just listen to me."

The line crackled with tension, and for a moment, I could hear the weight of regret in his voice, mingling with something darker, something unnamable that made my skin crawl. "Why should I trust you?" I whispered, the question hanging heavy between us, each word laced with the bitter taste of betrayal.

"Because I'm your father," he said, the words laced with a mix of authority and vulnerability. "And I won't stop until I find you. Until I find what we're looking for. You can't hide from the past, Ellie. It has a way of catching up with you."

His admission left a gaping silence, and I felt the weight of his words settle like a stone in my stomach. The forest outside was alive with rustling leaves and the distant call of an owl, a reminder that the world continued to spin, indifferent to my unraveling. "What if I don't want to know?" I challenged, but even as I said it, I felt the pull of curiosity, the undeniable urge to uncover the hidden truths that had shaped my life.

"You do want to know," he insisted, his voice softening, almost coaxing. "You've been searching for answers all along. Your mother's secrets—everything is tied to your past. You need to confront it, or it will always haunt you."

As the moonlight poured through the window, illuminating the cabin in a silvery glow, I felt an unsettling mix of dread and intrigue wash over me. What lay buried in the shadows of my family's history? Could I truly unearth the fragments of my past and piece together the puzzle that had been hidden from me for so long? With each passing moment, the tension in the air thickened, and I knew that whatever decision I made would ripple through my life, altering its course forever.

"Where do I start?" I found myself asking, the words slipping out before I could snatch them back. The thrill of the unknown surged through me, accompanied by the cold realization that I was stepping onto a path from which there would be no return.

I felt the warmth of the cabin retreat as the conversation deepened, leaving me surrounded by the chill of dread. The air became thick with unspoken fears and buried memories, swirling around me like the shadows that danced in the corners of the room. My father's voice, though familiar, was a siren call echoing through the dark chambers of my past, and I fought the urge to succumb to its pull.

"Ellie," he pressed, a note of urgency weaving through his words. "You need to understand. What I'm asking isn't just for me; it's for you. It's your legacy."

Legacy. The word struck a chord deep within me, awakening emotions I had buried under layers of resolve and denial. My mother had spoken of legacy, too, though her words had always dripped with warning. She had shared tales of our family's history, but the stories often twisted into dark fables, punctuated by her tear-streaked cheeks and trembling hands. As a child, I had believed she was merely overreacting, letting her imagination spiral into places of fear. But now, as the moonlight glinted off the old wooden table and shadows flickered like ghosts across the walls, I felt the weight of those stories bearing down on me.

"What exactly am I supposed to be looking for?" I asked, a shaky resolve lending strength to my voice. "You still haven't told me what it is."

"There's a box," he said, his tone shifting as if conjuring an image from the depths of his mind. "It's hidden in the old oak tree behind the house. Your mother thought it was safe there, away from prying eyes. But she also knew that one day, you'd need to find it. The key to understanding everything lies within."

I closed my eyes, a flurry of emotions colliding within me. The old oak tree—the one I used to climb as a child, its gnarled branches welcoming me into a world of imagination and play. But I had never considered it a repository of family secrets, a sanctuary for mysteries waiting to be unearthed. "What if I don't want to know what's in that box?" I challenged, feeling my pulse quicken with uncertainty.

"Then you'll remain shackled by your past," he replied, his voice low and firm. "You can't move forward until you confront what has been hidden from you. Don't you want to know the truth?"

His question hung in the air, wrapping around me like the chill creeping through the windowpanes. The truth. It was a double-edged sword—one side glittering with the promise of clarity, the other jagged and potentially harmful. I longed to push the thought away, to retreat into the comfortable life I had created in this cabin, far from the complexities of my family. Yet, a flicker of curiosity ignited within me, illuminating the corners of my mind I had kept shrouded in darkness.

"I'll think about it," I finally said, even though a part of me knew the wheels of fate had already begun to turn. The conversation faded, leaving a heavy silence in its wake. I lowered the phone, the weight of what had been said pressing down on me like the snow that blanketed the earth outside.

As the moon drifted across the sky, I paced the small cabin, its walls closing in with each step. The glow from the fire danced playfully, but it was a warmth that seemed distant, unable to reach the chill in my bones. Luke would return soon, and the normalcy of our life here would envelop me once more, offering a fragile comfort that felt like an illusion.

But could I allow myself that comfort while knowing a piece of my past lay waiting in the earth? I envisioned the oak tree, its bark rough beneath my fingers, the thrill of discovery mingled with the terror of what I might find. Perhaps the box contained letters, photographs, fragments of a life I had never known. Or perhaps it held something darker—secrets that could shatter the fragile peace I had fought so hard to create.

The door creaked open, breaking my reverie, and I turned to see Luke enter, his cheeks flushed from the cold and his arms laden with bags. "You won't believe what I found at the market!" he exclaimed, his enthusiasm brightening the room. I forced a smile, but the weight of my thoughts lingered, an invisible chain binding me to the reality of my past.

"What is it?" I asked, hoping to divert my mind from the conversation that had just taken place.

He unloaded the bags onto the kitchen counter, revealing fresh produce and the comforting aroma of baked goods. "I got some of that apple pie you love," he said, his eyes sparkling with mischief. "And I found the last bottle of that special wine we had at our anniversary."

"Wow, you really went all out," I said, my heart warming at his efforts to make our night special. Yet beneath the surface, my mind was a tumultuous sea, the waves crashing against the shores of my thoughts.

As he set about preparing dinner, I stole glances at him, the flicker of the flames reflecting in his eyes, highlighting the laughter lines that danced at the corners of his mouth. He was my anchor, grounding me amid the storm. "Did you have a good time?" I asked, trying to inject genuine curiosity into my tone.

"Yeah! I ran into Mrs. Thompson from next door," he replied, chuckling as he recalled her endless chatter about her garden. "She insisted on giving me some of her herbs. I think we'll be having a very aromatic dinner tonight."

I laughed, the sound bubbling up from my chest, but the laughter faded quickly, my thoughts drifting back to the call. Would I tell him? Would he understand the gravity of the situation, the weight of my father's words? The thought of Henry's looming presence turned my stomach, and I realized I needed to make a decision soon.

The smell of garlic sizzling in olive oil wafted through the air, the sound of Luke humming a tune blending with the crackle of the fire. I watched him move about the kitchen, lost in the rhythm of our life together, and for a fleeting moment, I felt the heaviness lift, as though the comfort of the mundane could ward off the shadows of my past.

But as I stirred the pot of simmering stew, I could not shake the sense that something was brewing, not just in the pot but within the very fabric of my life. The call had ignited a spark, a thread pulling me toward the mystery that awaited beneath the old oak tree. The door to my past was opening, and I had to decide whether to step through or close it forever.

As dinner progressed, the laughter and warmth filled the cabin, creating a tapestry of love and hope that I desperately clung to. Yet the pull of the unknown lingered at the edges, a siren song beckoning me back to the secrets that lay beneath the surface of my seemingly perfect life.

The cabin, once a sanctuary of warmth and solitude, now felt like a stage set for a drama I hadn't auditioned for. I stood in the kitchen, the rich aroma of Luke's cooking enveloping me like a comforting shawl, but the reality of the phone call loomed large, a specter in the room that refused to be ignored. My mind swirled with thoughts, each one more chaotic than the last, as I busied myself with the simple act of chopping vegetables. The knife glided through the soft skin of tomatoes, a sharp contrast to the turmoil within me, and I couldn't help but feel the weight of impending decisions pressing down.

The soft clatter of pots and pans created a symphony of domesticity, but each sound felt distant, muffled by the haze of my thoughts. Luke hummed a tune, blissfully unaware of the storm brewing just beyond the window. I glanced out, where the moon hung high, casting silver light on the snow-draped trees that surrounded our haven. It was beautiful, and yet, the scene felt like a painting with a hidden darkness lurking in the brushstrokes. I could almost hear the whispers of the forest, secrets buried beneath the surface, urging me to uncover the truth.

"Are you with me?" Luke called, his voice breaking through my reverie. I turned to see him looking at me with a curious expression, his brow slightly furrowed. He had a way of sensing when something was off, as if the air around me shifted in his presence.

"Yeah, just lost in thought," I replied, forcing a smile, the corners of my lips twitching in a semblance of normalcy. "What's for dinner?"

"Only the best stew this side of the Mississippi," he declared with a grin, his enthusiasm infectious. "You know I've been perfecting my recipe."

As he poured the stew into bowls, steam rising like little ghosts escaping into the air, I couldn't help but admire the way he moved. There was an ease about him, a natural rhythm that transformed the mundane into something magical. I could lose myself in the comfort of his presence, but the specter of my father's call loomed, a reminder that darkness could seep through even the sunniest of days.

Dinner passed in a blur of laughter and warmth, the rich flavors of the stew contrasting sharply with the chill that had settled deep in my bones. Luke regaled me with tales from the market, stories about the eccentric townsfolk who populated our small community, their quirks and idiosyncrasies becoming a thread that wove the fabric of our lives together. It was a delightful tapestry, but my heart was tugged by the darker threads I couldn't yet reveal.

As we finished our meal, I felt the warmth of the fire cradle me, yet my thoughts were still frigid. I had to confront my past, to unravel the mystery of that box buried beneath the oak tree, but could I really drag Luke into this? Would revealing my family's secrets taint the haven we had built together? My mind raced, darting between possibilities, and as I caught Luke's eye, the flicker of concern in his gaze mirrored my own uncertainty.

"Hey, you okay?" he asked, placing a hand on mine. His touch was grounding, a lifeline in the tempest of my thoughts. "You've been quiet all night."

"I'm fine," I assured him, but the word felt hollow even as it left my lips. "Just...thinking about some things."

"About your dad?" His voice was gentle, but there was a steeliness in it that told me he wouldn't let me sidestep the conversation for long. I hesitated, caught between the need to protect him from the storm brewing within me and the undeniable urge to confide in him.

"Yeah, he called." My admission hung heavy between us, and I watched as his expression shifted from concern to something deeper—a resolve to stand by me no matter what came next. "He wants me to find something my mother hid."

"Something hidden?" Luke's brow furrowed, his curiosity piqued. "What do you think it is?"

"I don't know," I confessed, my voice barely a whisper. "But it sounds important. He's convinced it has something to do with our family's history."

A thoughtful silence enveloped us as I struggled to gauge Luke's reaction. Would he see this as a mere curiosity or a dark cloud threatening to overshadow everything we had built?

"Ellie," he said, breaking the stillness. "Whatever it is, we can figure it out together. I'm not going anywhere."

His words wrapped around me like a protective cocoon, but they also ignited a flicker of fear within me. I didn't want to drag him into a mess that had been my burden for so long. But I also knew that denying him the truth would only build walls between us.

"Let's go for a walk," I suggested, desperate for a distraction, yet aware that my heart yearned for a deeper connection. The cold air would be bracing, but maybe the crispness of the night could clear my thoughts and open my heart.

We donned our coats, hats, and scarves, stepping outside into the crystalline air. The world around us was a winter wonderland, with the moonlight casting a silvery sheen over the snow, transforming the landscape into something ethereal. Each crunch of snow beneath our boots sounded like the universe acknowledging our presence, a reminder that we were part of something larger, something beautiful.

We walked side by side, the forest wrapping around us like an old friend, its dark secrets hidden behind layers of frost. As we ventured deeper into the trees, the world fell away, and for a moment, it felt as if we were the only two people in existence. I inhaled the crisp air, letting it fill my lungs, trying to drown out the echo of my father's voice, but the memories tugged at my mind like an insistent child.

"What's on your mind?" Luke asked, breaking the silence, his voice a soothing balm against the chaos within me. I turned to him, his features illuminated by the moon, and saw the earnestness in his gaze.

"I can't help but wonder what my life would have been like if things had been different," I admitted, my heart racing as I opened up. "If my father hadn't left, if my mother hadn't hidden so much from me. I feel like I'm standing at the edge of a cliff, staring into an abyss of what-ifs."

He stopped walking, turning to face me fully. "You're not defined by your past, Ellie. You're stronger than you realize. Whatever secrets your mother kept, you have the power to face them. And I'll be right there with you."

I felt the warmth of his words seep into my bones, wrapping around me like a comforting embrace against the chill of uncertainty.

"Thank you," I murmured, the sincerity in my voice resonating in the stillness of the night. We resumed our walk, the path ahead illuminated by the silver glow of the moon.

As we approached the oak tree, its gnarled branches reaching for the heavens, I paused, a sense of reverence washing over me. It stood as a guardian of memories, the keeper of secrets long buried. I hesitated, my heart pounding as the weight of the moment pressed down upon me.

"What if it's all too much?" I whispered, fear knotting in my stomach. "What if the truth shatters everything?"

"Then we'll put the pieces back together," Luke replied, his voice steady and unwavering. "Together, remember?"

I nodded, the resolve in his words igniting a flicker of courage within me. As I took a step closer to the oak tree, the air shifted, an invisible current of energy pulsing through the ground beneath my feet. I could feel it—the pull of the past, the whispers of family secrets beckoning me closer, urging me to unveil the mystery that had lingered in the shadows for far too long.

Reaching out, I placed my hand against the rough bark, its texture grounding me in the present while drawing me toward the past. Beneath its surface, I could sense the buried truths waiting to be uncovered. It was time to confront the secrets, to peel back the layers of my family's history and see what lay hidden in the depths.

As the wind rustled through the branches, carrying with it the echoes of generations gone by, I felt the weight of the world fall away. Whatever lay beneath this ancient tree, I was ready to face it. Together, we would embark on this journey into the heart of my family's legacy, unearthing the mysteries that had shaped me, not just for myself but for the love I shared with the man beside me.

With a deep breath, I steeled myself for the revelations to come, ready to confront the shadows of my past and embrace the light of my future.

Chapter 19: The Reckoning

The sun dipped low on the horizon, casting a warm, golden hue over the faded clapboard house that had been my sanctuary for years. As the shadows stretched across the porch, they seemed to blend with the remnants of a restless night, weaving tales of uncertainty that danced just out of reach. The wind whispered secrets through the swaying branches of the old oak tree, its gnarled limbs a testament to both time's passage and the countless storms it had weathered, much like my heart in this moment.

Luke's entrance jolted me back to reality, his familiar presence a grounding force in the tumultuous sea of emotions swirling within me. He stood there, framed in the doorway, the setting sun casting a warm glow around him. The light caught the contours of his rugged face, revealing a mixture of determination and tenderness that tugged at my heartstrings. His brown hair, tousled from the afternoon breeze, fell over his forehead, and for a brief moment, the world outside faded away, leaving just the two of us in our fragile bubble of existence.

"Hey," he said softly, his voice low and steady as if he had just emerged from a dream. "What did they say?"

The words spilled from my lips like a river breaking free of its dam, frantic and wild. I told him everything—the weight of Henry's ultimatum, the haunting implications of my mother's past that had begun to surface, and the sense of inevitability that coiled around my chest like a serpent. Each detail unfurled, painted vividly in the air between us.

"Henry wants to meet," I finished, the tremor in my voice betraying the bravado I desperately tried to maintain. "He says it's time we talked about what she left behind."

Luke's brow furrowed, and the warmth in his eyes dimmed for just a moment, replaced by an understanding that felt like a storm brewing on the horizon. "What does that even mean?" he asked, his grip tightening around my hand, as if the simple act of holding me could shield me from the chaos ahead.

I shook my head, frustration boiling just beneath the surface. "I don't know, Luke. I wish I did. But the more I think about it, the more I realize how little I actually knew about her." The anger and sadness intertwined, creating a complex tapestry of emotions that left me reeling.

He moved closer, his presence wrapping around me like a warm blanket on a cold winter night. "We'll figure it out together," he promised, his voice steady, the resolve in his tone igniting a flicker of hope within me. Yet, doubt gnawed at the edges of my mind. What could we possibly uncover about my mother that had been buried so deeply?

I could almost hear the laughter of children playing in the yard next door, their carefree giggles echoing through the air, a stark contrast to the turmoil roiling in my heart. How had my life devolved into a series of meetings and whispers about a past that seemed determined to catch up with me? I longed for the simplicity of those carefree days, when my greatest worry was whether I'd have time to finish my homework before dinner.

"I feel like I'm teetering on the edge of a cliff," I confessed, my voice barely above a whisper. "What if I can't face what's at the bottom?"

Luke stepped closer, his eyes locking onto mine, grounding me amidst the whirlwind. "You're not alone in this," he assured me, his thumb tracing gentle circles over the back of my hand. "I'll be right there with you, no matter what."

But as I gazed into his earnest eyes, a deeper fear nestled in my chest—a fear that perhaps I wouldn't be enough, that the weight of my family's secrets might crush the fragile bond we had built. My mother had always told me that love was a powerful force, but it also had a way of revealing the darker corners of the heart. What if my love for Luke wasn't strong enough to withstand the truths that lay ahead?

The soft patter of rain began, its rhythmic tapping against the wooden roof matching the racing tempo of my heart. The world outside blurred as droplets clung to the window, mirroring the tears I fought to hold back. "Henry knows something, doesn't he?" I murmured, the question lingering in the air like an uninvited guest.

Luke nodded, a serious expression settling on his face. "He's not just a threat; he's a piece of the puzzle." His voice was laced with conviction, yet uncertainty shadowed his features. "But we can't let him dictate our next move."

I appreciated his determination, but the darkness of uncertainty loomed large, wrapping its tendrils around my heart. "What if he reveals something that changes everything?"

He took a deep breath, his eyes searching mine. "Then we'll face it together. Whatever it is, we'll confront it side by side." His unwavering resolve washed over me like a balm, easing the tension in my chest, if only for a moment.

The wind howled outside, rattling the shutters and sending leaves spiraling into the air, a wild dance that mimicked the chaos inside my mind. I glanced at the old photograph on the mantle, my mother's smiling face a bittersweet reminder of what had been lost. I could feel the weight of her choices pressing down on me, every secret she'd kept intertwining with the reality I faced now. Would I ever understand her? Would I ever be able to forgive her for the shadows that haunted my existence?

As the storm raged outside, I leaned into Luke, seeking solace in his embrace. The warmth of his body contrasted sharply with the chill in the air, and I allowed myself to linger in the safety of his arms. In that moment, I knew the road ahead would be fraught with challenges, but I also knew that love—our love—might just be the light that pierced through the darkness.

The rain intensified, a symphony of droplets drumming against the roof, a stark reminder of the tempest raging not just outside but within my soul. With each heartbeat, the weight of my mother's unspoken truths pressed heavier on my chest, mingling with the echoes of Luke's comforting reassurances. It was a paradox, the warmth of his presence battling the cold chill of uncertainty, a battle I felt ill-equipped to win.

"Let's not think about Henry right now," Luke suggested, his voice cutting through the noise like a lighthouse beacon in the fog. He pulled me closer, and for a moment, the chaos of the world outside faded into a distant murmur. I could feel the tension in his muscles, a tightness that mirrored my own, as if we were two ships sailing in uncharted waters, navigating the same storm yet each grappling with our fears in isolation.

"Okay," I whispered, letting my head rest against his shoulder, inhaling the familiar scent of cedar and a hint of rain-soaked earth that clung to him. It was comforting, grounding. "What do you want to do instead?"

He pulled back slightly, his eyes sparkling with mischief as a smile tugged at the corners of his lips. "How about a little adventure? Something to distract us from the heavy stuff?"

My heart lifted at the thought, the notion of escape igniting a flicker of hope. Adventure had always been our remedy—our way of forging memories amid the chaos of life. "What do you have in mind?"

"I saw a place not far from here, an old bookshop that's supposed to be a treasure trove of forgotten stories," he said, excitement bubbling in his voice. "They even have a little café attached. I figured we could grab a cup of coffee and lose ourselves in some pages."

The idea was deliciously inviting. The thought of surrounded by the scent of aged paper, the faint whispers of stories long forgotten, was enough to stir a spark of joy in my heart. "I love that idea," I said, a smile breaking through the clouds of my uncertainty.

As we pulled on our jackets, the storm outside transformed into a gentle drizzle, the kind that kissed your skin like a lover's touch. We stepped out into the fresh air, the world around us glistening under the veil of rain. The streets shimmered, and the familiar sights of our small town took on an ethereal quality, bathed in the soft glow of the streetlights flickering like fireflies.

Hand in hand, we made our way through the winding streets, the rhythm of our footsteps blending with the soft patter of rain. The air was alive with the scents of wet earth and blooming flowers, a symphony that enveloped us as we ventured deeper into the heart of the town. The closer we got to the bookshop, the more the weight of my worries began to ebb, replaced by a sense of possibility.

The bookshop stood proudly at the corner of a cobblestone street, its window displays adorned with colorful covers that seemed to beckon us inside. A vintage sign swung gently above the door, creaking like a storyteller preparing to divulge secrets long held. As we stepped across the threshold, the world outside faded away, replaced by the warm embrace of wood and paper.

The interior was a labyrinth of shelves, each crammed with volumes that had stories to tell. Dust motes danced in the beams of golden light streaming through the tall windows, illuminating the spines of books that had weathered countless storms of their own. The air was thick with the scent of aged paper, an intoxicating blend of nostalgia and promise that tugged at my heart.

"Let's grab that coffee first," Luke suggested, leading me to a cozy nook in the corner where the café's warmth enveloped us like a well-worn blanket. The barista, a lively woman with streaks of purple in her hair, greeted us with a smile that felt like sunshine breaking through the clouds.

"What can I get you two lovebirds?" she asked, her eyes twinkling with mischief.

"Two coffees, please," Luke replied, his smile infectious. "One with a dash of adventure, if you have it."

"Coming right up!" she chimed, her laughter ringing through the space as she busied herself behind the counter.

We settled into plush armchairs nestled in the corner, the soft hum of chatter surrounding us like a comforting cocoon. I glanced around, soaking in the atmosphere. Everywhere I looked, readers lost in their worlds, their expressions a blend of wonder and contemplation. It was a reminder of the magic that stories could weave, a magic I yearned to embrace fully.

As the barista returned with our coffees, the rich aroma wafted through the air, wrapping around us like a warm hug. I took a sip, the warmth spreading through me, igniting a flicker of joy that pushed back the shadows lingering in my heart.

"Thank you for this," I said, my voice soft but earnest. "I needed to escape for a while."

Luke's gaze softened as he reached across the table, his fingers brushing against mine. "Anytime. We'll face whatever comes next together, remember?"

A warmth blossomed in my chest at his words, the reminder of our bond grounding me amidst the uncertainty swirling in my mind. I leaned back, letting the moment wash over me. "You know, I've always loved books," I mused, glancing around the shop. "They've always felt like a refuge, a way to explore lives that aren't my own."

"Is that why you chose to help people through their Salesforce journeys?" he asked, a hint of playfulness dancing in his tone. "To create a narrative for them?"

I chuckled, appreciating his perspective. "Maybe. I never thought of it that way, but it makes sense. Each client has their story, their struggles and triumphs. I just guide them through it, helping them unlock their potential."

As we sipped our coffees, time slipped away, each moment stretching like taffy, sweet and satisfying. The chatter around us faded, replaced by our shared laughter and the simple joy of being together. In that little haven, the looming shadows of my past began to recede, allowing light to filter through the cracks.

But as the rain continued to patter softly against the windows, a lingering whisper in the back of my mind reminded me that Henry was still out there, waiting, watching. And yet, with Luke by my side, the world felt a little less daunting. I couldn't change my mother's choices, but I could rewrite my own story—one filled with hope, love, and the promise of new beginnings.

And as I looked into Luke's eyes, I knew I was ready to face whatever came next. Together, we would navigate the labyrinth of my past, unraveling the threads of secrets and lies, weaving them into something beautiful. In the quiet sanctuary of the bookshop, I realized that love, much like the stories that surrounded us, was powerful enough to illuminate even the darkest corners of our hearts.

The quaint little bookshop became a sanctuary, a cocoon woven from the warmth of our shared moments and the rich stories whispering from the shelves. Each book seemed to hold its breath, waiting for someone to unlock the worlds within, and as we savored our coffees, I couldn't help but feel a sense of belonging in this magical place. Luke leaned back in his chair, a playful smirk dancing on his lips, and I marveled at how effortlessly he transformed the mundane into something extraordinary with just his presence.

"I think I spotted a section dedicated to hidden gems," he announced, his eyes sparkling with mischief. "What do you say we go on a little treasure hunt?"

A grin broke free as I nodded eagerly, the promise of adventure rekindling my spirit. We set down our cups, the remnants of coffee lingering like a warm memory, and ventured into the labyrinth of shelves. As we navigated through the narrow aisles, I felt a palpable sense of excitement. Each turn held the potential for discovery, each title a new doorway waiting to be opened.

"Look at this!" Luke exclaimed, pulling a tattered paperback from the shelf. The cover, faded yet vibrant, depicted a woman standing on the edge of a cliff, her hair wild in the wind. "The Sea of Secrets," he read aloud, his voice imbued with theatrical flair. "Sounds like my kind of story."

I chuckled, imagining Luke as the heroic figure leaping into the unknown, braving tumultuous waves and uncovering hidden truths. "You'd make a perfect protagonist," I teased, nudging him playfully.

"Only if you're my sidekick," he retorted with a wink, and for a fleeting moment, the weight of my worries lifted, replaced by the warmth of laughter and companionship.

We continued our exploration, weaving between the rows, our fingers brushing against the spines of countless stories. I reveled in the tactile joy of holding books, feeling their textured covers beneath my fingertips. The whispers of stories long forgotten intertwined with the rhythm of our conversation, each laugh and sigh a note in the symphony of our day.

Then, amid the sea of volumes, something caught my eye—a small, leather-bound journal tucked away on a lower shelf, its edges frayed with age. I knelt to retrieve it, the weight of its significance palpable even before I opened it. The cover felt warm against my palms, and I hesitated, as if the journal were a vessel containing secrets that demanded respect.

"Find something interesting?" Luke asked, kneeling beside me, his curiosity piqued.

I carefully opened the journal, revealing pages filled with elegant, looping script. The ink had faded, but the words leapt from the pages as if desperate to share their story. "It's someone's diary," I breathed, my heart racing as I skimmed through the entries. Each passage chronicled mundane yet intimate moments—sunsets watched from a back porch, the taste of fresh-baked bread, and whispers shared under star-studded skies.

"It feels personal," I murmured, entranced by the fragments of a life captured in ink.

Luke leaned closer, reading over my shoulder, his breath warm against my ear. "It's like we're peeking into someone's soul," he said, his voice low and reverent. The intimacy of the moment wrapped around us like a soft embrace, and I couldn't help but wish we could slip into those memories, escape into a simpler existence.

As I turned to a new page, the ink transformed into a scrawl, jagged and frantic. "There's something off here," I said, a knot forming in my stomach. The tone shifted, words cascading in a rush of anxiety and urgency. "There's mention of secrets, whispers of a past that won't stay buried."

Luke's expression shifted from curiosity to concern. "What does it say?"

"Something about a decision that must be made, about a truth that could change everything," I replied, feeling the weight of the words pressing against my chest. "It's eerie, like it's warning me."

A chill swept through the air, as if the very walls of the bookshop were closing in. The warmth of the café now felt distant, overshadowed by the weight of impending revelations. I snapped the journal shut, and the sound echoed like a thunderclap in the hushed space.

"We should put this back," I suggested, my heart racing as I struggled to regain my composure. The joy we had shared moments ago now felt like a fragile memory, one that could shatter with the right push.

"Wait," Luke said, a spark of determination igniting in his eyes. "What if this journal holds more than just someone's story? What if it connects to what we're facing?"

My pulse quickened. "You think it could be connected to Henry?"

"It's possible," he replied, his voice steady. "We've both been grappling with our pasts, and maybe this diary holds answers we need."

His conviction sent a shiver down my spine, both thrilling and terrifying. I weighed the possibilities, the allure of discovery warring with the fear of what we might uncover. "Okay, but we need to tread carefully. I don't want to stumble into something that could hurt us more."

"We won't," he assured me, his hand finding mine, anchoring me amidst the storm of uncertainty. "Together, remember?"

We returned to our seats, the journal cradled between us like a fragile bird. The café buzzed with life around us, but our world had shrunk to this moment—two souls entwined in the exploration of a past that felt both foreign and intimately familiar.

"Let's read a bit more," Luke suggested, his voice a mix of excitement and apprehension. We delved into the journal again, each word a breadcrumb leading us deeper into the author's life. The entries unfolded like petals, revealing layers of emotion and vulnerability.

There were mentions of friendships strained by secrets, the haunting specter of betrayal, and the yearning for truth that clung like ivy to the pages. As we read, the words began to resonate with my own fears—the ties of family, the weight of hidden truths, and the looming shadow of Henry.

"Look here," I pointed, tracing a finger over a particularly raw entry. "It says, 'Sometimes the truth is a mirror that shatters everything it reflects. But perhaps, in the shards, we find the pieces of who we really are.'"

"That's profound," Luke said, his gaze intense. "It feels like a call to action. Maybe uncovering our truths is the only way forward."

A surge of determination flooded my veins. The journey I had embarked upon, fueled by uncertainty and fear, suddenly felt like a path to liberation. The secrets that had loomed like dark clouds could be the very things that set me free.

As we closed the journal, I realized that I had shifted, like a flower reaching for the sun after a long winter. The burdens I carried began to feel lighter, as if the act of sharing my fears and uncertainties with Luke had somehow transformed them. "We need to confront Henry," I said, my voice steady and resolute. "Whatever he wants, we have to face it together."

Luke smiled, a blend of pride and admiration shining in his eyes. "That's the spirit. Together, we'll face whatever comes our way."

The world outside continued its gentle rain dance, and in that little bookshop, we forged a pact—a promise to unravel the mysteries that tethered us to our pasts. Together, we would sift through the fragments of truth, drawing strength from each other as we navigated the storm, armed with the knowledge that love, much like a well-worn novel, had the power to rewrite our destinies.

As we stepped back into the drizzle, hand in hand, the air buzzed with possibility. The world around us might still be filled with shadows, but we were ready to embrace the light, carving a new narrative from the remnants of the old. With each step, I felt the weight of my mother's secrets begin to lift, revealing a future that shimmered with hope and the promise of new beginnings. Together, we would write our own story—one filled with love, resilience, and the unwavering belief that the truth, no matter how tangled, could lead to the most beautiful of revelations.

Chapter 20: A Crack in the Ice

The crunch of snow beneath my boots broke the early morning silence as I made my way to the edge of the lake. The air was sharp and biting, each breath a reminder of the frigid reality that encased us. The sunlight filtered through the trees, casting fragmented shadows on the ground, creating an ethereal atmosphere that clashed with the turmoil in my heart. I drew closer to the lake, my gaze drawn to its icy surface. It gleamed like glass, reflecting the bright blue of the sky above, yet it was marred by jagged cracks that snaked through the ice, a chaotic testament to the chaos within me.

In that moment, I wished I could just peel away the layers of my confusion, like shedding a heavy winter coat, and reveal the warmth beneath. I could feel the tension simmering just beneath the surface of my skin. I had tried to act as though everything was fine, to play the role of the unwavering partner and friend. But beneath that facade, a storm raged, churning with memories of my mother's whispered fears, Henry's threatening voice, and the uncertainty that now surrounded my bond with Luke.

I found a flat rock near the water's edge and sat down, wrapping my arms around my knees, seeking solace in the stillness of the moment. The wind howled softly through the pines, a mournful sound that mirrored the ache in my chest. I could see Luke in the distance, his strong frame bending over the woodpile, muscles straining as he swung the axe. Each strike sent chips of wood flying, splintering into the air like pieces of my heart. How had we reached this point? The warmth we had shared in the quiet corners of the cabin now felt so distant, like a half-remembered dream.

As I watched him, a sense of longing washed over me. Memories flooded my mind—how his laughter would fill the air, his teasing remarks that would spark my own playful retorts. I remembered how we'd huddled together under the stars, talking about everything and nothing, our dreams interwoven like the constellations above. Those moments felt like lifelines, connecting us to a future I could no longer see clearly. Now, with Henry looming over me like a dark cloud, every joyous memory felt tainted by the shadow of impending doom.

The crackling of the ice drew my attention back to the lake. I leaned forward, pressing my fingers against the surface. The cold seeped through, a stark reminder of the danger that lay beneath. It seemed fitting, somehow, that the lake—once a refuge of peace and beauty—had transformed into a chilling metaphor for my life. I pulled back, a wave of despair washing over me. The frozen surface might look serene, but I knew all too well that it could shatter with just a little pressure.

A distant shout broke through my thoughts, startling me. Luke was calling my name, his voice laced with concern. I turned to see him striding towards me, his brow furrowed, the glint of worry in his eyes stark against his rugged features. For a moment, time suspended itself. He was like a knight emerging from the fog, an anchor in the turbulent seas of my mind. I wanted to reach out to him, to confess the chaos swirling inside me, but the words seemed to evaporate before they could take form.

"Hey, you okay?" he asked, concern etched on his face as he crouched down next to me. The warmth of his presence was undeniable, yet the distance I felt was palpable. It was as if an invisible barrier had risen between us, built from the unspoken words and unresolved feelings that clung to the air like the lingering scent of smoke from his woodpile.

"I'm fine," I replied, though the tremor in my voice betrayed me. I forced a smile, hoping to mask the turmoil within. "Just thinking."

"About what?" He leaned in closer, his gaze searching mine, as if trying to decipher the uncharted territory of my thoughts.

I wanted to tell him about Henry, the encroaching dread that gnawed at my insides, but the words stuck in my throat. Instead, I gestured to the lake, the way the sun sparkled on its surface, the way it looked so inviting yet felt so treacherous. "Just... about how everything looks so calm on the outside."

Luke followed my gaze, his expression softening. "You mean the lake?"

"Yeah." I swallowed hard, emotions swirling like the wind through the trees. "It seems perfect, but we both know how dangerous it is. It could crack at any moment."

He nodded slowly, the weight of my words sinking in. "I get that. Sometimes it feels like we're just walking on thin ice, doesn't it?"

A lump formed in my throat at his understanding. It was both comforting and terrifying, as though he could see the cracks in my facade. The air between us hummed with unspoken truths. "Exactly," I whispered, my heart racing.

He reached for my hand, his touch warm against the chill of the air, grounding me amidst the chaos. "Whatever's going on, you don't have to face it alone. You know that, right?"

I wanted to believe him, to take comfort in his words, but the truth felt like an immovable weight on my chest. The shadows of my past, the secrets I had inherited, loomed larger than ever. "It's complicated, Luke. I'm scared of what's coming."

"I can handle complicated." His voice was steady, a promise wrapped in sincerity. "Just tell me what you need. We can figure this out together."

His words were like a balm to my frayed nerves, and for the first time in days, I felt a flicker of hope amidst the dread. But the shadow of Henry loomed large, and I wasn't sure I could share that burden with him just yet. The lake shimmered, a deceptive beauty, reflecting the glimmer of the sun, but beneath its surface, danger lurked, much like the secrets hidden within my heart.

I took a deep breath, the icy air filling my lungs and momentarily clearing the fog in my mind. Luke's presence beside me was a comfort, a lifeline thrown in turbulent waters, but I feared that my truth might pull him under, dragging us both into depths we weren't ready to face. The sun shone brightly overhead, illuminating the world in a dazzling array of whites and blues, but the shadows of my past crept in, darkening my thoughts.

"Do you remember when we used to skate on this lake?" I asked, forcing a smile that felt strained at the edges. "We thought we were invincible, gliding across the surface without a care in the world."

Luke chuckled softly, a sound that warmed me despite the chill. "Yeah, until we fell through that one time. I still remember how freezing the water was." He grinned, his eyes sparkling with the memory. "You dragged me back to the cabin, and we laughed about it for hours."

I laughed, but the joy felt hollow. That laughter was a ghost of what we had once shared, a bittersweet reminder of innocence lost. "I thought you were going to give up on skating after that."

"Not a chance," he said, his expression earnest. "You were worth it. Besides, falling through the ice was just part of the adventure."

Adventure. The word hung in the air, heavy with irony. What kind of adventure awaited me now? I could feel the weight of my decisions pressing down, suffocating like a heavy quilt, reminding me that choices made in the name of love could easily become shackles of fear.

"Do you think we could ever go back to that?" I asked, my voice barely a whisper. "Back to the simplicity of skating and laughter?"

Luke's brow furrowed, the playfulness in his eyes giving way to a more serious demeanor. "I want that, too. But we have to face what's coming first. We can't pretend this isn't happening." His grip on my hand tightened, anchoring me to the moment.

The truth was, I wasn't sure if we could ever go back to those carefree days. The specter of Henry loomed larger with each passing hour, and the chill of impending danger seeped into my bones. I could feel the icy tendrils of fear wrapping around my heart, squeezing tighter with every unspoken word.

"I don't want to drag you into my mess, Luke," I confessed, the words spilling out before I could stop them. "This isn't just about us anymore. I feel like I'm in way over my head."

Luke's gaze softened, his thumb brushing over my knuckles. "We're in this together. Whatever it is, I can handle it." There was a determination in his voice that resonated with something deep within me, a spark of hope igniting against the dark backdrop of uncertainty.

But as I looked into his eyes, I wondered how much he truly understood. The depths of my turmoil were a vast ocean, teeming with secrets that I wasn't sure I was ready to share. "It's not just about Henry. It's everything that came before him—my mother, her choices, her fears. It feels like I'm carrying her legacy, and I don't even know if I want it."

The weight of my admission hung heavy in the air, a poignant truth that threatened to unravel the fragile connection we had forged in our time together. I could see Luke processing my words, the gears turning in his mind as he searched for a response that would ease my burden.

"I can't pretend to know what you're feeling," he finally said, his voice steady. "But you're not your mother. You're stronger than she ever was. You've got a chance to break that cycle."

His words resonated within me, stirring something deep in my core. The idea that I could choose a different path, that I wasn't bound to repeat the mistakes of the past, felt both terrifying and liberating. Perhaps I was standing at a crossroads, with one path leading to the familiar darkness of my mother's legacy and the other beckoning me toward a future that was still unwritten.

"I don't want to be afraid anymore," I whispered, the resolve solidifying in my heart. "I want to fight for us, for a life where I don't have to look over my shoulder."

Luke's grip tightened around my hand, a steady promise in a world that felt increasingly unstable. "Then let's do it. Let's confront Henry together. We'll figure it out as we go."

The warmth of his presence enveloped me like a cocoon, dispelling some of the shadows that had crept in. I had always admired his courage, but now it felt like an ember igniting within me, urging me to rise above the fear that had threatened to consume me.

"I'm scared," I admitted, my voice barely above a whisper. "What if he finds out where we are? What if he doesn't stop until he gets what he wants?"

"Then we'll outsmart him," Luke said, determination flickering in his eyes. "You're not alone in this. We'll find a way to protect what we have. I won't let him take you from me."

His unwavering belief in our strength together filled me with hope. I felt the icy grip of fear loosening, replaced by a warmth that radiated through my entire being. We were stronger together, a force of nature that could weather any storm.

The lake, with its cracked surface and deceptive calm, became a metaphor for my own life. Beneath the ice lay potential dangers, but there was also beauty in the struggle, the determination to rise above the chaos.

"I'm ready," I said, surprising myself with the strength of my conviction. "Let's confront this together. We'll face Henry, and whatever comes next."

Luke smiled, a radiant beam of light cutting through the lingering clouds of doubt. "That's the spirit. Together, we're unstoppable."

As we stood by the lake, hand in hand, I realized that the cracks in the ice didn't signify failure; they represented resilience, a reminder that even in the face of danger, there was beauty in breaking free. I took a deep breath, feeling the icy air transform into a catalyst for change. The path ahead was fraught with uncertainty, but I was no longer afraid. I was ready to carve my own destiny, one bold step at a time.

I could hear the rhythmic thud of Luke's axe biting into the wood, a steady metronome keeping time with the chaos in my heart. Each chop seemed to echo my internal struggle, a reminder that he was fighting for us, for a future I was afraid to imagine. The crackling of the logs breaking apart was almost soothing, but I found myself lost in thought, pondering what it meant to truly break free from the past. The morning sun bathed the landscape in a golden hue, creating an illusion of warmth that was at odds with the chill wrapping around my heart.

I turned my gaze back to the lake, the surface glimmering like shards of broken glass reflecting a million tiny suns. I thought about how it used to be a playground for our laughter and carefree moments, where the world felt uncomplicated. Now, it loomed large and dangerous, a reminder of the hidden depths beneath the frozen facade. The realization settled heavily within me: I was standing on the precipice of a choice, the kind that could irrevocably change everything.

"Hey," Luke's voice broke through my reverie, and I turned to find him approaching, his cheeks flushed from the cold and exertion. There was a sincerity in his eyes that made my chest ache with conflicting emotions. "You look like you're a million miles away. Want to talk?"

"I've been thinking," I admitted, the words spilling out before I could hold them back. "About us. About everything."

He stepped closer, brushing the snow off the rock beside me and sitting down. The warmth of his body radiated towards me, creating a fragile barrier against the icy world that surrounded us. "What about us?"

"I don't want to hide anymore, Luke. I don't want to pretend that everything is okay." My voice trembled slightly, each syllable laced with the weight of my revelations. "I've kept my mother's secrets for so long. I thought I could protect myself and those I care about by burying them, but it's exhausting. And Henry... he's not going to stop. He's determined to dig up the truth, and I fear what that might mean for us."

Luke's expression shifted from concern to resolve, the lines of his jaw tightening as if preparing for battle. "Then we face him together. We'll figure this out. You're not alone in this fight, and I don't plan on letting him disrupt our lives. We can confront your past and take back control."

His words hung in the air, both a promise and a challenge. But doubt nagged at me. Could we truly confront a force like Henry? He was relentless, and every moment he drew closer felt like a countdown echoing in my mind. "I wish it were that simple. Henry knows how to manipulate. He'll exploit my fears, my insecurities. He knows my weaknesses."

"And you know his." Luke's eyes were fierce, igniting something within me that had been flickering like a candle about to be snuffed out. "You're stronger than you realize. You've already faced so much. You can't let him win. You can't let him steal your future."

The passion in his voice ignited a flicker of determination deep inside me. Perhaps he was right; perhaps I was stronger than I thought. The warmth of his support enveloped me, a comforting cloak against the biting cold of my reality. I took a deep breath, feeling the icy tendrils of fear begin to thaw in the face of his unwavering conviction.

"Okay," I said, a newfound resolve hardening my voice. "Let's take control. Let's prepare for whatever comes next. Together."

The tension in my chest began to ease, and I felt lighter somehow, as if a weight had been lifted, if only slightly. We stood together, a united front against the impending storm. Luke squeezed my hand, grounding me, reminding me that I was not alone.

As we began to formulate a plan, I could almost envision the pieces of my life falling into place. We would gather information, unearth what my mother had buried, and fortify our defenses. With every step, we would reclaim the power that had been so easily taken from me.

Days turned into nights, and our resolve only deepened. We spent long hours huddled by the fireplace, poring over old documents and piecing together the fragmented history that had haunted my family. My mother's letters revealed a past filled with fear and resilience, a legacy that I had inherited but not yet embraced. The deeper we dug, the more I uncovered the nuances of her struggles, the sacrifices she had made to protect me from a world that had shown her no mercy.

Each letter was like a window into her soul, revealing her fears, her hopes, and ultimately, her failures. I began to understand that her silence had not been a sign of weakness but rather a desperate attempt to shield me from the chaos that had once consumed her life. In her efforts to protect me, she had inadvertently set the stage for my own battle.

Luke stood by my side through it all, his presence a steadying force. He listened without judgment, his quiet strength allowing me to unravel the complex tapestry of my past. As we worked together, my fears began to lose their power. The weight of my mother's secrets felt less burdensome when shared, like stones cast into a lake, creating ripples of understanding instead of waves of despair.

One evening, as the sun dipped below the horizon and painted the sky in hues of orange and purple, I decided it was time to confront my mother's legacy head-on. I sat by the lake, the icy surface now a serene mirror reflecting the vibrant colors of dusk. The air was thick with anticipation, and I could feel the pulse of the earth beneath me as if it were alive, resonating with my determination.

"Tonight is the night," I murmured, almost to myself. "I'm ready to face whatever comes."

Luke joined me, his warmth a comforting presence as we stared out over the lake. "You've got this. I believe in you."

With a final deep breath, I summoned every ounce of courage I had. I would not allow Henry to control my destiny any longer. My mother's legacy would not be one of fear and silence; it would become a testament to strength and resilience.

As the last rays of sunlight slipped below the horizon, I felt a shift within me. I was ready to confront my past, ready to carve a new path into the future—one that was undeniably my own.

Chapter 21: An Unwanted Visitor

The cabin stood defiantly against the relentless elements, its weathered wood and peeling paint a testament to years of solitude. As dusk fell, shadows danced along the walls, flickering like memories we wished we could outrun. I nestled deeper into the worn armchair by the fireplace, the warmth wrapping around me like an old friend, yet it offered little solace against the gnawing dread coiling in my stomach.

Luke had been quiet since discovering those tracks, a silence that felt heavier than the snow blanketing the ground outside. I watched him through the flickering light, his usually bright eyes now clouded with worry. He was an anchor in this storm of uncertainty, but even anchors could be pulled under. I could sense his unease, the way he clenched his jaw and flexed his fingers, as if he could physically dispel the tension building between us.

The cabin, once a haven, now felt like a trap. Each sound outside became magnified—the crunch of snow underfoot, the distant howl of the wind. I tried to convince myself that it was nothing but nature's symphony, but the paranoia clawed at my thoughts, each creak and groan of the old structure a sinister reminder that we were not alone.

As the fire crackled, casting shadows that twisted and elongated like the secrets we kept, I couldn't help but reflect on how we had come to be here, in this forsaken part of the world. It had started as an escape, a chance to breathe away from the chaos of our lives, but it felt more like a haunting now. Each flicker of the flames was a reminder of the light we once shared, now dimmed by fear and uncertainty.

I gazed out the window into the inky darkness, the trees standing like sentinels, their branches bare and skeletal, whispering secrets only they could understand. In the stillness, I thought of Henry. His name sent a chill down my spine, colder than the biting wind outside. The man had a way of inserting himself into the fabric of our lives, always lurking, always watching.

What had begun as a simple disagreement spiraled into something much larger than either of us anticipated. The cabin, nestled deep in the woods, had felt safe—our little sanctuary against the world. I had envisioned nights filled with laughter and quiet conversations, a reprieve from the chaos that had swallowed us whole. But now, with those tracks in the snow, I understood the folly of my naivety.

With every passing minute, my mind raced. I tried to push the fear away, to think rationally, but the possibilities spiraled out of control. What if he sent someone to find us? What if they came for Luke? The thought tightened my chest, a vice of anxiety squeezing the breath from my lungs.

"Do you think we should call someone?" I finally broke the silence, my voice barely above a whisper, as if speaking too loudly might attract attention.

Luke turned his gaze from the window, his expression unreadable. "And tell them what? That we're hiding from a ghost?"

His humor was sharp, cutting through the tension like a blade, but it did little to reassure me. I could see the resolve forming behind his eyes, the decision he was making even as I spoke. We couldn't stay here—not when the shadows outside seemed to thicken, pressing against the walls as if they sought to invade our sanctuary.

"Maybe we should leave," I suggested, my heart racing at the thought. The woods were dark and foreboding, a maze of trees and underbrush that could swallow us whole. But it felt like a better option than waiting for whatever fate Henry had in store for us.

He shook his head, running a hand through his tousled hair. "We don't know how many people might be out there. It's better to stay put for now."

The wisdom of his words hung in the air, a grim acceptance of our reality. We were trapped between fear and the unknown, and for a moment, the weight of it all threatened to crush me.

Night deepened, and the fire began to dwindle, the flames flickering as if they too were afraid. I wrapped my arms around myself, trying to stave off the chill that had crept into my bones. Luke sat across from me, his silhouette stark against the dying light, a guardian caught in a web of uncertainty.

Outside, the wind howled, a mournful sound that seemed to echo the turmoil within me. I closed my eyes, imagining the life we could have had, if only circumstances had been different. Days spent exploring the quaint little towns nearby, nights filled with laughter and whispered secrets beneath a blanket of stars.

But those dreams felt like fragile glass, shattering with the slightest tremor of reality. I opened my eyes and fixed my gaze on Luke, who stared into the fire, his expression distant. I wanted to reach out, to reassure him that we would find a way through this, but the words caught in my throat.

Instead, I settled back in my chair, letting the warmth of the fire wash over me one last time, holding onto the hope that we could reclaim the innocence of our escape. Even in the darkness, I clung to the belief that love could conquer fear, that we were stronger together, no matter the shadows that loomed outside the cabin walls. The night was far from over, and while the path ahead was uncertain, I knew that as long as we had each other, we would fight against the dark.

As the shadows lengthened, the fire's flicker began to dim, casting ghostly shapes against the walls. The remnants of the day's warmth clung to the air, but the chill of uncertainty seeped in through the cracks in the cabin's aging wood. I could almost hear the howling wind outside, its sharp notes a sinister reminder of the danger that lurked beyond our fragile sanctuary. My gaze drifted to Luke, who sat opposite me, a chiseled silhouette against the backdrop of the crackling flames. He seemed lost in thought, the weight of the world settling heavily upon his shoulders.

I shifted in my chair, attempting to catch his eye, but he remained transfixed by the flames, as if seeking answers from the flickering light. The lines of worry etched across his forehead only deepened, and I felt a familiar tug in my chest—a mix of concern and something else I couldn't quite identify. I wanted to reach out to him, to draw him away from the abyss of his thoughts, but what could I say that would ease the tension? In moments like this, words felt insufficient, almost trivial against the enormity of our situation.

"Luke," I finally ventured, my voice breaking the thick silence like a hesitant knife through butter. "What do we do now?"

He turned slowly, his expression heavy with the burden of responsibility. "We wait," he said, the simplicity of his words stark against the complexity of our reality. "We need to see what unfolds. If it is Henry or someone working for him, we have to be smart about our next move."

The resolve in his voice sent a shiver through me, both comforting and disquieting. He was right, of course. We had no choice but to play the waiting game, to sit in this purgatory until we could see what came next. I glanced toward the window, the darkness beyond thick and oppressive, and it felt as if the trees themselves were leaning in, eager to eavesdrop on our fears.

The fire sputtered, sending a shower of sparks into the air, and I leaned forward, feeding it a fresh log. The heat surged back, wrapping around us like a warm embrace, but my heart was cold. The flickering light illuminated the worn details of the cabin—pictures of past adventures hanging crookedly on the walls, and the scarred wooden beams that had seen far more joy than sorrow.

In that moment, the nostalgia surged within me, a bittersweet wave of memories that momentarily distracted from our present peril. This cabin had been our refuge, a place where laughter echoed off the walls and our troubles seemed distant, mere shadows on the horizon. I longed for those moments—the impromptu dance parties in the kitchen, the late-night confessions by the fire, and the quiet mornings spent wrapped in blankets, sipping coffee as the sun streamed through the windows.

But nostalgia was a double-edged sword, and with it came the sharp reminder of how quickly things could change. My thoughts turned back to the tracks in the snow, to the implications of that single discovery. What did Henry want from us? What was the price of our past? The air around us thickened, as if the cabin itself was holding its breath, waiting for the inevitable.

"Do you think we should barricade the door?" I suggested, my mind racing with possible plans of action. The thought of someone coming through that door sent a rush of adrenaline coursing through me.

Luke shook his head, a hint of a smile ghosting across his lips, though it didn't quite reach his eyes. "It's not like we're in a horror movie, Jess. Barricading the door would only trap us inside. We need to stay mobile."

His attempt at levity fell flat, and the moment passed, heavy with unspoken fears. I could see the gears turning in his mind, the strategies unfurling like the curling smoke from the fire. It was this side of him that I admired—his resilience, his unwavering determination to protect us both. Yet, I felt the familiar urge to take charge, to do something, anything, to reclaim some sense of control in a situation that felt all too helpless.

I stood up and paced the small living area, the worn floorboards creaking beneath my weight. Each step felt like a commitment to fight against the encroaching darkness, a promise to stand my ground. The walls seemed to close in around me, and the air was thick with unvoiced fears and what-ifs.

"Maybe we could create a distraction," I mused aloud, my mind racing. "If we make it seem like we're not here, it might throw them off the scent."

Luke raised an eyebrow, intrigued despite the heaviness of the moment. "Like what? A smoke signal? Set off fireworks?"

"Or we could create noise in another part of the cabin," I countered, a spark of inspiration igniting in my chest. "If they hear something, they might investigate that instead of checking here."

His expression shifted from skepticism to contemplation. "You're onto something. We could use the generator—make it sound like something's going on in the back room."

A plan formed between us, tentative yet full of possibility. The idea that we could outsmart the very fear that haunted us lent me a sense of strength I didn't know I possessed.

We moved swiftly, working together to set our plan into action. Luke grabbed the generator from the corner of the room, while I rummaged through the supplies, searching for anything that could serve as a makeshift diversion. The adrenaline coursing through me sharpened my senses, and for the first time that night, I felt a flicker of hope cutting through the cloud of dread.

With the generator humming to life, we created a cacophony of sound, the roar echoing through the cabin and spilling into the stillness of the night. I could feel my heart pounding in sync with the rhythmic thrum of the engine, a counterpoint to the chaos unfolding around us. Outside, the trees stood sentinel, their branches swaying in the wind, casting shadows that danced in the flickering firelight.

As we finished our preparations, a strange sense of camaraderie enveloped us, binding us in this moment of shared purpose. The threat of Henry loomed large, but we had ignited a spark of defiance within ourselves, refusing to be victims of circumstance.

Together, we stood at the threshold of uncertainty, ready to face whatever awaited us in the depths of that treacherous night. The cabin may have felt like a prison, but in our hearts, we were determined to fight for our freedom, our future, and each other.

The generator sputtered like a restless beast, its roar echoing through the stillness, drowning out the distant whispers of the wind. With every thrum, I could feel the pulse of hope coursing through me, a heartbeat synchronized with our shared determination. Luke stood beside me, his expression a mix of admiration and concern, as if the light of the generator had illuminated not just our immediate surroundings but the depths of our unspoken fears.

"Alright, let's move," he said, his voice steady despite the uncertainty looming outside. We took a moment to steady ourselves, exchanging a glance filled with unspoken promises. There was an electric charge in the air, a magnetic pull between us that seemed to strengthen with every heartbeat, grounding us even in the midst of chaos.

With the generator humming, we hurried to the back room. It was a small space, filled with the remnants of our escape—old furniture, dust-covered boxes, and the lingering scent of cedarwood. I glanced around, noting the shadows that danced ominously in the corners, seemingly alive with the weight of our anxiety. Luke positioned the generator to face the window, ensuring that the noise would carry into the night.

"Let's keep this door ajar," I suggested, the idea sparking in my mind as I wedged a chair against it. "If anyone's out there, they'll think we're in here, making all this noise."

He nodded, his eyes flicking back to the window, as if daring the darkness to reveal its secrets. "And if they come to investigate?"

I swallowed hard, my throat suddenly dry. "Then we'll figure it out," I said, feigning confidence. The truth was, I had no idea what we would do if someone actually stepped through that door, but the alternative—sitting and waiting in fear—felt unbearable.

As we settled into our makeshift strategy, the distant howl of the wind rose and fell like a mournful song. I tried to focus on the task at hand, but the nagging sense of dread clawed at my thoughts. Each minute felt like an eternity, every creak of the cabin's timbered bones a portent of doom. The darkness outside enveloped the world in an unsettling embrace, the trees standing as silent sentinels, their branches stretched like skeletal fingers clawing at the night sky.

Minutes turned into hours, and still, we remained in our vigil. Luke had taken to pacing the small confines of the room, his movement deliberate and rhythmic, while I settled against the wall, clutching my knees to my chest. I could feel the weight of uncertainty pressing down on me, a suffocating shroud that seemed to obscure the very air we breathed.

"Jess," Luke said suddenly, breaking the silence that had become our unwanted companion. "What do you think Henry wants from us?"

I pondered the question, the shadows of our past casting long, dark shapes across my mind. "Control, maybe? Or revenge?" The words tasted bitter on my tongue. Henry had always been the type to wield power like a sword, cutting through the lives of those he deemed unworthy. I had hoped we could escape that part of our lives, but it seemed naïve now. "He never took well to being ignored. And we've done a good job of that since we got here."

Luke nodded, his expression grave. "We underestimated him."

The acknowledgment hung heavy between us, a shared burden that we had carried for far too long. I didn't want to dwell on the implications of those words, but the truth gnawed at me. We had sought refuge in this remote cabin, thinking it could shield us from the storm of our past, but storms had a way of finding you, no matter how high the walls.

The generator sputtered again, an irritating cough that reminded me we were merely staving off the inevitable. I leaned forward, my eyes darting toward the window, half-expecting to see the outline of a figure approaching. The silence pressed in on me, every second stretching into an unbearable void.

"I wish I could just forget everything," I murmured, my voice barely above a whisper. "The fear, the memories... everything."

Luke paused in his pacing, turning to me with a thoughtful expression. "We can't erase the past, Jess. But we can shape our future. It's not over for us, not yet."

His words resonated deep within me, igniting a flicker of defiance I hadn't realized was still alive. Together, we could reclaim our narrative, wrestle it from the grip of those who sought to define us. I wanted to believe that, and in that moment, I found the strength to stand.

As the night deepened, I rose from my corner and joined Luke, our shoulders brushing as we faced the window together. The night was a thick curtain, hiding potential dangers, but also opportunities—opportunities to reclaim our lives. I could see the determination in Luke's eyes, the same fire that had drawn me to him in the first place.

"Let's not just wait for them to come to us," I said, my voice steady. "Let's take the fight to them."

A slow smile spread across his face, the kind that ignited something within me. "You're right. Let's make it so they don't know what hit them."

We began plotting our next move, the shadows around us fading in the wake of our renewed resolve. With each word exchanged, we laid the foundation for our escape from the clutches of fear. Luke gathered supplies, each item we collected becoming a symbol of our determination—flashlights, rope, even a couple of kitchen knives.

"Just in case," he added with a wry grin, and the gesture made me feel a surge of warmth.

The fire crackled in the background, providing a heartbeat to our plans. Outside, the wind howled like a distant warning, but we were no longer listening to its ominous tunes. We had forged our own soundtrack, a symphony of resilience.

With everything we needed within arm's reach, we positioned ourselves near the back door, ready to spring into action at a moment's notice. I felt the adrenaline coursing through my veins, heightening my senses, sharpening my focus. I glanced at Luke, and in that fleeting moment, we were two warriors preparing for battle, united by purpose and the unyielding desire for freedom.

Then, just as our plans crystallized, a sound broke the silence—an unmistakable crunch of snow beneath a boot, slicing through the thick air like a knife. I held my breath, my heart pounding like a war drum, as we exchanged a glance that spoke volumes. The time for waiting was over.

With a swift motion, Luke pulled the door slightly ajar, peering through the narrow opening. I felt my breath catch in my throat, the anticipation coiling within me as we braced ourselves for whatever lay beyond.

The night was dark and foreboding, but so was our resolve. Whatever awaited us outside that door, we would face it together. No longer would we be prisoners of our past; we were ready to step into the unknown, hand in hand, with courage lighting our way.

Chapter 22: A Deal with the Devil

The cabin stood behind us, a mere silhouette against the dawn sky, its rustic charm giving way to a tension that seemed to vibrate through the morning mist. The air was thick with the scent of pine and damp earth, the sun struggling to break free from the clutches of lingering fog. My fingers brushed against the cool wood of the cabin's porch railing, grounding me even as the tumult inside me surged. Luke, ever the protector, loomed in front of me like a human shield, his eyes fixed on the figure emerging from the shadows of the woods.

Henry's silhouette was that of a man hardened by time and secrets, the contours of his face sharpened by the flickering light filtering through the branches. As I stepped forward, I could feel Luke's unease radiating off him in palpable waves. "Please, don't," he pleaded, his voice low, meant only for my ears. But I had come too far, had faced too much, to retreat now. This confrontation felt like a necessary pilgrimage to the truth, and I could no longer ignore the pull of curiosity that led me closer to the fire.

"I just want to talk," Henry repeated, his voice a gravelly echo that mixed with the morning chorus of birds awakening in the trees. There was a weariness in his tone, a hint of desperation that drew me in, despite the caution screaming at me from every corner of my mind. He lowered his hands, and I caught a glimpse of the faint scars crisscrossing his palms, remnants of battles long past. The urge to understand flickered within me, bright and unrelenting.

"Talk about what?" I found my voice, trembling yet firm, cutting through the crisp air like a shard of ice. "What could you possibly have to say that's worth listening to?"

Henry sighed, the sound heavy with years of regret and burden. "Your mother," he said, and just like that, he had me. I felt my heart stutter at the mention of her name, a familiar ache resurfacing as memories flashed—her laughter, her warmth, her whispered promises in the dark. "She made a deal, and it's time you understood the cost."

I stepped further, past the protective barrier of Luke, who remained behind me, a silent sentinel. "A deal?" The words tumbled out, laced with skepticism and a simmering anger. "What kind of deal?"

He took a step closer, and I caught a glimpse of his eyes—fierce and glinting with something that resembled pain. "The kind that binds you, binds your family. She thought she could outrun it, but she was wrong. The moment you were born, it became your burden too."

My chest tightened at the implications of his words. This man, this embodiment of secrets, stood at the precipice of my mother's hidden life, and here I was, teetering on the edge of something monumental. "What do you want from me?" I whispered, the reality settling over me like a shroud.

His gaze flickered between us, assessing. "I want what she promised. You have something of great value, and I'm here to collect."

I felt Luke's presence behind me shift, a restless energy as he stepped forward slightly, instinctively protective. "We're not giving you anything," he said, voice steady and firm, but I sensed the cracks beneath his bravado. He had always been my anchor, my constant in a world swirling with uncertainty.

But Henry merely shrugged, a casual gesture that belied the seriousness of the moment. "You misunderstand. I'm not asking. I'm warning you. If you don't comply, I'll take what's mine in a way that you won't appreciate." His words hung in the air, thick with threat and foreboding.

My heart raced as the weight of his implications bore down on me. "What do you mean by that?" I challenged, the adrenaline pushing me forward. The sunlight broke through the clouds then, illuminating the edges of the trees, and in that golden moment, I caught the faintest flicker of vulnerability in Henry's eyes.

"I mean your life will unravel," he replied, the gravity of his words chilling me to the bone. "The people you love will be pulled into this dark web, and you'll have no choice but to watch."

His words twisted like a knife, sharp and searing. I thought of my father, of Luke, of everything I had fought for in the wake of my mother's absence. The world I had built felt fragile, like spun glass, teetering on the edge of shattering. I couldn't let him do that to me; I wouldn't allow him to manipulate my fate.

"And if I refuse?" I asked, though I could hear the tremor in my voice betraying my bravado.

Henry's lips twisted into a smirk, unsettling and cold. "You might find out what true chaos looks like. But I'm here to offer you a way out, a chance to end this cycle of torment."

In that moment, I felt the weight of destiny pressing down, heavy and foreboding. It was as if the universe had conspired to bring me to this very point, where choice and consequence danced like shadows in the light of dawn. I could choose fear, retreat into the safety of ignorance, or I could confront the darkness head-on, the choice clawing at me with urgency.

The sun rose higher, spilling gold across the landscape, illuminating the path ahead—a path fraught with danger yet pulsing with the promise of clarity. With a deep breath, I gathered my resolve. "What do I need to do?" I asked, my voice steadying, as if I had finally found my footing in a world that threatened to pull me under.

The moment hung in the air like a fragile promise, charged with the electricity of unspoken threats and the weight of choices yet to be made. I met Henry's gaze, my heart drumming a frantic tempo against my ribs as I wrestled with the gravity of his words. The woods behind him seemed to sway, shadows dancing like specters waiting for a signal, a primal instinct whispering caution into my ear.

"What do you mean by 'end this cycle of torment'?" My voice cracked slightly, betraying the tumult within, yet I held my ground, rooted in the earth beneath my feet. The morning sun peeked through the branches, casting dappled light on the gravel path at our feet, illuminating the stark contrast between our fates and the choices laid before us.

Henry took a breath, and for a moment, I saw a flicker of vulnerability. "Your mother thought she could sever her ties to the past, but you can't just walk away from a deal like that. It comes back, and it demands payment." He leaned closer, his voice dropping to a conspiratorial whisper. "It's like a shadow, always lurking, always waiting."

Luke stepped forward again, fists clenched, an unyielding force beside me. "You're not scaring her, Henry. Whatever your twisted game is, it ends here." But I could see it in Luke's eyes—the flicker of fear, the worry that the darkness Henry spoke of was more real than either of us could fathom.

I turned to Luke, the warmth of his presence a comfort, yet I felt the pull of curiosity. "What does he want from me?" I asked, needing to understand the contours of this new reality, the landscape of threats unfurling like a map of an uncharted territory.

"Your mother's secret," Henry replied, his voice steady, a practiced calmness settling over him like a well-fitted cloak. "The key she buried deep in her past. She promised it to me, and now I need you to fulfill that promise."

The weight of his demand crashed over me like a wave, the implications unfurling in my mind. My mother had always been an enigma, a woman of many layers. The way she navigated her world seemed almost choreographed, as if she had rehearsed her life's performance for an audience that never truly existed. "What is this secret?" I asked, desperation lacing my voice. "What do you think I can give you?"

Henry's expression shifted, an unguarded moment that revealed his ambition wrapped in regret. "It's about the artifact—something powerful that could shift the balance of control." He paused, gauging my reaction, his eyes narrowing slightly. "Your mother hid it from me, believing she could protect you from the consequences. But now it's your turn to choose, to step into the legacy she left behind."

"What makes you think I have any idea what you're talking about?" I shot back, a surge of defiance igniting within me. "I'm not my mother. I don't know what she did or why she did it."

He took a step back, the shadows deepening around him, morphing into a cloak of mystery. "You have her spirit. The same fire that fueled her decisions burns within you. That's why I came to you, not just for the artifact but to help you understand your place in this web."

A shiver raced down my spine, the truth of his words resonating like a haunting melody. I had always felt the weight of my mother's legacy, a burden draped around my shoulders like a heavy quilt woven with unspoken stories. "And what happens if I refuse?"

"Then the shadow will consume everything you love." His voice dripped with a foreboding chill, and I could see the flicker of a cruel smile ghosting across his lips. "And you'll be left standing alone, watching the pieces of your life shatter."

A knot tightened in my stomach, dread pooling like lead in my veins. I glanced at Luke, whose eyes held a mixture of determination and concern. I could feel his silent plea for me to walk away, to reclaim the safety that lay just beyond the boundaries of this conversation. But as I stood there, heart pounding, the desire for answers clawed at my insides, demanding to be heard.

"I won't let you hurt anyone," I said, my voice stronger, bolstered by the conviction swelling in my chest. "I'll find a way to protect my loved ones from whatever darkness you're threatening us with."

Henry regarded me with a strange mix of admiration and annoyance, as if I were a puzzle he couldn't quite solve. "Protecting them might not be an option if you don't understand the full scope of what you're dealing with. Knowledge is power, and you're standing at the precipice of something monumental."

I took a deep breath, centering myself in the chaos swirling around us. "Then tell me what I need to do to make this right," I demanded, my voice rising in defiance against the uncertainty threatening to engulf me.

"Seek the artifact," he replied, his gaze sharpening. "It lies where the past converges with the future—where your mother once found refuge."

A flicker of recognition ignited within me. I thought of the old cabin my mother had always spoken about, a place tucked away from prying eyes, where memories hung like ghosts, waiting for someone brave enough to breathe life into them again. "The cabin," I murmured, realization dawning.

Henry nodded slowly, a satisfied smile creeping across his features. "You're clever. It's a start. But remember, this journey won't be easy. Shadows linger, and the deeper you delve, the more you risk losing."

With those words hanging ominously between us, I felt a resolve crystallize within. I was done living in fear, done allowing the past to dictate my present. The stakes had never been higher, and as the sunlight broke through the trees, illuminating the path forward, I knew I had to embrace my mother's legacy, no matter the cost.

"Then let's begin," I said, feeling the weight of determination settle over me like armor. "I won't shy away from this."

As I turned back to face the path that would lead me to my mother's truth, I felt Luke's hand find mine, a tether grounding me to the warmth of loyalty amidst the chill of uncertainty. Together, we stepped into the unknown, ready to face whatever lay ahead.

The woods around us held their breath as I faced Henry, the weight of his presence a tangible force that seemed to suck the warmth from the morning air. I could hear the distant rustle of leaves, the chirping of birds trying to reclaim their morning songs, but their melodies felt distant, almost trivial against the backdrop of the confrontation unfolding before me. Luke's protective stance radiated an energy that both comforted and constrained me, his unspoken worries clawing at my resolve.

"What do you need?" I found myself asking, my voice steadier than I felt. I wanted to sound bold, but beneath the surface, my pulse raced with a mix of determination and apprehension. Henry's eyes glinted with a knowing light, as if he held the key to a locked door in my mind that I had yet to discover.

"Your mother hid something valuable, something meant for me," he replied, his tone smooth but carrying the weight of a long-guarded truth. "It's time you understood the gravity of what's at stake."

As he spoke, the forest around us seemed to whisper secrets. I could almost feel the trees leaning in, their gnarled branches twisting like eavesdropping sentinels. My mind raced, drawing on fragments of childhood memories. My mother often spoke of shadows, of hidden things buried beneath layers of time and regret, yet she had always kept the specifics from me, her expressions veiling a world I had not been prepared to enter.

"What is it? What does it do?" I pressed, urgency suffusing my voice as I stepped forward, determined to break down the wall of mystery that had surrounded my mother for far too long.

Henry inhaled sharply, a flicker of something like nostalgia flashing across his features. "It's an artifact, an object steeped in power. It could tip the scales of balance in ways you can't yet comprehend." He leaned closer, his breath mingling with the crisp morning air. "But it's not just a thing; it's a piece of your legacy, and now it's entwined with your fate."

"Entwined?" The word felt heavy, laden with implications that sent a shiver up my spine. "You think I'm just going to hand over something I know nothing about?" The anger rose within me, hot and bright, against the backdrop of his calm demeanor. "You may be intimidating, but I'm not a pawn in your game."

He chuckled, a low rumble that resonated through the air. "No, you're not a pawn. You're a player, whether you like it or not." He stepped back, allowing the sun to illuminate his figure more clearly, and I could see the lines of a life lived in pursuit of shadows etched across his face. "Your mother thought she could shield you from this world, but it's like trying to contain a wildfire with a bucket of water. It only grows larger."

The metaphor sank in, painting vivid images in my mind of flames dancing, consuming everything in their path. Fear clutched at my heart, but beneath it lay a current of anger. I was done being fearful. "So, what do you want from me?" I demanded, crossing my arms defiantly. "What do I need to do to end this?"

Henry's smile widened, revealing a glimmer of teeth that felt more predatory than friendly. "You need to find the artifact. It lies within a sanctuary of memories—your mother's sanctuary. The place where she once sought refuge when the shadows of her past closed in."

"I have no idea what you're talking about," I replied, frustration bubbling to the surface. "You think I'm going to blindly search for something that might not even exist?"

"Perhaps you should consider the possibility that you already know its location," he replied, his voice a soft, persuasive whisper. "The cabin she would often visit, tucked away from prying eyes, filled with the echoes of her past."

The realization struck me like a bolt of lightning. Memories flickered back—the stories she told of her childhood, of a small cabin near the lake, hidden by the forest's embrace. "The cabin," I breathed, the words spilling out like an incantation. "But I thought it was just a story."

"It was her refuge, a sanctuary from the chaos," he said, his gaze piercing through me as if he could see the thoughts swirling in my mind. "She sought to protect you from the very darkness she had danced with. It's time for you to reclaim that which she hid."

"No," I said, shaking my head. "You want me to dredge up painful memories and unearth shadows? That's not happening."

Luke's hand tightened around mine, a silent reminder that I was not alone in this. "We don't have to do this," he whispered. "We can leave right now."

But something deep within urged me to stay, to face this challenge. The truth of my mother's past was a tangled web, and I was the only one who could unravel it. "What if I find this artifact?" I challenged Henry, my heart pounding with equal parts fear and determination. "What happens then?"

Henry's expression shifted, a glimmer of something resembling hope flickering in his eyes. "Then you have the power to rewrite your narrative, to forge a new path, free from the chains of your mother's decisions."

His words hung in the air, heavy with the promise of liberation. Yet, the threat that lingered like smoke in the background was a constant reminder that my choices came with consequences. I could sense the struggle within myself, the tug-of-war between the desire to protect my loved ones and the growing curiosity about the depths of my heritage.

"I'll find it," I declared, the decision cementing in my mind like the unyielding roots of the trees surrounding us. "But you'll leave my family alone. I won't allow you to threaten them."

Henry regarded me, a flash of admiration lighting his features. "Very well. You have your terms. But remember, the shadows never sleep."

With a nod, I turned to Luke, who was watching me with a mixture of concern and pride. Together, we moved away from the clearing, back toward the cabin, the weight of our pact settling heavily on our shoulders. As we walked, I felt the woods close in around us, a sanctuary holding secrets that would soon be unearthed.

Arriving at the cabin, I pushed the door open, and the familiar scent of aged wood and memories enveloped me like an embrace. Dust danced in the beams of light filtering through the windows, and I felt the ghosts of my past urging me forward. I had made my choice. I would face whatever shadows lay ahead, guided by the strength of my resolve and the flickering light of hope that still burned within.

As I stepped deeper into the heart of the cabin, I knew this was only the beginning. The journey ahead would be fraught with challenges, but I was no longer just a passive observer. I was a participant in my own story, ready to reclaim my legacy, and finally understand the truth that had long been hidden in the shadows.

Chapter 23: The Hidden Map

A gust of wind swept through the kitchen, sending a shiver down my spine and rustling the old curtains that hung limply by the window. I stood at the table, the flickering light from the overhead bulb casting a warm glow over the map, but the darkness outside felt almost alive, pressing against the house as if it wanted in. The scent of the jasmine my mother used to grow wafted through the air, mingling with the sharp, acrid smell of fear that lingered around us like an unwelcome guest. Luke leaned over the table, his brow furrowed in concentration, tracing the faded lines with his finger, but it was hard to focus on the map when my thoughts kept darting back to Henry.

"Can you believe he just left this?" Luke muttered, his voice low and edged with disbelief. "What does he think this is, a treasure hunt?" His sarcasm hung in the air, thick as the tension that wrapped itself around us.

I didn't answer immediately, caught in a swirl of emotions that tangled in my chest. My mother had been a quiet woman, full of secrets wrapped in layers of soft laughter and gentle smiles. It had always felt like she was protecting me from something, though I could never pinpoint what. Now, as I stood there with Luke, the implications of Henry's visit—his threats, the map, the hidden past—loomed larger than life. I felt like an explorer uncovering buried treasure, yet every discovery sent an icy finger of dread tracing its way down my spine.

"Look here," Luke said, breaking me from my thoughts. His finger landed on a series of jagged lines that resembled mountains. "These contours seem to match the terrain of that town your mom grew up in. It's got to mean something."

I squinted at the paper, the ink a washed-out sepia against the yellowing parchment. It felt ancient, like it had been waiting patiently for decades for someone to breathe life back into it. "It has to be Willow Creek," I whispered, the name tasting foreign on my tongue. It was a place that existed only in stories my mother told me—of creaky wooden porches and fields that stretched on forever, a childhood painted in soft pastels and whispers of nostalgia.

"Willow Creek," Luke repeated, letting the name roll off his tongue as if tasting the sweetness of honey, something so distant yet so close. "We need to get there. Whatever Henry is after, it's likely tied to your mother and that town. We can't just sit here."

As the reality of our mission began to settle in, I felt an inexplicable thrill rush through me, mingling with my fear. It was as if the very essence of adventure had taken hold of my spirit. I imagined driving down winding country roads, the scent of sun-warmed earth filling the car, laughter spilling from our lips as we navigated through the heart of America. But that vision was soon overshadowed by the reminder of Henry, a man whose presence felt like a storm cloud gathering at the edge of a clear blue sky.

"What if he follows us?" I asked, biting my lip, my thoughts spiraling again into anxiety.

Luke straightened, his blue eyes piercing through the dim light. "Then we'll deal with him. We can't let him stop us from finding out what's at Willow Creek." His confidence was infectious, pulling me closer to the edge of courage. It reminded me of those childhood days when I would climb to the highest tree in our backyard, daring myself to jump into the unknown.

I nodded, but the weight of uncertainty lingered. Luke's resolve helped to fortify my own, yet doubts still flickered in the recesses of my mind. I turned my gaze back to the map, studying the way the ink had bled into the paper, as if the very heart of the map had been drawn with emotions instead of mere lines. My fingers traced the contours, each mark a potential clue to unlocking my mother's past and the treasure it held.

The late afternoon sun dipped low, casting a golden hue through the kitchen window, the shadows dancing across the walls as the light waned. With the map laid before us, it was as if time had collapsed around us, allowing no space for hesitation. Every tick of the clock felt like a countdown, pushing us toward an uncertain future where secrets would be unearthed and fears confronted.

"Let's go tonight," I declared, surprising even myself with the firmness of my voice. "We can drive through the night. The sooner we get there, the sooner we'll find out what this means."

Luke grinned, a smile that ignited something deep inside me—a flicker of hope intertwined with an exhilarating thrill. We began gathering supplies: flashlights, snacks, a map of the surrounding roads—tools for our journey into the unknown. My heart raced with anticipation as we loaded the car, the anticipation crackling in the air like static electricity before a storm.

As we pulled away from the familiar warmth of home, the world outside morphed into a tapestry of darkness, punctuated by the occasional glow of streetlights and the distant shimmer of stars. The roads twisted and turned, each curve a potential fork in our journey, each mile a step closer to Willow Creek and the truth that awaited us. I leaned back against the cool leather seat, letting the rhythmic hum of the tires against asphalt lull me into a contemplative state.

"You okay?" Luke asked, glancing over at me, concern etched on his features.

I took a deep breath, inhaling the scent of leather mixed with the lingering smell of the jasmine that had clung to my clothes. "Yeah," I replied, allowing a small smile to form. "I just... I can't shake the feeling that we're being watched."

"Then let's find whatever it is that's hiding in the shadows," he said, his determination igniting a spark within me. "We'll face it together."

With those words, I felt the weight of the world shift slightly, as if the road ahead held not just danger, but a promise of revelations and perhaps a path to healing.

The miles stretched out like a dark ribbon unfurling beneath us, the landscape shifting from urban sprawl to vast open fields, dotted with the occasional flicker of farmhouse lights breaking the horizon. The car hummed steadily, a comforting sound that masked the tension woven into the fabric of the night. I found myself lost in thought, tracing the lines of the map in my mind, envisioning what lay ahead—Willow Creek, a name so ordinary yet wrapped in the extraordinary weight of my mother's secrets.

"Do you think your mom ever talked about this place?" Luke broke the silence, his voice slicing through my reverie.

I turned to him, caught off guard by the question. My mother's stories were like fireflies flitting in and out of focus—vivid, yet elusive. "Only once or twice," I admitted. "She spoke about the river that ran behind her house, how it sparkled in the sun, and the massive oak tree she used to climb. But the details were always vague, like she was afraid to let too much slip."

Luke nodded thoughtfully, his eyes fixed on the road, the dim light from the dashboard casting shadows across his handsome face. "Maybe she wanted to keep it safe, to protect it from whatever happened after."

The unspoken heaviness of that thought lingered in the air between us, and I could almost feel the weight of my mother's unvoiced fears pressing against my chest. It wasn't just the journey ahead that filled me with apprehension; it was the mystery of my mother herself, the woman I had thought I knew. What had she hidden? What had she faced? As I stared out at the passing scenery, the darkness thickened, swallowing the stars, but in my mind, I clung to the idea of that river, that tree—a world that felt both foreign and achingly familiar.

As dawn broke, the horizon erupted in shades of pink and gold, a soft promise of renewal. We pulled into a small diner just outside Willow Creek, the kind that seemed to have sprung straight from a postcard. The neon sign flickered, welcoming us with a warm, inviting glow that stood in stark contrast to the biting chill of early morning. The air inside smelled of fresh coffee and sizzling bacon, grounding me in the moment, and I couldn't help but smile as I watched the waitress shuffle between tables, her laughter infectious.

"Let's fuel up before we dive into this mystery," Luke said, his voice brightening as he slid into a booth. I followed suit, feeling a mixture of nerves and anticipation swirl within me. We were about to unearth pieces of my mother's life, her past, and perhaps even confront the very ghosts that had haunted her.

As we settled in, I scanned the walls adorned with photographs of the town's history—grainy black-and-white images of bustling streets, smiling families, and faded storefronts. My fingers danced over the map in my pocket, a silent promise to uncover the truth hidden within its inked lines. The waitress approached, her smile warm and genuine, and I ordered a stack of pancakes while Luke opted for a hearty breakfast platter.

"Where are you two headed?" she asked, pouring steaming coffee into our cups. Her curiosity sparked a feeling of comfort, a sense of belonging that washed over me.

"Just passing through," Luke replied casually, but I could feel the excitement thrumming beneath his calm exterior.

"Willow Creek has a charm of its own," she continued, wiping her hands on her apron. "Not much happens here, but folks around these parts hold on to their stories tight. It's a town built on secrets and memories."

My heart raced at her words, a thrill of recognition flooding my senses. "What do you mean by secrets?" I pressed, the question tumbling out before I could think better of it.

She leaned in, lowering her voice conspiratorially. "Oh, everyone knows about the old mill on the edge of town. Rumor has it that it was the heart of Willow Creek once, but it's been abandoned for years now. Some say it still holds treasures from the past. Others believe it's haunted."

Luke and I exchanged a glance, the unspoken connection solidifying the urgency of our mission. The old mill—it was another piece of the puzzle, another place that felt woven into the fabric of my mother's story.

As our plates arrived, I felt a surge of energy. Each bite was filled with the warmth of home-cooked comfort, but it was the buzz of anticipation that truly fueled me. We wrapped up our meal, leaving behind a few crumpled bills as a tip, and stepped outside, the sun now fully rising, casting a golden hue over the quiet streets.

Willow Creek spread before us like a canvas, the quaint houses lined with picket fences, the rich smell of earth mingling with blooming flowers. I felt as if I were stepping into a dream, the air alive with possibility and the haunting echoes of my mother's past.

"Where to first?" Luke asked, peering at the map I unfurled between us.

"The mill," I replied, my voice steady with determination. "It's time to confront whatever awaits us there."

We walked, side by side, the path beneath our feet crunching softly with gravel. As we approached the mill, its silhouette loomed against the backdrop of an azure sky, the once-proud structure now crumbling and draped in ivy like an aging actor refusing to leave the stage. The large wooden doors hung slightly ajar, creaking ominously in the gentle breeze as if inviting us into its depths.

"Are you ready?" Luke asked, his voice a whisper, reverberating against the silence surrounding us.

I nodded, my heart pounding like a drum, a blend of excitement and trepidation coursing through me. With each step, I felt a connection to the place, as if the very ground remembered my mother's footsteps. We crossed the threshold into the cool, dim interior, where dust motes danced in the slants of light breaking through the broken windows.

The air was thick with memories, and I could almost hear the laughter of children playing and the bustling energy of a town that had once thrived here. Every corner held a fragment of history, and as I inhaled the musty scent of wood and decay, I sensed we were on the cusp of unraveling the truths buried deep within these walls.

With a mix of anticipation and fear, we ventured further inside, driven by an unyielding need to uncover the hidden pieces of my mother's past—and perhaps, our own destinies intertwined in the shadows of Willow Creek.

The interior of the mill was a world frozen in time, each step reverberating with the whispers of its past. Dust motes floated lazily through the air, catching the weak light that filtered through cracked panes of glass, illuminating the wooden beams above us. The scent of damp earth mingled with the sweetness of nostalgia, invoking memories I didn't fully possess but felt deep within my bones. Every creak of the floorboards seemed to echo with the laughter of children who had once played here, their joy now replaced by silence, punctuated only by our tentative movements.

I glanced at Luke, his expression mirroring my own sense of wonderment and trepidation. We ventured deeper, navigating through remnants of machinery, now rusty and lifeless, yet still holding the charm of their bygone utility. My heart raced at the thought that my mother might have wandered these very floors, perhaps dreaming of escaping to places far beyond Willow Creek.

"This is it," I said, the words tumbling from my lips as if they were a declaration of independence from the past that had so long held me captive. "This is where the answers are."

The mill's vast open space began to narrow as we approached a wall that had long succumbed to decay. Here, the bricks were crumbling, and patches of ivy crept in like silent guardians, eager to reclaim their territory. I noticed a subtle indentation in the wall, a section that seemed different, almost purposeful in its disarray. The map's lines swirled in my mind, guiding my instincts.

"Help me with this," I murmured, gesturing to the wall. Luke stepped beside me, and together we pushed against the weathered surface. A cloud of dust erupted, obscuring our view momentarily. I held my breath, the anticipation crackling in the air like static electricity before a storm.

With a final shove, a piece of the wall gave way, revealing a small alcove tucked away from the world's scrutiny. I felt a rush of adrenaline as we stepped forward, curiosity propelling us into the shadows. Inside, the alcove was surprisingly dry, sheltered from the elements, and at its center rested a wooden chest, worn but sturdy, as if it had been waiting for us to arrive.

My fingers trembled as I approached it, each step weighted with the significance of what might be contained within. Luke stood behind me, a silent support, grounding me as I knelt before the chest, the air thick with the anticipation of discovery. The latch was tarnished but still functional; with a gentle tug, I opened it.

Inside, I found a trove of my mother's past: yellowing letters tied with a frayed ribbon, a collection of photographs that seemed to shimmer with life, and a delicate silver locket that sparkled faintly even in the dim light. Each item was a thread woven into the intricate tapestry of her history, and I could feel my heart swell with emotion as I carefully lifted each piece.

I held the locket up to the light, the surface cool against my skin. It bore the initials "M.E."—my mother's name and the mystery of a life that had been tucked away from me. With a shaky breath, I opened it, revealing a tiny photograph of a young woman with bright eyes and a radiant smile, the resemblance unmistakable. It was my mother, but the woman in the picture radiated a vibrancy I had never known in the quieter, more guarded version of her that I grew up with.

"Wow," Luke breathed, stepping closer. "Is that…?"

"It is," I whispered, my voice barely audible, the significance of the moment settling heavily around us. "This is my mother."

The letters beckoned to me next, each one a window into her life—a glimpse of her hopes, dreams, and the fears that had lingered just beneath the surface. I carefully unwrapped the ribbon, and as I read, each line poured forth her emotions like an overflowing river, rich and raw. She wrote of friendship, of love lost and found, and of the heartbreaking choice to leave this place behind, choosing safety over the shadows that lurked in her past.

As I absorbed the words, I felt an unbreakable bond forming between us, even across the years and through the distance she had chosen. The chest became a time capsule of her life, each item pulsating with the stories I had never heard, leaving me awash in both grief and gratitude for the woman she had been.

"Do you think this is what Henry was looking for?" Luke asked, his voice cutting through my reverie, bringing me back to the present.

I paused, considering. "It has to be. He wouldn't have left this behind if it weren't important to him." My heart raced at the thought that whatever power Henry sought was tied to these treasures. My mind raced, swirling with possibilities, but one thing was clear: we had to protect this legacy. Whatever he intended to do with this knowledge, we wouldn't allow it.

"Let's take everything," I said resolutely, gathering the letters and photographs with a fierce determination. "We need to get out of here and figure out our next steps."

As we made our way back through the mill, I felt lighter, empowered by the connection to my mother that I had forged within those dusty walls. Yet, the shadows remained, a constant reminder of Henry's threat, lurking at the fringes of our newfound understanding.

Outside, the sun hung high, casting long shadows as we loaded the treasures into the trunk of the car. I felt a mix of exhilaration and dread. This place had been a sanctuary of memories, yet I knew we weren't safe. My pulse quickened as I glanced back at the mill; its weathered facade, once inviting, now felt ominous, as if it bore witness to something dark and hidden.

"We should head to the diner and figure out a plan," Luke suggested, his tone urgent but steady.

I nodded, sliding into the passenger seat, clutching the letters tightly against my chest, as if they were the key to unlocking not just my mother's past, but my own future. With the engine's rumble, we pulled away from the mill, the town fading behind us. But the specter of Henry lingered like a dark cloud, and I knew we had to face him.

Driving through Willow Creek felt different now, the familiar streets transformed by the weight of my discoveries. The world outside the car window buzzed with life, yet all I could hear was the pounding of my heart and the echo of my mother's voice whispering through the pages of the letters. She had fought for her secrets, and now it was my turn to safeguard her legacy.

Arriving at the diner, I stepped inside, and the familiar smell of coffee washed over me, mingling with the fragrance of freshly baked pies. The waitress who had greeted us earlier offered a smile, but this time, I felt a different energy in the air, a sense of urgency that drew me forward. I slid into a booth, the leather warm against my skin, and spread out the letters on the table. Luke sat across from me, his expression focused, eyes scanning the words as if they held the key to unraveling the danger that Henry posed.

"Let's see what we can find," I said, my voice steadying. "If there's anything in here that can help us understand why Henry wants these so badly, we need to know."

As we began to decipher the stories woven into the letters, the essence of my mother came alive, each word a brushstroke on the canvas of her past, revealing not just her life, but the resilience and strength that had defined her. The shadows of the mill lingered in my mind, but the warmth of her spirit infused me with determination.

"We'll figure this out," Luke said softly, leaning closer, his confidence a balm to my racing thoughts. "Together."

I looked up, and for the first time since embarking on this journey, I felt hope bubbling within me, igniting a fierce resolve. Together, we would confront Henry, unearth the truth, and ultimately discover who my mother had truly been—a woman not defined by her secrets, but by her bravery in the face of them. And with that, we would reclaim the story of her life, turning the pages to a new chapter where the shadows could no longer hold sway.

Chapter 24: The Road to Nowhere

The sun's feeble light crept over the horizon, casting an ethereal glow upon the blanket of snow that enveloped the world outside our window. It was a silent farewell to the warm, woodsy cabin we had shared, a place where laughter and quiet moments had intertwined seamlessly, now left behind like a forgotten dream. Luke, with his furrowed brow and tightly clenched jaw, seemed more a statue than a man, fixed in a trance of concentration, the steady thrum of the engine a mere whisper against the stillness that hung in the air.

The landscape outside morphed into a winter wonderland, an unyielding white canvas speckled with the dark silhouettes of pines standing guard over our path. I leaned closer to the window, the cold glass numbing my fingertips as I traced the shapes of distant peaks dusted with fresh powder. Each mountain seemed to tell a story, tales of those who had dared to traverse their rugged terrain, now lost to time. My heart raced with a mix of trepidation and thrill—were we destined to be mere footnotes in a greater saga, or would we carve our own legend from the same unyielding spirit that had shaped this land?

I could sense Luke's tension vibrating through the vehicle, like a tightly strung bow ready to snap. His eyes, once vibrant with the warmth of adventure, now held the weight of a thousand unspoken thoughts. I wondered what haunted him so deeply. Was it Henry's relentless pursuit, or perhaps the burden of our quest? The map nestled in the glove compartment seemed to pulse with a life of its own, a siren call luring us deeper into the wilderness and further away from safety.

"Are you okay?" I ventured, my voice a gentle ripple in the silence. He flicked his gaze towards me, an ocean of emotion swirling in those stormy depths.

"I'm fine," he replied, though the way he clenched his teeth belied his words. "Just... thinking."

"About Henry?" I asked, carefully threading my own anxiety into the open space between us.

"More about what we'll find." The tension in his voice mirrored the tightness in my chest. The mysteries surrounding the map had begun to weave themselves into the fabric of our lives, a tangled thread of fate binding us to the unknown.

As we drove, the trees blurred past like ghosts, shadows flitting in and out of view, their presence both comforting and foreboding. It felt like we were entering a world untouched by time, each bend in the road leading us deeper into a realm where echoes of the past whispered secrets only the mountains could comprehend. I allowed myself a moment of quiet reflection, the serene beauty surrounding us offering a temporary reprieve from the storm brewing in our minds.

The sun rose higher, painting the sky in hues of lavender and gold, a palette so enchanting that it momentarily distracted me from the gravity of our mission. But with each passing mile, the landscape shifted, becoming harsher and more desolate. I could almost hear the echoes of our own doubts reverberating against the towering cliffs, a reminder of the perilous path we had chosen.

Suddenly, Luke's voice cut through the silence like a knife. "You remember the first time we saw this place?"

I smiled at the memory, warmth flooding through me despite the chill in the air. "How could I forget? You nearly crashed the truck when you saw that moose."

His laughter broke the tension, a bright spark igniting the dim cabin. "That was not my finest moment, I'll admit."

It felt like an eternity since we had shared such moments, where joy bloomed effortlessly between us. Yet, as quickly as it came, the laughter faded, swallowed by the reality we faced. The seriousness of our mission lay heavily upon us like a shroud, suffocating the lightness we had just momentarily reclaimed.

The road twisted ahead, flanked by sheer cliffs on one side and yawning chasms on the other. My fingers fidgeted nervously with the fabric of my jacket, a tangible reminder of the uncertainty that wrapped around us. A gust of wind howled through the mountains, carrying with it a chilling sense of foreboding that made the hairs on the back of my neck stand on end.

"Do you think we're doing the right thing?" I asked, breaking the silence once more, my voice quaking slightly.

He glanced at me, his expression unreadable. "We have to find out what this map leads to. There's too much at stake."

His resolve was admirable, but I could feel the tremors of doubt creeping in. We were not just chasing shadows anymore; we were seeking answers that could change everything we thought we knew about our lives, each other, and the haunting specter of Henry looming in the distance.

The mountains loomed ever closer, their jagged edges stark against the brightening sky, as though they were daring us to approach. A sense of inevitability washed over me, an understanding that the choices we had made could not be undone, that we were on a collision course with our destinies. The weight of the map felt heavier in my heart, not just a piece of paper, but a tether to all that was uncertain, dangerous, and tantalizingly out of reach.

As the miles unfolded beneath us, a new determination took root within me, a fierce longing to confront whatever lay ahead. Together, we would unravel the threads of our lives intertwined with this map, forging a path through the snow and uncertainty toward whatever awaited us. The road was long, and the journey was fraught with peril, but the promise of discovery was worth every heartbeat. I glanced at Luke, ready to face whatever lay ahead, my heart beating in time with the engine's rhythmic pulse, a reminder that we were alive and very much in this together.

The road undulated like a frozen serpent, twisting and curling through the majestic peaks that towered above us, their granite faces glistening under the cold morning sun. The silence was profound, punctuated only by the crunch of snow beneath the tires and the distant whisper of the wind threading through the trees. Each bend in the road felt like a new revelation, an unveiling of secrets hidden in the folds of the landscape. I stole glances at Luke, his profile carved sharply against the soft glow of the dashboard lights, and wondered what battles raged in his mind.

"Do you think Henry knows where we are?" I ventured, breaking the quietude that had settled like a thick fog. The question lingered in the air, heavy and unyielding.

"Knowing him, he probably has a good idea," Luke replied, his voice low and measured, a stark contrast to the churning turmoil within me. The thought sent a shiver down my spine. Henry was a specter, lurking at the edges of our reality, a constant reminder that we were not alone in this vast expanse of wilderness.

I turned my gaze back to the map, its edges crinkled from use, the ink slightly faded but still legible. I traced the winding line that snaked across the paper, leading to a point that seemed both tantalizing and ominous. My fingers itched to unfold the layers of mystery contained within its folds, but each glance only heightened my unease. The map was more than a mere guide; it was a symbol of our reckless pursuit of answers in a world shrouded in uncertainty.

As we ventured deeper into the mountains, the scenery shifted subtly, the trees growing denser, their limbs heavy with snow. The air thickened with the scent of pine, earthy and alive, a contrast to the chilling reality of our journey. I inhaled deeply, hoping to absorb some of that vitality, but it felt fleeting, slipping through my fingers like grains of sand.

"We need to stop soon," I said, the uneasiness of the road pressing against my ribcage. "I could use a break."

"Good idea," he said, relief washing over his features. He maneuvered the vehicle to the side of the road, where a small clearing opened up, framed by towering pines that swayed gently in the wind. As I stepped outside, the cold air enveloped me, invigorating and biting, and I took a moment to appreciate the wild beauty surrounding us. The mountains loomed like ancient guardians, their majesty both comforting and foreboding.

I brushed the snow from a fallen log and sat down, feeling the coolness seep through my jeans. Luke joined me, the crunch of snow under his boots echoing in the stillness. We sat side by side, the silence stretching comfortably, broken only by the occasional rustle of the trees. I watched as a hawk soared overhead, its wings outstretched against the azure sky, a fleeting symbol of freedom that seemed to mock our own entrapment in this quest.

"What do you think is waiting for us at the end of this?" I mused, allowing the question to linger in the crisp air.

"Whatever it is, I hope it's worth it," he replied, his eyes scanning the horizon, as though searching for answers in the vast expanse of blue. "This feels bigger than us, like we're part of something we don't fully understand."

His words resonated within me, echoing the tangled thoughts I could barely articulate. We were two souls, bound by fate, hurtling toward an uncertain future, propelled by a force neither of us could comprehend. The air felt charged, almost electric, as if the very universe conspired to weave our destinies into the fabric of something greater.

"Do you think we'll ever escape Henry's grasp?" I asked, the name slipping from my lips like a curse.

Luke turned to me, his expression serious. "We have to. We can't let him control us. This journey is about reclaiming our lives, our choices."

I nodded, though the weight of his words lingered, a reminder of the darkness that hung over us. As we sat in companionable silence, I allowed the stillness to wash over me, the mountains standing witness to our resolve. In that moment, I realized how deeply intertwined our fates had become, like the roots of the ancient trees surrounding us, firmly planted yet reaching for the sky.

Eventually, I broke the silence again, my voice soft yet determined. "No matter what happens, I believe in us. We'll find a way to beat him."

Luke met my gaze, and in his eyes, I saw a flicker of hope, a shared determination igniting between us. "Together," he affirmed, and the simplicity of that word wrapped around me like a warm blanket against the cold.

After a brief respite, we climbed back into the truck, the engine humming to life, and continued down the winding road. Each mile brought us closer to the unknown, and I found comfort in the rhythm of our shared purpose. The map felt less like a burden and more like a guiding star, illuminating the path ahead, even if the destination remained shrouded in mystery.

The terrain began to change again, with sweeping valleys giving way to jagged cliffs, and soon, the outline of a small town emerged in the distance. The buildings were quaint, nestled against the mountains like colorful gems scattered among the boulders. I felt a flicker of excitement at the prospect of civilization, a reminder that we weren't alone in this vast wilderness.

"Let's stop and grab some supplies," I suggested, my spirits lifting at the thought of warm coffee and a few familiar comforts.

As we entered the town, the air shifted, imbued with the scent of woodsmoke and fresh bread. The streets were lined with charming shops, their windows adorned with twinkling lights that fought against the early dusk. I could see a small café tucked between two rustic storefronts, its warm glow inviting us in.

Luke parked the truck, and we stepped out into the crisp air, the bustle of the town swirling around us like a warm embrace. For a moment, I let go of our troubles, allowing the laughter of children playing in the snow and the cheerful chatter of townsfolk to wash over me. It felt good, fleetingly, to be a part of something so ordinary and alive.

We entered the café, the warmth wrapping around us like a hug, instantly banishing the chill from our bones. The smell of fresh coffee mingled with the scent of baked goods, a heady mix that sent my senses into overdrive. We placed our order, and as we waited, I took in the eclectic decor—a mixture of rustic charm and modern flair, with photographs of the town's history lining the walls. Each image seemed to tell a story, whispering of lives lived and dreams chased against the backdrop of these unforgiving mountains.

As we settled into a cozy corner, I felt a sense of peace settle over me, a reminder that amid the chaos and uncertainty, there were still moments of beauty and connection. The chatter around us faded into a comforting hum, and I found myself leaning closer to Luke, our fingers brushing against each other, a quiet acknowledgment of the bond that had been forged through this tumultuous journey.

In that small café, with the world outside fading away, I allowed myself to dream of what lay ahead, the uncertainty transforming into a tapestry of possibilities woven with threads of hope, courage, and an unwavering belief that together, we could face whatever awaited us on the road ahead.

As the last of the warmth from the café clung to us like a lingering hug, we stepped back into the biting chill of the outside world. The air had an invigorating sharpness that cleared the cobwebs of doubt lingering in my mind. Luke and I exchanged glances, a silent agreement passing between us, a mutual understanding that whatever lay ahead, we would face it together. The truck sat waiting, sturdy and reliable, a faithful steed in this rugged landscape.

I slid into the passenger seat, the familiar scent of leather and pine enveloping me. The map lay like a secret waiting to be revealed in the glove compartment, a tangible representation of our quest. I couldn't shake the feeling that it was more than a guide; it felt like a promise, a pathway to something transformative. Luke started the engine, the roar breaking the silence and propelling us back into the wilderness.

As we wound our way through the narrow streets of the town, I took in the charming facades of the buildings, their rustic wood siding painted in faded pastels, each telling a story of generations past. Small, twinkling lights draped over porches lent an air of magic to the evening, and I found myself wishing for a moment longer in this quaint haven, a sanctuary from the uncertainty that awaited us on the road. But destiny had other plans, and as the mountains loomed larger in our rearview mirror, I felt the weight of the map pressing against my conscience.

The road turned once more, the mountains now a backdrop to our thoughts, and I let my mind wander to the many possibilities that lay ahead. Luke's focus remained steadfast, his grip on the steering wheel fierce, and the tension radiating from him was palpable. He was a man on a mission, propelled by a sense of urgency I could hardly grasp. I leaned back, studying the contours of his face, the way his jawline tightened with each mile. How had we ended up here? Two people on the brink of unraveling a mystery that could either bind us together or tear us apart.

"Do you ever think about what happens after this?" I asked, my voice softer than I intended, almost lost amidst the hum of the tires against the road.

256

"What do you mean?" he replied, glancing at me briefly before returning his gaze to the treacherous path ahead.

"I mean, if we find what we're looking for... will it be worth it? Will we still be us?"

His eyes flickered with surprise, as if my words had pried open a door he had been reluctant to approach. "I guess I've been too focused on the end goal. I haven't really considered what comes after."

"Maybe we should," I said, my heart racing with the weight of the question. "What if we're different people once we reach the end? What if it changes everything?"

He sighed, the sound a heavy release of breath. "Change is inevitable. But what matters is how we adapt, how we choose to move forward."

I nodded, feeling the sincerity in his words, yet the uncertainty lingered like fog in my mind. Our future felt like a sprawling landscape before us, full of forks in the road and uncharted territories. I closed my eyes for a moment, imagining the life waiting beyond this quest—a life where the shadows of Henry and the map no longer haunted us.

As we ventured further into the mountains, the landscape transformed dramatically. The towering pines gave way to rugged cliffs, and the air grew colder, laced with the scent of impending snow. Each turn of the road revealed breathtaking vistas, sweeping valleys dotted with glistening rivers that carved their paths through the wilderness. I felt an exhilarating rush at the sight, an appreciation for the beauty surrounding us, even as we were driven by darker motives.

The tension in the air thickened, charged with unspoken fears and hopes, and I glanced at Luke, who appeared lost in thought. "What do you think Henry really wants?" I asked, probing deeper into the shadows that lingered between us.

He hesitated, the lines of his face taut. "Power, control... whatever he thinks he can gain from this map. It's never been about the treasure; it's about what it represents to him."

I felt a shiver run down my spine. The notion that our journey might be a pawn in someone else's game was unsettling. Yet, somewhere within me, I recognized that we were not merely victims of Henry's ambition. We were the architects of our own fate, capable of steering our lives in a direction of our choosing.

As the sun began to dip below the jagged peaks, the world around us transformed into a canvas of oranges and purples, painting the sky with strokes of fire. I felt a yearning to capture this moment, to hold onto the beauty even as the darkness crept in. "Let's stop here," I suggested, my finger pointing toward a wide-open overlook where the mountains fell away into the valley below.

Luke obliged, parking the truck at the edge of a precipice that offered an unfiltered view of the stunning landscape. We stepped outside, the cold biting at our cheeks as we stood side by side, absorbing the majesty of nature unfurling before us. The silence was profound, wrapping us in a cocoon of tranquility amidst the chaos that lay ahead.

"This is incredible," I murmured, my breath clouding in the crisp air.

"Yeah," Luke agreed, his eyes trained on the horizon. "It's hard to believe we're really here."

As twilight descended, the stars began to twinkle against the deepening blue, a celestial map unfolding above us. In that moment, everything felt possible. The challenges that loomed over us shrank in the face of such beauty, reminding me of the resilience that lived within both of us.

"Whatever happens next, we'll find a way through it," I declared, my voice steady, grounded in the strength we had nurtured together.

Luke turned to me, his expression softening. "You're right. We're in this together, no matter what."

In the heart of the mountains, beneath the vast expanse of the universe, I felt a sense of belonging, a fierce connection that anchored me to him and to the journey we were undertaking. The fears that had threatened to consume me faded into the background, overshadowed by the light of hope and shared purpose.

As we made our way back to the truck, I sensed the impending challenges, the storm brewing on the horizon, but it no longer felt insurmountable. Together, we would unravel the secrets that awaited us, forge our own destiny, and emerge from the shadows stronger than before. The map was not merely a pathway; it was a catalyst for transformation, a journey that would lead us to the truth about ourselves and each other.

With renewed determination, we climbed back into the warmth of the truck, ready to confront whatever awaited us on this unpredictable road. The map now felt like an extension of our shared story, one we would navigate together, step by step, mile by mile, as we ventured into the great unknown, hearts aligned and spirits unyielding.

Chapter 25: Ghosts of the Past

The house groaned under the weight of time, each creak of the floorboards echoing through the stillness like whispers of forgotten memories. Dust motes danced in the dim light filtering through the grimy windows, swirling in patterns that felt almost deliberate, as if they were guiding us deeper into the secrets this place harbored. I could almost hear the laughter of children long gone, their voices weaving through the air, blending with the faint rustle of leaves outside, a reminder that life once thrived here amidst the decay.

The scent of mildew mingled with the stale remnants of old wood, creating a heady mix that evoked a strange sense of nostalgia. It was more than just an old farmhouse; it was a mausoleum for dreams unfulfilled, a sanctuary for the echoes of those who had come before. I inhaled deeply, trying to absorb the essence of this space, knowing it was the very fabric of my mother's past, woven together with threads of love and heartache.

As Luke and I ventured further, I felt the weight of history pressing against my chest. Each room we explored was like stepping into a time capsule, revealing glimpses of lives once lived. Faded wallpaper peeled away, revealing layers of stories hidden beneath. I brushed my fingers against the rough surface of a mantle adorned with long-burned candles, remnants of warmth that had once filled this place. I could almost picture my mother here, a young woman with dreams in her eyes, laughing as she lit candles for special occasions, her joy illuminating every corner.

"Can you feel it?" Luke's voice broke through my reverie, low and reverent. He stood in the doorway of what I assumed was the living room, his silhouette framed by the dim light spilling in from the window. There was a certain vulnerability in his gaze, as if he, too, was touched by the weight of this house. I nodded, unable to articulate the mix of emotions swirling within me—curiosity, dread, and an inexplicable longing for something just out of reach.

We climbed the narrow staircase, its steps worn smooth by generations of footsteps. The air grew cooler as we ascended, the light dimming, and I felt a shiver run down my spine. Reaching the attic, we were greeted by the scent of aged wood and memories buried under layers of dust. I took a cautious step forward, my heart racing with anticipation, and that's when I spotted it—a small, weathered box nestled beneath the floorboards, as if it had been waiting for someone to unearth it.

"Do you think it's what we're looking for?" Luke asked, his voice barely above a whisper. I could see the hope flickering in his eyes, mingling with the unease that had settled between us like an unwelcome guest. I knelt beside the box, heart pounding in my chest, and lifted it gingerly from its resting place. It felt heavy in my hands, filled with the weight of untold stories.

With trembling fingers, I pried it open, the lid protesting with a low creak that echoed through the attic. Inside lay a collection of letters, their edges yellowed with age, and photographs, some faded to a ghostly blur. A small key glimmered in the dim light, its presence both intriguing and ominous. As I sifted through the contents, my breath hitched at the sight of my mother's familiar handwriting, each loop and swirl resonating with memories of late-night conversations and shared secrets.

The letters were addressed to Henry, a name that sent a shiver through me, stirring something deep within my memory. I had heard whispers of him in my childhood—fragments of conversations between my mother and her friends, words laced with both affection and sorrow. I read through the first letter, my heart racing as I immersed myself in her thoughts, her dreams, and the unfulfilled promises that lingered like a bitter aftertaste.

My mother wrote of love, of a future that had slipped through her fingers like sand. She spoke of laughter shared under starlit skies and the gentle caress of warm summer nights. Yet, beneath the romance, there was an undercurrent of loss—of decisions made and paths not taken. Each word felt like a thread pulling me closer to her, unraveling the mystery of the woman I had always yearned to understand.

"Julia," Luke's voice broke the silence again, softer this time, almost reverent. I glanced up, meeting his gaze, and found him watching me with a mix of concern and curiosity. "Are you okay?"

I nodded, though I wasn't sure if it was the truth. The words on the page resonated within me, creating a chorus of emotions that I struggled to navigate. This was my mother's story, and yet it felt like a part of my own—a narrative woven into the very fabric of who I was. As I turned the pages, I caught glimpses of a life I never fully grasped, moments crystallized in time like the photographs that surrounded them.

In one faded snapshot, my mother stood by a lake, sunlight dancing on the water's surface, her laughter captured in the moment. She was beautiful and carefree, her spirit radiant against the backdrop of the vibrant American landscape. The wildflowers swayed gently in the breeze, a reflection of her youth and the untainted joy she once held. I longed to reach out and touch the image, to bridge the gap between our worlds, to understand the girl in the picture and the woman who had raised me.

Another photograph showed her with Henry—smiling, their hands intertwined, eyes sparkling with an affection that felt almost tangible. I studied the image closely, trying to decipher the emotions etched across their faces, the unspoken connection between them. The depth of their bond radiated through the photo, an invisible thread that tied my mother to a time and a person I had only known through whispers and half-remembered stories.

As I flipped through the letters and photographs, I felt the weight of the key in my hand, its purpose shrouded in mystery. My heart raced at the thought that it might unlock not only a physical door but the door to my mother's past—a past that might hold the answers I desperately sought. I glanced at Luke, who watched me with an understanding that made the air between us hum with unspoken possibilities. In this moment, we were not merely two people navigating the remnants of history; we were explorers on the brink of discovery, searching for the truths that lay hidden within the echoes of the past.

The key felt cold against my palm, a simple piece of metal that seemed to resonate with the weight of untold stories. I turned it over, letting the light catch its edges, hoping for some revelation that would explain its significance. Luke leaned closer, his curiosity palpable, his breath quickening as he caught sight of the letters spread out like a patchwork quilt of secrets.

"Should we open the box?" he asked, his voice tinged with a mix of excitement and trepidation. I nodded, though my heart was a chaotic symphony of nerves and anticipation. This was not merely an act of curiosity; it was an invitation to delve into the very core of my mother's existence. Each letter was a thread woven into the tapestry of her life, and now I had the chance to unravel it, to see the world through her eyes.

With shaky hands, I gathered the letters together, their crisp edges feeling fragile under my fingertips. I chose another at random, my heart pounding as I began to read. The ink, though faded, was still vibrant enough to convey the intensity of my mother's emotions. She wrote with a raw honesty that made my chest ache—her hopes, dreams, and fears spilling onto the pages like inkblots of her soul.

One letter in particular caught my attention; it was filled with poetic descriptions of summer evenings spent at the lake, a place where laughter mingled with the sound of water lapping at the shore.

She described the golden glow of the setting sun casting a warm light over everything, transforming the mundane into something magical. It felt as though I were there beside her, a ghost in her memories, experiencing the joy and longing that danced in her words.

The more I read, the clearer it became that Henry was not merely a name; he was a presence woven deeply into her life. She spoke of him with a reverence that suggested he was more than just a passing figure; he was a force that had shaped her in ways I had yet to comprehend. There was mention of their dreams—plans to travel the world, to create a life filled with adventure and love. Yet, woven into that dream was a subtle undercurrent of heartbreak, as if she were mourning a future that had slipped away from her grasp.

"Do you think he was... important to her?" Luke asked, his voice almost a whisper, as if afraid to disrupt the fragile atmosphere that surrounded us. I glanced up, meeting his gaze, and saw a flicker of understanding there—an acknowledgment of the emotional gravity of this moment.

"More than I think I realized," I replied, feeling the ache of connection grow within me. My mother had carried this piece of her life with her, tucked away like a secret too precious to share. I could only wonder what had happened to sever that bond, to lead her to bury these letters in a place where they would lie in silence for years.

Determined to discover the truth, I pushed aside the remaining letters and rummaged through the box, my fingers brushing against the cool metal of the key. There was a slight tremor of anticipation as I held it up to the dim light, wondering what door it would unlock. A sudden urge to find that door—whatever it might lead to—spurred me on.

"Do you think there's a place in this house it belongs to?" I asked, my eyes scanning the attic's nooks and crannies, the shadows that seemed to beckon me toward discovery. Luke shrugged, his brow furrowing in thought.

"Maybe the old cellar? It's down at the end of the hallway. I saw a door there that looked like it hadn't been opened in ages."

The idea sent a jolt of excitement through me. The cellar. It was as if the very word thrummed with possibilities, resonating with the secrets the house kept hidden. I tucked the letters safely back into the box and closed it gently, an unconscious promise to return to them later. With the key clasped tightly in my hand, I motioned for Luke to lead the way.

We descended the staircase, the air growing heavier, thick with the memories of what had once been. The sunlight barely penetrated the narrow windows, leaving shadows to linger in the corners like specters watching our every move. I felt an electric tension in the air, a charged atmosphere as if the very walls held their breath, anticipating what we might uncover.

The cellar door loomed ahead, aged wood splintering in places, a testament to years of neglect. My heart raced as I approached it, and I could feel Luke's presence behind me, a comforting anchor as I reached for the doorknob. It resisted my touch at first, stubbornly refusing to yield, but the key slid into the lock with a satisfying click.

With a deep breath, I turned the knob, the door groaning open to reveal the darkened space beyond. A musty scent wafted up, a blend of damp earth and rotting wood. We stepped inside, the darkness wrapping around us like a heavy blanket, obscuring whatever lay ahead. I fumbled for the light switch, my heart pounding, and when the bulb flickered to life, I felt a rush of triumph mingled with apprehension.

The cellar was cluttered with remnants of the past—old furniture draped in dusty sheets, stacks of boxes teetering like unsteady towers, and cobwebs stretching across the rafters like gossamer curtains. It was a world frozen in time, a repository of memories waiting to be rediscovered.

"Look at that," Luke said, pointing to a small trunk nestled in the corner, half-hidden beneath a pile of boxes. It was adorned with intricate carvings, faded but still beautiful, like a relic of a bygone era. My breath caught in my throat as I approached it, the anticipation building with each step.

"Let's see what's inside," I said, my voice barely above a whisper as I knelt beside the trunk, the wood cool against my fingertips. The latch was stubborn, but with a little coaxing, it sprang open, revealing a trove of treasures that seemed to pulse with life.

Inside lay a collection of items—old jewelry, tarnished but still glimmering with a hint of their former glory, delicate silk handkerchiefs, and a few books that had clearly been cherished. But it was the small velvet pouch tucked in the corner that captured my attention. My heart raced as I reached for it, my fingers brushing against the soft fabric.

Opening the pouch, I found a collection of trinkets—each one a piece of my mother's history. There were charms that seemed to tell a story, a tiny silver locket that might have once held a photograph, and a delicate bracelet that glinted in the light. I felt a connection to her in that moment, as if I were piecing together the fragments of her life, each item a whisper of who she had been.

As I sifted through the contents, I sensed that this trunk held not just remnants of her past, but pieces of my own identity waiting to be uncovered. My heart swelled with an overwhelming mix of gratitude and sorrow, knowing that within these walls lay the truth of who my mother was—a truth that had been buried, waiting for someone to find it.

In the silence of the cellar, I could almost hear her voice, resonating in the air like a gentle breeze, urging me to continue my search. And as I stood there, surrounded by the ghosts of the past, I understood that the journey to uncovering her story had only just begun.

The velvet pouch lay heavy in my hands, each trinket nestled within it like a carefully guarded secret, each one holding the weight of memory. I delicately lifted a tarnished silver charm shaped like a crescent moon, the surface dimmed with age yet still reflecting the faint glow of the bulb overhead. As I traced the curves with my fingers, I imagined my mother, young and spirited, threading it onto a chain, a piece of her world carried close to her heart. I could almost hear her laughter echoing in the corners of this dusty cellar, mingling with the past, urging me to delve deeper.

Luke leaned closer, his breath mingling with mine as we examined the treasures. "Do you think these were important to her?" he asked, his voice barely above a whisper, as if raising it might disturb the spirits lurking in the shadows. I nodded, a swell of emotion rising within me. Each item felt like a fragment of her soul, and I could sense the stories buried within them, waiting to be uncovered.

Setting the charm aside, I reached for the delicate bracelet, its intricate links sparkling as I held it up to the light. "This must have meant something special," I murmured, lost in thought. The way the metal caught the light reminded me of those fleeting moments when laughter erupted over dinner, my mother's voice ringing like the chimes on our porch in a summer breeze. I had always taken for granted her presence, her warmth, and the way she filled every space with joy. Now, standing in this forgotten cellar, I felt the echoes of her love, vibrant and alive, urging me to explore her history.

"Maybe we should keep looking," Luke suggested, his voice grounding me in the present. I knew he was right; the trunk was only the beginning. I carefully returned the trinkets to the pouch, a sense of urgency rising within me. "Let's find out what else this place has hidden."

Together, we began to sift through the remnants of the cellar, moving boxes aside, revealing relics of the past: a rusted bicycle, its tires flat and covered in dust, a weathered fishing pole, and a collection of faded family portraits, their subjects gazing into the distance as if watching over the remnants of their lives. Each discovery felt like a breadcrumb leading us toward a greater understanding of my mother—a map drawn by her own hand, guiding me through the labyrinth of her memories.

It was during this exploration that I noticed a faint outline on the wall, a door obscured by a tangle of boxes and old furniture. My heart quickened, a sense of destiny tingling at the nape of my neck. "What do you think is behind there?" I asked, excitement bubbling in my chest. Luke moved closer, peering at the door with a mixture of wonder and apprehension.

"Only one way to find out," he replied, determination lining his features. Together, we began to clear the path, pushing aside years of neglect until the door stood fully revealed. It was a simple wooden door, much like the others in the house, but this one held an air of mystery, as if it guarded secrets too sacred to share.

As I reached for the handle, I felt the pulse of history beneath my fingertips, the resonance of countless stories waiting to be told. I turned the knob slowly, the door creaking open to reveal a small, dimly lit room that appeared untouched by time. Inside, I found shelves lined with dusty books, their spines cracked and faded. An old desk sat against the far wall, littered with scattered papers and an ancient typewriter, its keys worn from use.

"Wow," Luke breathed, stepping inside and letting the door close softly behind us. The atmosphere felt electric, charged with the essence of creativity and dreams long unfulfilled. I could almost envision my mother here, fingers dancing across the keys as she poured her heart onto the pages, capturing her thoughts in ink that had since dried but never faded.

"Look at this," I said, pulling out a dusty journal from the shelf. Its leather cover was worn but still held a promise of the stories within. I opened it cautiously, the pages crackling like autumn leaves beneath my touch. The handwriting was unmistakable—my mother's elegant script danced across the page, the words flowing with emotion and urgency.

With each entry I read, I felt like I was stepping into her world, understanding the struggles and triumphs she had faced. She wrote of her dreams, of wanting to escape the confines of this town, to find a place where she could truly belong. There were tales of laughter shared with Henry, dreams whispered under starlit skies, and the shadow of something darker that loomed over her—a struggle that was palpable in the weight of her words.

In one entry, she recounted a moment of doubt, revealing a painful conflict between her love for Henry and the expectations placed upon her by family and society. I could feel her heartache in every line, the agony of choosing between love and duty, between passion and safety. The vulnerability of her words enveloped me like a warm embrace, igniting a fire within me to uncover the truth behind her decisions.

As I flipped through the pages, I noticed a recurring theme—a sense of longing, of searching for something just beyond her reach. There were mentions of dreams to write, to create, and to break free from the chains of her past. It struck me that, in many ways, she was still searching for herself, even as she raised me, her own dreams tucked away like the treasures we had just uncovered.

"Julia, come look at this," Luke called from across the room, his voice a mix of excitement and urgency. I glanced up, my heart racing as I crossed the room to where he stood, peering at a faded photograph that hung on the wall, framed with care.

It was a picture of my mother and Henry, taken on what appeared to be a summer's day. They stood close together, arms around each other, radiant smiles lighting up their faces. The background was a sea of sunflowers, their golden faces turned toward the sun. In that moment, they looked impossibly happy, their joy infectious.

"I can't believe how young they look," I murmured, captivated by the image. "It's like they were caught in a moment of pure bliss."

"Do you think they were together when this was taken?" Luke asked, his brow furrowed in thought.

"Probably," I replied, my heart swelling with a bittersweet ache. "But what happened after this? What made her hide all of this?"

The questions hung heavy in the air, tangible and unsettling. I turned back to the desk, the typewriter looming like an artifact from another era, waiting for someone to breathe life into it once more. "Do you think she wrote about him?" I asked, my fingers brushing the keys gently, as if the act of touching them would summon my mother's spirit to guide me.

"Let's find out," Luke suggested, his enthusiasm reigniting my resolve. Together, we began to sift through the scattered papers on the desk, a treasure trove of thoughts and emotions waiting to be unearthed.

As we explored, I stumbled upon an envelope, yellowed with age and addressed to Henry, the handwriting unmistakable. I held it up, my heart racing as I turned to Luke. "This must be it," I said, my voice trembling with anticipation.

With cautious hands, I opened the envelope, revealing a letter that felt fragile in my grasp. I unfolded it, my breath hitching as I read the familiar loops of my mother's writing. Each word resonated with her longing, her desire for connection, and the ache of what could have been.

She poured her heart onto the page, recounting her dreams, her fears, and the unshakeable bond she had with Henry. "I wish I could tell you how I truly feel," the letter began, and I could almost hear her voice, filled with emotion. "There are parts of me that you know, and parts that I fear you never will."

Tears pricked at my eyes as I read her words, feeling the depth of her vulnerability. The letter was both a confession and a love letter, a bridge between two hearts entwined in a dance of uncertainty. She spoke of the future they had envisioned, yet acknowledged the barriers that stood in their way—family expectations, societal pressures, and the weight of a world that often felt too heavy to bear.

"Why didn't she ever talk about him?" I whispered, the words escaping me like a breath I didn't know I was holding. The answer hung in the air, heavy with unfulfilled dreams and lost love, a melody of sorrow that echoed in the silence around us.

"Maybe it was too painful," Luke suggested, his voice softening, understanding the emotional storm swirling within me.

"Or maybe she thought it was better to forget," I replied, the ache of my mother's unspoken truths weighing heavily on my heart. In that moment, I realized that this journey was about more than uncovering her past—it was about understanding her choices, her sacrifices, and ultimately, my own identity.

As the light flickered above us, illuminating the dust motes swirling in the air, I felt a profound connection to the woman who had given me life. Each discovery, each letter, and each photograph was not merely a piece of her past; they were fragments of me, reflections of the legacy she had left behind.

In the midst of the dust and shadows, I began to see the contours of my mother's spirit—her laughter, her dreams, and yes, even her ghosts. And I knew that this journey would not only help me understand her better but would also allow me to embrace my own story, weaving together the threads of our lives into a tapestry

Chapter 26: The Key to Everything

The moment the key turned in the lock, an electric jolt coursed through me, a visceral response to the mysteries it promised to unveil. Dust motes danced in the shafts of sunlight streaming through the cellar's small window, their slow twirls like whispers of the past, urging me to confront what lay hidden in the trunk. I pulled the creaky lid open, each groan echoing through the shadows of the dim room, the scent of aged wood and old secrets wafting up to greet me.

As I peered inside, the atmosphere shifted, heavy with anticipation. The trunk brimmed with yellowed papers, their edges curled and frayed, as if they had absorbed the essence of time itself. I sifted through them gingerly, careful not to disrupt the fragile remnants of my mother's life. Each document I touched felt like a connection to a world I had only glimpsed through fragments of her stories.

There, at the bottom of the trunk, was a leather-bound journal, its surface worn and supple, the corners frayed as if it had been clutched tightly during moments of fear or joy. I lifted it gently, feeling the weight of countless words pressed between its pages. My heart raced; this was my mother's voice, preserved like a fossil in amber, each line a testament to her struggles and triumphs.

The first few entries were filled with the mundane details of daily life—grocery lists, weather notes, the excitement of my first day of school—but soon the tone shifted. As I delved deeper, her penmanship became frantic, the ink splattering in her urgency, as if she were racing against time itself. She wrote about Henry, a name that now burned like acid on my tongue. In these pages, he transformed from a mere figure in my childhood stories to a specter of terror that loomed over her life.

I felt a growing unease as I read about the entanglements of their past—a whirlwind romance soured by betrayal and manipulation. Henry was painted not just as a lover turned foe but as a man whose ambition spiraled into a dark obsession. My mother had orchestrated an elaborate charade to shield me from his reach, crafting a life that was part illusion, part survival strategy. Each entry unveiled another layer of her fear, her determination to protect me, and the sacrifices she had made in the shadows of our suburban life.

In the quiet of that cellar, surrounded by remnants of a life I didn't fully understand, my perception of my mother began to transform. She was not merely the caregiver who had held me through childhood fears, but a warrior in her own right, waging battles that I had never perceived. I could almost hear the echoes of her footsteps as she navigated a life filled with secrets, always glancing over her shoulder, fearing the consequences of the truth.

I stumbled upon a passage that sent chills racing down my spine. My mother detailed a hidden fortune, an inheritance entwined with her family's history, something Henry believed he was entitled to. The papers corroborated her claims—deeds to properties scattered across the state, each tied to a lineage riddled with complexities and betrayals. My hands trembled as I realized the weight of the responsibility now resting squarely on my shoulders. This was not just about me anymore; it was about safeguarding her legacy and dismantling the power Henry had wielded over her life.

My thoughts spiraled as I considered what this meant for my own future. Would I have to confront him, this ghost of my mother's past? Would he try to take back what she had fought so hard to protect? The thought left me breathless, my mind racing through scenarios that seemed ripped from a thriller novel. What if he came looking for me? What if he still had allies in the shadows, waiting for the perfect moment to strike?

The sun began to dip lower in the sky, casting elongated shadows that crawled across the cellar floor. I closed the journal, cradling it against my chest, as if holding a fragile artifact of my mother's spirit. I needed time to process this newfound reality, this intricate web of family history laced with danger. I could feel the chill of dusk creeping in, an unsettling reminder that I wasn't just an observer in this story; I was a player, thrust into a game of high stakes.

In that moment, the weight of the trunk seemed to expand, filling the space around me with its quiet gravity. I could hear the faint echoes of laughter from upstairs, the sound of my younger sister playing, blissfully unaware of the storm brewing beneath our feet. I longed to protect her from the truths I had unearthed, to shield her from the darkness that threatened to seep into our lives.

As I emerged from the cellar, leaving behind the weight of the past, I resolved to confront this reality head-on. With my mother's words as my armor and her courage as my guide, I would unravel the threads of our legacy and stand firm against the shadows. I owed it to her, to the memory of her strength, to carve out a future untainted by fear. Little did I know that my journey was only beginning, a path paved with revelations that would reshape everything I believed about family, love, and the ties that bind us.

The trunk closed with a definitive thud, sealing away the whirlwind of revelations that churned within me. The air felt thick, laden with the weight of history and the urgency of decisions yet to be made. I leaned against the wall, trying to ground myself in the present, but the chill of the cellar lingered like a specter, a constant reminder of the past I had stumbled into.

As I ascended the creaking stairs, I could hear the faint strains of laughter filtering through the open door of the living room. The mundane sounds of life—my sister's giggle, the rustle of my mother's knitting needles, the soft hum of the television—seemed at odds with the tempest brewing inside me. I paused on the threshold, watching as my mother sat on the couch, her gray hair falling in soft waves around her shoulders, her hands deftly weaving colorful yarn. She was the picture of serenity, blissfully unaware of the storm brewing beneath the surface of our lives.

A pang of guilt twisted in my stomach. I wanted to shield her from the truth, to cocoon her in the comforting illusion of our ordinary existence. But I also understood that the illusions were crumbling, and the truth would claw its way to the surface no matter how tightly I clutched at the fragile threads of our family tapestry.

I stepped into the room, forcing a smile as I joined them. My sister, ever the beacon of innocence, bounced over to me, her bright blue eyes sparkling with mischief. "Can we have pancakes for dinner?" she chirped, her enthusiasm infectious.

"Pancakes?" I echoed, the absurdity of the request bringing a smile to my lips. "How about pancakes with a side of whipped cream and chocolate syrup?"

"Yay!" she squealed, darting back toward the kitchen, her little feet pattering like a joyful drumbeat against the hardwood floors.

"Sometimes I think she just likes the idea of pancakes more than actually eating them," my mother said, her voice warm and melodic. I sat beside her, pulling my knees to my chest, grateful for this moment of normalcy even as the shadows loomed in the corners of my mind.

"Maybe," I replied lightly, though a heaviness settled in my chest. "But at least it gives us an excuse to indulge a little."

As we prepared dinner together, I lost myself in the rhythmic motions of cooking. The scent of sizzling batter filled the air, a tantalizing aroma that wrapped around us like a warm embrace. Each flap of the spatula seemed to erase the weight of the world, if only for a moment. But as I flipped the pancakes, my thoughts slipped back to the trunk, to the secrets it held, and to the responsibilities I could no longer ignore.

The conversation flowed easily, peppered with laughter and stories of our day. I savored my mother's laughter, the way it brightened her face, making her seem years younger. But a nagging thought persisted; how could I keep this façade intact when the truth was clawing at the edges of my mind?

After dinner, as my sister scampered off to play with her toys, I found my mother in the living room, settled into her favorite armchair, a novel resting in her lap. The flickering light from the lamp cast a warm glow around her, but my heart felt cold. The cozy ambiance seemed incongruous with the tumult within me.

"Can I ask you something?" I said, my voice a mere whisper, hesitant to disturb the fragile peace.

"Of course, darling," she replied, looking up from her book, her eyes reflecting concern. "Is everything alright?"

"More or less." I took a deep breath, the words rolling in my mind like a storm, threatening to break loose. "Do you remember when you told me about your past? About Henry?"

Her expression shifted, shadows crossing her features as she set her book aside. "It was a long time ago. Why do you ask?"

"I found something in the cellar," I confessed, my heart racing. "Something that made me realize there's so much more to your story than you've ever told me."

Her silence was heavy, a palpable tension filling the space between us. I could see the emotions flicker across her face—fear, anger, sadness, a whirlwind of feelings that had long been buried. "What did you find?" she finally asked, her voice steady yet cautious.

"The trunk—inside it were legal documents and your journal. It talks about Henry, about the inheritance you were protecting." Each word felt like a stone dropping into a still pond, sending ripples through our conversation.

Her eyes widened slightly, a myriad of thoughts playing across her face. "I didn't want you to know," she said quietly, her voice barely above a whisper. "I wanted to shield you from it all. Henry was... dangerous, and I thought I could keep you safe."

"I understand that," I replied, my tone softening. "But I need to know. I need to understand why you had to protect us, what he meant to our lives. I can't fight a battle without knowing the stakes."

A long pause enveloped us, stretching on like a horizon that refused to meet the sky. Finally, she spoke, her voice thick with emotion. "It wasn't just about protecting you. It was about the choices I made, the mistakes I tried to bury. I thought if I kept you away from it all, you could have a normal life. But now..."

Her words hung in the air, heavy with implications. "Now, you're in the thick of it. I can't let Henry take anything from us again. I'll help you face this, whatever it takes."

I could feel the warmth of her love washing over me, grounding me in the present even as the specter of the past loomed large. Together, we were not merely mother and daughter; we were allies in a battle that had been waged long before I had even drawn my first breath. And as the realization settled in, a flicker of hope ignited within me. We would uncover the truth together, and in doing so, we would reclaim our lives from the shadows that had threatened to engulf us.

The weight of my mother's revelation hung heavy in the air, twisting my thoughts into a chaotic jumble. I stared at her, searching for reassurance, for the calm she had always exuded when life spiraled out of control. Instead, I saw something more vulnerable—a flicker of fear in her eyes that mirrored my own. In that moment, it became painfully clear that I wasn't just inheriting the burden of a fortune; I was stepping into a labyrinth of emotional intricacies and dark histories that threatened to engulf us both.

"Do you think he knows?" I asked, my voice barely above a whisper, as if the very mention of Henry's name might conjure him from the shadows.

She shook her head slowly, a frown etching deeper lines across her brow. "I don't know. I haven't heard from him in years, but I can't ignore the fact that he was always obsessed with what he believed was rightfully his. This inheritance—it's not just money to him; it's power."

The air thickened with unspoken fears, swirling around us like the dust motes that floated lazily in the golden light of the late afternoon. I leaned back in my chair, allowing the reality of our situation to settle within me. My mother had fought so fiercely to keep me safe, and now the very thing she had shielded me from was crashing into our lives with all the subtlety of a freight train.

The next few days blurred into a haze of activity. My mother and I spent hours pouring over the contents of the trunk, the yellowed papers revealing the intricate web of our family's history. Each deed we unearthed told a story—a testament to the lives that had been intertwined, to the sacrifices made for the sake of family. The properties were not merely possessions; they were pieces of our legacy, scattered like breadcrumbs leading back to a past that refused to remain buried.

As we pored over the journal, I felt an unsettling kinship with my mother, a bond forged in shared secrets and newfound resolve. Her words became a guide, illuminating the shadowy corners of our family's history. I learned of her childhood dreams, ambitions that had been suffocated under the weight of obligation. Her determination to protect me began to resonate deeply within me, fueling a fire I hadn't known existed.

Each revelation peeled back another layer of my mother's life, revealing the sacrifices she had made. She had moved from town to town, always a step ahead of Henry, crafting new identities and new stories, desperate to shield me from the repercussions of her past choices. Yet, as the pages turned, I sensed the toll it had taken on her spirit. There were entries that hinted at loneliness, moments when she had longed for connection but had chosen safety instead. I saw a woman who had been both my shield and my prison.

The urgency to reclaim our narrative surged within me. If Henry believed this inheritance belonged to him, we had to be proactive. I had to learn everything I could, not just about our family's past but about the man who had left scars on my mother's heart. Armed with this knowledge, I resolved to confront him, not just for the fortune that seemed to shimmer tantalizingly out of reach but for the legacy of resilience my mother had forged.

That Friday evening, as shadows lengthened and the air grew cool, I found myself in the local library, a refuge of knowledge that had long been a sanctuary for me. The scent of aged paper mixed with the crispness of newly bound books enveloped me in a familiar embrace. I sought out every resource I could find about Henry—newspaper articles, court documents, anything that might paint a clearer picture of the man who had haunted my mother's life.

Hours slipped by, the fluorescent lights casting a sterile glow that paled in comparison to the warmth of the sun outside. The library was eerily quiet, save for the rustle of pages turning and the soft tapping of my fingers against the keyboard. My focus narrowed, each click a step closer to uncovering the truth. As I dug deeper, a tapestry of connections began to unfurl before me—old business dealings, failed partnerships, and a trail of emotional wreckage that followed in Henry's wake.

Finally, I came across a clipping that made my heart stutter. It detailed a high-stakes lawsuit involving Henry, accusations of fraud and deceit swirling around him like a dark cloud. The words leaped off the page, illuminating the layers of his character I had yet to fully grasp. He was not merely a man scorned; he was a master manipulator, weaving a narrative that would ensnare anyone who dared to cross him.

That night, as I returned home, the weight of knowledge pressed down on me. I had unearthed a lineage filled with deception, a labyrinthine narrative that had ensnared my mother. I glanced at her, sitting at the kitchen table, her knitting abandoned, lost in thought. I wanted to reassure her, to tell her that we would confront this together, but I feared the truth would only deepen the shadows in her eyes.

The following week, I felt the familiar pulse of anxiety return as I prepared to face Henry. My mother had insisted on accompanying me, her steady presence a balm against the nerves that threatened to spiral out of control. We met in a small café, the kind that was quaint but carried the air of whispered conversations and hushed secrets. The clinking of coffee cups and the soft hum of voices created a deceptive comfort, masking the tension that hung between us.

When Henry entered, the atmosphere shifted. Time seemed to slow, and the air grew thick with unspoken history. He looked older than I had imagined, lines etched into his face like the very documents that had bound our fates together. He carried himself with an arrogance that radiated through the café, a man who believed himself above consequence. As his gaze met mine, a shiver coursed through me. This was the man who had haunted my mother's life, the shadow that loomed over our family.

"Interesting to see you both," he said, a smug smile playing at the corners of his mouth. "I had almost forgotten about you."

"Henry," my mother began, her voice steady yet laced with an edge of defiance. "We need to talk."

His expression shifted, curiosity piqued, and I felt the tension escalate, the weight of our unspoken history pressing down on us. I stepped forward, drawing on the strength my mother had shown me through the years.

"Let's not dance around it. We know about the inheritance. It doesn't belong to you," I stated, my voice unwavering, carrying the conviction of all the truths I had uncovered.

His eyes darkened, a storm brewing beneath his cool facade. "You really think you can just waltz in here and claim what you believe is yours? You have no idea the lengths I'll go to protect what is rightfully mine."

In that moment, I realized that the path before us was fraught with danger, but it was a journey I was willing to take. My mother and I had weathered storms before; we could navigate this tempest together. I felt the embers of hope spark within me—a determination to reclaim our narrative, to step out of the shadows and forge a future unfettered by the chains of the past. Together, we would face whatever lay ahead, bound by the threads of resilience and the legacy we were determined to protect.

Chapter 27: Betrayal

The soft hum of the city buzzed outside my window, an orchestra of life playing just out of reach. I gazed through the glass, watching as the neon lights flickered like stars fallen from the night sky, illuminating the damp streets of Chicago. Raindrops raced down the windowpane, blurring the lines between the world outside and the storm brewing in my heart. Each droplet whispered secrets of betrayal, a chilling reminder of the shadows lurking in the corners of my once-sparkling life.

It wasn't supposed to be like this. Luke had swept into my life like a summer breeze, warm and inviting, promising adventure and companionship. We had shared countless evenings filled with laughter and hope, strolling hand in hand along the waterfront, the sound of waves lapping against the shore providing a melodic backdrop to our dreams. His deep voice would wrap around me like a cozy blanket, assuring me that everything was right in our world. I had been naïve, wrapped in the sweet fabric of our romance, oblivious to the undercurrents pulling me toward darkness.

Now, as I stood alone in my small apartment, the familiar warmth of our shared moments felt foreign, tainted by the stark truth that had crashed into my life like a runaway freight train. The inheritance had been a whisper of fate, a promise that had grown from my grandmother's dusty old trunk, hidden away in the attic for decades. When I learned of the small fortune awaiting me—a quaint cottage by the sea in Maine, along with a collection of her cherished antiques—I felt like I had stumbled upon a treasure map leading to a life unimagined. I thought of how Luke would react, envisioning the glimmer in his eyes as we plotted our escape from the chaos of the city to a quiet life filled with Sunday brunches and beach strolls.

But now, that dream lay shattered, the pieces scattered across the floor of my heart, sharp and jagged, ready to cut deep. Luke's confrontation played over and over in my mind, a twisted film reel of disbelief and pain. The accusation hung in the air like a dark cloud, his words striking me with the force of a thunderbolt. "You think I'm in this for you? It's about the money, isn't it? It always has been." I could still see the betrayal etched on his face, his expression a blend of anger and disappointment as if I were the one who had wronged him.

With every passing second, the warmth I once felt for him cooled, transforming into a bitter chill that seeped into my bones. How had I allowed myself to become so blind? The warning signs had been there, hiding behind his charming smile and sweet nothings. Late-night phone calls that seemed a little too secretive, his distracted gaze whenever I mentioned my grandmother's name—it all clicked together like the pieces of a malicious puzzle.

I paced the room, my bare feet meeting the cold, hardwood floor, grounding me in this moment of clarity amidst the chaos. The sunlight struggled to break through the thick, gray clouds outside, casting the room in a muted light that echoed my mood. I needed to reclaim my power, to find the strength buried deep within me that had allowed me to rise above challenges before. I refused to be a victim of Luke's greed, nor would I let his betrayal define my story.

As I rummaged through the clutter of my mind, I began to remember the promise I had made to myself long before Luke had arrived, a promise to always prioritize my own happiness and dreams. I took a deep breath, inhaling the scent of fresh coffee wafting from the kitchen, mingling with the damp air. The aroma pulled me back, reminding me of mornings spent savoring solitude and indulging in the luxury of my thoughts. I reached for my journal, its pages filled with hopes, dreams, and the raw emotions I had poured into it like a lifeline.

The pages were soft under my fingers, and as I flipped through them, the ink seemed to glow with the potential of new beginnings.

I found a blank space near the end, a white canvas begging for fresh words. I scribbled furiously, letting the anger and pain flow out of me like a river breaking free from the confines of its banks. This was my moment to reclaim my narrative, to take back the parts of my life that Luke had tried to claim as his own.

"Dear future," I wrote, my pen gliding across the paper, "I am done with darkness. I am done with betrayal. I choose light. I choose freedom." Each word resonated with a strength I had almost forgotten I possessed, igniting a fire within me that I hadn't felt in far too long. I could feel the weight of Luke's betrayal lifting, the energy around me shifting as I embraced the truth of my worth.

The afternoon faded into evening, the sun dipping below the horizon and painting the sky in vibrant hues of orange and pink. I could see the reflections of the sunset dancing on the buildings, mirroring the vibrant resurgence within me. I looked out once more, this time not as a victim, but as a warrior ready to reclaim her territory. I would not allow the past to dictate my future; I would rise, stronger and more determined than ever.

I pulled on my jacket, the fabric familiar and comforting against my skin, and stepped out into the bustling streets of the city. Each footfall echoed my newfound resolve, the energy of the city embracing me as I wove through the crowd. The laughter and chatter of strangers surrounded me, the air electric with possibility. I was ready to face the world, to forge my own path without the shadow of betrayal looming behind me.

The streets buzzed with life as I navigated through throngs of pedestrians, each step heavy with the weight of revelation yet buoyed by a flickering sense of purpose. Chicago had transformed into a canvas painted with vibrant strokes of determination and fleeting joy, each passerby a character in my evolving narrative. The air, rich with the scent of roasted coffee and fresh pastries from nearby cafés, beckoned me into its warm embrace. I needed that warmth, the steady rhythm of life to remind me that the world still turned, even when mine had been thrown off balance.

As I strolled past the bustling open-air markets, the colors of autumn enveloped me—a riot of reds, yellows, and browns swirling together like an artist's palette. I allowed myself to get lost in the crowd, reveling in the anonymity it offered. I spotted a flower stall brimming with sunflowers and dahlias, their vibrant hues competing for attention. A sudden impulse seized me, and I reached out to purchase a bouquet, its cheerful disposition a counterbalance to the darkness that had seeped into my life.

Clutching the flowers tightly, I wandered into a nearby park, a serene oasis amidst the urban chaos. The trees, their leaves rustling softly in the gentle breeze, seemed to whisper secrets of resilience and renewal. I found a weathered bench beneath a sprawling oak and settled down, inhaling the floral fragrance that mingled with the crisp autumn air. With each breath, I absorbed the tranquility around me, allowing it to wash over the tumult in my heart.

The park was alive with laughter—children scampered about, their joy infectious as they chased one another, while couples strolled hand in hand, their intimate conversations mingling with the sounds of rustling leaves. I watched as a young girl, no older than six, stopped in front of me, her big brown eyes wide with wonder as she clutched a plush teddy bear almost as large as she was. She glanced at my bouquet, a look of longing flitting across her face, and in that moment, I realized how much I had taken for granted.

"Are those for someone special?" she asked, her voice bright and curious.

I smiled, the innocence of her question momentarily lifting the weight on my heart. "They're for me," I replied, surprising myself with the honesty. "Sometimes we need to treat ourselves, don't you think?"

Her face lit up like the sun breaking through clouds. "You should give them to someone! Flowers make people happy."

"Maybe you're right," I mused, suddenly inspired. "What's your favorite flower?"

"Sunflowers!" she exclaimed, jumping on her toes as if she might take flight. "They're like little rays of sunshine!"

"Then they'll be perfect for you," I said, plucking a single sunflower from my bouquet and handing it to her. Her eyes sparkled with delight, and I felt a warmth spreading through my chest, the first genuine flicker of happiness I had experienced since the confrontation with Luke.

"Thank you!" she squealed, cradling the flower as though it were a fragile treasure. As she bounded away, I couldn't help but smile, feeling a sense of lightness seep into my bones. Perhaps there was magic to be found in the simplest moments—a spark of joy that could ignite a fire within, even when the world felt bleak.

I spent the next hour in that park, watching the tapestry of life unfold before me. I jotted down my thoughts in my journal, pouring out the remnants of hurt and confusion that clung to my spirit like damp fog. The more I wrote, the clearer my path became, and with each stroke of the pen, I slowly unearthed pieces of myself that had been buried beneath the weight of Luke's betrayal. I wasn't just a victim; I was a survivor, and I had the power to create my own narrative, one that celebrated resilience and rebirth.

Eventually, the sun began to set, casting a golden hue across the park, the sky morphing into a watercolor of oranges and purples. It was time to return to my apartment, to gather the pieces of my life and start anew. I stood up, stretching my limbs, feeling the lightness that had taken root in my heart. I wasn't done yet; there was still so much to explore, to learn, and to reclaim.

As I made my way home, I decided to take a detour through a small neighborhood filled with quaint shops and boutiques. Each storefront had its own unique charm, and I found myself wandering into a vintage shop, its windows filled with relics of the past. Dust motes danced in the beams of sunlight filtering through the glass, and the scent of old books mingled with the musky fragrance of antique furniture.

I was drawn to an ornate mirror hanging on the wall, its gilded frame intricate and elegant. I leaned in closer, examining my reflection. The woman staring back at me seemed different somehow—her eyes were bright with a newfound spark, and her shoulders, once hunched in defeat, stood tall and proud. It was a subtle transformation, but in that moment, I saw the potential of who I could be—a woman reborn from the ashes of betrayal, ready to carve her own path.

The shopkeeper, a woman with silver hair and kind eyes, approached me with a gentle smile. "It has a way of finding those who need it most, doesn't it?" she said, glancing at the mirror. "A reminder that beauty lies not just in how we see ourselves, but in how we choose to live."

I nodded, the weight of her words settling into my soul. "I think I'm beginning to understand that," I replied, a small smile playing on my lips. "It's time for a change."

I left the shop with the mirror's reflection etched in my mind, a constant reminder of the beauty in resilience. Back in my apartment, I arranged my flowers in a vintage vase that had once belonged to my grandmother, its delicate design a connection to the roots I had almost forgotten. I lit a candle, its soft glow flickering against the walls, and filled the space with music that spoke of hope and renewal.

The phone buzzed on my table, interrupting my reverie. It was a message from a friend, an invitation to join a small gathering at a local gallery showcasing emerging artists. I hesitated, the remnants of doubt creeping back in. But then I remembered the laughter of the children in the park, the joy of giving, and the mirror's promise.

I typed a quick response, accepting the invitation, and felt a surge of excitement, mingling with the thrill of the unknown.

This was my moment—a chance to embrace life with open arms, to step into a world that was both familiar and foreign, and to dance once more in the light of possibility. Each step forward would be a declaration of my resilience, a vibrant brushstroke on the canvas of my life, and I was ready to paint a masterpiece.

The gallery buzzed with energy, the air thick with anticipation and the scent of fresh paint, mingling with the sweet aroma of wine. As I stepped through the doorway, the cacophony of laughter and chatter enveloped me, an invigorating contrast to the solitude I had felt just hours before. The walls were adorned with vibrant canvases, each one telling its own story, a reminder of the beauty that could emerge from chaos. I took a deep breath, the thrill of possibility coursing through me, igniting a spark of excitement that pushed back the shadows of betrayal.

I spotted a group of friends clustered near the bar, their laughter rising above the soft notes of a jazz trio playing in the corner. They were a motley crew, each one brimming with creativity and charm, and I felt a surge of relief at the familiar sight. It was comforting to know I wasn't entirely alone in this vast city, that there were people who cared, who would help me navigate this new chapter of my life.

"Hey! You made it!" shouted Sarah, her curly hair bouncing as she waved me over. She had a knack for bringing light into any room, her laughter contagious as she introduced me to a couple of new faces. We shared stories, and in that moment, I felt a sense of belonging that had eluded me for far too long. As the night wore on, I allowed myself to indulge in the warmth of friendship, laughing and chatting, letting the wine loosen the edges of my heart.

But amidst the laughter, an undercurrent of uncertainty lingered. I couldn't help but feel the ghost of Luke trailing behind me, a phantom from my past trying to creep into my present.

Whenever someone mentioned love or trust, the weight of his betrayal pressed down on me like a heavy blanket. I found solace in art, immersing myself in the vivid colors and bold strokes of the paintings around me. Each canvas seemed to whisper encouragement, reminding me that life could be transformed even in the wake of hurt.

My fingers brushed against the cool surface of a painting, its vibrant swirls echoing the turmoil within me. The artist had captured the essence of chaos and beauty, intertwining them seamlessly. I stood transfixed, as if it were a mirror reflecting my own internal struggle. A voice broke through my reverie, pulling me back to the present.

"Beautiful, isn't it?" A tall man with an easy smile approached, his gaze locked onto the painting. "The artist really captures the turbulence of emotions."

I nodded, appreciating his insight. "It's fascinating how art can convey feelings we often can't express in words."

He turned to me, his expression earnest. "Exactly. Sometimes, we need to channel our pain into something beautiful, something that can resonate with others." He extended his hand. "I'm Jake, by the way."

"Claire," I replied, shaking his hand. His grip was warm, solid, a contrast to the coldness that had gripped my heart for weeks. There was something about his presence that felt refreshing, as if he brought a breeze of optimism into the room.

We spent the next hour discussing our favorite artists, our conversations dancing from one subject to another. Jake's enthusiasm was infectious, and I found myself laughing freely, the heaviness in my chest lifting with each passing moment. He shared stories of his own struggles and triumphs, painting a vivid picture of a life steeped in creativity and resilience.

"What about you? What drives your passion?" he asked, his gaze steady and curious.

I hesitated, the words forming a tight knot in my throat. "I've always loved writing. I used to dream of becoming a novelist, but..." I paused, the shadow of Luke's betrayal looming over my aspirations. "I guess life had other plans."

His expression softened, and he leaned closer, his tone sincere. "You know, it's never too late to reclaim your dreams. Don't let anyone dim your light."

His words resonated deep within me, like a gentle reminder of my worth and potential. Perhaps this was the shift I had been waiting for—the realization that I could still forge my own path, even after betrayal. As the evening progressed, I felt a renewed sense of hope blossom in my chest, blooming against the odds like a wildflower in the cracks of concrete.

Later, as the gallery began to empty, I found myself standing alone at the edge of the room, watching the last few guests filter out into the cool night. The moon hung low in the sky, casting a silvery glow over the city, and I felt a sudden surge of gratitude for the unexpected turn of events. This gathering had sparked something within me, a flicker of ambition that refused to be snuffed out.

Jake approached me once more, his smile bright against the dimming light. "What's next for you, Claire?"

I hesitated, a wave of uncertainty washing over me. "I don't really know. I guess I'm still figuring things out."

"Why don't we brainstorm? I'd love to help," he offered, genuine warmth radiating from him. "Sometimes, talking it out can illuminate paths we never considered."

His kindness was disarming, and I felt a flutter of excitement at the idea. "I'd like that," I replied, a genuine smile breaking across my face. "I think I need a fresh perspective."

We exchanged numbers, the connection feeling like a new thread woven into the fabric of my life. As I stepped out into the crisp night air, the world seemed to shimmer with possibilities. I looked up at the stars twinkling above, each one a beacon of hope, a reminder that even the darkest nights give way to light.

In the days that followed, I poured myself into writing, the words flowing from my heart as if they had been waiting patiently for me to set them free. My journal became a sanctuary, a space where I could explore my thoughts and emotions without fear of judgment. I embraced the chaos of my feelings, weaving them into stories that reflected my journey of healing and resilience.

As I wrote, I could almost hear my grandmother's voice, guiding me through the process. She had always believed in the power of storytelling, often reminding me that words could bridge the gap between sorrow and joy. Inspired by her legacy, I began to shape my experiences into narratives that celebrated the beauty of overcoming betrayal and finding strength in vulnerability.

One afternoon, as I sat in a cozy café nestled in my neighborhood, the familiar sound of clinking cups and soft chatter surrounded me, offering a sense of comfort. I sipped my coffee, the rich flavor enveloping my senses, and glanced around, absorbing the life bustling around me. A familiar face caught my eye—Sarah was walking in, her smile as bright as the sun spilling through the window.

"Hey! Mind if I join you?" she asked, sliding into the seat across from me.

"Not at all! I could use the company," I replied, excitement bubbling within me.

"How are things going with your writing?" she inquired, her eyes sparkling with genuine interest.

I hesitated, still feeling vulnerable about sharing my journey. "It's been liberating, actually. I've been exploring my feelings, you know, channeling everything into stories."

Sarah leaned in, her expression encouraging. "That's amazing! You've always had a way with words. I can't wait to read something!"

The warmth of her enthusiasm lit a fire within me. "I'm working on it. I think I've found my voice again, despite everything."

"Of course you have! You've got this fierce spirit inside you," she said, her words a balm to my soul. "And don't forget—you have so much support around you."

Her unwavering belief in me reignited my determination. I realized that my journey was not just about healing from betrayal but also about reclaiming the dreams I had once put on hold. I wanted to share my stories, not just as an outlet for my pain, but as a testament to resilience and the beauty of life's twists and turns.

As we chatted and shared our dreams, I felt a sense of clarity wash over me. The scars of betrayal would always be part of my story, but they no longer defined me. I was not the sum of my past; I was a tapestry of experiences, rich and complex, each thread contributing to the vibrant narrative of my life.

With renewed purpose, I began to outline the stories that had been waiting within me, weaving together threads of heartbreak, hope, and the transformative power of love. Each word I penned was a step closer to my dreams, a chance to connect with others who had faced their own challenges. I was ready to embrace the unknown, to explore uncharted territories of my heart and creativity.

And as I dove deeper into my writing, I knew one thing for certain: the road ahead would be paved with both challenges and triumphs. I was ready to face them all, for I had emerged from the shadows, stronger and more vibrant than ever before. My story was far from over; it was just beginning.

Chapter 28: Running Toward the End

The headlights sliced through the darkness, illuminating the cracked asphalt of the country road that wound like a serpent through the heart of nowhere. I could feel the tension in my chest tightening with every mile, the rhythmic thud of my heart syncing with the pulsating beat of the engine. With each passing moment, the distant glow of the farmhouse faded into obscurity, a haunting reminder of what I was leaving behind. Luke's face lingered in my mind—his laughter, the warmth of his presence. But there was no time for sentiment. I had a mission, and my mother's ghost seemed to whisper a steady mantra in my ear: "Finish what I started."

The night wrapped around me like an inky shroud, punctuated only by the occasional flicker of stars above, glistening like shards of glass against the vast expanse. This was a world that was both familiar and foreign, echoing with the memories of childhood summers spent chasing fireflies, the scent of freshly cut grass mingling with the sweet tang of nostalgia. But that innocence had long since dissolved into the shadows of my reality, replaced by the specter of Henry—a looming threat whose very name sent shivers down my spine.

The journal lay beside me on the passenger seat, its pages worn and frayed, filled with secrets that felt both intimate and heavy. It was my mother's legacy, a roadmap of her fears and desires, the ink a testament to her struggles. Every line told a story, and each story was another thread connecting me to a woman I had barely known. As I flicked through the pages, I could almost hear her voice rising above the chaos, urging me forward, pushing me to uncover the truth buried beneath layers of deceit. It felt absurdly reckless to think that a mere notebook could hold the key to my salvation, yet here I was, clinging to its fragile existence like a lifeline.

The landscape outside the car transformed from rolling hills into dense thickets, the trees pressing in on either side of the road as if they were silent sentinels guarding the secrets of the night. With every passing mile, the familiar sights of home morphed into an alien wilderness, shrouded in mystery and peril. My fingers drummed nervously on the steering wheel, tapping out a rhythm of uncertainty as thoughts of Henry danced like shadows in my mind. He was relentless, a force of nature hell-bent on claiming what he believed was his. And now, as the darkness thickened, I couldn't shake the feeling that he was closer than I cared to admit.

Ahead, the road dipped into a hollow, a place where the trees parted to reveal a forgotten diner, its neon sign flickering like a distant star. The kind of place where stories were traded over coffee and pie, a refuge for lost souls seeking solace in the arms of grease and nostalgia. I felt an irresistible pull, a whisper of familiarity that beckoned me to stop, to breathe, to gather my scattered thoughts before plunging deeper into the unknown. Pulling into the gravel parking lot, I killed the engine and stepped out into the crisp night air, the scent of rain-soaked earth mingling with the faint aroma of fries sizzling on the grill.

Inside, the diner was a time capsule, adorned with checkered tablecloths and vintage jukeboxes. The walls echoed with laughter, and the soft clinking of silverware danced in harmony with the soft country tunes wafting through the air. My presence seemed to break the rhythm for a moment, and a few heads turned, curiosity etched on their faces. I settled into a booth in the far corner, the vinyl seat cool against my skin, and glanced at the menu—unassuming and simple, just like the place itself.

The waitress approached, her smile warm and genuine, eyes sparkling like the stars I had left behind. "What can I get you, hon?" she asked, her Southern twang wrapping around each word like a comforting embrace.

"A coffee, please," I replied, my voice barely above a whisper. I needed the caffeine to fuel my racing thoughts, to steel myself against the impending storm.

As I waited, I studied the patrons around me: a couple sharing a slice of pie, an older man nursing a cup of coffee while scribbling in a notebook, and a group of teenagers animatedly debating the best burger on the menu. For a brief moment, I was a spectator in their world—a world untouched by the turmoil I was racing toward. The waitress returned, placing a steaming cup before me, the rich aroma wafting upward like a balm to my frayed nerves.

"Everything okay, sweetie?" she asked, concern etching her features as she noticed the shadows lurking in my eyes.

I nodded, forcing a smile that felt foreign on my lips. "Just... a lot on my mind."

She studied me for a moment, as if weighing my words, before giving me an understanding nod. "Well, you know where to find me if you need anything." And with that, she turned, her kindness lingering in the air like the warmth of a summer afternoon.

I took a sip of the coffee, letting the bitter richness swirl through me, grounding me in the moment. Yet, even as I savored the fleeting taste of normalcy, I could feel the weight of my mother's legacy pressing down, a palpable reminder that time was running out. Henry's shadow loomed ever closer, and I had to summon the strength to face him, armed with nothing but the truths unearthed from those ink-stained pages.

The diner, once a haven, now felt like a ticking clock. I knew I had to move. The world outside was waiting, and my past was chasing me like a predator on the hunt.

With a deep breath, I paid the bill and slipped back into the night, the cool air wrapping around me like a shroud. The road ahead was fraught with uncertainty, but I was no longer just a girl running away; I was a woman fueled by purpose, ready to confront the shadows of my past. The headlights flickered back to life, illuminating the path that would lead me toward the reckoning I had been preparing for all my life. The end was near, and I was finally ready to meet it head-on.

The wheels of my car sang against the asphalt, a low, rhythmic hum that blended seamlessly with the quiet symphony of the night. The landscape outside transformed from dense woods into sprawling fields, the moon casting an ethereal glow over the landscape, illuminating patches of wildflowers that swayed gently in the cool breeze. Each flicker of my headlights revealed a different scene, a snapshot of the world I was leaving behind. The fields, once a canvas of golden hues, now appeared shrouded in a silver mist, each blade of grass whispering secrets of what had come before.

As the road unfurled before me, my thoughts danced between memories and fears. The journal remained a steadfast companion, its presence both comforting and intimidating. I imagined my mother sitting at a small wooden desk, the sun streaming through the window as she penned her thoughts, her fears spilling onto the pages like ink bleeding through the fibers. I could almost see her, brow furrowed in concentration, her fingers smudged with ink, crafting her legacy in a world that had turned its back on her. What had she faced? What battles had she fought? It was a puzzle I was desperate to solve, and the pieces were scattered across the terrain of my life.

The gentle rumble of the engine was interrupted by a sharp ping from my phone. Glancing down, I saw Luke's name flash across the screen. My heart constricted, torn between the ache of longing and the steel resolve that propelled me forward. I had left him behind, not out of anger or indifference, but because the weight of my journey could not be shared. I couldn't allow myself to be distracted by the warmth of his gaze or the safety of his embrace. There was a fire in my belly now, a desperate need to unravel the threads of my past, and I would face it alone.

I silenced my phone and drove on, the wind whipping through the open window, carrying with it the scents of earth and wild blooms. Somewhere along the way, I had traded my safety for purpose, and now every mile felt like a step toward liberation. As the hours slipped away, I became acutely aware of the darkness pressing in around me, a palpable entity that threatened to suffocate. I pressed my foot against the accelerator, the car leaping forward as though it, too, sensed the urgency of my quest.

A sign loomed ahead—"Welcome to Crestwood"—the words faded and peeling, like the town itself had long been forgotten. I could see the silhouette of the main street, dotted with flickering lights from the few businesses that still stood, defiantly resisting the encroaching shadows. My instincts urged me to pull in, to gather my bearings before plunging deeper into the uncertainty that awaited me. I parked outside an old gas station, its neon sign sputtering like a dying star. The smell of gasoline mixed with something earthy, almost nostalgic, filled the air as I stepped out of the car.

Inside, the gas station felt like stepping back in time—a small, cramped space filled with the sweet scent of freshly brewed coffee and a hint of motor oil. The linoleum tiles, yellowed with age, seemed to sigh underfoot as I made my way to the counter. The cashier, a middle-aged man with a gray beard and tired eyes, looked up from a crossword puzzle, his face breaking into a smile that was both welcoming and weary.

"Evening, miss. What can I get for you?" His voice was gravelly, like the gravel underfoot.

"A coffee, please," I said, my voice steady despite the whirlwind within. "And maybe some directions to the old Thompson estate?"

The mention of the estate drew his gaze, his brow furrowing slightly. "That place hasn't been lived in for years. You sure you want to go there?"

"Just a family matter," I replied, trying to sound casual while every nerve in my body hummed with tension.

He nodded slowly, pouring the coffee into a chipped ceramic cup. "It's a straight shot down Pinewood Road. Can't miss it. Just be careful. The woods have a way of swallowing people whole out there."

I took my coffee, the warmth radiating through the ceramic and into my palms. "Thank you."

As I stepped back outside, the wind tousled my hair, sending a chill down my spine. I looked at the sky, a vast canvas of midnight blue sprinkled with stars, each one a reminder of the countless choices that had led me to this moment. With the coffee cradled in one hand and the journal tucked under my arm, I made my way back to the car, determination coursing through my veins like wildfire.

Pinewood Road was narrow and winding, flanked by towering trees whose branches twisted and knotted, forming a dark canopy overhead. The further I drove, the more I felt like an intruder in a world that had forgotten me. Shadows danced along the edges of the road, the headlights of my car barely piercing the gloom that enveloped everything. My heart raced as I navigated the path, the weight of expectation heavy on my shoulders.

The Thompson estate loomed ahead, its silhouette emerging like a ghost from the mists of memory. It stood defiantly at the end of the road, a relic of a bygone era, shrouded in an aura of mystery and decay. Ivy crawled up its crumbling facade, nature reclaiming what had once belonged to humankind. The windows, dark and vacant, seemed to watch me as I approached, and I could almost hear the whispers of my mother echoing from within the walls, urging me forward.

I parked the car, the engine's hum fading into an eerie silence that enveloped me like a heavy fog. The air was thick with anticipation, a tangible reminder that I was on the precipice of something monumental. As I stepped out into the night, the cool breeze kissed my skin, a stark contrast to the heat of my racing heart. The ground crunched beneath my feet as I walked toward the entrance, each step bringing me closer to the secrets waiting to be unveiled.

The front door creaked open under my touch, a reluctant invitation into the depths of my family's past. The darkness inside was profound, the air musty with the scent of age and neglect. My heart pounded in rhythm with the whispering wind, the journal clutched tightly in my hand as I took my first step inside. I was ready to face whatever lay within these walls, determined to uncover the truths hidden in the shadows. This was my moment to reclaim not only my mother's legacy but my own identity—a journey that began in this very house, waiting for me to finally unlock the door to my past.

The interior of the Thompson estate was a museum of memories, each room steeped in silence, where time had folded in on itself. Dust motes danced lazily in the thin beams of moonlight that filtered through the grimy windows, illuminating the remnants of a life once vibrant. I stepped carefully, wary of the creaking floorboards beneath me, each groan echoing like a warning in the stillness. The air was thick with the scent of aged wood and something metallic that lingered, reminiscent of forgotten echoes and buried secrets.

As I ventured deeper into the house, my fingers brushed against the walls, tracing the contours of faded floral wallpaper that had lost its color, much like the stories of my family that had faded from memory. The living room, once a gathering place filled with laughter and warmth, was now a mausoleum of the past. An old fireplace loomed in one corner, its bricks cold and grey, and a mantle lined with cracked picture frames—faces of my ancestors staring back at me, their expressions a mixture of pride and sorrow. Each gaze felt like a judgment, a reminder that I was standing on hallowed ground, a descendant of a lineage woven with both triumph and tragedy.

In the far corner of the room sat a grand piano, its surface cloaked in a thin layer of dust, keys yellowed with age. I could almost hear the soft notes of a lullaby floating through the air, a melody my mother might have played during happier times. I approached it, compelled by a nostalgia that wrapped around me like a familiar shawl, and brushed my fingers across the keys. They were cold, unyielding, yet they resonated with a haunting beauty that echoed in my chest. I imagined her here, her fingers dancing over the keys, filling the air with music while we sang along, blissfully unaware of the darkness lurking just beyond the light.

Shaking off the reverie, I turned my attention back to the journal tucked under my arm. The leather cover felt warm against my skin, a heartbeat of its own, pulsing with the energy of the secrets it contained. It had guided me thus far, and I was determined to extract every fragment of truth it held. I sank onto a plush, moth-eaten armchair that had seen better days, the fabric worn and faded. I opened the journal, flipping through the pages filled with my mother's delicate script, her thoughts flowing like a river of ink.

As I read, fragments of her life spilled out: her dreams, fears, and the ghosts that haunted her. She wrote of a love once vibrant that had dimmed under the weight of expectations and regret, of the way Henry's charm had ensnared her in a web of desire that soon turned suffocating. My heart twisted as I read her words, the pain and longing palpable, as though she were speaking directly to me across the chasm of time. I could feel the urgency in her pen strokes, a desperate plea for someone—anyone—to understand the battle she had fought against the tide of darkness.

A sudden noise jolted me from my reverie—a sound like glass shattering from somewhere deep within the house. My heart raced, adrenaline coursing through my veins as I snapped the journal shut and rose to my feet. I strained to listen, the silence that followed thick with tension, suffocating yet electric. The wind outside picked up, howling through the cracks in the old windows, a mournful tune that sent a shiver down my spine.

I made my way cautiously through the house, each step calculated as I navigated the labyrinth of memories and shadows. I knew that I was not alone in this place, that Henry's presence lingered like a specter, just out of sight. My mind raced with possibilities; he could be lurking behind the heavy drapes, hiding in the corners, waiting for the opportune moment to strike.

I found myself in the dimly lit kitchen, the air thick with the scent of rust and decay. The countertops were covered with dust, the remnants of forgotten meals lingering in the air like ghosts. My gaze fell upon a series of photographs pinned to the corkboard above the counter, the edges frayed and yellowed with time. They depicted family gatherings—smiling faces, laughter frozen in time. My mother, radiant and young, stood at the center of it all, her eyes sparkling with joy. But as I examined each image, a creeping sense of unease washed over me. In the background of one photograph, a shadow lurked—too dark, too ominous to belong.

Before I could fully process the implication, a loud crash echoed from the hallway. My heart thundered in my chest as I darted toward the sound, adrenaline surging through my veins. The journal felt like a weight in my pocket, a reminder that I was armed with knowledge, but I was also woefully unprepared for what lay ahead.

As I stepped into the hallway, I spotted a door swinging ajar, the wood splintered at the frame. Cautiously, I approached, my breath shallow, anticipation and fear entwined in an uneasy dance. I pushed the door open wider, and my stomach dropped. The room was an old study, littered with papers, a desk overturned as if a struggle had occurred. The dim light revealed a trail of shattered glass leading toward the window, where the curtain billowed like the wings of a trapped bird.

In the center of the chaos stood Henry, his back turned to me, framed by the broken shards of glass. He was a dark silhouette against the moonlight, tension coiling in the air around him like a snake ready to strike. I could feel my heart racing, pounding in my ears like a war drum. My instincts screamed at me to retreat, but a deeper, primal force propelled me forward, demanding confrontation.

"Henry," I called, my voice steadier than I felt. "What are you doing here?"

He turned slowly, his expression a mask of amusement tinged with something darker, something that made my skin crawl. "Ah, the prodigal daughter returns to claim her inheritance," he said, his voice smooth as silk, yet laced with menace. "How noble of you. But do you really think you're ready for this?"

I straightened, determination igniting within me. "I'm not afraid of you."

He chuckled, a low, rumbling sound that sent chills racing down my spine. "Fear is a natural response, darling. But you're right about one thing. You shouldn't be afraid. You should be terrified."

I took a step back, the weight of his words hanging in the air, thick and suffocating. "What do you want, Henry? This isn't just about money; you know that."

His eyes narrowed, calculating, as if sizing me up like a predator assessing its prey. "It's about legacy, my dear. The Thompson name has always been worth something—wealth, power, control. Your mother thought she could escape it, but legacies don't fade; they persist. You have something I need, and I intend to take it."

The realization hit me like a blow. He wanted the journal—the very thing that could expose him, unravel the web of deceit he had spun around my family. And suddenly, I understood my mother's fears, her warnings echoing in the recesses of my mind.

Before I could respond, he lunged toward me, and I stumbled back, adrenaline surging as I narrowly avoided his grasp. My instincts kicked in, propelling me into action as I bolted for the door. The estate was alive with the chaos of my flight, the shadows chasing me as I dashed through the winding halls. I could hear his footsteps pounding behind me, a relentless reminder that I was not alone in this fight.

I raced through the rooms, each one a prison filled with memories and secrets, desperately seeking an escape. My heart pounded as I turned a corner, sprinting down a narrow hallway that seemed to stretch endlessly before me. The journal, my mother's voice, urged me forward, whispering courage into my ears, guiding me through the maze of darkness.

Finally, I reached the staircase, my feet pounding against the wood as I descended into the dimly lit foyer. I had to get outside, into the open air where I could breathe again, where I could find a way to fight back. But just as I reached for the door, Henry appeared, blocking my exit, a predator cornering its prey.

"Did you really think you could run from me?" he sneered, his voice dripping with malice. "This is just the beginning, sweetheart."

I stood frozen for a moment, adrenaline coursing through my veins as the weight of my fear collided with a fierce resolve. I wouldn't let him take what was rightfully mine. I wouldn't let him extinguish the flicker of hope that burned within me. My mother had fought her battles; now it was my turn to stand and face the darkness head-on.

"Get out of my way," I demanded, my voice low but steady, echoing with the strength I had found within.

He chuckled darkly, stepping closer, the shadows wrapping around him like a cloak. "And what are you going to do, little girl? You have nothing."

But in that moment, something shifted. I felt the weight of the journal in my pocket, its very presence igniting a spark of courage within me. I was not defenseless; I had the truth on my side. The echoes of my mother's voice resonated in my heart, fueling my determination.

"I have everything," I said, meeting his gaze with fierce defiance. "And I will not let you win."

With that, I launched myself forward, ready to confront the darkness that had plagued my family for far too long. The night was far from over, and as the storm brewed outside,

Chapter 29: The Final Stand

The clearing where the forest thinned was an unlikely stage for a confrontation, yet there it was, dappled in the muted light of a winter afternoon. A smattering of pine trees stood sentinel around me, their branches weighed down by fresh snow, creating a stark contrast against the dark, almost sinister trunks. I could feel the chill seeping into my bones, but the bite of the cold was nothing compared to the turmoil raging within my heart. This was the ground where my mother had spun stories of her childhood, filled with laughter and warmth, now cloaked in an eerie silence that echoed with the weight of expectation.

As I stood there, my boots crunching softly on the snow, I was reminded of her—how she used to twirl me around in circles, her laughter bright enough to pierce the gloom of winter. I could almost hear her voice in my mind, urging me to find strength, to remember the lessons woven into every bedtime story. "Courage doesn't mean you're not afraid," she had said, her eyes sparkling with conviction. "It means you stand your ground even when your heart feels like it's ready to burst." I clung to those words, feeling them wrap around me like a protective cloak as the wind whispered secrets through the trees.

The minutes stretched like hours, each one filled with anticipation and dread. The sky turned a muted gray, the clouds heavy and low, as if the heavens themselves were holding their breath. I felt the air shift, and the hairs on my neck prickled—a sign that Henry was near. I had imagined this moment countless times, rehearsed every word I might say, but nothing could prepare me for the reality of standing here, staring into the face of someone who had once meant everything to me.

When he finally emerged from the woods, it was as if the world around us had faded into the background. Henry's tall figure cut a striking silhouette against the pale canvas of snow. His dark coat flared slightly in the wind, framing a face I had come to both love and fear. There was a strength in his demeanor, an unwavering resolve that was unsettling, and I felt my heart pound in response to his presence. But alongside the fear, there was something else—an ache for the boy I once knew, who had played in these woods with wild abandon, who had shared whispered secrets under the stars. The boy who had made promises that now felt as distant as the setting sun.

"Emma," he said, his voice steady but tinged with something I couldn't quite place. Regret, perhaps? Or was it an echo of longing that matched my own? I forced myself to stand tall, to meet his gaze head-on, even as a storm of emotions churned within me.

"Henry," I replied, keeping my tone neutral, despite the tempest of memories and feelings battling for dominance. I was here to confront him, not to wallow in nostalgia. "You came."

He took a step closer, the crunch of his boots breaking the stillness. "You know I would. You're the only person who matters to me, even now."

I wanted to scream, to demand why everything had spiraled out of control, why our lives had been thrust into this chaotic dance of shadows and secrets. But instead, I stood still, forcing myself to breathe, to collect my thoughts. This was not just a reunion; it was a reckoning, and I could feel the weight of our shared history pressing down on us.

"What do you want, Henry?" The words felt foreign on my tongue, laced with an intensity that mirrored the tension in the air. "What could you possibly say that would change anything?"

He looked away, his jaw tightening as if he were battling with demons I could only imagine. "I want to explain. I want you to understand why I did what I did."

"Understanding doesn't change the past," I shot back, my voice sharper than I intended. The truth was, I didn't want to understand. I wanted to rage against the choices that had ripped us apart, that had led to the devastation that now loomed over us like a dark cloud.

"Emma, please." His voice softened, and for a moment, the steel in his gaze melted away, replaced by something raw and vulnerable. "I never meant for it to come to this. You have to know that."

I felt a flicker of hope, a brief and tantalizing notion that beneath the layers of betrayal and hurt lay the boy who had once promised to stand by my side. But hope was a double-edged sword, and I hesitated, caught in the web of my own emotions. "Then tell me why. Tell me why you left, why you made the choices that shattered everything."

As the words hung in the air, the wind picked up, swirling around us like the chaotic thoughts in my mind. Henry drew a deep breath, and for the first time, I saw a crack in his facade. "It was never about you, Emma. I was trying to protect you—"

"By abandoning me?" I interrupted, the bitterness spilling out. "You call that protection? You don't get to twist your actions into something noble."

The intensity of our exchange crackled in the air, a palpable energy that threatened to ignite the very ground beneath us. I felt the coldness of the snow beneath my feet, the sharpness of the air as it pierced through my jacket. But within me, a fire raged, a determination that had been stoked by months of unanswered questions and painful silence.

"I had no choice," he insisted, his eyes pleading. "You have to believe me. If I had stayed, I would have put you in danger. Everything I did was to keep you safe."

"Safe from what?" I shot back, my voice rising as frustration bubbled to the surface. "Safe from the truth? Because that's all this has ever been about, hasn't it? Hiding from the reality of what we became."

Henry stepped closer, invading my personal space, his breath warm against my skin. "I wanted to shield you from the darkness. I didn't want you to become a part of it."

I felt the heat of his presence, and the memory of our shared laughter and stolen kisses wrapped around me like a tender embrace, battling against the walls I had built. But I couldn't let myself be swayed. "You don't get to decide what I can handle. I've fought my own battles, Henry. I can face whatever is out there."

He searched my eyes, a tempest of emotion swirling in his gaze. "But this is different. It's bigger than us. And it's not just about you anymore."

As the realization settled in, a chill ran down my spine. I was here to face him, yet somehow, the stakes had been raised higher than I had anticipated. The darkness loomed, and I could feel its presence in the wind, the trees standing silent witnesses to our confrontation.

The silence that enveloped us felt heavy, as if the air itself was pregnant with the weight of our unspoken words. I could hear the distant rustle of branches swaying gently, and the soft thud of snowflakes landing in silent surrender. Each moment stretched taut, a thread poised on the edge of snapping. It was a strange juxtaposition, this tranquil setting contrasting sharply with the storm brewing between us.

Henry shifted his weight, breaking the spell of silence. "I didn't want to come back here, Emma. Not like this." His voice carried an edge of vulnerability, a crack in the armor he had worn so well. "This place—it holds too many memories."

"And yet here you are," I replied, crossing my arms against the chill, trying to create a barrier between his warmth and the cold reality of our situation. "You can't escape what you've done by avoiding it."

He nodded, his expression conflicted as he took a step back, almost as if my words were a physical blow. "I know that now, but I thought I could protect you. I thought leaving was the right thing."

"And what was I supposed to do?" I challenged, my voice rising as the anger bubbled to the surface. "Just sit back and wait for you to return like some fairy tale princess? I'm not a damsel in distress, Henry. I'm not waiting for a knight to save me."

The rawness in my tone hung in the air, and for a heartbeat, I thought I saw a flicker of admiration in his eyes, as if he finally recognized the strength I had forged in the fire of my abandonment. "You're right," he admitted, his voice low. "I underestimated you. I thought I could shield you from the truth, from the darkness that I couldn't escape. But the truth is... it's already here. And it's bigger than either of us."

The revelation hung between us like the heavy clouds above, threatening to spill their contents. It was unsettling, the way his words stirred a recognition within me. The danger wasn't just a specter lurking in the shadows; it was a living, breathing entity, woven into the fabric of our lives.

"I don't want to be part of this anymore," I said, my voice trembling slightly, the strength I had summoned beginning to wane. "I don't want to carry the weight of your choices or the consequences of your past."

Henry took another step closer, the desperation palpable in the space between us. "You don't have to. But if you turn away now, you'll be leaving behind a part of yourself. We've always been intertwined, Emma. Our fates are linked, whether we like it or not."

The realization settled heavily upon my chest, an anchor that threatened to drag me down into depths I wasn't ready to explore. I wanted to deny it, to push away the truth that had been hiding in plain sight. But I could feel it—a deep-rooted connection that bound us together, a thread woven through our shared history that could not be easily severed.

As I stared into his eyes, I saw the remnants of the boy I had known. The mischief, the laughter, and even the pain danced behind the surface, and I felt a pang of longing for the simplicity of those days when the world hadn't seemed so complicated. The innocence of our youth was lost, replaced by this tangled web of choices and regrets.

"I can't carry your burdens, Henry," I said, my voice steadier now, tinged with a resolve I hadn't anticipated. "You need to face them. And if you're going to bring me into this, you need to let me in completely."

The flicker of determination in his gaze ignited something within me, a fire that surged against the cold. "I want to fight, Emma. I want to stand with you, not just against whatever is coming, but beside you. But I need you to trust me."

"Trust is earned, Henry." The words tasted bitter on my tongue, a reminder of all the times that trust had been shattered. "You can't just expect me to leap into the unknown because you say it'll be okay."

He stepped closer still, his presence an intoxicating blend of warmth and urgency. "I know I've failed you, but please—believe in me just this once. There's a storm coming, and we can either face it together or let it tear us apart."

The weight of his plea settled over us like a blanket, and I could feel the tension shift, the air crackling with an electric energy that made every hair on my body stand on end. The very ground beneath our feet seemed to tremble in anticipation, as if nature itself was holding its breath, waiting for us to decide.

"I don't want to lose you again," he murmured, his voice barely above a whisper, as if confessing a secret meant only for my ears. The vulnerability in his tone struck a chord deep within me, resonating with a fear I had buried beneath layers of pride.

"I don't want to lose myself," I replied softly, the truth spilling forth like a torrent. "I've spent so long piecing together my life without you. I can't just throw it away."

"Then let's find a way to weave our lives together again," he urged, his eyes alight with determination. "This is our chance, Emma. We can rewrite our story. We can confront the shadows, uncover the truths, and reclaim what's ours."

In that moment, I felt a flicker of hope igniting in the darkest corners of my heart. Perhaps there was a way through this maze of confusion—a path we could carve out together. I searched his eyes for the boy I had once loved, hoping to find a spark of the light we had shared.

With a deep breath, I made my choice. "Alright," I said, the words laced with a mixture of trepidation and resolve. "I'll trust you, but only if you promise me one thing: no more secrets. We face whatever is coming as a team, and you share everything—no matter how dark."

Henry nodded, his expression earnest, relief washing over him like sunlight breaking through clouds. "I promise, Emma. No more secrets. Just us against the storm."

The moment hung between us, charged with the weight of our shared history and the uncertainty of what lay ahead. I could feel the world shifting, a new chapter unfurling as the snow fell silently around us, wrapping us in a cocoon of possibility. The shadows loomed, but we were no longer alone. Together, we would face whatever came next, ready to reclaim our story and rewrite the narrative of our lives, hand in hand, heart to heart.